GHOST TOWN

Kevin Chen

GHOST TOWN
A NOVEL IN 45 CHAPTERS

*Translated from the Mandarin
(and the Taiwanese) by Darryl Sterk*

Europa
editions

Europa Editions
27 Union Square West, Suite 302
New York, NY 10003
www.europaeditions.com
info@europaeditions.com

This book is a work of fiction. Any references to historical events,
real people, or real locales are used fictitiously.

Sponsored by the Ministry of Culture, Republic of China (Taiwan)

Library of Congress Cataloging in Publication Data is available
ISBN 978-1-60945-798-3

Chen, Kevin
Ghost Town

Art direction by Emanuele Ragnisco
instagram.com/emanueleragnisco

Cover design and illustration by Ginevra Rapisardi

Prepress by Grafica Punto Print – Rome

Printed in Canada

CONTENTS

"The past is never dead. It's not even past."
—WILLIAM FAULKNER, *Requiem for a Nun*

"We are all in the gutter,
but some of us are looking at the stars."
—OSCAR WILDE, *Lady Windermere's Fan*

For my hometown, a non-existent Yongjing

GHOST TOWN

PART 1
MOM'S GONE MISSING

1. *The first row of townhouses*

"Where are you from?"

That was the first question T asked him. T gave him a lot: a German passport, a new home, an escape route, and a lot of questions. Right from the start, T liked to ask questions. What's your hometown like? How many brothers and sisters do you have? How hot does it get on the island in the summertime? Are there cicadas? What about snakes? What do the trees look like? What are they called? Are there any rivers? What about canals? When is the rainy season? Are there ever any floods? Is the soil fertile? What all gets planted? Why can't I accompany you to your father's funeral? Why go home? Why not go home?

The question marks caught on his hair and nicked his skin. T's questions were hard to answer, so he didn't. He dodged, or lied, until his made-up biography was full of holes and contradictions, like a badly written novel. And so he wrote one. The first chapter opened with a table on which a few objects had been placed: one gun, two knives, and three diaries. The gun would have to be fired in a subsequent chapter, the knives should be used to dismember and flay, and the diaries would solve the riddle at the heart of the story. But the novel of his life was a total mess. He wrote and wrote and forgot about the gun, the knives, and the diaries. Instead, he obsessed over an assortment of trash that was strewn on the table and littered his narrative with irrelevant clues, like a mural on a factory wall, a pair of bright red shorts, and a face with a plastic bag over it. When a person is rotten, his novel will be, too, full of holes.

He was a guy who was all holes from his mouth on south, holes he stuffed with everything he didn't want to talk about—all the incidents that had made a mess of his memory and which he claimed to have forgotten. When the holes ripped, as they did from time to time, sundry stories would come tumbling out.

How should he tell these stories?

Unable to get them off his chest and out of his mouth, he could only keep writing: I grew up in a small town.

A rural backwater in central Taiwan, his hometown was first settled by immigrants from Guangdong Province in China early in the nineteenth century. On level wasteland, they built their settlement, a street surrounded by homesteads. Soon the land was traversed by artificial waterways that probably resembled T's German *Kanäle*. The oldest of these "canals," or "ditches," had drawn muddy water from the longest river in the country since the late eighteenth century for farmers to irrigate their fields with. Early on, there were internecine brawls, not to mention never-ending disasters that put the fear of Fire and Flood in people's hearts. No wonder the settlers called the place Yongjing. It was an expression of their aspiration for eternal (*yong*) peace (*jing*).

The terrain around Yongjing was flat, not rolling, but gazing east you could see green hills and, on a clear day, the mountains of the Central Range beyond. Gawping west, you couldn't see or even hear the Muddy Waters, but the old-timers used to say that if you walked thataway you'd eventually hit the Taiwan Strait. Few did. The inhabitants left this patch of prairie seldom if ever. Most of them never went mountain climbing, never saw the sea. They stayed home and farmed the land. The soil retained moisture relatively well and was passably fertile. Local produce included flowers, betel leaf, and rice. After several centuries of settlement, it still looked like a farming community. The buildings were low-slung, single-story. A few of the old, three-wing residential compounds were declared national heritage sites, but not many tourists made the trip. Prosperity still hadn't arrived.

In the 1970s a contractor came to Yongjing and obtained a piece of land for a row of townhouses, a first for the township. Ten units, three stories each. The project was supposed to be a prelude to prosperity. When tall buildings start going up it means that a place is going to escape from poverty. At the time, a lot of folks had never seen taller! The building materials and methods were also unprecedented: reinforced concrete, ceramic flush toilets, and crushed granite floor tiles, Taiwan-style terrazzo.

He grew up in one of those townhouses, the fifth from the left. The sixth from the left used to be his eldest sister's place, but now it was sitting empty. The seventh was once a VHS video rental store, but now the whole building was charred black. There was a 出售 "For Sale" sign on the balcony. The place had been "For Sale" for years. The top half of the second character 售 had fallen off, leaving a yawning 口 "mouth" that transformed "For Sale" into "Way Out." The phone number on the bottom of the sign was too mottled to make out.

He stood looking at the sign, lost in thought. After many years in prison, he could really use a way out. Instead, he'd come back here. He knew better than anyone else that this place could never be a way out, not for him. Could that ruined sign lead him all the way back to those bright red shorts?

His eldest sister was the only one who stayed. She now lived in the fifth house from the left, his old home.

The small town was also a ghost town, to him.

A ghost town is deserted. His hometown was indeed out of

the way, remote from civilization, far from any metropolis. Nobody had heard of it. When Taiwan's economy ran wild in the 1970s, Yongjing didn't keep up with the pace of development. There was a brain drain. When young people like him left the countryside they never came back. They forgot the place, they even forgot what it was called. They left behind an aging generation that could never leave. Originally a blessing, the name became a curse. Intended to signify Eternal Peace, Yongjing came to mean Always Quiet. It was really, really quiet.

The summer he got out, there was a drought in central Taiwan. The roads were like stovetops in the afternoon. He could fry eggs, stir-fry rice, or simmer congee on the asphalt, no need to fire up the range. It'd been so many years, but everything matched his memory of the place. The weather certainly did. Boy was it hot! The afternoon heat could slow the second hand of the clock. The trees took an afternoon snooze, the wind died down. If you held your breath and listened you could hear the earth snore, the thick, heavy sound of hibernation. Not until the next rain would the land even consider waking up. As a boy, he'd find a tree and fall so deeply asleep in the shade that absolutely nothing—neither the crowing cock nor the throbbing cicada, neither the squealing pig nor the hissing snake nor even the baaing sheep—could wake him. Truly, he slept like the dead. But after he grew up, he often suffered from insomnia, especially as an inmate. In prison the scarcest commodity is noise. You can't hear the rain fall or the wind blow. The fluttering leaves are inaudible. He told the prison doctor it was too quiet, how was he supposed to get to sleep? Would medication help? He thought of asking if there was a pill that could help him hear the rain. Back home, the rain struck the "ironskin" roofs, playing a bright, brassy, percussive symphony. If he heard rain falling on sheet metal shingles, he could fall asleep for sure.

He came back because he really wanted to hear the rain.

What he heard now was a sewing machine.

That was his eldest sister Beverly.

As her foot worked the treadle, a midday soap opera played on the television beside the sewing machine: the nasty mother-in-law had just slapped her poor daughter-in-law on the cheek. Cocks were crowing, electric fans whirring. He faintly heard firecrackers from the next neighborhood. He hadn't slept in a quite a few days. He'd taken quite a few connecting flights. His mind was so muddled he didn't know where he was, but the sound of the sewing machine was unmistakable. He'd really come home to this ghost town.

Ghost towns are deserted, but where are the ghosts? Are there any?

There were a lot of ghosts in the countryside, living in people's oral accounts. Folks used to tell him never to go near the copse of bamboo out in front of the townhouse. There was a lady ghost lurking in there, a poor daughter-in-law who was driven out of her husband's home after her chastity was compromised. She walked into the bamboo and hanged herself. She had haunted the bamboo ever since, hanging in wait for young men to seduce. When the dogs howled at the moon, they were "blowing the dog conch" according to the Taiwanese idiom, meaning the beasts had seen a ghost. So go to sleep, Mother would say, and don't open your eyes, cause if you do, you'll see it, too. Even if you see it, you can't say it. If you see it, run away—try to outrun it if you can. Don't look when you should not: if you do, you're gonna get caught. The kids said the most ghosts were to be found in the willow trees that lined the irrigation ditch along the field. Don't touch the leaves, they used to say, or you'll get mixed up with a ghostly maiden. You're certain to get zero on every examination, and the only way out of the mess would be matrimony. The maidens in the willows were actually lonely old spinsters waiting for some unlucky sod to come marry them. There was another ghost in that ditch, a beautiful lady who jumped in a well after she was abused by a Japanese soldier. She was rescued, but then she got raped by the doctor she was taken to. In the end she drowned herself in the Muddy Waters. But instead of being washed out to sea, she ended up stuck in the irrigation network. She floated all the way to Yongjing, where she stopped in the middle of the ditch. There she stayed, no matter how fast the water flowed. A temple in her honor was built on the shore, at the foot of the old town wall. His friends said that the moss along the waterline was fresh green blood from her ghostly body. The ditch reeked so bad because of her ghastly stench. As for the mushrooms budding on the banks, don't touch them, let alone eat them, those are her nipples. If you touch one, your luck will turn. If you eat one, your guts will become a haunted house. You'll die, blood spraying from your eyes, before seven days are up. If you see a red envelope on the road, don't go anywhere near it. It contains the Eight Characters of that lady ghost's birth. If you pick it up hoping to find money inside, you'll have to take her as your wife.

Later on, another lady ghost joined the others, a member of his own family. She ran around disheveled, yelling her head off, until she drowned in the ditch.

That reminded him of an old saying, "Hang the cat in a tree, throw the dog in the stream." One time, Mom rode her scooter with him on the back and a pet dog in his arms. He was supposed to toss it in when they got to that irrigation ditch. Afraid of the ghosts, he cried and cried. His mom told him to hurry up. Here, the ditch was practically a slough, because the locals treated it as a gutter: it was clogged with dead dogs and hogs, rotten watermelons, old scooters, even a betel nut stand. Everything stank in the hot sun. A million flies cavorted in celebration, enjoying an all-you-can-eat feast. He made out the putrid carcass of the neighbor's dog, Yeller. Crying, he refused to toss their dog in. He said he wanted to bury it and erect a grave marker. Mother grabbed it out of his arms and threw it into the dead water with a splash. A cloud of flies scattered and immediately reformed with an ear-splitting buzz, as if to say thanks. They hadn't finished with the rotten dogmeat, and here they'd been served fresh.

How was he to tell T? That this was the kind of hellhole that he was from?

How was he to tell T about his absurd upbringing? Five elder sisters, one elder brother, a father who never talked, and a mother who never stopped. The snake killer. Red Shorts. The irrigation ditch. The Wedding of the Century. The bishopwood tree. The White House. The hippopotamus. The Eternal Prosperity Pool. The secret basement. The starfruit orchard. The temple to the Lady at the Foot of the Wall. The Tomorrow Bookstore. The silver water cistern.

In jail he often dreamed about the doggie cemetery behind T's place. As a boy, T raised three dogs, which he buried one by one in the back yard. On each wooden grave marker he pasted a picture. That was the kind of dog burial he had fantasized about growing up in Taiwan. He'd finally seen it in Germany. He also dreamed about the slough Mother threw the dog into, but he never saw a shadow of a ghost. Now that he was all grown up, he didn't believe in ghosts anymore. He was no longer afraid of them. Ghosts weren't scary, people were. The living were the cruelest, not the dead. In his dreams the slough didn't stink, the water wasn't dead. The lotus flowers bloomed, the mushrooms grew in dense mats, and from the heat and the hue of the willows and the silvergrass, he could tell it was high summer. Drawing water from the ditch to irrigate the fields, was, his father, a white-toothed, dark-skinned youth, the most respectable eldest son in town. He smiled in the sun, teeth twinkling. The lotuses were all bashful in his presence.

Pity that he killed T.

If T were still around to ask, he would point to that row of townhouses and say, "This is where I grew up. It's Ghost Festival today, the Day of Deliverance. The ghosts are coming. I've come back, too."

2. *Stuffed into the crack in the floor*

"What'll we do? What'll we do?" Fourth Sister hollered over the phone. "Mom's gone missing!"

Beverly ended the call and collapsed on the floor. It didn't matter whether she hung up or not. Barbie wouldn't even notice. She'd just keep hollering.

The hot summer raged, without rain or cloud to bring relief from the sun, which shone munificently on the town. This heat would be the death of her, but she still couldn't afford to turn on the air conditioner. She forced herself to save on electricity because she hadn't had enough work this month. The floor was nice and cool. She pressed herself against those terrazzo tiles to give her sweaty, aggravated body some relief. A long crack had appeared in the floor after the big earthquake a few years back. She had decided not to repair it. Everything in an old house falls apart, no matter what. The wall cancer—mold and peeling paint—had metastasized. Rats ran rampant. The pipes were often blocked. Sheet metal shingles had been blown off several times. She still remembered what the house looked like when it was brand new: off-white tiles on the exterior walls, snow-white paint inside, shiny floor tiles. The tiles looked pebbly, like they would poke your feet, but they were smooth to walk on, even slippery. The freshly waxed floor was like a slide.

She rolled over and eyeballed the crack. Today was Ghost Festival, which meant that the Gate of Hell was wide open.

Maybe she could see hell through the crack. It was right by her sewing machine, a sign of vitality. Every time she looked, it seemed to grow a bit bigger. She checked a few more times, hoping to see it widen. Maybe one day it'd get so wide she'd be able to stuff herself in. Then nobody would be able to find her.

She remembered the day of the earthquake. Her husband Little Gao tore into the back yard, grabbed a few potted orchids, and ran out, without a glance at her. She hadn't gotten up at all. She just kept treadling. She had a batch of garments to deliver the next day. The earthquake didn't matter. The walls could fall, the house could collapse, she didn't care. But please don't let the power go out. Because then the sewing machine will stop working and I won't be able to fulfill the order and get paid. She hadn't paid the bills that month. The only other thing she was hoping for was that her husband would keep running with those orchids, out of town, to disappear and never to return.

When she was young, she wished she were an orchid. But after that earthquake she felt sorry for those orchids.

How old was this house? The year baby Keith was born, they finally left the three-wing compound and moved into one of the new houses in this row. Counting on your fingers, it was the fifth from the left. Back in the day, this row of townhouses was a construction project to welcome the future to the town. Out back, a fishpond; in front, a rice paddy. The contractor said the feng shui was ideal, that it was a den for dragons, a place to raise a family and make a fortune in. Whoever moved in would take off, just like the town. The small town would grow into a big town, then a city. Tall buildings would go up in the fields, neon signs would flash. At the time, Father was making deliveries around the clock in a beat-up flatbed. Watermelons, potted tree seedlings, garments, you name it. For a time, he mostly delivered betel nut and betel leaf, which reminded him of all the raw red mouths he saw around town. He, too, wrapped nuts in leaves, and chewed his way to a bloody good business plan. He would wholesale green gold. Local farmers grew tons of leaves, and although the quality and texture didn't compare to the leaves from eastern Taiwan— Yongjing leaves were thin and bland—production was steady and they went cheap. The betel nut stands in central Taiwan depended on leaves from the fields of Yongjing. Father cut deals with the farmers, who sold him their harvest, which he drove around selling to the stands. He negotiated the price and pocketed the profit, proving that in Yongjing money grew not only on trees but also on vines. Less than a year in, all five daughters' tuition was paid on time. There was white rice and pork loin on the dinner table. At the beginning of the year his first son was finally born, and at the end of the year, in a race against the clock, his second. With seven kids, the bedroom in the three-wing compound wasn't just crowded anymore, it was cramped, so Father got the down payment together and bought one of these townhouses. He bid his mother farewell and moved out.

Beverly carried her baby brother in on moving day, the first happy day she could remember. Mom was relieved. She finally had two sons and didn't have to face Grandma anymore. Beverly was excited. She walked into a multi-story house for the first time in her life. She took the stairway leading up. There was even a third story. My goodness! She would have her own room. The first evening, Heath slept with Mom and Dad, while Beverly and her second sister Betty took care of Baby Keith. They were both too wound up to fall asleep. They snuck out of bed, picked up their baby brother, and sniffed the fresh paint on the wall. They went up and down the stairs. They rolled around on the floor. They kept stroking the first phone they'd ever had at home, picking up the receiver and listening to the dial tone. They put the receiver to Keith's ear, and he smiled; it sounded like cooing. There was even a sit-down toilet. They sat down and peed—how comfortable it was compared with the outhouse over that smelly cesspit. They used to have to run out in the middle of the night when their tummies cramped up. They'd see snakes squirming on the door in the moonlight. Actually, they weren't scared of the snakes. What scared them was the lady ghost of the outhouse that everyone talked about. In the bathroom of the new house you could lock the door. A press of a plunger and the filth was gone in an instant. Everything was fragrant. There weren't any snakes or ghosts. When Keith cried in the middle of the night, the two sisters made a formula from milk powder. They had no idea how to do it. All they knew was that it was "top notch" Japanese powder according to the pharmacist. They thought the thicker the better, the thicker it was the more nutritious it would be. So they went easy on the water and added a couple of extra spoonfuls. Keith wolfed it down and barfed it all back up again. Beverly and Betty thought he looked funny when he did that. They'd never been anywhere. They'd certainly never seen a waterfall before, but when Keith spit up that milk, well, it was the most amazing waterfall they had ever seen.

Suddenly Beverly thought about her baby brother. How was he doing? Every time she thought of him she would get a hankering—a hankering to smoke a joint.

It was Ghost Festival today, but try as she might, she couldn't see any ghostly revelry through the crack in the floor. At least she could hear Barbie's ghastly shrieks over the phone. They suited the occasion. Beverly looked up at the table she had set with lavish offerings in front of the door. She hadn't eaten the whole day. Putting on a feast for all the lonely souls had turned her into a hungry ghost. The souls should have eaten their fill now that the incense sticks had burned down. She crawled over, opened a packet of crackers, and started munching. They were god-awful. She couldn't understand why these White House food products were so popular when they tasted as dry as cracked earth in the hot sun and when one bite of the sweet kind gave you diabetes, two bites of the salty flavor kidney failure. Course she hadn't bought them herself, it was Little Gao who brought them home from the superstore in the next town. She told him, buy anything for the offering, just don't buy that brand. And wouldn't you know it, he bought a whole bunch. She knew he did it on purpose. They tasted like bricks—why were folks so keen on eating bricks? Brick by brick, the cookies and crackers had been stacked so high they had turned into the White House, the only mansion in town.

They tasted terrible, but she made herself finish. Can't waste food. Chewing for her had never been about enjoyment, it was a burning compulsion. No matter how gross it was, she had to swallow it. Even food that's well past its expiration date is still edible. Spoiled New Year's cakes? Just trim the mold. As a girl, she was well acquainted with the bitter taste of hunger. It was a bottomless privation, a lifelong fear.

In the three-wing compound Beverly lived in when she was a girl, her mother, as the eldest daughter-in-law, was in charge of making meals for Grandma, who often belittled her cooking. Once Grandma splattered hot soup on her and suggested she try feeding it to the pigs to see if even they'd eat it. As she was carrying the soup out, Mom heard some of her daughters calling out in hunger, so she poured the whole pot on them. Beverly didn't find it scalding, just that it was a pity. They'd had nothing to eat the whole day. That pot contained enough soup to fill their bellies. She licked the hot soup off her skin, wanting to get down on all fours and lick up the splashes that were spreading all over the dirt floor. She recalled those hard times after Barbie was born—not just *another* girl, but also the fourth in a row. Father's brothers all had boys first, but her mother kept having useless girls. The failure of several business ventures had left Father totally broke. The table was sparsely set, without grain or meat. Back then Grandma kept a big black dog that Second Sister raised. Sometimes Grandma gave it a second helping. It had more to eat in its bowl than they did on the whole table! Later on Grandma slaughtered that dog and fried it up with garlic in the wok. Father's nephews were called over to have a bite, while his own daughters were ordered to remain in their room. They wept silently when they smelled that intensely meaty smell. They didn't know if they were crying out of hunger or because they'd seen Granny knock the dog unconscious with a brick and toss it in boiling water. The brick, which was stained with the dog's blood, got thrown into the spirit hall, the room where the family altar was kept. From then on, every time Beverly saw that brick, she would hear the dog's pitiful whines.

Today being Ghost Festival, Beverly was reminded that she was the only daughter in the family to inherit the full set of her mother's rituals. She'd been praying with her mother since she was a girl. She was familiar with all the taboos around the different festivals. Of course she knew the dos and don'ts for Ghost Festival. The big round table had to be set up in the entrance and laid with chicken, pork, duck, instant noodles, dried foods, and an incense burner, facing out. In front of the table, a little towel had to be dipped in a pail of water for passing spirits to wipe their hands and feet with before enjoying the food. Three sticks of incense had to be stuck in every dish. The harder the year, the bigger the meal. You burned spirit money as an offering to the lonely souls, so that they'd leave you be. You weren't supposed to dig, move house, or travel for the whole of Ghost Month. One year she wanted to switch jobs, from one garment factory to another. The pay and the atmosphere were so much better there, but her mother absolutely forbade it, reminding her that any girl who switched jobs during Ghost Month would spend the rest of her life picking duds; she was sure to marry the wrong guy. She obeyed and stayed. If she hadn't, she never would have met Little Gao.

The heat had woken her up at four in the morning. The ancient air conditioner died after running for two hours. You had to tap it over and over, and reason with it, and it took its own sweet time coming back to life again. Why not get up, Beverly thought, and slaughter the chicken? She was raising a few in the back yard. The day before she'd chosen it and tied up its feet as advance notice of execution. It was a cock with glowing feathers. Mean and boisterous, it often flew over the walls and fought with the neighbors' dogs. The neighbors complained about it left and right. It cockadoodledooed every morning, rain or shine. By slaughtering it and offering it, she could let everyone have some peace and quiet. The cock knew its time was up and struggled mightily, pecking her arms and squawking piteously. While she tied its legs up tight, the other chickens voted with their feet; they knew their back-yard companion was dead meat. Her mother had taught her how to do the deed. Grab its neck, slit its throat, and let its blood drip into a rice-filled bowl to make pudding with. Pluck the feathers and scald it. Then go to work on the filaments with the tweezers. A few friends were always saying that she was thick in the head but clever with her hands. She'd grown her brain in the wrong place. Either that or it had grown in the right place and then moved to her fingers. She was good at patchwork, sewing, and alterations. She was swift and nimble when she defeathered a chicken. It would end up smooth and shiny, prettier than a market-bought one. But what good is a clever pair of hands? She knew that she was an old-fashioned girl, a reject from an older era. She'd dropped out of school at fifteen years old to go to Shalu to work as a seamstress. Now she was in her sixties, her hands callused. She did piecework at home. If she sewed a hundred garments for export to Europe, she still couldn't buy a single piece of clothing for herself. She often wondered what Europeans were doing in the clothes she had sewn. Drinking coffee by the side of the road? Taking a river cruise? Smoking a joint? Window shopping on vacation with a brand-name purse in hand? No way, Keith said, Europeans were just like her, working hard. But how could she believe him when she'd never been? At least they could afford the clothes she made, unlike her.

So she got out of bed at four in the morning and washed her face with soap from thirty years ago. She'd found it sorting out the mess on the third floor. The packaging was smudged, but stick a magenta bar in the water and you still got suds. The sickening artificial floral fragrance didn't waft, it barged into your nostrils. One year, Little Gao announced he was going to invest their life savings in a soap factory, another of his get-rich-quick schemes. A few days later the factory called to say they'd stopped production. The investment evaporated. All they got out of it was some boxes of strongly scented soap. She hated that soap. But couldn't toss it, it was useful. You could use it in the laundry or the shower, on the dog or the floor. The whole house smelled like cheap perfume. One day the next year on a trip to the supermarket, she saw an entire shelf of the stuff. The factory hadn't stopped production at all. She confronted her husband, who admitted the investment was a ruse to pay a gambling debt. There was no factory, no investment. He'd bought those boxes himself. She remembered her husband's expression during the interrogation. It was as if to say: "Is there anything you wouldn't believe?" That evening she put soap in his soup. It was a bizarre color, not to mention the aroma, but he just slurped it down, without any change of expression. He didn't get sick or die. All he did was belch.

Her husband was immortal, of that Beverly had no doubt. There was no help for it, he couldn't be killed. Or could he? This was her biggest reason to carry on. What kept her alive was the off chance of seeing her husband die with her own eyes.

3. *Without a plastic bag*

I can't remember her face.

Without a plastic bag.

I can't remember her face without a plastic bag.

Memory drifts, volatile, deceitful, self-expunging, fact-distorting. But my memory is stuck to skin. In the hot sun of the seventh month in central Taiwan, sweat erupts, and a plastic bag sticks to my youngest daughter's skin, leaving her silent and blurry.

I do have a good memory for certain facts, especially numbers. I remember the first phone number in the new house we moved to from the three-wing compound. I remember that I was the first son in a country clan, and that I had three younger brothers, five daughters, and two sons. I remember that I got married one time. I remember how much a certain customer owed me in a certain year and how many big cargo trucks I owned. I remember my liver function index before I died.

I've completely forgotten her face. Did she have a prominent nose? How high was her hairline? Big or small eyes? Thick or thin lips? The arrangement of her teeth? I have no idea.

But I remember all kind of numbers in her life. The day, month, and year she was born. That she was the fifth daughter. The score she got on her high school entrance exam. The digits on her scooter plate. That she slept on the third floor. That she sneezed a record fifteen times when she woke up in the morning. That she'd been in hospital six times on suicide attempts before she finally did herself in. That she was 165 centimeters tall.

I only found out her height when I ordered the coffin next door. The coffin maker came over to measure the corpse. "165 centimeters," he said. "She had fine bones and a good figure." The make-up artist applied lipstick and eyeshadow. I'm sure she looked fabulous, but at the time all I could think of was the plastic bag.

We were the first family to move into this row of houses. I was the eldest son of a gentry clan. Before the Japanese left in '45, Mother used to walk me to the public school. Holding my hand, she would point out all the fields that belonged to our family. "We've received a share of the crop from those fields for generations," she'd say. "We've never gone hungry. Just study hard and it'll all be yours." After the Japanese left, I was sent off to boarding school for junior high. Then the Nationalist government carried out land reform. When I came home after graduation, we weren't rich landlords anymore. The family fortune was in decline. Yongjing at the time couldn't be described as barren, but the meadows were weedy, the roads muddy, the snakes fat, the mosquitoes nasty.

That contractor came out of nowhere with truckloads of rebar and cement, gravel and sand. It was an omen of civilization. The bamboo in front of the fish pond had to be cleared for a construction site. Ten townhouses were about to be built. The contractor advertised for temp workers. I signed up and followed the foreman like everyone else. Everyone said there was a lady ghost in the bamboo, but all we saw was a bunch of dead cats hung up in there, along with colorful, lustrous snakes. A bamboo grove that had stood there for a century disappeared almost completely in a week, leaving only a clump. Who in those days wanted a view of bamboo? It was just a smudge of green that signified underdevelopment. Worthless, inedible bamboo was replaced with rebar. Smoke and dust billowed from the construction site. I took a deep breath and got a noseful of metal dust. Boy, it smelled good. This must be the smell of progress.

When I picked up my paycheck, I asked the foreman, "How much are these houses selling for?"

They were three stories, partitionable. Master bedroom for

me and Cicada, a room for each child. When we died we'd leave it to our eldest son.

At the time I had a premonition that this was the house for the Chen family to make a fresh start in. We were no longer members of the landed gentry. I was an eldest son with little money. But I believed that this house would be the beginning of our escape from poverty.

We were the first household to move in. The second was the coffin maker. Not long thereafter, a hardware store opened next door. When a daughter married out or in, we would go to the store to buy the necessities for the ceremony: a pair of "double happiness" cushions, satin streamers, colored ribbons, nametags, and gift baskets, as well as candles and the rest of the Twelve Ceremonial Observances—we could take care of everything in one purchase. When an elder died we could go to the coffin maker to select the wood and the style. It would be great. I had five daughters to marry off and two sons to bring daughters-in-law home for. When I arranged my mother's funeral, and when it was my turn to go, there was no need to go far. Life and death, all in the same row. There was no need to go anywhere. We could live here and die here.

Who would have thought that the first funeral I arranged would be hers?

I have no recollection of her face, but I remember everyone said my youngest daughter was the prettiest.

The year I married Cicada, the matchmaker lady said she was the prettiest in the neighborhood.

Our prettiest daughter, the youngest, looked the most like her mother: big eyes, big chest, thick eyebrows, pale skin. They looked the most alike and hated each other the most.

My little girl's murderer was actually my wife.

So, it's for the best that I have forgotten my youngest daughter's face, though that means I have also forgotten my wife's face.

4. Household Registrar Chen

Betty had gotten off work and walked out of the office before realizing that today was Ghost Festival.

Many stores had set out tables of offerings and smoking braziers. Betty hadn't done that in years. How was she supposed to, living in a small apartment in Taipei? In the first few years after moving in she'd put a little table out on the balcony, but it was too narrow to burn spirit money on. She was afraid she might burn the whole building down. Her only offerings were chicken boiled in brine and seasonal fruits. Without even lighting incense, she put her palms together and pumped her hands up and down to pray for good luck and a good life for the family. The family in the apartment across the narrow lane had also set out an offering, but they sure weren't afraid of a fire. They fed the brazier with a pile of spirit money, until a gust of wind ballooned the flames out of the balcony, raining ash into the lane. Betty noticed a tableful of those crackers. Why was it that everyone loved to buy that brand? The White House crackers reminded her of her fifth sister Plenty's funeral. The spirit money was piled up into a little hill. Father lit the pile and the blaze began. The other sisters threw Plenty's clothes into the fire. The flagrant tongues of flame sucked greedily at her tears. "Plenty," Mother yelled in Taiwanese at the edge of the fire, "remember to come back and get him when you're a ghost!" Mother's mourning had melody, probably because she'd been in the sutra recitation group for such a long time. "Come back and get him" kept repeating, in a different tune each time, and "him" got more and more strident. The sound was high and ringing, like a long, sharp flathead screwdriver boring a hole in her eardrum. The fire burned a few hours until a squall blew up and the ash went flying, swirling all over the sky. Mother didn't break, didn't tire. She ate a mouthful of ash, but her *dantian* opened even wider, allowing her to really belt it out. Talk about a chest voice. "Him" flooded the countryside in waves. Where was he? Too far away to hear, but maybe the ash would find him. It wafted with Mother's wails on the wind, tainting every low-slung abode, every betel nut tree, and every ditch. But the ash avoided the White House entirely—the fence wall, the columns, the roof, everything was just as spotlessly clean as before, without a speck of dust. Embellished with gold, the building glittered.

The ground was wet. Had it rained today? Busy apologizing to angry callers all afternoon, Betty hadn't heard the rain at all. She looked up at the sky. The dark gray clouds bore down, announcing another big shower. She had always liked the sound. In the countryside the raindrops poured down as if from a pail, striking the earth so hard they forced various critters out. The smell of grass floated in the air. Rat snakes rolled around in the mud. Spiderwebs glistened with millions of water droplets. With all the ironskin additions on the rooftops of Taipei, a rainstorm sounded like an air raid. Bombs exploded in the air and debris clanged crisply on the roof, burying the traffic noise and the bustle of the city for a while. "Is there anything you miss in Taiwan?" she'd asked Baby Keith. "I can mail it." In his reply he wrote that he didn't know why but he missed hearing the rain in the countryside and in Taipei. There weren't any ironskin roofs where he was, so you couldn't hear the rain. It was so quiet, too quiet. How could you buy the sound of the rain? She wanted to record it on her mobile phone and send it to him, but he wasn't allowed access to email. The truth was that she had no idea how to get the audio file from her phone onto the computer. How was she going to send the sound of rain?

Waiting for the bus on the sidewalk, she stepped in a big puddle to dodge a bicyclist. She was up to her ankles in dirty water. She imagined the dissolved dust and filth and acid rain seeping into her leather shoes and cotton socks and inviting fungus to take up residence between her toes. But she didn't want to step out. The hot summer weather made the foul water feel surprisingly cool. They'd implemented energy-saving measures at work, limiting the use of the air conditioner. The whole day she sat soaking in her own sweat. Stepping into the dirty puddle reminded her of jumping in the mud as a girl, sometimes stepping on a slippery stink snake. She'd spent the whole day in a muggy office and the only consolation turned out to be a puddle of putrid water. A sour reek of decay wafted from the armpits of the male colleague who sat to her right. To top it off, he'd gobbled down two boxes of stinky tofu at his desk for lunch. When the female colleague to her left took her shoes off, her feet putted stinking shots at her nasal cavities, one precise hit after another. The odor was strong enough to annihilate civilization. From the mouth of the balding director who yelled at her for not being flexible enough flowed a garbage-laden river of halitosis. The supervisor who consoled her had only to scratch at his scalp to pour a pail of slops for the hogs. The citizen who stuck his finger in her face and accused her of disrespecting animals stank like a dog. Body odor was a deadly weapon, a blade with which all these people had been slitting her throat all day long. She didn't actually mind dogs, not at all. The wild dogs in the countryside reeked even worse. She always liked burying her face in a dog's belly or grabbing its paws and getting a good sniff. In the three-wing compound she lived in when she was a girl, Granny had raised a black dog and made her responsible for feeding it, until she bashed it over the head with a brick, cooked it up, and ate it. She knew Granny didn't especially like dog meat. It was because of her that Granny killed that dog.

Now she lived in a small flat in Taipei. Three bedrooms, one family room. With her, her husband, and their daughter and son, one more cockroach would make it insufferably crowded.

There was simply no space for a dog. Her daughter was out of work, her son out of school. They were probably waiting for her to come home and make them dinner right now. She liked dogs! But today she'd gotten onto a lot of people's news feeds because of them. She stood accused of discriminating against dogs.

Her window handled household registration. She updated registers, issued transcripts, and replaced ID cards. It was simple work, an ideal job. It was perfect because it was all of a piece and the pay was regular. It wasn't complicated. Once you got the hang of it, the tasks you had to perform from day to day didn't change much. This was the kind of life she wanted. She got up at six every morning and made breakfast for her family. She had to be out the door before seven-thirty to catch the MRT and make her bus connection. She got to work before eight-thirty, sat down with a freshly steeped cup of tea, turned on the computer, and waited for the public to come in. People took slips of paper and waited for the number to be called. Everything was so orderly she took it for granted.

But in the past few years, her "ideal job" had gone haywire. Civil servants of her generation had to learn to use a computer as adults. Technology crashed over her like a tidal wave. She surfed it as best she could by learning to use the new word processing software. After everything went electronic, the pace of work increased. A volume of work that once took several days now had to be done in an hour, so people wouldn't complain about "bureaucratic inefficiency." She managed to work faster, but she couldn't get used to all the cameras. They were all over the place, and always in your face. Many citizens would start recording her with their phone cameras when she told them they couldn't get the document they wanted. They were "gathering evidence," they said, to show the whole world how awful Taiwanese civil servants were. Everyone carried a smartphone around. Anyone could start recording at a moment's notice.

The threat was that if she didn't hurry up, they'd upload it to the internet or hand it over to the media.

One time a pretty young woman with big, shining eyes and long hair came in. She reminded Betty of Plenty, her baby sister. She looked bashful, like she hadn't seen too much human filth. She was there to apply for the maternity grant but hadn't brought all the required documents. There wasn't any way they could get it done for her that day. She lost it. She started throwing documents at the window and yelling. "I'm going to give birth any day now! I don't have any money, why won't you people help me!" It was just a brief outburst. Betty and a few colleagues came out from behind the counter to comfort her. They steeped her a tea and had a friendly chat. They told her what to watch out for when she went into labor and what to pay attention to when she sat out her month of recuperation, what she should eat more of. Congratulations by the way! They recommended obstetricians. They talked and talked. Finally, she smiled, her big eyes shining even brighter. She would come back the next day. That evening the crying girl made it onto the television news. A few of her fellow citizens had livestreamed her outburst. The spectacle of a hysterical girl sent some sparks out into the tedium of daily life. One video went viral. "Who's the Toughest Customer? Watch This Pregnant Girl Go Berserk!" read the clickbait title. She got doxxed. A reporter went to the open-air market where her mother worked, focused his camera on a lady who was slaughtering a chicken, and stuck a microphone in her face. "Did you know your daughter is expecting? Have you seen this clip?" The reporter got out his tablet and played the viral video of the daughter screaming at the household registration office. The mother looked shocked. She was still holding the chicken neck she had just cut. Fresh blood was spurting out onto the chopping block.

Betty hid in the bathroom and watched the video of the screaming girl over and over, thinking about Plenty.

She didn't come the next day, or ever again.

Later, in response to the public's proclivity to "record video evidence," her boss demanded that in addition to the CCTV cameras in the office everyone on staff had to shoot each interaction for self-protection.

That morning, Betty forgot to turn her camera on.

There was a sudden disturbance in the waiting area. A child burst out crying. Betty was at the photocopier. She came out to see what the matter was. A man had brought five big dogs in, taken a number, and was now waiting for it to be called. A child who was afraid of dogs happened to be waiting with his mother, who took one look at Household Registrar Chen and demanded that she deal with those dogs. "My son is terrified of them. Isn't this a public agency? Shouldn't dogs stay outside? They can't be allowed in, can they?" When Betty went up to communicate with the guy, he took out his phone, started shooting, and said: "These are guide dogs, I'm a trainer." She offered an immediate apology. "Oh, I'm so sorry, I didn't realize you were visually impaired." "You think I'm blind?" he asked, raising his voice. "Didn't I just tell you I was a trainer? Not blind. The dogs have to follow me around for me to train them. They can't stay outside. I'm going to lodge a complaint that you're not seeing-eye dog-friendly."

The boy sobbed, the man yelled, the dogs stayed. Betty went back to the photocopier and didn't think too much about it.

A few hours later, calls for "Household Registrar Chen" started coming in. Soon her extension was ringing off the hook. People started yelling as soon as she took the call. A reporter showed up to ask: "Why do you hate seeing-eye dogs so much?"

It turned out that after leaving, the trainer had edited the video and uploaded it to a seeing-eye dog society's social media account. Betty's colleague played it for her. It was really well done. He'd added a special effect, a red arrow pointing at her face, and a line of narration: *Household Registrar Chen is no friend to seeing-eye dogs.* No surprise, he cut the part where she'd said "visually impaired" and he'd said "blind." With her frown and furrowed forehead, she became the face of discrimination. One shot was of his cowering dogs, the next was of her apathetic expression.

The insults hit her like a tsunami. Bitch! Trash! You got no fucking respect for dogs! Taiwan can't get ahead because of civil servants like you. Weevil! My taxes pay your salary. You'll quit if you know what's good for you. Lousy bureaucrat. Cunt! I'll loose my dogs on you, they'll tear you to pieces. You have no sympathy. Don't you know fur babies are man's best friend?

The last call she got before clocking off started out with a dog barking. Then someone said: "Fucking bitch! You better watch out!"

All her regular work was put on hold. Her boss told her to write a report and hand it in the next day. She knew it was a letter of contrition. She probably didn't have a ghost of a chance of even a "Satisfactory" on this year's performance review. He patted her on the shoulder. "Ms. Chen," he said, "you're something else. You didn't even cry." She was thinking, for what? I grew up getting yelled at. What's so bad about this?

The bus was taking forever to come. Betty couldn't help it; she swiped her phone and watched the clip again. She paused it at the close-up of her face. So that's how she looked now. A collapsed blob and an icy gaze. What a contrast she made with those excitable canines! No wonder everyone thought she was a bitch who discriminated against dogs.

Shops all along the street were burning spirit money. Her eyes scanned the tables. On almost every one sat a box of White House crackers. They were inescapable. Two years before she'd gone to China on a group tour. As they took in a sea of cloud from the peak of Huangshan, the local guide got out those crackers and asked, "Care for a treat from Taiwan? A taste of home?" Nobody took him up on it, until he said they were complimentary. Then everyone fought for one, afraid there wouldn't be any left. Strolling through the immaculately preserved village of Hongcun to the southeast, they saw a little girl eating the same kind of cracker. Dining on crab on West Lake several hundred kilometers to the east, you guessed it, she saw those crackers again. Last year, she found a shelf full of them in a Japanese pharmacy while buying vitamins for her husband. She wrote a letter asking Keith if they had this kind of cracker in the jail in Germany. She wouldn't be surprised if they did. Wasn't everyone talking about globalization?

A few high school girls at the bus stop were watching a video on their phones with the volume turned way up. She had no trouble making out "Household Registrar Chen." It appeared she was famous. She stepped out of the puddle. When she got close enough to listen in, she overheard them cursing "that terrible civil servant who hates man's best friend." One of them eyed her, as if to say, "What's this *obasan* doing getting so close to us? Ew, look at her feet, they're filthy!" They didn't recognize her as the star of the clip they were watching. She'd been worried that after a day spent getting yelled at over the phone there'd be no way to escape insult in her daily life. But she squeezed on the bus and the MRT and pushed her way through the crowd in the evening market, and absolutely nobody recognized her along the way.

She told the pork peddler to give her the same as yesterday. He looked at her, searching through the faces of his regular customers in his mental rolodex without finding a match. That's funny, don't I come here to buy meat almost every day? Betty wondered. He obviously doesn't know how to do business.

She had no idea that she was colorless and transparent, the easiest kind of existence to overlook in a crowd.

A few days before when she was doing yoga stretches on the

bedroom floor, her husband walked in and didn't even see her. He picked up the tablet, lay down on the bed, found an adult video, pulled his pants to his knees, and started jerking off. Holding her upward-facing-dog, she didn't dare to exhale forcefully. Her husband moaned and wiped himself off with the blanket. Soon his moans turned into snores. Without risking a glance, she stood up as quietly as she could and tiptoed out of the room. The covers and the blanket will have to be steam-cleaned, won't they? How come he didn't notice me? I was lying on the floor by the bed! Not that it wasn't for the best that he didn't.

As she was leaving the evening market with the pork, her phone started yelping. She looked down at the screen. It was Barbie.

"Betty! Betty! Come home right away! What are we going to do? Mom's gone missing!"

She took a deep breath. "Mom's been dead a long time," she said in her most indifferent tone.

Barbie wasn't even listening. "Hello? Betty? Hey, come home as quick as you can. Can you hear me? Mom's gone missing!" Betty had no idea that Barbie hadn't heard her reply. She didn't know that she was colorless, her voice too soft to hear. Transmitted through the phone, it was light as a feather, weightless even, and unable to reach her sister's ear. "Mom's dead," she said. "Quit yelling. I'm busy at work in Taipei, I don't have time to go home." But her sister just kept hollering, not having heard a thing.

Household Registrar Chen was like a ghost, floating formlessly about. Her existence was automatically edited out of people's vision and hearing. Actually, this was the lifestyle she wanted: to be invisible in a crowd, blending in with the background. She saw no reflection in the mirror, left no prints on the ground. She just drifted around. She hadn't disappeared yet, but she didn't fully exist anymore.

5. The baby boy in the starfruit tree

Keith wished he could tell T: There are trees where I come from, lots of them.

Several fields had been planted with betel nut palm trees until poor harvests turned farmers to planting betel vines. There was a flamboyant phoenix tree in the school grounds of Yongjing Elementary that the sun had lit on fire every summer for over a century. When it burst into gorgeous red bloom overnight, the children would pick the scarlet calyxes and corollas and make butterflies, with sepal bodies and petal wings. That reminded him of one weekend when the family went into the fields to weed and water. When Ma went to Main Street to buy bowls of crispy tofu soup, rice flour pudding, and *bah-uân*—"meat circles," those saucer-shaped dumplings with a minced pork filling—the kids sat making butterflies and waiting for lunch under the phoenix tree. Suddenly a cloud of cabbage whites flew over, and Beverly muttered, Don't move! Everyone froze. The butterflies alighted upon them, until the sound of Ma's scooter and the scent of those *bah-uân* dumplings prompted a mad scramble for lunch that frightened them away. Heath was the first to get his, as usual, and he got the biggest portion. "Boys need energy," Ma said. Heath could have an extra *bah-uân* and two extra bowls of soup. His soup was sure to have chunks of tofu and a pork ball or two, while his sisters only got tofu, sometimes only broth. Keith was also a boy, but maybe Ma had noticed something funny about him, the baby of the family. He ate tofu soup just like his sisters.

Besides the phoenix trees, there was a bishopwood tree by the junior high school that was regarded as sacred. It was supposedly a thousand years old. The townsmen had tied a red banner on it that read: *A thousand years Lord Bishopwood has reigned, a mighty king. Reflecting sun, reflecting moon, He shines all through Yongjing.* There was a tiny temple by the tree, with another red banner: *Let the birds sing! Long live the king!* There were also rainbeans, banyans, and clumping bamboos. His mother told him never to play around in that clump of bamboo in front of the house: it was haunted by an evil spirit, a ghostly maiden waiting for little boys to catch, to say nothing of the venomous green bamboo vipers. But Dragon Boat Festival was an exception. Then she'd take him into the bamboo to pick leaves to wrap sticky rice cakes with for the steamer. He kept his eyes peeled but didn't see any lady ghosts or snakes. There were just cat corpses hanging from some of the stalks.

He knew T would go on to ask: What about winter? How cold does it get? Do the leaves wither on those trees?

T's family lived in a small town called Laboe on the Baltic Sea in northwestern Germany. The snow buried everything in winter, leaving the trees bald, the grass brown. New buds and sprouts only appeared in March or April. Keith recalled that penetrating icy cold, the winter wind that cut like a knife, slicing off the tip of his nose. One year, they visited T's old home for Christmas. It was the coldest winter since reunification, but the air around the dinner table was even colder, bone-chilling. T and his father didn't talk the entire day, until they couldn't hold it in any longer. They started to fight at dinner. T's father threw a plate on the floor, kicked over the Christmas tree, and hurled colorful German vocabulary in Keith's direction, spittle flying. He didn't understand a thing. Words he didn't understand shouldn't have done him any damage, but the man's fury was clearly directed at him, the foreigner. He managed to make out a couple of the slurs, sure he was the intended target. When T's mother ran outside, Keith followed her, closing the door behind him to insulate himself from the heated argument inside. Without shore lights, or even moonlight, he and T's mother stood in the front yard in the dark. Night was all-consuming. There was a big expanse of black sea before them, but absolutely no waves that he could hear. He wondered whether the water at the edge would freeze at ten below Celsius. T's mother tried to light a cigarette, but a blatant gust threatened to swallow the flame. He held out his hand to block the wind. Right after she succeeded in lighting it, the wind left, leaving everything deathly still: the swing hanging limply from the leafless bough of the apple tree, the brown grass under the snow, the tide, the sea itself. T's mother seemed to have died, too. Her eyes flickered out; he couldn't hear her breathing. She was holding a cigarette without smoking. She was crying without tears. He wasn't sure if he was still alive. He'd come running out without a jacket on, and now the cold drilled up into him through the soles of his feet. His hands were numb. The world was pitch black. The only sign of life was the lit end of that cigarette, silently aflame.

T kicked the door open, suitcases in hand. He was lobbing grenades of abuse at his father inside. T found his hand in the dark and said: Let's get out of here! I'm never coming back to this cursed place. They ran pulling the suitcases behind them along the road in the freezing wind, which invaded their bodies through their nostrils. They didn't run too far. They stopped by the sea and held each other, panting. He still didn't know what father and son had been fighting over. All he knew was that T was crying.

They sat down on the shore, pulled out all the clothes in the suitcases, and put them on. T said a bunch of things in his mother tongue, then switched to English when he remembered Keith didn't understand. Sorry, I got so worked up fighting with my father in German that I forgot I needed to translate. Welcome to my home, Laboe. Come on, say it three times, Laboe, Laboe, Laboe. Hard to say, no? Put an o and an e together and, sorry, it's a strange sound. German is a strange language. You'll know what I mean as you pick it up. This is Laboe. The city on the other side of the strait is Kiel. This strait is the Kieler Förde, an inlet of the Baltic Sea. This is where I grew up. You can't see it, but there's a beautiful white sandy beach right in front of us where I spent many summers swimming, soaking up the sun, chasing girls, chasing boys—until I found you. I used to lie on the beach the whole summer watching the ships in the strait, especially the big cruise ships that set out from Kiel for Scandinavia, thence for the world. I loved this beach, but I hated it, too. The sand trapped me here, I couldn't go anywhere. There's a beached submarine, a U-boat from Second World War, down there. As a boy I dreamed of driving off in it and going all around the world. Thank goodness I took the train to Berlin instead, or I wouldn't have met you.

T talked a lot, and for a long time, as if he couldn't stop. Talking through his tears, he pointed out a row of bare trees there that would bud out beautifully in spring. They were always so fine and so green. The dead trees would come to life again overnight. What about back home? What kind of trees grow there? Do the leaves fall in winter?

Keith didn't answer. Using the cold as an excuse, he said he was freezing to death. Let's go find a hotel to spend the night in. Or should we walk over there and sleep inside the sub? Have a good night's sleep, then pilot it all the way to Taiwan?

Now that Keith had finally come home, he wanted to tell T how green it stayed all winter. The leaves didn't fall, the grass didn't wither. The days were shorter, but the nights never got dark, because of all the chrysanthemum fields. Those flowers were a cash crop, a mainstay of the local economy. To inhibit blooming until the time was right, the farmers outfitted the fields with millions of bulbs. It was like a sun shining at night, a sea of light. There was no need to look up at the stars and moon: this ordinary little patch of countryside sparkled with stars. The yield increased annually. More farmers took the plunge, until an incredible area was under cultivation. A fantastic number of bulbs lit up at sundown, driving the night away, all year round.

There's a stupendous inland sea of chrysanthemums not far from the townhouse I grew up in, T. I'm from a small town on which the sun never sets. Can you imagine? There are so many trees and flowers. The kind he wanted to tell T about most of all was a flowering tree whose fruits were shaped like stars.

He'd taken the train back first thing in the morning. It was a slow train, the kind that stops at every station, even in Yongjing. Yongjing Station was unmanned and usually deserted. Around it in the flat farmland of central Taiwan were hovels with rusted sheet metal shingles and siding, fallowed rice paddies, and dry irrigation ditches. He'd grown up here, but somehow he couldn't get his bearings after disembarking. When he ran into an old man shouldering a sack of corn into the station, he had to use his rusty Taiwanese to ask: Which way to Main Street? The old man opened his mouth to reveal raw red teeth and a chewed-up cud of betel nut. He pointed the way and said that was where he'd just walked from. "Young man, don't you have a cellular phone? Check the map."

Keith shook his head. They weren't allowed in prison. Only now that he'd gotten out did he realize that everyone, even an old man bringing corn into a deserted train station, carried one around, staying constantly connected, while he was out of touch, a lost soul. For now he had no desire to return to the human realm, so he hadn't picked one up.

He started walking in the direction the man had pointed him in, deciding not to return to the row of townhouses right away. Instead he would take a tour, and if he got lost he would ask for directions. He was afraid of being recognized, even after all these years. His aunts and uncles had never left, let alone his grandaunts and granduncles. So he hid behind the downturned brim of his hat. Only when he was sure the coast was clear did he dare look up. He passed the Eternal Prosperity Temple. A tiny building in his memory, it was now an imposing, almost palatial, three-story edifice. In front there was a square in which tables were often set out for roadside banquets. He remembered attending a temple fair with his father, marching in the procession, and praying to the Lords of the Three Mountains. Then he passed by the Qingfu Temple; it had been built during the Qing dynasty for the blessings, the *fu*, it might bring. It used to be a little light brown temple to the neighborhood god of the earth. Why didn't it match his memory at all?

T, now I'm an atheist, just like you, but I want to show you the temples I frequented as a boy. Later on you'll see the Eternal Peace Temple, the Sweet Rain Temple, and the Lady at the Foot of the Wall. So many temples for such a small town! When I ran a fever as a boy, my mother wouldn't take me to a doctor, we'd go burn incense at temple and *siu-kiann*, "collect my wits," while we were there. She took the bright yellow paper talisman from the temple keeper's hand, lit it, and tossed it in the water. Then she fed me the water. I imagine that if you heard me explain all this, your jaw would drop, and a bunch of question marks would tumble out of your mouth.

So many temples, and the one he wanted to see the most was the Lady at the Foot of the Wall. It was a little temple where Mother used to recite scripture. It was a place to watch films, to slaughter pigs, to grill sausages, and to kiss. It was the temple he dreamed about the most in his prison bed in Germany. In his dreams the temple expanded until it was a hundred stories high, and the big tree behind it grew until it reached up into the sky, while in the square they replayed the first film he ever saw in his life over and over again. He'd forgotten the name, but remembered it was an anti-Japanese epic, about the war of resistance. He watched the film sitting on Red Shorts's lap. He could feel something mysterious in those shorts getting slowly hard.

Next he walked to the open-air market, which was crowded with shoppers buying offerings for Ghost Festival, but the stand selling the *bah-uân* he'd loved most as a boy was gone, and the market was noticeably smaller. He recalled a hundred vegetable and meat stalls; why were there so few now? Maybe the market was the same size and it was his memory that had shrunk. He continued several blocks. It turned out that a chain supermarket had opened a location and erected a billboard advertising goods from all over the world. A lot of grandmas and grandpas came here to buy groceries. No wonder! The new supermarket had taken the place of the traditional market.

He got to the Mainlander Noodles stand and ordered bowls of meat stew and sesame noodles. The taste was off. He could tell from the first bite that the boss from Sichuan hadn't made it. The boss had come to Taiwan after the war. Now he was sitting in a wheelchair, hooked up to an oxygen tank, without the old sparkle in his eye. Now it was his son who was preparing the noodles. The flavor of the stew and the noodles was much diminished. The hot sauce had no kick. Taste had not been handed down. After finishing the noodles, he went walking across the fields. A lot of the old betel leaf fields were gone, a lot of farmland left fallow. There were "For Sale" signs stuck in the soil. A chrysanthemum field he used to play in was now occupied by a ramshackle building, an abandoned motel. There were no flowers to be seen, only overgrown weeds, some taller than he was. The elementary school building was new, at odds with his childhood memory. Betty had mentioned it in a letter. The earthquake had caused a lot of scary cracks to appear in the walls, and the old three-wing compound to collapse. The school had been rebuilt, but the compound was razed. Good riddance, wrote Betty. Now that it was finally gone, there was one less reminder of her childhood. She would be in a better position to forget. She'd tried her hardest to turn her childhood off, but when it got dark and she closed her eyes, the three-wing compound stood there glowing. At least after demolition there was no physical evidence. She wasn't just afraid of earthquakes, she was in awe of them, especially the one that had caused walls that in her memory seemed indestructible to collapse, in just a few seconds.

Of course he couldn't miss the Wang family mansion, the White House, with its Ionic order columns and ornate golden balustrades. It was blindingly bright. It must have just been whitewashed again. He observed it from a distance, not daring to approach. To him, it was a gore-splattered White House, the setting of a badly acted soap opera. Every time he dreamed about it in prison, it was bloody.

Dear T, I'll tell you about the White House later. First, the starfruit trees.

It was still there. He followed the path through the field and found the familiar orchard. Although the fence had fallen, and overripe starfruits littered the ground without anyone to come collect them, the trees were still standing. The trunks and boughs looked even thicker, and even more heavily laden with fruit. He picked a ripe one with translucent flesh and took a big bite. It took him back to when he was seven years old. He was playing hide and seek with the neighborhood kids. He always ran the fastest and found the best hiding places, where nobody would ever find him. That time, he raced behind the townhouses, by the fishpond, through a patch of purplish globe amaranth, around the slough, and past a three-wing compound where someone was drying grain in the courtyard. He took a shortcut through a duck farmer's yard and another through the soy-sauce factory grounds. He ran and ran, until he finally reached the starfruit orchard. It was a frontier where his little seven-year-old body had never ventured. Where is this? How long did I run for? Am I still in Yongjing? If I hide here my playmates might never find me.

A low fence around it, blossoming starfruit trees inside. The little purplish-red five-petal flowers were spaced out, as if they were shy of one another. It was so clean inside the orchard, without a single dry leaf on the ground. Outside the summer was oppressive, but in here a cool breeze was blowing, and a bouquet was in the air, at once sweet and tart. He chose the tree with the biggest trunk to climb up, not daring to breathe aloud. He was afraid that if he made any noise he would get caught for sure. But if he could only stay quiet, this was the safest corner of the world. Nobody could find him here.

He waited and waited, until he fell asleep. When he woke up and looked down, he saw red.

Under the starfruit tree sat a tall, tanned, topless fellow in red shorts. He was reading.

The man looked up. "Are you Cliff Chen's baby boy?" he asked in Taiwanese.

The red shorts kept expanding in his field of vision, until they occupied his mind. He stared at those shorts, speechless.

"Hey, don't be scared. You're safe here. They'll never find you."

Dear T, right then and there I fell in love with that man in red shorts under the starfruit tree.

6. The life-eating third daughter

Belinda had a sudden craving for starfruit soup.

Steaming hot. Served in a creamy porcelain bowl. With two heaping tablespoons of sugar. When you've got a cold, it clears your sinuses and soothes your throat. In winter, when the steam off the turbid brown broth hits your eyes, it's like you're holding an alpine lake with mists swirling up from the palms of your hands. You can serve it cold in summer with ice cubes and longan flower honey, stirring it clockwise and counter-clockwise to get it all mixed up. Then you quaff it in big refreshing gulps. Your forehead freezes and you forget you've ever heard of summer before.

There were always starfruits at home when she was a girl,

sent by the basket, beautifully ripe. Mother washed them gently with a soft brush, sliced off the edges, and cut them crosswise. Voila, a tangy plate of amber stars, topped with condensed milk, plum powder, and brown sugar. She would brine the leftovers in a big glass jar. The pickles were ready in a week. You could stew them with jujubes and wolf berries to sweeten a chicken broth. They went nicely with black tea. Belinda's favorite was starfruit soup. To make it, Mother strained the dregs, simmered the juice, and served it with sugar or honey.

Every time she got hit, she felt like drinking starfruit soup.

But now she wouldn't let herself.

Mother taught her and her sisters how to plant all kinds of fruit: papayas, bananas, eggfruits, passion fruits, and guavas. They didn't keep any for themselves, just took the harvest to hawk at the market. Folks said that "the third girl eats life," meaning that the third daughter in a family is fortunate. She's born into privilege. Indeed, Belinda's parents doted on her. Knowing how much she liked guavas, they always saved a few for her. She found a corner to eat them by herself, not sharing even a bite with her sisters.

But now she didn't eat guavas at all. Everything she used to love, she never ate anymore. The things she used to hate, now she forced herself to chopstick into her mouth, serving herself a heaping bowl, sometimes without rice. Smiling, she chewed slowly until she swallowed the last bite. Growing up in Yongjing, she particularly loathed green pepper, eggplant, bitter melon, and broccoli. She found them monstrous in color and appearance, ugly and deformed. She could have overlooked the deformity, but they were the same on the inside: strange in taste and texture. She would throw up every time. But now she ate all these vegetables, especially bitter melon, and the bitterer and bumpier the better. She hid in the kitchen, closed her eyes, and felt the skin. The bumps were like tumors, a precipitous terrain. She wondered if her insides would feel the same to the touch. The silky-smooth surface she presented to the world concealed countless tumors. Each was stiff and hard, recalcitrant and dry. Day and night, they slowly grew, impervious to any drug, getting more and more malignant. If she could turn herself inside out like a sweater, she'd show her true colors: she was actually a gruesome green tumor monster. So she wore brand-name clothes and accessories, reading the materials tag carefully when she tried things on. If it was pure wool, mohair, cashmere, or silk she would swipe it, and if she saw polyester she would put it back on the rack. She needed the softest, smoothest, classiest armor to hide the bruises, or else the world would discover that she was actually a bitter melon, tumorous from head to toe. Tumors grew on her skin, swollen black and blue. After a period of rehabilitation, they hid in the recesses of her body. She couldn't feel them from the outside, but her bones, veins, and organs could feel them. She forced herself to eat more bitter melon, with a smile, because she herself was a metastatic bitter melon. Eating bitter melon was like eating herself. One bite after another, she chewed herself up. Eventually she would disappear.

To eat bitter melon, green pepper, and eggplant was also to make a clean break with the girl she used to be.

Knowing how much she hated eggplant, Mom wouldn't make it. She served it exactly once on the round dinner table in their bedroom at Grandma's place. They ate the poorest fare in those days: sweet-potato congee, three times a day, fish and meat hardly ever. One time her father carried in a crate of purple eggplant, a gift from her granduncle. Her mother heated a hunk of lard in the wok, sizzled minced garlic, and stewed chopped eggplant. Right before serving, she seasoned it with sugar and soy sauce. Each chunk of purplish brown eggplant was shiny with oil. Everyone ate it heartily with congee, except for her. She'd rather go hungry. She wouldn't eat a single bite. That was the last time eggplant appeared in the house.

Now she ate it all the time. She found Italian eggplants in a high-end supermarket in a posh department store. They were round as bowling balls, with violet skin. Sometimes there were pure white eggplants from Israel. No matter, into the basket they went. She never looked at the price, just bought a basketful of expensive ingredients that she hated, took them home, and forced herself to swallow.

One time she wore a dress that exposed a bruise on her back. On the way out the door to a wedding banquet, her husband grabbed her arm. "You trying to get me in trouble? What are you going to say when someone asks you how you got it? We're going to be late. You have five minutes to get changed."

Her husband counted every second, demanded speed in all things. Every evening at seven o'clock sharp, he appeared at the news anchor's desk. Never late, he divided time into precise slots and tolerated no procrastination. They were leaving in five minutes. He'd been invited to speak at the banquet, they had to be on time. He snipped the backless dress off her with a pair of scissors, got her a long-sleeved red dress out of the wardrobe, and ordered her to change into it. Without a second to waste, she didn't cry or yell, she just put on the dress. Without a hair out of place or a flaw in her makeup, she headed out the door before the five minutes were up. Her husband was a marionettist; she was the marionette hanging on the string. The arms weren't hers, or the legs, and the expression was painted on. Her limbs might jerk violently around, but she never stopped smiling.

When they got home after the banquet, he got a call from the station. There was a major murder story, he had to rush to the studio to go live with a reporter at the crime scene. She immediately fetched two clean suits with a matching shirt and tie and put them in a bag with vitamins and Ginseng Chicken Essence. She went down with him to the basement parking lot, where they met their neighbor, a legislator. Her husband kissed her cheek and drove away. The legislator looked envious. "I get so depressed every time I see you two. How can you be that lovey-dovey, an old married couple? Do you have a sister you could introduce me to?" She laughed. Her laugh sounded too dry. Can't have that, no, no, no. A laugh should be moister. Inject some feeling, don't let your secret out, that you're dry inside. Adjust your smile! She tried to make small talk. "I'm an only child, and you're welcome wherever you go, Legislator, how could you need an introduction? Didn't I see you with that starlet in the last issue of *Entertainment Weekly*? Right in front of our tower?"

She rushed into the elevator and checked herself in the mirror. Was her pleasantry just now—did it sound sincere? Was the smile demure enough? What about the accent? Did she enunciate? Did she talk like a hick? Her husband often commented on the earthiness of her accent, her funny twang. She announced her shameful background every time she opened her mouth.

When she got back to the apartment, she went into the kitchen, opened the fridge, and saw an aubergine lying like a snake on a tray. She grabbed it and started chewing, right away, without rinsing or cooking or throwing up. She didn't cry or yell. She was a good wife, well trained. There was nobody to see her, but she was still a good wife. If she could eat that awful eggplant while looking out at the lake, a good wife she could remain. She was eating too slowly. Gazing at a white water bird, she told herself she had to finish before it flew away. She stuffed the rest of it down her throat. The bird shook itself, beat its wings, and flapped over the water.

Nobody from her family had attended her wedding. Her husband wouldn't allow them to set foot inside that hotel. If he laid eyes on anyone from her family the wedding was off. He showed her a polished press release. If the wedding got canceled, he'd send it to the major stations. The tone was coldly impartial, based on the gory real-life event, but with enough embellishment to spin a yarn that put himself in the best light possible and threw her family under the bus. His expression was cool and composed. He said he was a newsman—the right to speak was in his hands. "You think you can explain away that farce last night?"

"She's my baby sister!"

He lit a cigarette. She had no idea he smoked. "Count me lucky. Watching the video clip, I was thinking, thank God I didn't choose your sister. Too bad, such a pretty face. Hurry up, call your father, tell him to stay at the hospital in Changhua, don't rush up to Taipei. He's old, lots of health problems, right? What are you waiting for? Call. Do it. If I see your father at the hotel, or if you let anyone know that my fiancée's family is your family, then I'll do it. I'm a man of my word."

She'd kept that press release, all these years. Her husband was a storyteller. She had no voice. She didn't have a narrative function.

One year on Ghost Festival, the building manager had set out round tables for the residents to place offerings on. Of course, she knew her husband would forbid her from taking part in such a superstitious congregation. She joined his church after the wedding. She got baptized, converted to Christianity. But she'd helped with the tables and talked with a few ladies about the festival. Growing up in the country, she dreaded Ghost Festival but also looked forward to it. It was scary because the Hellgate was agape. At the thought of all those lonely souls flitting around I would have to snuggle close to my mom and dad at night—lucky for me I was their favorite, they always let me sleep with them. But I loved it, too, you know? My parents bought all kinds of food for the offering, whatever I liked to eat. Everything on the table was my favorite.

As soon as she came in the door she got pushed down on the floor.

"I saw you holding incense."

Her husband hit her with such skill and just the right amount of force, but without touching her face and arms. It would hurt, she would bruise, but never bleed. A few times, when he'd let his nails grow, he scratched her back and blamed her for having thin skin. Since then, he'd aimed at parts of her body that she would cover with clothing, so that no black, blue, or red would show.

"How many times do I have to tell you? 'Thou shalt have no other gods before me!' You just don't want to listen, do you? Don't do anything boorish like that again, you're not a country girl anymore. I have to go to work. You're not to leave the flat today. I'll bring you a midnight snack when I come home." She got ice cubes out of the freezer and pressed them on her injury. Her fourth sister's name flashed on her phone.

"Hello? Belinda? Come home quick, Beverly and Betty are ignoring me, you know me the best. Please come home! Mom's gone missing! Mom's gone missing! She's really gone this time. I can't find her anywhere. Can you hear me?"

Fiddling with the ice cubes, she wanted a bowl of starfruit soup so bad. It was so hot out, she needed a cold fix.

Living in the three-wing compound as a girl she had never heard of ice. One day her father took her with him in the pickup to a factory. It was hot and muggy outside, but inside there was another world. It was so cool in there. The workers were carrying bags of white rocks. She'd never seen anything like it. Belinda, her father said, those are "ice 'cubes.'" He picked one up off the floor, showed it to her in the sunlight, and popped it in her mouth. Ah, she'd never forget the taste. It was the loveliest, yummiest treat in the world! She guessed only rich people could afford it. After she grew up, she'd make a pile of money, pile up those beautiful ice cubes around her house, and eat them every day. Dad, she said, I want to make a bed of ice to keep us cool at night.

Later on, after her two baby brothers were born, the family moved into the townhouse, which was equipped with their very first fridge. She recalled opening it over and over with her sisters, waiting for the water to freeze in the tray. They had to wait until everyone else was asleep. Finally the cubes formed. Arranged on the table, they sparkled appealingly, giving off an alluring frosty mist, until they disappeared down the sisters' throats. The girls stuffed themselves with ice cubes, ate them with meatball stew, rice, stir-fried rice noodles, sweet red bean soup, *bah-uân*, pot-stickers, and noodles with sesame sauce. They called it a science experiment. They fed an ice cube to their little brother, who wasn't even one yet. He ate it, frowned, smiled, frowned, and cried. Then he smiled again. He looked so cute! How are you, Keith? I keep saying I'll go to see you in Germany. I'd like to see that big lake you told me about. But you've visited me here, you know how it is. I can't go anywhere. Now, and in the future, this is the only lake I'm going to be able to see.

She pressed the ice on her sore spot, but it quickly melted, no match for the heat that the anchor's fist had left behind. She didn't have to look in the mirror, she knew she was smiling.

7. Ghostspeak

I'm a ghost.

How appropriate, for a ghost like me to speak about ghosts?

I died, but I still "exist." Here I am, talking to myself. My "existence" isn't in light, sound, or shade. It's not a physical phenomenon. Science cannot prove it. There are no units to count it. It is unquantifiable, immeasurable.

Memory is the medium of my existence and my transmission. Through my memory and others' memories, I am "present," here and now. I cling to memory, like a parasite. Anywhere there is memory, and stories to be told, that's where I reside. Whenever history is told orally, I am in people's throats and mouths, on the tips of their tongues. When stories are written out by hand, I ride the tip of the pen, plunging onto the paper. Unless the sheet is burned, shredded, or crumpled up, that's my dwelling place. But even if it is destroyed, people can memorize a text, making a perfect mental copy of a page. In that case I dwell in the mind. Memory, full of secrecy, is my breeding ground. Concealed, undivulged, anonymous. Dirty, nasty, rotten. Secrets buried for an entire lifetime, that's the softest, most inviting medium for me.

Not to mention trees and streams, earth and grass. That banyan I used to climb remembers me, as does the bishopwood tree to which I prayed. The bamboo grove I helped cut down remembers me, as does the field where I lay down to sleep. This small town remembers me, for I lived here and died here. Where else was I going to be a ghost?

But memory is erratic. That pot of porridge on the table, a family of nine ate it. If you asked Cicada, then me, then the five daughters, then the two little sons: Was the congee you just ate thick or thin? Then everyone would remember it differently. And the answers wouldn't just be thick or thin, because between thick and thin lies an expanse of "in-between." Imagine a crooked line. Between thick and thin there is a line that no external force can straighten. It is warped, following a roundabout route with endless twists and turns. In some places, it's knotted up. There's a place in every flexion where shadow provides protection and lies can be lodged. Those who said it was thin actually thought it was thick. Those who said it was thick actually wanted it to be thicker.

But because of all that in-between, I can find an ideal medium whenever I want, a dark place that is piled high with secrets. If it stays warm and damp, I'll stay, too.

I'm just a farm boy who lived and died in central Taiwan. I harvested crops in the field. Later I drove a truck, making deliveries. With only a junior high school education, I could never have expressed myself so articulately in life. But death induces incredible transformations. After I became a ghost, all linguistic boundaries instantly dissolved. Everything I could not say before, I can say now.

In "ghostspeak," the nonsense that makes sense, the truth in fiction.

When I was still alive, I actually never spoke.

My mama always said I was too quiet. I didn't cry or make a fuss. I didn't snore or turn over in my sleep. I barely seemed alive. Many times, she shook me awake when I slipped into such a deep sleep after she nursed me that she worried I had suffered SIDS. I'd wake up wide-eyed and unblinking, but still silent. She wondered whether her eldest son might have some mental impediment, or was he a deaf-mute? It was a herbal balm that convinced her that I didn't, and wasn't. My earliest olfactory memory is of a pungent herbal balm. My mother used it every time she got chewed out by my paternal grand-mother, for instance, for messing up the dishes for the spirit offering. You can't cook this kind of meat like that, Grandma said. You can't fry this sort of vegetable like that. If you offer it to the ancestors, they won't like it. If some misfortune should befall any of their descendants, how will you take responsibil-ity? You're just a daughter-in-law! She did as Grandma said, cooked up a new table of dishes, but then she got yelled at for missing the opportune moment. She must have let the ances-tors go hungry on purpose, Grandma said. Then she slapped her. Every time she got hit, she would lock herself in the room, get a vial of bright green balm out of the cabinet, hold it under her nose, and breathe it in as hard as she could. It was a cure-all, effective for scalds and snakebites, for aches and pains, even for rheumatism. Mother loved the smell. She would use it every time she got a panic attack, taking a mighty sniff and rubbing it all over herself. One time she was crying as she applied it. She saw me sitting there, watching her expressionlessly. So she applied it to the insides of my nostrils. I can still remember the scent, even now that I am a ghost. It's as if someone is kicking or punching around in my nose. At the sight of my forehead bunching up, she stopped crying. Then she stuck her fingers, still covered in that balm, in my eyes. It was like a knife or sword dancing on my corneas. Finally I cried, finally she smiled and burst out laughing. My granny heard her. She pushed in the door, charged up, and gave her ear a pinch. Dinner's not cooked yet, and here you are laughing. Listen to yourself, you sound like a ghost! Who the hell are you trying to scare?

The herbal balm was concocted at the Lady at the Foot of the Wall. The temple keeper said it was a natural herbal prescription, rub it wherever it doesn't feel right. Every time Mama went to the temple, she bought quite a few vials. Every time she got hit or yelled at, every time she felt anxious, she would get it out. She was always giving off a powerfully minty aroma. She liked to make the rounds of the temples, praying to all the gods. Whenever she heard that a certain deity had the power to answer prayers, she made a trip to the temple with me in tow. She prayed for Granny to meet an untimely demise, for a bountiful harvest, and for her four sons to grow up and bring home brides and have another bunch of sons, don't let them have any useless girls. She liked taking me to pray, because I was the quietest. I never complained no matter how far it was. I didn't cry or fuss. One time at a temple fair at the Lady at the Foot of the Wall, she handed me over to the keeper. She busied herself burning spirit money, tossing the crescent-moon blocks, and murmuring to the spirits. When is the old crone going to croak? she asked. Only when she passed on would she see some better days. I sat listening to the tipsy keeper babble. When he pinched me, I didn't respond. He pinched me harder, but my expression didn't change. Then he took a few lit incense sticks from the burner and poked me in the arm.

It hurt, but I didn't cry.

When my mama got back and saw the burn, the keeper said, "This son of yours has no respect for the gods. He was playing around with incense." When we got home, Mama got the balm from the basket and told me to lick it off her fingers. It was so bitter, so spicy. I threw up and got the runs. She cursed me, but in a quiet voice. While I was praying for your Granny's early demise, you were insulting the gods. No way Granny's going to die now. If she doesn't die, how am I supposed to live?

Granny didn't die early, she lived to a hundred.

I bought the first townhouse in the row. A couple of doors down a coffin maker moved in. When she died, I could go next door and buy her a coffin, to fulfill my responsibility as the eldest son.

But, to my great surprise, Mama, too, lived to be a centenarian. I predeceased her. The next coffin I had made after Plenty's was my own.

My memory of my mama is still of scent. When I smell a herbal balm, or whenever someone crushes mint leaves, I think of her. Yes, a ghost that exists because of memory is itself full of various memories, of scent and touch and pain.

After I married Cicada my mama had a whipping girl, someone to take to task. She repeated the same things to Cicada that Granny had said to her. The minty smell got fainter and fainter. Cicada was the eldest daughter-in-law in the compound, but she kept having girls. My mama yelled at all of them from Beverly and Betty to Belinda and Barbie. Then came Plenty, or Ciao, as we called her then. By that point, Mama didn't smell minty at all.

Once that herbal odor had worn off, she stopped visiting the Lady at the Foot of the Wall.

Now it was Cicada's turn.

It was her turn to go beg the Lady: Please, please, let my mother-in-law die, as soon as possible.

One summer day, Cicada looked up at the sky and said, It's not rained here in Yongjing in a long time. The dirt in the ditch is going to crack. The vegetables in the field are all shriveled. If this continues, will we have a good betel leaf harvest? She announced a big ritual at the Lady at the Foot of the Wall. She would recite scripture with her friends. I had a funny feeling. Who would hold such a ritual first thing in the morning? Had someone made a pile of money and come back to fulfill a vow? Or had someone died? Someone, whoever it was, had arranged to thank the resident deity bright and early.

That morning, right after dawn, Cicada and the rest of the reciters picked up their microphones and started to chant. All the male cicadas in the big tree behind the temple got woken up by the chanting, and they woke up cranky. They flexed the tymbals in their tummies for all they were worth, producing a deafening roar. There were twenty pigs to slaughter that day, but the butcher had a funny feeling, too, when he heard them chanting, a group of them, and so early in the morning. It was a sleepy chant, with the occasional yawn. But he hadn't the time to worry about what was going on in the little temple next door. He was in a hurry to do his job. When the first slung-up hog felt the tip of the knife it squealed pitifully before dyeing the gray floor red.

The male cicadas, the butcher, and Cicada sang in a raucous chorus, waking up the sleepy town. The cocks started to crow, the dogs to blow the conch, the dead cats hung up in the bamboo to meow, the geese to honk, the ducks to quack, the mushrooms on the banks of the irrigation ditch to grow furiously, the light-controlled chrysanthemums to bloom on cue, and country folks like me to come to. My fifth daughter Plenty suddenly woke up and sneezed fifteen times. The ghosts in the public cemetery all woke up, too, as did the weeds, the tree snags, and the fallowed fields, along with the molds, the rice stalks, and the wildflowers. All the living and the dead, including the living who wished they were dead in that small town were woken rudely up.

I woke up, like everyone else. Damn! I said, lying in bed. What a racket!

That was the day those police slipped into Yongjing without anyone noticing.

8. A room without a view

Barbie feared windows and refused light.

She remembered how they all used to sleep like tinned sardines in that bed at Grandma's place. With no space for pillows, she lay her head on Betty's calf, Belinda lay hers on her stomach, and Beverly lay hers on Plenty's butt. By the bed was a window with a wooden frame, with a view of a rice field. She liked lying by it, pretending to sleep, but actually hungry for the sight of the moon and stars. In those days she was so afraid of the dark that if she had to go at night, she would hold it in until morning. She was terrified of the ghost in the outhouse, too. Now she was no longer afraid of ghosts or the dark. She felt her way to the bathroom in the dark. She fiddled with her phone in the dark. Now she knew the thing you should be scared of in the dark isn't a ghost, it's yourself.

When she was a girl, Yongjing suffered a rash of burglaries. Beverly said she'd heard that the burglars were a couple of strangers who only struck on moonless nights. If they saw a woman they would rape her. When Mother went shopping at the market, she, too, heard these terrifying rumors. So in the evening before she went to sleep, she bolted the wooden door and leaned a couple of chairs against it. The rumors got more and more terrifying. So the neighbors formed a militia that patrolled the paths through the countryside. One dark night, Barbie was startled out of sleep by a clamor, the sound of pursuit. Men were running around and cursing outside. Everyone else was fast asleep. Looking outside, she could not see the rice field, just a dark shadow that loomed towards the window until it burst into a blinding flash of light. She rubbed her eyes. The flash disappeared. A man with shadowy features stood in front of the window, looking at her. She wanted to scream, but he placed his forefinger on his lips to shush her, a gesture somehow so forceful it snapped her vocal cords. Like a candle that had been snuffed out, she watched the man outside, mutely and motionlessly. He took a couple of steps back, pulled down his pants, and started to fiddle with himself.

The clamor came closer and closer. The man's hand moved faster and faster, until a shiny white substance spurted onto the window. The man put his finger to his lips again, waved at her, pulled his pants up, and ran away, just before a group of yelling men arrived. Shadowy figures ran back and forth waving batons. "Call the cops!" someone yelled. Finally her parents and sisters awoke along with all the farming families in the neighborhood. It turned out that the militia had almost caught that thief. The Wang household had suffered a break-in. All Grandma Wang's gold was gone.

The next day Mother spent a week's grocery money on an air gun to use for self-defense. She said, we can go hungry a couple of days, nobody will die. But who knows? We might be next. Placed by the bed, the air gun had an inauspicious metallic odor, like it was waiting for those evil-doers to show up at any moment.

Barbie wasn't sure if an air gun could protect their family. She had another idea. She asked her mother whether they could install a set of curtains. Busy cooking Grandmother's lunch, Mother slapped her in reply. Barbie blamed herself for her stupidity. She should have gotten her third sister to talk to Mother about it—both Mother and Father loved her best. If Belinda asked for curtains, there would be curtains. Every night, as soon as she lay down, she saw that milky white fluid spurting onto the window. If there were curtains, she wouldn't see it anymore.

She started to fear windows. At night, she lay as far away as she could get. In class, and on the bus, she sat by the aisle. If the task of wiping the windows for spring cleaning fell to her, she did it with her eyes shut. But she could still see that strange white goo that glowed in the dark.

After they moved into the townhouse, she finally had her own room. Wooden partitions separated the space on the third floor into six cubicles, one for each daughter plus one for Baby Keith. When Plenty said she wanted the one by the balcony, Barbie wasn't going to fight her for it. She chose the next one down, which had a tiny window of matte glass that looked out on the hallway. This reassured her. Finally she had a room without a view. Finally she could get a good night's sleep.

She went to a fabric shop to ask for scraps, as cheap and dark as possible. The shopkeeper gave her some for free. She asked Beverly to sew the scraps together and Heath to nail up a wooden pole. That was her curtain. It was good enough to block the light. When she called it a night she made sure that the curtain covered every corner of the window and that Plenty was in the next room. Only then did she feel safe enough to go to bed and get to sleep.

Now she lived in a spacious upstairs room at the White House with an en-suite bath and a full-length window that overlooked the entire town. But actually she had no idea what Yongjing looked like now.

Were the fields the same as before? Was the Mainlander

Noodles stand still in business? Had the Lady at the Foot of the Wall been torn down? Betty said the three-wing compound collapsed in the big quake. That was for the best, for whenever she thought of the window she slept by as a girl, she got a full-body rash. The compound had collapsed, but was that row of townhouses still standing? She hoped the same earthquake would be the end of the White House. She was actually happy when it started, because she thought that was going to be the end of her. It turned out that the White House was almost completely intact. There were some cracks, but no structural damage at all.

As if, her husband Baron said, we used only the best materials, top quality. We're not afraid of any earthquake. Even if all the houses in Taiwan collapse, don't worry, Barbie Chen, our White House will still be standing.

Barbie Chen, he said, you never go out, you'd never guess how much the world has changed. Open the curtains, Barbie Chen! Take a frigging look outside.

Barbie Chen, I'll open the curtains while you're asleep. Okay?

Barbie Chen, oh Barbie Chen, have you heard anything go bump in the night lately? My workers are digging a foundation. Guess what, I'm going to build the biggest building in the world right here in Yongjing.

Bar! Bie! Chen! We're all moving when it's done. You don't want to stay here by yourself, do you? Will you come? You'll have a floor to yourself. An entire floor! But I won't let you install curtains.

The past few years he'd taken to calling her by her full name, as a provocation. Sometimes he'd sing it do re mi, turning her name into a tune. A number of times he called her by the wrong name. He called her Plenty instead.

What's with the names of the five sisters in your family? he'd asked her one time before the wedding day. Beverly, Betty,

Belinda, Be, Be, Be. Why switch to Barbie for you, and then Ciao for your little sister?

Because she and her sisters were unwanted. Hoping for boys, Mom and Dad kept having girls, three Be-s in a row. To their astonishment, the fourth child was another girl. They thought they had better not call her Beth, Bernice, or Beatrix. So they broke with tradition and called her Barbie, in order to break the girl curse. Who would have expected that the fifth child would also be female?

At the time, she would answer Baron no matter what he asked. Now when he kicked in the door and yelled at her in the darkened room, she did not pay him any mind. He would yell and make a fuss, and when he got drunk he would kick at the piles of newspapers and magazines. She actually wasn't worried that he would find her. Her room was like a maze, and he did not have the patience to find his way around. She could hide in some corner of the room making phone calls and he would never be the wiser.

She knew that he could threaten her all he wanted, but he'd never dare draw the curtains. For a while, he disappeared. She heard from the groundsman that he was in China on business. He kept making the news. Baron Wang Snaps Up Electronics Firm, read one headline. He was hoping to diversify, to build an Oriental Silicon Valley. Several months later, he suddenly returned from China, bringing a bunch of friends for a late-night party at the White House. The next morning he broke the door down and jerked the curtain open. Sunlight flooded in. Dust danced densely in the air. When she saw the light she lost it. Roaring like a tigress, she jumped on his back and hammered at his head. He threw her off onto a pile of newspapers and magazines, but she jumped immediately back on and clawed at his face with fingernails she had not cut in several months. He cried out in pain and begged for mercy. She jumped off and bellowed, "Close the damn curtains or I will claw your eyes out and burn your house down, starting with these newspapers and magazines! I doubt you used asbestos in the White House walls."

Since then, he'd just holler her name at the door, but no longer dared to open it. He would say something sarcastic and leave. She finally had the room all to herself. Nobody else was allowed to come in. When the groundsman delivered her meals, he was only allowed to quietly open the door, set the meal on the floor, close the door, and leave. She'd even ordered him to turn off all of the lights outside before he made his delivery. She knew there was a crystal chandelier from Paris twinkling like the Milky Way right outside the door. Baron *still* hadn't removed it. That chandelier was one of Plenty's demands.

Barbie had chosen the fabric for the curtains herself. Jet-black and heavy, they would totally block the light. One layer wasn't enough for her, she ordered three. She had a set of three-ply curtains made, so that she could be sure that no light would get in. She had heard of villages north of the Arctic Circle that experienced polar night in winter. She had created eternal night in the White House.

Between her and the outside world, the air-tight window blocked sound, and the curtains light. Sun, moon, and wind could find no crack to enter. The curtains hadn't been taken down and washed since installation. Sometimes, to make sure she wasn't dead, she buried her face in them and took a deep breath. The dust particles and mites in the fabric entered her body and triggered her allergies. She started sneezing. Achoo, achoo, achoo, achoo, achoo, at least five times. By the fifth sneeze, she had confirmed that she was indeed still alive. The sneezes made her think of Plenty, who used to sneeze when she woke up. She would sneeze and sneeze and sneeze. At least ten times a day.

Another way to be sure that she was still alive was to call

someone. She was always calling her elder sisters. Is Beverly still working in the garment factory? Betty and Belinda live in Taipei, but didn't they say they were coming to the White House to see me? Why haven't they come? She had a phone to make all the calls she wanted. Her sisters would answer no matter how busy they were.

When the groundsman brought breakfast that morning, he asked her if she wanted to come down to pray, seeing as it was Ghost Festival and her husband wasn't at home.

She replied with silent refusal.

The Hellgate was open. She wasn't afraid of ghosts anymore, but she still believed in them. What to do what to do? The ghosts were coming, she had to make an offering. Otherwise the ghosts would be angry! What about Mom? Where had she gone?

"Where's Mom?" she bellowed. "Have you seen her? It's Ghost Festival today, I have to ask her how to make the offering! Only she knows how to do it right!"

The groundsman just closed the door.

She felt her way in the dark to the desk, turned on the only light in the room, a dim table lamp, and started to read the paper. There were piles of newspapers and magazines in her room. They were bound into reams, the reams piled up into mountains that grew and grew until they crowded the ceiling. That paper mountain range dominated the room, leaving only narrow winding passageways for her to crawl through. She washed her clothes in the bathroom and lay them out to dry on the slopes. Leftover chicken bones and condiments she would toss at the peaks. The newspapers and magazines got moldy, though you could still tell that the newspapers were from the same date, the magazines the same week. When they stank up the hallway outside, the groundsman came knocking. The boss, he announced, said that something had to be done about it. The smell would be difficult to explain to the VIP guests.

The groundsman promised not to touch the piles. All he'd do was clear off the chicken bones and the other leftovers and install a dehumidifier. The dehumidifier operated industriously all day long, but started to beep in the middle of the night. She hit it as hard as she could but it would not hold its tongue. She opened it to find it full of water. She happened to be thirsty. So she drank the entire pail. When she shoved it back in, the machine finally shut up.

She still had to make an offering. To do that she had to find her mother. Only she knew how to do it. Barbie had no idea. And there was no way the groundsman would know. She took a look at a tabloid by her desk. "Is Cracker Jack Junior's Wedding Off? Or On Again With Another Sister?!" the headline read. She must have read it a thousand times. She always thought she might have missed something.

She heard an infant crying.

As if there could be an infant in the White House. It must be a ghost. Mom!

It must be because the White House had not made a spirit offering today that a ghost had come.

What should she do? Mom would know. Oh my God. Mom's gone missing. Unable to recall where Mom had gone, she made calls to her elder sisters.

"Mom's gone missing! Mom's gone missing! *Mom's gone missing!*"

Her yells echoed in the room and woke up all the mites and the spiders, the roaches and the rats. In the past few years the moldy publications had absorbed all of her yells, which would come back out again whenever she nudged them, along with a menagerie of corpulent vermin.

When the newlyweds moved in, the echo was really loud. When they were writhing on the bridal bed, the shrieks of ecstasy resounded in the room. They often forgot to close the window. And so the sounds of newlywed pleasure seeped out over the balustrades and the fence wall, through the rice fields, and down the highways and byways of the township. They woke up domestic animals and even reached Plenty's ear. Sometimes he would yell "Plenty!" when he climaxed. Barbie felt the ecstasy of victory. What with the window refusing to close and all, Plenty must have heard it. It was because this room would leak secrets that she later had to seal it up like a crypt.

In those days he did not call her by her full name, he just called her Barb.

"Barb," he said, "I built the White House for you. It's your wedding gift. Do you like your bridal suite? From now on, I'm going to buy you whatever you want. So tell me, what do you want?

At the time she only wanted one thing. For Plenty to disappear.

9. *The mayor on the factory wall*

Will you please just tell me what you want?

T would start off quietly, then raise the volume. What do you want?! He went from questioning to bellowing. The curtain had to come down on the shouting, which always turned into crying. T would cry and say sorry.

He wanted to answer, but there was tape over his mouth, and he was tied up. T would tear the tape, loosen the bindings, and say sorry. Sorry, I know I should see a doctor. Sorry. Does it hurt?

That glue was really strong. His lips had been ripped off, and his mouth was gone. So much the better. He would not have to reply to T's question. Yes it hurt, his whole body hurt. T held him tight, which hurt even worse. Teary-eyed T started to kiss him, but he could not return the kiss. His mouth was gone, how could he kiss? Sometimes the tape was stuck to his nose; then he couldn't breathe at all. When he had almost asphyxiated, T cut it. What an artist T was. When he took a sharp blade to the tape he'd stuck to his lover's skin, he could avoid his flesh, adroitly cutting a passageway for air.

T, I've come home. I know you always wanted to go home, back to that small town by the Baltic Sea. There you had a beach to race down, ships to gaze at, and snow to wait for. You would wait for the end of summer and then for spring. You would wait for the fish to come onto the hook, and for the next train. You always wanted to get away but kept coming back to that little seaside cottage to see your parents and your old dog and eat smoked saltwater fish: trout, eel, salmon, mackerel, speckled dogfish, and Kiel herring the color of caramel. Anytime you smelled fish, you would think of the Baltic Sea. Fish were your childhood and your adolescence. You always complained that you could not buy fish anywhere near as tasty in Berlin.

Before he was released, a cellmate asked him: Where will you go after you get out?

He didn't have friends or family in Berlin, or any place to stay. He would probably go to a halfway house. But first he had to go home. Home? that cellmate asked him. Where are you from? There was a globe in the prison. He put the tip of his finger on Germany, started it turning, and traced the route he would fly through Europe, central Asia, all the way to East Asia. He opened a flight route home to an island destination. The finger-drawn flight route passed through China and arrived at the Pacific Ocean. But there was no island for it to land on. There was nothing, just a blank. On that globe, Taiwan did not exist. He pointed at that patch of sea and said, I'm from a little island around here. The island is my home, my home is on that island. That island must be so small the globe in the Berlin prison forgot to include it. Looking into the sea, he wondered: Is it possible that the island has sunk beneath the waves while I've been in prison? Has a massive earthquake hit my distant homeland, rearranging the tectonic plates, while I, in the parallel space-time of prison, have no idea?

But now he had really come home, to the center of this non-existent island. He left the starfruit orchard and headed even further out. He wanted to go pay his respects to his father. The graveyard was near the township line. Death was inauspicious, unclean. It might disturb the regular order of society. So they put it on the outskirts. The remoter the better, so that the living did not have to see the tombs. Maybe that way they could avoid death.

His mother had refused to let him attend his father's funeral. Many years ago his father had been diagnosed with terminal liver cancer. He went to a few big hospitals, but the doctors all said he only had a few months to live. So he gave up on chemo. He didn't check into hospital, but he did not go home, either. He said he wanted to go live out his days at the temple. Mother had always kept him on a short leash. "I've only got a few months to live," he said. "Please." She bellowed her opposition. "I'm dying," he said. "Just let me go." The Mother Matsu Temple in Yongjing was really quiet, without many pilgrims. Following the keeper's schedule, he kept early hours. He nursed his illness and waited for death to come.

And wouldn't you know it, a man who, according to his doctors, only had a few more months to live ended up holding on for a decade in that temple.

When his father finally left the world, Keith was in Germany. "Father passed away yesterday," Betty called to say. "Can you come back for a visit? You know Mother, she's volatile. She said that if you come back for the funeral, she'll be the next one to die. I've thought it over and come to the conclusion that this is Father's funeral, he would want you to be there. So come back anyway. I'll figure out how to handle Mother. He needs at least one of his sons to hold his spirit tablet, right?"

"What about Heath? Didn't he get out of prison?"

"Who knows? He said something about making a comeback, going back into business with the Wangs. But we can't find him anywhere."

He flew back the very next day. It was almost midnight by the time he arrived in Yongjing. Beverly, Betty, and Belinda were sitting at the round table folding paper lotus flowers in Father's makeshift mourning hall. "Thank goodness you're late," Belinda said when he showed up. "Mother's gone to bed. She still doesn't know you're coming home."

The hall was austere, in accordance with his father's wishes. The simpler the better, he said. The ceremonies didn't have to be elaborate. They didn't have to burn anything for him. They could just pray a bit and cremate him. The photograph of the deceased was of Father in middle age, smiling. With shining eyes and thick eyebrows, he was handsome, even with wrinkles. Father had kept a lot of secrets in his life, but in this photograph he looked at peace. The deceased was at peace, while the living were evasive. His three daughters and his baby son were all beating around the bush, stuffing tricks up their sleeves. Father's body had not been placed in the coffin yet. They had to wait for the opportune moment. Until then, his corpse had to be kept on ice. They could see Father lying silently inside the cooler in a death gown. Keith put his hands on the transparent lid and said, "Dad, it's me." In death, Father looked just like he did in the photograph: his wrinkles had relaxed, and his hair was black.

Keith volunteered to keep the vigil. After all, his body was still on German time. He wasn't sleepy at all. "You can all go to bed, I'll stay up."

Yongjing was really quiet after dark. The air was autumnal. A cool breeze brought the faint buzz of insects. It had been a long time since he'd seen his sisters, hadn't it? Why was everyone so aloof, without a hug, without any bodily contact at all?

They even avoided eye contact. They didn't express any emotion. They just kept carrying things out for him to eat. "You should eat more! What are they feeding you in Germany?"

The door of the hall was wide open, and the lights were on for the wake. Behind the incense burner a little radio was playing a scripture recitation loop. Mercy, Amituofo Buddha, ran the weak refrain. He sat by himself folding lotus flowers and eating instant noodles. His sisters had reminded him to look out for animals. There were lots of wild and feral cats and dogs in the countryside that, by custom, could not be allowed to approach the hall. He kept his wits about him, watching out for creatures that might be lurking out of sight. That's when he noticed how wide the road out in front had gotten. It was freshly paved. The asphalt glittered under the lights of the mourning hall.

The first to wake up the next morning was Mother. She took one look at her youngest child and threw shade: "Where's your brother? Is he still on the mainland? When a father dies, a son has to come back to carry his spirit tablet. You're back, but you're useless. You don't count."

She was just getting started. "Spendthrift!" she cried. "Wastrel! Prodigal! I never want to see you again!" After ordering her youngest child away, she trampled on her husband's last wishes. The undertakers arrived to lower the body into the coffin and take it for cremation. "The coffin is too shabby," she howled, throwing her arms around Cliff's corpse. Even though the Chen family were no longer well off, it was not as if they could not afford a decent coffin. She would go choose one herself. Beverly explained he'd gone next door to order the coffin himself, and he'd made a point of choosing a cheap wood and a simple design. It was just going to get burned, he'd said. All that mattered was that it was flammable. But Mother wouldn't listen. Father would be cremated over her dead body. "We're going to bury him in style!"

She was still embracing Father and alternating between howling, crying, and chanting a bunch of scriptures and spells when Keith finally left.

So he missed his father's funeral. Soon after he returned to Germany, he went to prison. He'd never visited his father's grave, but he knew where he must be buried. Now that he was back for Ghost Festival, he should make the trip.

He walked and walked but must have taken a wrong turn, because he could not find the way. The country roads were nothing like he remembered. He remembered dirt or gravel roads; now they were paved. You came out of the orchard, went past the soy-sauce factory, around a few bends, then you'd see the graveyard. His brain must have overheated, as he couldn't navigate by memory. After numerous wrong turns he finally found the factory. It was abandoned. The sheet metal shingles were gone, the grounds overgrown with weeds. As a boy he could find it by the sour, salty smell. Ah, that smell. His apartment in Berlin had been close to a candy factory. He smelled a sweet odor every time he opened the window. The day he killed T, a thick honey fragrance floated in. "Oh, they're making honey candy today." He was covered in blood, T's blood. And his own. It hurt a lot. He felt so sleepy. The honey made him think of the beautiful spring, when flowers bloomed and bees buzzed. He smelled the honey, lay down on the cool floor, and fell into a deep sleep. Before killing T, he hadn't slept in a long time. Finally he could sleep, a dreamless sleep approaching death.

Smell was the sense by which he would orient himself. The orchard smelled of ripe starfruit, the Lady at the Foot of the Wall of stick incense, the graveyard of spirit money ash, and the soy sauce plant of the mellow sweetness of fermenting soybeans. Now that the factory was abandoned, there was nothing to smell, but something to see. The outer wall was covered in a mottled canvas mural, an assortment of posters, and sticker advertisements. He took a closer look at the palimpsest. The mural had come first, a monstrosity that touted the mayor's achievements. The brushwork was execrable, the palette exaggerated. It was a harvest scene, with beautiful grain, blooming flowers, and farmers grinning ear to ear to celebrate the bounty of the year. That was the background. The figure was the mayor. He had a big round head and gleaming white teeth. A banner carried his message to the citizens: "When will all the winning stop? Let's celebrate a bumper crop! Mayor Heath and the Wang Foundation thank you for your support."

Heath.

The township mayor was his elder brother. Sixth child in the family. Finally, a boy after five girls.

That was his brother's face all right. A full forehead, thick eyebrows, big eyes, curly hair. Like Mother. The mural was weathered. Flecks of paint had fallen off. The lips were gone. From close up, Keith could see a lot of insults had been written on his head. Fuck your mother! Corrupt bastard! Greedy bugger! Go to hell! Give us our money back! Then the campaign posters and the sticker advertisements had occupied the wall, covering up the mural bit by bit. He read the names on the posters one by one, and the positions the candidates were running for: alderman, representative, county mayor . . . Then the adverts: Fortune Teller. Commune With Master Ji Gong. Used Car? Car Loan. Sofa Refurbishing. Factory Direct. Farmer-Direct Guavas. No Frills Divorce. Catch Your Spouse in the Act. Professional Male Matchmaker. Non-Surgical Boob Job. Crack Control. Cistern Repair. Gutter Cleaning. Professional Loan Collector. Scrivener. Investment. Vietnamese Brides. God is Life . . . It wasn't out with the old, in with the new. The old might be peeling off, but the new just kept getting stuck on top. The wall was a riot.

The posters and adverts were his home. His home was charlatans and usurers, gangsters and matchmakers. It was politics and corruption. Whatever your situation or symptom, you could find something here. Every ad had a phone number at the bottom. There was an answer to every question in life at the other end of the line.

"Hey Classmate!"

A little truck pulled over by the side of the road. The driver popped his head out and greeted him.

"Keith Chen?" He hopped out and walked over. It was Sam.

Sampan Yang. The sampan that made him seasick. His classmate from junior high. The second country boy he fell in love with after Red Shorts.

10. Thank you Paris

Her phone rang, again.

Beverly crawled up from the terrazzo floor, assuming it must be Barbie. Several months ago she'd read a news story on the Internet about a European vacation the White House Wangs had taken. What they wore to the airport, what airline they flew on, what hotel they stayed in, what brand of car they drove—the reporter listed all the travel details, specifying brand and price. "Baron came along, but with his new squeeze, not his wife." The reporter did a family tree that included the tycoon's Taiwanese wife and his mistress in Beijing, both of whom received the same bespoke Paris brand-name purse. Of course it included his eldest son Baron. Baron's wife had not been seen in many years. His new girlfriend was a twenty-year-old model who'd recently made her catwalk debut. The insert at the top of the page showed the missing wife, looking distraught.

Baron's wife was Barbie. This picture was taken many years before, at Plenty's funeral, by a paparazzo with a telephoto lens. What did Barbie look like now? Beats me, her eldest sister thought. So she went to the White House with a basket of fruit, pressed the electronic doorbell, and noted the CCTV cameras in the gateway. No-one answered, but she knew she was being watched. Suddenly the groundsman popped his head out of a side door and waved for her to come in.

Beverly hurried over. "Don't worry," she said. "I'm not that dumb. I know that they're on holiday in Europe. I saw it on the Internet."

The groundsman frowned. "You make my life difficult showing up like this. Baron might ask to see the CCTV videos. Now I have to edit them. Hurry up, come in. I don't want anyone to see you."

He led her through the flower garden and into the White House. Beverly stood in front of Barbie's door, knocked, and said, "Barbie, it's me. I'm here to see you."

Barbie didn't open the door. She dialed Beverly's number and started yelling before Beverly had even taken the call. "Are you out of your mind? Didn't I tell you never to come here? It's disgusting! It's filthy! He'll kill you! Don't put it past him!"

Filtered through the door, Barbie's voice sounded like muffled thunder. It'd be nice if the thunder were real, Beverly thought. It hadn't rained in such a long time. The air was cloudy and gray, smelling faintly burnt. Beverly knocked on the door and repeated what she'd just said to the groundsman. "Open the door! I've brought your favorite fruit, papaya. We can eat it together. What do you say?"

Barbie didn't open the door, just kept calling her and telling her to hurry up and leave. "Get out! If you don't go now it will be too late! Haven't enough people died in our family?"

On the other side of the door, Beverly stood listening to Barbie yell and her phone ring. This time, she didn't take the call.

That morning, the morning of Ghost Festival, Barbie had

called to yell: "Mom's gone missing!" It'd been several years since Barbie mentioned Mom. Why today? Now her mobile rang again. She found it in a pile of scrap fabric beside the sewing machine. The caller wasn't Barbie, it was Paris.

This time she took the call. "Hi Paris, aren't you busy getting the offering ready? You got time to give me a call?"

"Beverly! Come quick! There's been an accident. Your husband's truck turned over. He spilled a load of milk on the highway."

She didn't panic, just calmly asked where it had happened and said she would be there as soon as she could. He'd done it again. In the past few years, he'd been causing trouble everywhere he went. Nothing he did could surprise her anymore. From Paris's tone just now, she knew he was still alive. It was so hot today, she decided to take it easy. In any case, Paris was there.

She changed in front of the mirror. The perm she had gotten half a year before was limp and faded. She looked bitter, like she'd had a hard life. Her eyelids drooped, her wrinkles were deep. Her face was quaking night and day. She really needed to refresh and touch up her curls, not to mention the roots, but she hadn't had the money lately for another trip to Paris.

There were three beauty salons in town. The oldest one did not have a name, just a musty wooden Hair Cut sign that turned around in the evening into Fried Chicken. The boss lady had not changed the oil in the deep fryer in over a decade. There were often hairs in the chicken, which the locals therefore dubbed Frizzy Fried Chicken. The second one was called Four Sisters. Just like her parents, theirs kept on having girls, four beauticians in a row. They had the same father, but four different mothers. The father tried out different women, hoping to have a son, without success. When the fourth daughter was born, he had a heart attack and died of apoplexy. Whether cutting or curling, the sisters always did a half-assed job. They wouldn't bother opening on a special day. Instead they would run off to dance in some funeral procession. The day their father was buried, the sisters led the way, guiding him to Soul Mountain. The third one was called Paris Coiffure Workshop. It was the most popular of the three among country ladies of a certain vintage. There were posters of the Eiffel Tower on the walls inside. The beauticians were a mother-daughter pair from Taipei. They couldn't speak Taiwanese. They'd apparently gone to Paris on a package tour, three days and two nights. The mother had pale skin, long lashes, and a pert nose. She didn't walk, she floated across the floor. When Beverly saw the boss, she realized why people said country folks were "earthy." Paris, a city girl, didn't have any grime on her face. She was clean cut. Not like Beverly with her dull, sticky skin. When she washed her face, the sink would end up full of foul water. She guessed the boss's washing-up water was clear. Paris's daughter was pretty, too. She helped out washing hair or sweeping it up, but she never spoke. Apparently she went to a famous girls' high school in Taipei, where she studied her way into a depression. She dropped out and came with her mother to the countryside. "When my daughter gets better," Paris said, "we'll go back to Taipei."

Actually, only one style of permanent wave ever came out of Paris Coiffure Workshop. But there was a picture of the two beauticians in front of the Eiffel Tower, and who in the countryside had gone abroad? Who had a passport? Paris was the epitome of Europe in the small-town imagination. When you came here to get a perm, you felt European. Every customer got the same look. You only had to take a gander at the housewives buying groceries at the market. They all looked the same from behind: just as collapsed, equally weathered, all Paris. "Beverly, didn't I hear that your youngest brother was in Europe?" the lady boss asked one time. "Is he in Paris? Good for him! Paris is really pretty. Look, I bought this blouse in Paris, isn't it divine?" "He's in Berlin," Beverly replied. "Berlin? Where's that? Why haven't I heard of it? Have you been there yourself?"

Beverly shook her head. "I wish." When she left home at fifteen to work as a seamstress in Shalu, she thought she could go really far in life, but she didn't end up going anywhere. She just came back here. She envied the boss lady for having gone to Paris. Even though Beverly had seen the blouse she had bought in Paris at a stall in the evening market in the next town. That was the first time she'd smelled dirt on her.

At eighteen years of age Beverly met her future husband in the garment factory. His surname was Gao, meaning "tall." Little Gao, they called him, because he was short and slight. But his surname suited him, because his job at the factory was loading and unloading fabric and garments with a forklift, a *duigaoji*. Little Gao made it look easy. He seemed more comfortable driving than talking, but every time she went into the warehouse for fabric to sew into garments, the normally taciturn Little Gao would come over and ask, "Hey, Bev, wanna go for a spin?" He meant to ride her around in the forklift when the foreman wasn't there. Life was hard and dull for seamstresses like her. A dozen young women crowded into a narrow dorm by night and sat in front of the sewing machine for a dozen hours a day. They only had one day off a week. To be able to swing around the warehouse in a forklift, sitting pressed up against a young driver, was the factory version of romance. Beverly always refused, afraid the foreman would find out.

She'd quit school and come to Shalu to work at fifteen. Exports were booming that year. There were constant orders for textile mills and garment factories to take. She heard about the boom from a classmate who'd left school a few months before. Home on a visit in snazzy new clothes, she told her that they were looking for seamstresses in Shalu, which wasn't really that far away. The foreman wouldn't even ask how much education she'd gotten. Room and board included. If you were willing to work hard you would get hired. She hated school, she was dumb. Having heard her mother's daily complaints about how poor they were, she wanted to go out and make some money. And she really couldn't keep living at home, not after the incident that Father didn't know about, or anyone else in the world for that matter, besides her. All she wanted to do was run away, but Mother wouldn't let her go. Beverly couldn't understand why. She wanted to go make money, and would be bringing money home for sure. Without her there there'd be one fewer child at home to feed and educate. What was wrong with that? Her mother slapped her and wouldn't allow her no matter what. Mother wasn't actually opposed to her going off to work. The truth was that Mother hated her and wouldn't agree to anything she wanted. Of course, Beverly knew that her mother hated her because of what she had seen. So when her classmate told her about all the boys she'd met on the job on her next visit home, Beverly made up her mind. She went to Shalu the very next day and found work in a garment factory.

She had actually never heard of the place before, Shalu, though Taichung City was familiar, and Shalu was to the north-east of the train station in Taichung. She had to take the train and then the bus to get there. She saw a lot of factories along the way. That told her that it was going to be easy to find a job, that there was money to be made. She was a country girl. She had never seen so many cars before in her life, or so many people. Of course Shalu was better than her hometown. It had a little night market, even a university. It had the smoke and dust of a prosperous city. And her mother was about fifty kilometers to the south. She didn't have her own room anymore, though, she had a dozen dormmates, all teenagers from poor families. All of them had dropped out of school to come to Shalu and learn to sew.

When she got her first month's pay, she was so excited she took the bus and the train home to see her mom, who took the money but didn't so much as look at her. She counted it, frowning, but didn't say a thing. Obviously, she didn't think it was enough. After that Beverly seldom visited. She dutifully sent money home every month. But she spent her Sundays in the dorm, crying and listening to the radio. Her sisters wrote her letters telling her about all the little things that had happened around the house. Keith would draw a picture and write, "Big Sister, come home soon, I miss you." He had always had such neat handwriting. From an early age he copied his sisters' characters. He liked to read, too. No wonder he went on to become a writer when he grew up. She didn't understand the books he'd written, but that hadn't stopped her from buying them. She rode her scooter to the bookstore in Yuanlin and asked the cashier for each book by title. When she purchased one, she announced, "My little brother wrote it. Can you please help us promote it? Thank you so so much!"

After she met Little Gao, he would come to the dorm on working days at ten o'clock in the evening with a midnight snack. Whoever answered the door would yell, "Beverly, it's for you!" The two of them would sit outside, eat fried chicken, and look up at the sky above Shalu as gravel trucks roared by, trailing plumes of dust. Under cover of dust, she finally dared to take a good look at him: small nose, small eyes, small frame, dark skin. He was a good driver. By day he drove the forklift. In the evenings he often drove a truck, taking odd delivery jobs. He carried concrete, watermelons, or Chinese cabbage. He almost never spoke. He reminded her of her father.

One day, one of the racks in the warehouse cracked and collapsed. A domino effect brought down the whole framework and then a sheet metal wall. Several tons of fabric crashed into a mountain of dust and debris. It was rush hour in the warehouse. All the forklift drivers who had been hard at work to get all the deliveries out were now buried alive. She'd never forget what they were making that day for export in a shipping container: red polo shirts. All the seamstresses dropped what they were doing, jumped into the red fabric mountain, and pushed the fabric frantically out of the way, trying to find the drivers. Beverly dug and dug until she finally felt a warm body. She grabbed ahold of it and pulled with all of her might, but could not budge it. She kept digging and finally the guy's head appeared, half caved in. Then another head popped into the tunnel of red that she had excavated. It was Little Gao, smiling from ear to ear. She took another look at the head in her hands. She knew who he was. He had three kids. His wife was a seamstress just like her. She sat right across from her. She held the head and bawled. Little Gao crawled out, sat beside her, and waited for her to stop crying.

"Hey Bev, wanna go for a spin?"

The next day all of the red fabric was gone. The wall had been repaired overnight. There was a new seamstress across from her, who started working as soon as she sat down. "This is a rush job," the foreman hollered. "No slacking!" She asked a colleague about the seamstress who sat across from her. The wife of the guy whose head collapsed, where did she go? Her colleague didn't tell her anything, except to shut up.

A few months later, she was pregnant. As soon as the foreman found out, he came to her dorm and told her to pack up and leave. She had no place to go, besides home. "Didn't you say you were going to go out and make some money?" her mother yelled. "You were out there living it up, until you got yourself knocked up." Having a child out of wedlock was scandalous in a small town like Yongjing. It so happened that the next townhouse in the row was for rent. Father put up the money for the damage deposit. That was their bridal suite. The wedding was rushed, the dowry shabby. She had been working for three years, planning to save some money and settle down in downtown Taichung. She didn't want to spend her whole life as a seamstress. She wanted to open a store and sell pretty clothes. But now she'd come full circle. Her time in the city was like a dream. Here she was, back in this row of town-houses. She tried her best to get away from her family and ended up living next door to them. Now her mother was only a wall away.

Little Gao quit his forklift driver job in Shalu and fol-lowed her back to Yongjing. He did odd jobs at construction sites around town. Only after the wedding did it dawn on her that her quiet husband was a gambling fiend: rummy, mahjong, baseball, he was game for anything. He had a bookie the way an addict has a dealer. After nine months of pregnancy, not a penny remained of her years of savings. She had to go next door to ask for a loan. A distance of a few steps, it was the longest, and most humiliating, journey. Her mother got out a wad of bills and shot her verbal daggers. "At fifteen you went out to make it and here you are, still bor-rowing money from me. Silly girl, you're the only one who doesn't know that he's been gambling behind the god-of-the-earth temple." Beverly ran home, stashed the money, grabbed a cleaver, and charged over to the temple. She overturned tables. She pushed bystanders out of the way. She hacked at a few would-be peacekeepers. She even hacked at the holy statue of the god of the earth, but she never got close enough to her husband. Little Gao slipped out and ran into a rice field. She chased him, knife in hand, and the police chased her, blowing their whistles as they went. She ran across the rice field and the chrysanthemum field. She was running across the swamp spinach field, the future site of the White House, when her water broke. She gave birth in that field before the ambulance arrived. Frogs were croaking, in harmony with her labor cries. Every onlooker's face was clear as day in the moonlight on that summer night, but she couldn't find the one that belonged to the father of her baby girl. Dammit all! she thought. I almost got him. I was gaining on him. A few more steps and he would have been within hacking distance. Two days later she came home from hospital to sit out her month of postpartum recuperation. She wasn't surprised to find that the money that her mother had loaned her was gone.

She couldn't hack him to death with a knife or poison him with soap. Today's traffic accident wouldn't kill him, either. She knew that lately her husband often stayed at Paris's place after doing the deliveries of produce, fish, and dairy for the supermarket he'd been working at the past few years.

A couple of close friends tipped her off after seeing a woman in the passenger seat of her husband's truck. They didn't get a good look at her face or a photo op. They urged her to hire a private investigator and sue the bitch. She laughed along bitterly with them and cursed the slut, whoever she was. But she actually had no wish to know. She felt grateful the silly woman was willing to take her husband in. Obviously, Mother Matsu had answered her prayer. One time when she was getting her hair shampooed at Paris's, nature called, so she excused herself. She was sitting on the toilet when she saw her husband's polo shirt hanging on the door. That polo was actually his uniform from the defunct garment factory in Shalu. He had worn it for over thirty years. She had gone into the bathroom to pee, but when she saw that polo shirt, she felt a shit coming on. Her entire body relaxed, and she defecated vigorously into the bowl. In an instant she felt very light. She skipped back to the chair. She couldn't help smiling while Paris washed her hair. "Having a good day?" Paris asked. "It's you," Beverly replied, still beaming. "You're so good with your hands. When it's someone who's been to Paris doing it, you can feel the difference. It feels so good." She'd actually been constipated for a week.

She decided not to change or even go out. It was such a hot day. Her mouth curdled at the thought of all the milk on the road. Paris was there, that was enough. Paris had been to Paris. She had not. She could let Paris handle it. Thank you Paris.

11. Pare a pear

Betty felt like writing a letter to Keith.

So she stopped in at the stationary shop in the evening market. The shop had seen better days. Overhead, fluorescent tubes flickered. The inventory on the sagging shelves was antiquated. The ballpoint pens wouldn't write, the ink had gone dry. The red envelopes had faded in the sun. The past few years this neighborhood had been inundated by a few typhoons. Letter paper that had gotten soaked in the flood stayed on the shelf once it was dry, still for sale.

The boss was from Changhua, just like Betty. He was thirteen or fourteen when he came to Taipei as an apprentice, and had not been home in fifty years. His family members and relatives had all died. He had nothing left, besides this lousy old store. He lived here and ate here. He didn't mind that business was bad, he wasn't getting any new inventory in. When the remainder sold out, he would sell the store, go back to the countryside, and plant a garden.

Betty often came here to buy letter paper. It was white paper with fine red vertical guide lines, just as simple as that. It had gotten so much sun it was brittle. Betty often punctured it by pressing too hard with her pen. Although she had bought a lot of letter paper, there was still a big pile left. Judging by the size, she guessed the boss was going to be trapped here for the rest of his life.

If all you do is talk about going home, you're probably

never going to. People who can go home will just go home,
they don't have to talk about it. They don't even have to think
about it. They can get themselves there on autopilot. And they
don't have to hunt around for the keys, there's someone inside
to open the door. The lights are on, the water's hot, the linen's
fresh. Dinner's served. Even when it's gone cold, a friendly
chatterbox will warm you up like a microwave oven.

Betty could relate. She often told her husband and children
the same thing. "Tomorrow I'm going home to Changhua, see
you in a couple of days!" Actually she went and stayed in a
cheap hotel in Taipei. Everyone says that you have to knock
before entering a hotel room, to tell the ghosts inside to make
themselves scarce. She, too, would knock, but then she'd whisper, "I'm back!" When she got inside, she'd keep breaking
taboos, by peeling a banana and paring a speckled *lâi-á* pear,
or maybe a pair. Then she'd spend two nights in the dim hotel
room, doing whatever she felt like. She'd lie in bed watching
pornos. She'd take a hot bath. She'd read a thick novel. She'd
write a letter to her little brother in Germany. Occasionally she
would text her husband. "It's really hot and sunny here in
Changhua, is it still raining in Taipei?" In the middle of the
night when she was trying to get to sleep, she would listen to
the Taipei rain outside and breathe in the humidity in the
room. She would imagine a ghost lying sleepless on the bed,
right beside her. For her, knocking on the door wasn't to drive
the ghosts away, it was an invitation. It was as if to say: Hey
ghosts, come out, come out, wherever you are.

The stall operators in the evening market did not remember
her, but the boss of this stationary store did. He even knew that
she was from Changhua, just like him. He never forgot her.
Little did she know that it was because she was practically the
only customer. "Hello, Ms. Chen," the boss always said. "How
nice to see someone from back home! I saw another news story
about the Wang clan on TV. The pride of Yongjing! The Wang

Foundation! They're amazing! Look how far they've come sell-ing those crackers. Do you know them?" She shook her head, hesitated a few seconds, then nodded. "We were neighbors." Which elicited follow-up comments and questions. "Wow! Neighbors! Then your family must also be well off. Or are you rich? I saw that White House they built on *Lifestyles of the Filthy Rich*. It's even whiter than the one in Washington. It's so bright and shiny, with a golden roof. So you know them? Are you still in touch with them? Have you been to the White House? Is it open for tours? Oh boy, next time I go home to Changhua I want to go have a look." She had a reply to every question, but she didn't say a thing. She quietly went through the letter paper, looking for sheets that weren't quite so yel-lowed and wrinkled up.

The boss was getting the offering for the Ghost Festival ready when she walked in. Unsurprisingly, the centerpiece was a box of White House crackers. He hadn't had a customer in days. As soon as he saw her, the words came flooding out. "Have you seen the offering next door, what a travesty! Imagine, setting out *lâi-á* pears! These young people in Taipei, they just don't understand. Last year it was a bitter melon! If elders don't hand down the old ways, then I reckon they might just disappear someday." Betty first heard about the taboo when she was living in the three-wing compound. Her mother bought *lâi-á* one time for Ghost Festival, but before she could even set them out, Grandmother slapped her and fired verbal daggers at her. Cicada was ignorant and unwilling to learn! She was a disgrace to the Chen household she had married into! It sounded like she was inviting the lonely souls into the house! "Don't you know you're not supposed to offer *lâi-á* to the 'goodfellas'?" The "goodfellas" were the spirit mafia who came round once a year to collect spirit protection money and enjoy a feast.

When Cicada dropped the beautiful *lâi-á* on the ground,

Betty went to pick them up. But before she had even touched them, her cheek had crashed into grandmother's palm. Picking them up was not allowed, or even touching them, let alone eating them. Grandmother's leathery palm was covered in hard calluses that scratched her tender cheek. She whispered the word over and over: *Lâi-á! Lâi-á! Lâi-á!* It sounded just like the Taiwanese word for "come," in other words: come on out and eat. When you set out offerings weren't you inviting the ghosts to come and eat them? So weren't *lâi-á* pears the perfect invitation? She bought them on purpose for Ghost Festival. The fruit retailer always reminded her of the taboo, and she would smile and nod. And then she would go home and put them right in the center of the table. Under her breath, she would say: "*Lâi-á*, one and all."

With all the old-fashioned stationary, the shop reminded her of the bookstores in Yongjing when she was a kid. There were three of them. The names of the first two were variations on the first character in the place name: Yongchang, meaning Eternal Prosperity, and Yongnan, meaning Eternal South. As for the third, it was called Mingri, meaning Tomorrow.

Located by the swamp spinach field, the Yongchang Bookshop was run by Betty's junior high school music teacher's husband. In 1979, the year that America broke off diplomatic relations with Taiwan, the music teacher and her husband suddenly absconded. Apparently assuming Taiwan was doomed, they moved to Argentina, leaving the bookstore behind. After Jack Wang made it big selling crackers, he came back to Yongjing and bought the field and all the buildings around it, as a site for a mansion. The ownership of the building in which the Yongchang Bookstore was located was uncertain, and difficult to ascertain. Wang decided to tear it down first and ask questions later. The backhoe easily picked it apart. It was full of reference works from the 1970s. Cracker Jack had a fire set, a bonfire of all those old books.

The boss of the Yongnan Bookstore was mean and nasty. Anyone who tried to test out a ballpoint pen before buying it was sure to get rebuked. But business was pretty good, because all the boys knew that behind the curtain at the back of the store there was a dimly lit little room stocked with pornographic publications. One time when the store was empty, Betty ventured into the forbidden zone herself. Inside, she was shocked to see her homeroom teacher. When he looked up and saw her, he got up to make his getaway and bumped into a shelf on his way out. She still remembered the girl, legs open wide, in the glossy magazine that happened to fall wide open upon her lap. She did not go and help her teacher, who was lying on the floor moaning in pain, because she herself had fallen, in between those legs. Only when the boss came back did Betty snap out of it, just in time to catch sight of the teacher's ass. In that era, before sex education class was invented, she had seen both men's and women's private parts in a single day, killing two "birds" with one stone. The next morning the teacher came shuffling into the classroom with a cane to announce a seating change. She was assigned to one of the far corners, as far away from the lectern as possible, right behind a big boy who limited visibility to about three feet. Years later, Keith's homeroom teacher came over to force him to switch schools. She was yelling at the top of her lungs, Mom and Dad were apologizing. But when her husband saw Betty he ran straight outside. He was her homeroom teacher, the one who fell down in the bookstore! What if he fell down a second time and had to use a cane again?

The bookstore she frequented was the Mingri Bookstore. There were two bosses, one thick, the other thin. The thick one was called Ming, the thin one Ri. They put their names together into *mingri*, "tomorrow." *Ri* happens to be part of the Mandarin for Japan, Riben. And the bosses were Japanophiles. They stocked the store with a lot of Japanese ballpoint pens, erasers, and compasses, along with magazines and language learning materials. Although she couldn't afford those Japanese products, she often came in to buy white paper with red guidelines for letters to Beverly in Shalu. On the counter lay a plate of home-made cookies, compliments of Boss Ri. Sitting behind the counter, the two bosses would listen to Japanese language tapes and eat Taiwanese popcorn chicken. Sometimes they would read, especially literary books. There was a whole shelf for novels and collections of lyrical essays. Betty could stand at that shelf and while away an afternoon. The thick boss would smile at her. "Good book?" he would ask. She didn't have money to buy a book, at least not on her own. She and her sisters used to save up and pool their cash to buy a book. Then they would take turns reading it. At the time owning a book was a luxury. The first thing you did was sign your name on the first page. And the date. One time she spied the thin boss holding the thick boss's hand behind the counter. When a customer came in they immediately let go.

They had to let go for good the day the police came to town. That was the last day of operation for the Tomorrow Bookstore. The building was cordoned off, the shutter rolled down. Betty stood on the other side of the Do Not Cross line until the shutter rolled up again and the thick boss and the thin boss were dragged out in handcuffs and pushed into cruisers, after being pulled apart by the police. "Ming!" the thin one cried out in anguish, right before a cop landed his fist on his face. "Pervert!" the policeman yelled.

That was the last time she ever saw them.

Every time she came to this old stationary store in the evening market in Taipei she would think of Boss Ming and Boss Ri, thick and thin.

Carrying the groceries and stationary home, she tried to think of a first line for her letter. Keith had always had such a way with words. Every previous letter she'd written him had begun as follows: "I know I have a poor prose style, please forgive me." She really meant it. One of his stories was about a studious junior high school student who got caned by his homeroom teacher. "You damn faggot!" she yelled at him in front of the class. "Every time I discipline you I worry about getting AIDS!" Betty burst out crying when she read that part. Sorry, Keith, nobody protected you. Nobody believed you!

Leaving the stationary shop, she went home to an empty apartment. She took a quick shower to wash her dirty feet. But she could hardly wash off those curses, which stuck to her like crazy glue.

While showering, she finally thought of an opening. "Keith, is everything all right in prison? Today at the office I got yelled at because of seeing-eye dogs. I even made the news. I probably don't have a hope in hell of passing this year's performance review. As soon as I got off work I felt like writing you. I wanted to ask if there are dogs in your prison in Germany. Before you were born, when we were still living with Grandma, I raised a black dog. It was Grandma's dog. But I was in charge of feeding it. I fed it and fed it, and the dog followed me wherever I went."

There was a dog in almost every three-wing compound in the countryside. Theirs was no exception. One day, a bitch had a litter of puppies in the courtyard. Grandma drove the bitch away and started to weed the puppies out. Most were inauspicious white-paw puppies. One by one Grandma grabbed and tossed them into the field, grab, toss, frown, grab, toss, frown. In the end she chose only one, a black one. "Look at the size of its paws!" Grandma said. "It'll be a big 'un when it's grown. We can keep it as a guard dog and sic it on the burglars." Betty happened to be there. So Grandma ordered her to take care of Blackie with a glance. She didn't have to say a thing.

Betty had no idea how to take care of a dog. Nobody in the family ate a square meal. What was she to feed the dog with?

She went to the kitchen to sort through the trash and asked at the neighbors for leftovers. She added water to the spoiled food scraps and fed the mixture to the puppy, which promptly barfed. It threw up and kept right on eating. It was so cute. She raised it every which way. It was a vital little animal. It grew really quickly. In a few months it was a big dog that enjoyed gnawing on pork bones. It used to follow her around. When she went into the field to weed, when she fed the pigs in the sty, when she went to the outhouse in the middle of the night, the black dog would accompany her across the courtyard. It would sit obediently outside the door for her, wagging its tail and squinting into the field. It was like the moonlight was petting its head.

She was that dog's keeper and its killer.

One morning in grade three before the first class was over, Grandma charged into the school and demanded to see Betty Chen. As soon as Grandma saw her in her seat, she ran over and gave her a vicious tug on the right ear. "What'd you do with my pearl necklace?" she shouted.

Grandma had gotten up that morning planning to go to the temple to pray for a baby son for her eldest son. His wife had not had any boys, just useless girls, five in a row. On a whim she wanted to wear her necklace. Her husband had bought it in Tokyo. Those were real Japanese pearls, you know. When she could not find it anywhere in her room, she remembered that a few days before her granddaughter had come to her room to clean up. Was it the second or the third? In any case it was a useless girl. To think she had the gall to lift the necklace!

Grandma went to the school and searched class by class, for Beverly, Betty, and Belinda. She dragged them outside one by one and interrogated them in front of their teachers and classmates. Kneeling, the sisters were crying and shaking their heads as Grandma's palm walloped their bodies. When she got tired of hitting them with her hand, she ran into a classroom and grabbed a cane.

The three sisters didn't have the chance to get their book bags, they were yelled at and shoved off the school grounds. The whole school watched them go. At home they knelt in the courtyard, where, with endless endurance, Grandma continued flogging them. Mother rushed out carrying Barbie and Ciao, who were crying and fussing in her arms, only to have to kneel down beside her three eldest daughters. "I don't care about the necklace!" Grandma yelled. "I just want to know who it was! If somebody admits it, we'll call it a day."

Betty stood up sobbing and said, "It was me!"

Grandma picked up a big broom and walked closer and closer to Betty, who was thinking: "I'm a goner!"

The broom handle hit her in the gut, sending her little body flying.

She bounced off the brick wall and fell face down on the ground. She braced herself for more broom handles. Suddenly Grandma screamed. Blackie had bit her arm and would not let go.

Later that day Grandma stunned the dog with a brick. Then she dumped it in a cauldron of boiling water. She skinned it with gusto, chopped it up with a cleaver, and cooked it, while Betty and her sisters cowered in their room. They shut the window as tightly as they could, but they still smelled it.

Her second uncle came home with his son just in time for the dog-meat feast. Through the window, Betty saw her cousin with that necklace around his neck. Although she couldn't hear the conversation, she could see her uncle remove the necklace and hand it back. Everyone took a bowl and enjoyed the meal. They were all smiles.

Betty sat down and started writing the letter.

"Keith, it was because of me that Blackie died. Blackie still appears bright-eyed in my dreams. But the fur fades a bit every time. Lately it's been almost white. Today being Ghost Festival and all, I felt like writing you. For no reason at all. I wanted to talk to you. It's been a long time since I got a letter from you. Are you feeling well? Did you enjoy the books I sent you? Today I also thought about the Tomorrow Bookstore. Do you remember the thick boss and the thin boss?"

Betty knew that she, Household Registrar Chen, had hurt a lot of people.

When she was young, she often thought, why not just die and get it over with. She would rather be a ghost. One fewer girl at home wouldn't make any difference. So she told Grandma she took the necklace. Her lie condemned the dog to death. After she grew up she kept on hurting people. If back in the day she had not said anything, if she had not told on them, then maybe bosses Ming and Ri would still be alive today. Later on, she saw the thick boss's picture in the newspaper. His face wasn't so round anymore. In fact, he was thin as a rail. She initially thought that the reporter had got the wrong man. But she did a double take and, yes, that was the thick boss's face. It had just been a few months. She shuddered to think about what might have become of the thin boss.

It was all her fault.

12. *Changhua Migrants Association, Neihu Chapter*

Lately Belinda had been trying to lose weight. Her husband complained that she looked bloated. That must mean she lacked discipline in daily life. She was letting herself go. He pinched her love handles between thumb and forefinger, slowly adding force. She held her breath and clenched her hands. She knew it was punishment for that photograph. At a recent opening ceremony for a new television station, a paparazzo caught her with her tummy sticking out. The entertainment news

headline was: "Is the Anchor's Wife Rocking a Baby Bump?"
That evening, she was wearing a dress her husband's designer
friend had provided her with. Only when she got there and
squeezed into it did she realize it was too small. She had a premonition of pain.

Her husband went into the kitchen and threw all the noodles, the sugar, the flour, and the snacks in the bin. He threw a
packet of candies at her face. "Are you sneaking sweets when
I'm not looking? No more sugar for you! Are you just like your
mother, illiterate? From now, read the nutritional information!
If there's any carbohydrates, whether sugar or starch, you're
not allowed to eat it.

In mentioning her mother he meant to humiliate her.

Cicada was born late in the Japanese colonial era, but early
enough to start school before the war ended. She only went for
two days. She didn't learn a thing, besides what to do in the
event of an American air raid. She'd always regretted her lack
of education, because her illiteracy turned the modern world
against her. When she deposited money in her post office
account or visited the household registration office, she had to
bring a daughter along. The motor vehicles office made an
exception by allowing her to take the exam for the scooter
operator's license orally. Please don't ask her to read the street
signs! She still had to take it a dozen times before she finally
passed. She couldn't even write her own name, especially the
character 蟬 in her given name. That character means cicada,
and so she went by the name of Cicada Lin, but for all she
knew it was an occult symbol. Why did there have to be so
many strokes? It was so difficult to write. Her daughters took
turns teaching her but she ended up so frustrated she ripped
up the paper.

How come she went to school for only two days? She kept
changing her story. Sometimes it was because of the expense,
especially for a girl, who was only going to get married.

Sometimes she quit after her teacher, a freedom fighter, got shot in the classroom by the colonizer. Sometimes she just couldn't memorize the fifty sounds of the Japanese language. Sometimes the school closed after an American air raid bombed the building to smithereens, killing a lot of the kids. According to Mother, another bomb fell into a nearby fish-pond and rained fish all around. Everyone ran out to get some. The roads, the fields, and the trees were covered in the stuff. She came home with an armful, hoping to contribute to the family livelihood, but so did her sisters and brothers. There was a hill of raw flesh in the kitchen.

Mother was garrulous, as illiterates often are. She could talk your ear off! And yell. Boy could she yell. She was always yelling at her daughters or at Father. She was always telling stories, too. In that era of privation, when families like theirs often couldn't feed their children let alone buy them picture books, and when the institution of the "bedtime story" didn't exist yet, she went on and on about something or other before bedtime. Her prattling was like an airborne suspension of some dust-like material that floated into Belinda's ear and put her to sleep. Finally she could forget the rumbling of her empty stomach. "There was a snake in the field today." "We're short on grocery money this month." "So and so's getting married. We'll have to give them a red envelope." "Such and such died. We'll have to give them a white envelope." "Guess who had a son?" "Know whose son brought a wife home?" "We're short on money this month, I mean really short." "The roof is leaking." "Those pearls of hers are actually plastic." "Just wait until I have a son." "I can't believe I will never have a son!" Asleep, she was just as loud, with the explosions of her snores and the thunder of her somniloquy. Her sleep exacerbated her cursing, opening the floodgates on a stream of expletives. Her throat had its own verbal system, of cutting rebukes, comforting incantations, tall tales, and resounding chants. She could make up a complicated family history at the drop of a hat. She could murmur magical spells: "a bowl of rice that's shaken thrice" could calm a bawling infant. One moment she was amiably collecting a child's wits, and the next moment she erupted, spewing lava at whoever happened to offend her until the poor soul was a blubbering mess.

Belinda had the highest level of education in the Chen family. Of the five sisters, she was the only one who went to university. In Taipei, the capital city! Nobody in the Chen family had ever been. "Things must be expensive there," her family said. "Where will you live? What will you eat? How much will it cost?" None of the other Chen daughters had dared to take the entrance examination. They'd all found a job right after graduating from vocational school. How could Mom and Dad let a daughter go to university? Because as the third daughter, Belinda led a charmed life. No surprise that she would end up going to the top university in the country. Her father bought a box of fireworks to celebrate. He set them off morning, noon, and night, three days in a row. The top student in Yongjing that year, and the only one to win test-based admission to National Taiwan University, turned out to be a girl.

The day before the first day of class, her father drove the whole family up in the truck. It was an old story: country bumpkins visiting the big city for the first time. Belinda, her two brothers, and Mom and Dad sat up front in the cab, while the other daughters sat in the trailer. When they drove onto the freeway, the next stop was Taipei. There was a thundershower along the way, but no rain shield for Beverly, Betty, Barbie, and Ciao to sit under. They tried to take shelter under the plastic crates Dad shipped betel leaf and betel nut in. Even when they were completely soaked, nobody complained that it wasn't fair that Belinda got to ride in front. She had gotten into university. She was the only reason they got to go to Taipei.

The truck flew through Taipei's bustling downtown core

but got flagged down at the front gate. Such a big vehicle was not allowed on campus! Dad got out, handed out cigarettes and betel nut, and told his daughters in the trailer to unload a crate of fruit. "Mr. Security Guard," he said, "please, Sir, my daughter is going to university, she's moving into the dorm. The whole family has come up to help her settle in. Can you please make an exception?"

They made a scene lugging luggage. People were staring. Belinda was mortified. When she got into the dorm room, she put a rush mat and a cotton blanket on the bed. "I'm hungry," someone hollered. Mother got out the portable gas stove and the wok. "Must be expensive to eat out in Taipei," she said. "I'll just cook a quick meal in here. I'll be done in no time." She served dinner on beds of precooked rice in metal containers. While everyone was eating elbow to elbow, the delicate fragrance of garlic escaped under the door and down the hall, until it reached the nostrils of the hall monitor. Knock knock! "No cooking allowed in the dormitory!" Mother invited her in and set off verbal firecrackers, launching a spirited assault that left the poor woman unable to get a word in edgewise. A bowl of rice appeared in her hands, and meat in her mouth, and when she had swallowed the meat, Mother fed her stir-fried swamp spinach. "We planted it ourselves in Yongjing. Pesticide-free, I promise!" The other three roommates arrived one by one, with parents in tow. Faces contorted at the spectacle of dinner in the dormitory. Belinda ate without daring to say a word of greeting to her new roommates. Looking down, she counted how many people had managed to squeeze into that little four-bed room. One, two, three, four, five, six, seven, eight . . . in the end she counted all the way to twenty. The dormitory only quieted down after her family left. Belinda sat on her bed, glancing over the fruit, dried tofu, and soy sauce piled on her desk, her roommates sleeping in their beds, and the moonlight that, sifted through the palm trees, was spraying onto the floor. It started to drizzle. Soon it was raining. The rain rang crisply on the illegal ironskin additions in the neighborhood. Her blanket smelled like dinner—garlic, pork chops, luffa, and prawns. With the sound of her mother stir-frying dinner in the wok ringing in her ears, she burst out crying. She cried the whole night.

It had cleared up the next morning. The sunlight was golden. She realized it gave her away as soon as she stepped out of the dormitory. She saw her classmates' clothing and accessories, their shoes and socks. They were so simple and elegant. Then she took a look at herself. She looked poor. She was wearing a floral print dress patterned, cut, and sewn by Beverly as a present for getting into university. The coloration was loud, the fabric heavy. In class, she heard that kids who had grown up in the capital spoke the National Language clearly, hicks like her in a sluggish drawl, as if the speech sounds were generated from a different phonology. Every time anybody opened his or her mouth, accent drew a map that was marked for social class topography. She ran back to the dormitory after class to change. She'd already decided to turn herself into a Taipeier.

Now she was a Taipeier. After many years of adjustment she'd buried every trace of her twang. Her attire was stylish, the lines clean. She made up her face and sprayed perfume on her wrists. She got around in a German sedan. She lived in a luxury apartment with a view of a lake.

There were no lakes back home, only smelly gutters, irrigation ditches, and fishponds. She'd read about lakes in a book, but could not imagine the form that one would take. What amount of water accumulation would count as a lake? After the wedding, she moved with her husband to Neihu. The apartment had a full-length window with a view of Dahu, "big lake." That was the first "lake" she'd seen in Taipei. Her husband invited a bunch of friends to come over and make merry.

They drank French champagne and German white wine with Spanish ham. Expressions of admiration and envy were tossed at her. One of the guests brought a photographer along to take pictures of the newlyweds sitting in their custom Italian leather sofa and standing in front of their handmade Swedish liquor cabinet. The color photos would appear in the paper the next day. After everyone left, Belinda gazed at the lake and at Egret Hill beyond, lost in thought. The night was so quiet, the moonlight so clear. The stars were bright. All the buildings, from here to the horizon, were luxury apartments, without an iron-skin addition in sight. Each one cost a fortune, which didn't make them any easier to come by. It was Taipei in the glory days. And she was lucky enough to be part of it. Finally she had made it. She was a Taipeier.

The silvery moonlight took her back to the night she moved into the dormitory. "I'm going back to Changhua tomorrow," she said quietly. "Plenty's funeral procession is in a few days."

"You're not going anywhere."

A leaden cloud blocked the silvery moon. It was pitch black in the apartment.

"I will arrange the elegiac couplets and the floral wreath. Don't worry, it'll be covered in high-profile names, of famous stars, legislators, the president. It'll be an event. You won't be there, though, because the paparazzi will be out in force. You stay put for now. You can go home when it's all over."

Her husband's tone was harsh. Every utterance was an order. When it started to pour, he pulled her onto the couch. She pulled back and said, "No, not tonight." That cloud, it turned out, didn't just obscure the moon. It also drowned out her repeated refusals. He didn't hear her beg him to stop. He entered her forcibly from behind, stabbing her like a knife, drilling into her like a bit into dry ground, penetrating her posterior like the tip of a ballpoint pen a flimsy piece of paper. That was a pain she had never experienced before.

The next morning she could barely walk. Every step tore her apart. Her mother called. "When are you coming back?"

Mother had never yelled at her, not even when she was a girl. She doted on her. But she finally got angry at the news that Belinda wouldn't be attending any part of Plenty's funeral. She yelled obscenities over the phone, which Belinda listened to gazing out at the lake, trying to keep herself awake. She was exhausted. She hadn't slept since the wedding. Mother's verbal assault was like a bedtime story. It made her drowsy.

She slept a long, long time. When she woke, there was no sign of the anchor. She decided to go for a stroll. Walking along the lake, she still felt a bit sore, but much better. She sat on the bench by the shore. Beside her on the lawn was a food stall. A red banner read: Changhua Migrants Association, Neihu Chapter. She went to the stall, bought a *bah-uân* dumpling, and took a bite. It tasted fake, like a Taipeier's idea of a Changhua *bah-uân*. A beautiful white waterfowl approached her on long, thin legs. "It doesn't taste too good," she said, "I'm afraid it might kill you." She took another bite of her pseudo-Changhua *bah-uân*. As the Changhua migrants sang karaoke, she said a lot of things to that water bird. It just wasn't going to fly away. The rest of the *bah-uân* just wasn't going to get eaten.

Keith came for a visit while he was back from Germany. "You should come see me in Berlin," he said. "There's a lake close to my place that's several times bigger than this one."

"Can you see it from your window?"

"No, but you can smell candy if you leave the window open. You'll see."

When she heard that he'd killed a man, she went to the supermarket and bought a packet of German candies.

She checked the address of the factory. It was actually in Berlin. She opened it up, stuck her nose in, and took a deep breath. Keith, is this the smell you were telling me about?

Staring out at the lake, she ate the whole packet. She envied Keith. He had the courage to kill.

She wanted to, too. To kill the anchor.

13. *Saucy Cicada*

Just listen to those cicadas.

It's been a hot, dry summer. It hasn't rained in so long, all the irrigation ditches have dried up, and the fallowed fields are cracked. In front of every household a brazier full of spirit money sends up clouds of smoke, making the weather even more insufferable. The land sizzles like a skillet. The male cicadas in the trees call with all their might. The sun rages in a cloudless sky. I'm a ghost, without hair, skin, or organs. I have no body, so I don't have to regulate my temperature. Cold and hot mean nothing to me. But since I'm here, I can sense the heat vicariously. Through the crack in the townhouse floor, I can watch my eldest daughter Beverly. I know it's hot, because she's burning up. In the dark master bedroom in the White House, I can watch my fourth daughter Barbie making calls to her siblings. I know it's hot, because she's covered in sweat. In front of the soy-sauce factory, I can watch my younger son Keith looking at the mural of his elder brother Heath. It's so hot that he's about to faint. Otherwise he wouldn't have lost the way. When he left Berlin, it was fifteen degrees. When he got to Yongjing, it was thirty-eight. It's the hottest day this year.

But no matter where I go, I still can't remember my fifth daughter's face. I thought that after I became a ghost I would find her. But I've been floating around my hometown, and I can't find her anywhere. She's just not here. I can't find any other ghosts, either. When I was alive I thought that ghosts could see each other. But when you really become a ghost you discover that being a ghost is the loneliest existence. Without fixed form, odor, color, or temperature, I can't relate to any person, place, or thing, any animal, vegetable, or mineral, anywhere in space and time. I can only circulate in the tiny crack between tick and tock, hanging inverted with the bats from the branches or hibernating with the cicada nymphs in the soil.

When people put a table of offerings out, they say that they're feeding the hungry ghosts, the lonely souls. But those offerings feed a private, human desire for safety and security. The more they fear death, the more deprived they feel, the more extravagant the offerings on the table will be. The more extravagant their offering, the lonelier they are.

Now I can hear the little truck that drives around broadcasting local government decrees. It sets out from the township office with the volume set to max, competing with the cicadas to see who is the loudest. It drives down all the little lanes, driving the voice of the township mayor into everyone's ears. "Hello, fellow Yongjingites, it's me, your mayor. Today is Ghost Festival. Yongjing is a tinderbox these days, so please keep the fires in your braziers under control. The reservoir is low, water is running short, so please don't let the tap run! I beg you, I beg you again. Never fear, I will be with you every step of the way. Together we can wait out the water shortage."

This policy truck was an innovation of my eldest son. He came up with the idea when he was mayor. His successor has followed suit. Heath had big posters of himself printed, which he hung on the sides of a little truck. On the roof he installed a loudspeaker to broadcast the decrees that he spent an entire day recording in his office. At the time he wore a suit with a vest that said Mayor Heath, At Your Service. He would drive the truck himself, smiling the whole way as he heard his voice resound throughout Yongjing.

Back at the office, he made a rule against speaking Taiwanese that for the time being he was the only one to follow.

Under his leadership, Yongjing was going to take off. Agriculture would soon be upgrading, along with local industries, betel nuts and leaves, and cultural and historic sites. He would lead the way towards internationalization, attracting tourists from all over the world. How could Yongjing globalize if people kept speaking Taiwanese?

When he called for a general "upgrade," he meant that the original or traditional approach was bad. It needed to be phased out, at least improved on. So he took a delegation to Paris and New York, came back, and reported to his citizens in his policy truck. He wanted to turn Yongjing into a petite Paris of the Orient, a miniature New York in the East. Corner grocery stores were backward; he'd introduce American superstores. The big open-air market was too old; he'd invite designers to come in and design some new stalls for vegetable vendors, fishmongers, and pork peddlers. He'd inject some European style, minimalist design, low-key luxury, to create the charming scenes he'd seen in a traditional market in France. The century-old exterior walls of the three-wing compounds were too plain; he'd invite international graffiti artists to come in and decorate them. Otherwise, old buildings weren't tall enough; he would build towers. Slaughtering a sacred pig in a temple fair was detrimental to the township image. Animal welfare groups would protest. He announced that they were forbidden. Road signs were to be bilingual in English and Chinese. How else would all the tourists be able to navigate? An English class was held at the Township office, which the mayor attended along with everyone else. The rice paddies, the betel leaf and chrysanthemum fields, and the horticultural nurseries started to transform into leisure farms. Mayor Heath invited the entire world to come to Yongjing to be his guests. Guests would only spend the night and money there if there was somewhere to stay. He would appropriate fallow farmland and build a five-star hotel, where tourists from different lands could listen to the cicadas cry soaking in the spa during the day and the frogs croak sipping cocktails at the bar in the evening.

That was the happiest time in Cicada's life. Her eldest son had been elected by a landslide. She was the mother of the mayor! It was like golden powder had been sprinkled all over her. No matter where she went, she glowed. We'd kept at it, having five girls before we managed two boys. The eldest boy was like his mother, with a round face and a fortunate, well-fed physique. And the baby of the family is like me, with a narrow face and a delicate build. After the eldest served as township mayor the next step was county mayor. And then he was going to go to the capital, the city of Taipei. "Mom," he told her, "wait for me, one day I'm going to be the president." Cicada laughed like a mighty bell.

The summer I met Cicada, the sound of cicadas and the smell of soy sauce were in the air.

Before I died, I labeled the people around me according to scent. Everyone had a special odor. My ma smelled like mint, the coffin maker like sawdust, Beverly like fabric, Nut like starfruit. Baby Keith like books. Heath started out smelling like a coffin, but later, after Baron convinced him to run for township mayor, he smelled like a suit.

At eighteen, Cicada smelled like soy sauce.

The matchmaker told my mother that the suitable girl was the eldest daughter of the owner of the soy-sauce factory. The mother was a widow, the daughter had just turned eighteen. She was hardworking and obedient, and round in face and ass. One look at her would tell you she would bring good fortune into her husband's household, that she'd have sons for sure. Her name was Cicada Lin, her nickname Saucy. She was the prettiest girl in town. She was illiterate, but she was frugal and hard-working. She was born to be a good daughter-in-law. The matchmaker pointed at the soy sauce on the table and said, "Meals in every household in the township are seasoned with this brand of soy sauce. That tells you the family's financial situation is decent. Her dowry will be generous." She'd compared the Eight Characters of her birth and mine. According to her, a marriage between the eldest son of the Chen family and the eldest daughter of the Lin family was a match made in Heaven.

I only saw Saucy Cicada twice before I married her. The first time was at the factory, where the two clans met. The matchmaker brought Cicada in. She served oolong tea and betel nut to the guests, but she didn't say a thing. She didn't even look up, so I couldn't see what she looked like. I couldn't smell the tea—the sour, salty odor of fermenting soybeans was too strong. The soy sauce apparently sat in vats in the courtyard for six months before bottling. I could follow the conversation, barely, over the sound of the cicadas that were crying in the trees outside the factory. One of her relatives mentioned that the cicadas cried just as loud on the day she was born. They cried so loud nobody heard her mother cry that it hurt so much, that the baby was coming. So they called her Cicada. Fragrant Soy Sauce was a family concern that dated back to the Japanese era. A lot of Japanese soldiers made the trip to Yongjing to buy a bunch of bottles before catching a ship to Yokohama back in '45. They said they were going to dip their sushi in it in Tokyo. It was around that time that Cicada started learning to make soy sauce, working by her mother's side. She had skills. She knew how to select and boil the beans, how to sprinkle the yeast. But a daughter had to be married off, the business handed down to a son. Her mother had to hurry up and find a suitable boy.

The second time I saw her we had a black-and-white prenuptial photo taken in front of the factory. I was wearing a shirt and suit pants, she a form-hugging floral print dress. She held a little purse in her hand. My ma had gone to the only studio in the township and gotten the photographer to come out. When our bodies finally came into close proximity for the photo shoot, I finally got a good look at her face. Big eyes, round cheeks, curly hair. When she noticed I was looking at her, she looked down. I inhaled deeply, taking a surreptitious sniff. Truly, she smelled just like the soy sauce on the dinner table! She still hadn't said anything. She was staring at the ground. I asked her what was down there. She thought about it for a long time. "Cicadas are small and white when they first crawl out of the ground," she whispered. "If you grab a handful and deep-fry them, they taste real good. They taste even better if you dip them in soy sauce. Many people don't know." Having finished speaking, she looked down again.

The third time we saw each other we were man and wife. On the wedding night she sat on the bed in our three-wing compound and started to talk. And once she started she never stopped.

Just like the cicadas that never stop crying.

14. The sampan's passed the piled-up peaks

Keith and Sam sat shoulder to shoulder outside the abandoned soy-sauce factory eating *bah-uân*.

The factory courtyard was piled with shards from the soy-sauce vats, but the scent of fermenting soybeans was nowhere to be smelled. The roof was gone, leaving leaning iron pillars. Keith took a deep breath. There was a heavy metallic odor, redolent of rust. He remembered, when the soy-sauce bottle ran dry, Ma would tell him to ride his bike to his grandma's house to get another bottle. Grandma would put three or four bottles in a burlap bag and tell him to ride safely. At the time, the factory was bustling. Taiwan's economy had taken off. The Fragrant brand, which had been available only locally, was now shipped around the island. The orders poured in. They kept expanding and hiring.

Soy sauce usually ran out from five to six in the evening, an hour in which night and day had a tug of war and in which the country sky turned from blue to purple and orange. He minded his ma and grandma, but there were too many fun things to do on the way. He rode the bicycle all around, everywhere but home.

He rode by someone standing in front of the bishopwood conveying gratitude to the spirit of the tree. It turned out to be his neighbor the snake killer, who had spent a lot of money to have a stage built under the tree for the Three Sisters Burlesque to thrash about on. They were called the three sisters, but actually they were a grandmother, mother, and daughter. It was a three-generation family tradition. At every wedding and funeral in town you were sure to catch sight of them. The smallest "sister" on the stage was Keith's elementary school classmate. She didn't stop stripping when she saw him there, just hollered, "Hey Keith, have you finished your math homework yet? Can I copy it? It's so hard, I can't do a single question!"

He rode by a chrysanthemum field that the farmer was outfitting with bulbs. A fuse had blown. Tens of thousands of bulbs were flashing, like all of the stars in the sky had fallen down to earth.

He rode by the Yongnan Bookstore, which was crowded with students after school. The owner was at it again, giving some kid who had tested out an eraser an earful. A group of older boys had appointed an envoy, who had gotten up the courage to part the curtain at the back. Everyone was holding his pocket money. They were all hoping to get a load of the new stock they'd heard about. Full color. Buck naked. "Wanna see a Japanese lady with no clothes on?" asked one of those boys, who were a lot older than him. "If you do, then hand over your allowance." He shook his head. "I just came out to get soy sauce."

He rode by the corner grocery store under the banyan tree and stopped to buy a taro ice pop. He leaned his bicycle against a streetlamp and let the pop melt in his mouth as he counted one, two, three silently. One, the lamps turned slowly on. Two, bugs gathered to dance under the lights. Three, bats dove at the bugs, as applause rippled in his mind. He really liked bats. They slept all day, hanging upside down amongst the luxuriant foliage. They looked so cute, cuddling close to one another. When they flew out at dusk to catch bugs, their wings were translucent, and their flight like forked lightning.

He rode by the starfruit orchard and saw Red Shorts getting ready to go home. Red Shorts took one look at him and said, "While you've been out on a joyride, your mom has been yelling for you in the kitchen. I can hear her from here. Don't just stand there, get your ass home. How can she make dinner without soy sauce?"

Sweaty and tanned after a day in the sun, Red Shorts came walking out, a book in one hand and a ladder in the other. Red Shorts was big and tall, like a tree compared to him. A few days before he had read about the Amazonian jungle in a picture book. There were caimans, piranhas, vicious monkeys, venomous spiders, toucans, and butterflies in gorgeous hues—all animals he had never seen or heard about before. He imagined that this starfruit orchard was like a little local version of the Amazonian jungle, with a boa constrictor wrapped around a starfruit bough. Red Shorts put down the ladder, grabbed him by the waist, and whirled him around in place until he begged him to stop. Giggling, he hugged him tight. "No more, please, or I'll be sick!" He took a deep breath to get a whiff of his armpit, then slid down to his waist. It smelled like a tree or an herb or a river, faintly pungent. He took another sniff and there it was, the dense jungle, the perfume of sharp-toothed alligators and piranhas. Their jaws clamped onto his body, leaving bite marks that he would never be able to forget.

According to the story in the picture book, the tortoises and the butterflies were bosom buddies. The butterflies had a taste for tortoise tears, and as the tortoises had no way of cleaning away the crud around their eyes themselves, they let the butterflies land on their heads and suck. They loved each other. He imagined that he was a butterfly, that Nut was a tortoise, and that the starfruit orchard was their secret Amazonian jungle.

Actually Nut was a tortoise that shed no tears, not even in the cruelest moment of his life. He just picked up his pen and wrote.

"What do you think of the *bah-uân*?" Sam asked him. "Not the same, is it?"

Keith nodded. He noticed when he took the first bite. The skin was too flaky. He had to chew it a long time before swallowing. He couldn't smell bamboo shoots in the filling.

"It's actually the same stand. The one we ate at when we were kids. Remember? We used to ride our bikes there after class. That old boss is dead. He left the stand to his two sons. The taste has been a mess ever since. The two sons had a falling out, and isn't it always because of the money? One of them stayed put, and the other opened another stand across the street, going head to head with his brother to see whose dumplings tasted the worst."

Sitting on the steps in front of the factory, Sam and Keith ate their *bah-uân* with chopsticks out of the plastic bags. Without bowls or spoons to eat the tofu and pork ball soup with, they looked up, held the bag to their mouths, and trickled the liquid in. The last time the two of them had eaten together like this was in the third year of junior high.

"It's mainly the sauce. Without Fragrant brand soy sauce, the *bah-uân* taste different. But sometimes I still feel like having one. I know it's not going to taste good, it's not going to be the same as when we were kids, but I still drive the truck over.

Fortunate that I bought extra today, isn't it? Considering that I ran into you."

Keith gave Sam another glance. Short hair, swarthy, lean. He was wearing a sports vest, khaki shorts, and muddy trainers.

"Have you come home for Ghost Festival? Why didn't Beverly mention you were back?" Not knowing how to reply, Keith just shook his head.

"You really stand out, from a mile away. I took one look at you, and from the way you walk and the way you're dressed, I was thinking: outsider. Seeing as how the Hellgate is open wide and all, I thought I'd seen a ghost. Around here folks drive or ride. Nobody would walk along the field like you were doing. Fortunate that it was daytime. Take a look at the clothes you're wearing, a blazer? Classmate, anyone could tell you're not from around here."

Keith was wearing a navy blazer, a white shirt, black jeans, black shoes, and black socks. He really did stand out. It's just that he didn't have much of a wardrobe left when he got out of prison. This was basically it.

"When did you get out? Or did you break out? Beverly says you still had a couple more years left in your sentence? Are you on parole?"

Staring at the cracked vats, Keith chewed his *bah-uân* and sipped the soup out of the plastic bag, which he folded and folded again when he was done. He licked the sauce off his fingers. He was moving really slow. Sam's gaze had come to rest upon him. It was light, that gaze, like a butterfly alighting on a fingertip, like a willow catkin skirting the surface of the river, like a spider's thread falling on silver hair. Sam really was like a sampan, rocking gently back and forth. It always made him dizzy. He looked slowly up. He had eaten his fill and regained his strength. All right. Tensing up his abdomen, chest, and throat, he forced those words, which were as hard as stones, through his larynx, up his pharynx, and out his mouth. "I got out."

"I. Got. Out." The I, the two ts, and the g had sharp edges that scraped the sides of his throat and the walls of his oral cavity. It hurt. But now that he'd said it, he felt lighter.

Sam rested his hand on his shoulder but didn't speak. Keith took a look at that hand. It was deeply lined, with dirt around the fingernails. In thirty years, small hands had gotten big, and pale skin crow-black.

He'd met Sam in junior high school, on the first day of the second term. The first day of the first term was a written intelligence test, on which basis the students were assigned to classes. The highest scoring students were assigned to two A-plus classes, Class One and Class Two. The next highest were assigned to two A-minus classes, Class Three and Class Four. It was all downhill from there. Keith had never taken an intelligence test in his life. He had no idea how to answer. There were seventeen classes that year, and he ended up in Class Seventeen, though he only realized that students in the "grazing water buffalo class" were considered unteachable until he went home and his sisters told him. Expressions twisted, features distorted, they wondered how he'd gotten assigned to the most marginal frontier of secondary education, as he wasn't dumb.

Class Seventeen was a lot of fun. Half the class ate the proverbial duck egg—they got a big fat zero—on exams, which were races to the bottom. There was a spirit medium classmate who held a séance in math class. The teacher prostrated himself and begged him to reveal the winning numbers in the lottery. There was a classmate with tattoos who brought a samurai sword to class, saying he was going to go settle a score right after they got let out. That evening he got hacked to death. The next day he was in the news. There was another round-faced, slow-moving boy who was always smiling. There was a classmate in a wheelchair. There was a classmate who was missing an arm. His elementary school classmate who did strip teases for the spirits was also there. Class Seventeen was always a blast. The teachers didn't really teach. The math teacher wrote the Heart Sutra on the blackboard. The English teacher admitted that she couldn't speak any English. The physical sciences teacher often didn't show up. The history teacher spent classes nursing a glass of sorghum liquor. The geography teacher, a former soldier from Sichuan province, kept hollering: "Retake Mainland China!" The National Language teacher showed the class a nude album he'd bought in the Yongnan Bookstore, of a mixed-race AV idol from Japan. Keith's classmates always brought lots of snacks to class. Pork sausages with raw garlic. Taiwanese popcorn chicken. *Bah-uân*, *bah-tsàng*, and *bí-ko*: deep-fried saucer-shaped dumplings with a pork filling, pyramids of sticky rice steamed with chunks of pork in a bamboo leaf, and cylinders of sticky rice that looked like they'd been steamed in sections of bamboo. Everyone was always eating. You share with me and I'll share with you. Everyone was always laughing, too. Good times.

Some shit had happened by the end of term. A few girls got knocked up. A couple of tattooed boys got hauled off by the cops. The classmate in the wheelchair slit his wrists in the boys' bathroom, flooding the floor with blood. A girl gave birth in the girls' bathroom. More blood. Only half the students made it back after winter vacation. The first day of class, the director of academic affairs walked in and patted his shoulder. "Keith Chen," he said, "you're transferring! Pack your bag and come with me."

It turned out that he had been scoring higher on the monthly grade-wide Chinese and English exams than students in the top two classes. The educators in charge of such matters decided to summon him from the margin to the center. He was reassigned to Class Two.

The first class of the day was English. The diminutive

homeroom teacher stood in front with a rattan cane in her hand and razors in her eyes.

"There is a new student in our class today, who goes by the name of Keith Chen. I hear his English is really good. He got a higher mark on the last test than all of you dumbasses. Keith, stand up. Now that you're here, someone else is going to get the boot. If you slack off, it might be one of you. Keith, you have to study hard, too. If you don't, then back you go."

What a strange class! Nobody kicked the desks. Nobody played poker for money and mahjong for fun. Everyone was so quiet and tired-looking.

"Sampan Yang, you sit next to Keith. You're responsible for helping him adjust to his new environment. He'll have a lot of adjusting to do. His old class was basically a bunch of hoodlums and whores."

He'd heard Sampan Yang was the teacher's son. Sampan got the highest marks in the school. He was going to be a doctor. Keith would always remember how he introduced himself. "My name's Sampan, as in 'The sampan's passed the piled-up peaks.' You know, the boat that carried that poet out of exile down the Yangtze through the Three Gorges. Nice to meet you!"

Everyone besides his mother called him Sam for short. Sam was the same height as him. He had a big nose and little eyes. "We're not like the other classes," said Sam. "Other classes start at 7:30, but the teacher said we had to come early for quizzes on English vocabulary at 6:30 and math at 7:00. If you get less than ninety you get the cane, once for every point you fall short. No exceptions. We have art class, shop class, home economics, and music, but all we do is more math and English to prepare us for the grade-wide test that establishes the all-important ranking. If we don't get at least five classmates in the top ten, we all have to do the frog jump around the track.

On the first test, Class Two swept the top ten. That didn't mean that the teacher was satisfied, because her son Sam wasn't on the list. After all the other teachers and students had left, Sam stayed behind, to get a cane to the palm or the behind, to squat in place or frog jump around the track while his mother berated him. "Sampan Yang, how are you going to get into medical school if you can't even get into the top ten in this backwater? I'm not going to ride you home today. You can walk yourself home." Keith was hiding behind a phoenix tree the whole time memorizing the English words for the morning quiz and spying on Sam.

After the teacher rode off, Keith appeared from behind the tree and went over to sit down beside Sam. Noting the cane marks on his friend's white uniform, Keith got out a steamed taro cake for him to eat. "My ma made it, it's really good. Go ahead, have it." Sam gobbled it all up. Smiling, he said, "You dumbass, I forgot to tell you, you can't bring snacks to school. She goes through our bookbags while we're out of the classroom. If she found this, hehehe, you would be worse off than I was just now. Golly, this is so good. Your ma's amazing!" Pushing his bicycle, he left the empty school grounds with Sam and walked him slowly home. There were lots of bats to see in the golden evening sky.

"It's good that you got out. You haven't been home yet, I guess. Don't go for the time being. Let me call your sister and tell her to prepare a stove. You'll have to firewalk before you can cross the threshold."

"Sampan Yang," Keith asked, "what are you doing here? Didn't your entire family move away? Wait a minute, how do you know my sister?"

Sam took out his phone and winked his right eye. "You can come back from Germany, so why can't I? Wait a second, I'm going to give her a call."

Suddenly he felt really sleepy. What time was it now? In the summertime, Germany is six hours behind. So that makes it . . . Where was he? Where was this?

"Beverly, hi, it's me, Sam. I'm going to drop by in a bit. I'm bringing a mystery guest. . . . Don't ask so many questions. Let's just say it's a guest. Have you finished setting out the offering yet? . . . Okay, listen, go get a stove, a small one. . . . Oh it doesn't matter, whatever. Just not too big. . . . Uh-huh, yeah. Do you have pig trotters at home? . . . No? I'll pick some up on the way."

Hearing Sam talking, he felt almost seasick.

"You want to go to sleep, don't you? Must be jet lag. Come, sleep in my truck. I'll drive you home." He sat in the passenger's seat. The engine engaged, his eyelids slammed shut.

The seat was really plush. He sank into it, and then swiftly into an abysm of sleep. He hit bottom, and bounced back up off a soft, viscous, flexible surface. "Ah!" he cried and woke up in surprise. Ah? Aren't I in prison? Where is this? Who is driving the car? Sam? Sampan Yang? How'd you get so old? Sam, is it really you? Where am I? The flowers in that field, are they chrysanthemums?"

"You rest, Classmate, we're going to buy *mī-suànn* vermicelli. Your sister will have guessed by now that her baby brother has finally come home."

15. The suicide note(s)

Keith:

I haven't written you back, but I got your letters. All the letters you've written me the past few years. You sent them to the old townhouse. Beverly snuck them over to me. Baron doesn't know. He really doesn't. He thinks that it's shameful that there are people in my family, two of them, who are locked up. What a moron! As if no one from his family has ever seen the inside of a cell. Moron. He can go to hell.

I didn't answer your letters, I didn't. Because I can't. You know how dumb I am. It's really hard for me to write a letter. I can't do it. I'm dumb, so dumb I married the wrong guy.

Now I'm replying to your letters late, too late. But I read all the letters you sent to me. I read all the books you wrote. I don't go out anymore, but I'm always reading. I read old newspapers and magazines, and your letters and books. Sometimes I wonder whether you've written about me in any of those novels you wrote. I've read them a lot of times, every one. The dumb girl must be me, right? But maybe not. Keith, your books are great, but they often go way over my head. That means I'm dumb. You're not dumb. They say you killed a man and that you're going to be behind bars for a long time. When I heard that I was so envious. Know why? You must, you're smart. Not like your fourth sister.

I'm just dumb. Those letters that you wrote me, I received them all. And I kept every last one. A lot of the paper in my room is mildewed. But I didn't want your letters to mildew. I asked the groundsman what to do. He got me a dry box. Electric. I plugged it in and put your letters to bed. They're so well-behaved, they haven't mildewed. After you get out I will return them to you. All of them. You can go through them. Make them your next book. I've read them a number of times. I'm not lying to you. I bought all of your books and read them. I keep reading your letters.

Mom's gone missing. I tell you, Mom's gone missing. I keep on calling our Beverly, our Betty, and our Belinda, but nobody pays me any mind. I want to call Plenty, too, but I'm too dumb, I just don't know how.

We have to go find Mom. If we can manage to do that, everything will be all right. The White House

Beverly just called to say you were back.

"Barbie, get your ass out here," she said, "Keith is back!" He's come all the way from Germany. You dumbass, what did you come back for? Seriously, why? What are you going to do here? You really are dumb.

I

'm done for. I'm ruined. It's all over. That's how it is. I'm dumb as a post. I can't leave, I really can't. I want to burn the White House down. If I burn it, it won't be white anymore. It'll turn into charcoal. The white will be black, and all the gold will melt away.

There's a letter, and another letter. Two letters.

In my dry box, in addition to the letters that you wrote, there are two other letters. Really old letters. From a long time ago. Handwritten. I found them at the Wang place. The Wangs don't know I have these letters. I hear that nobody is writing letters anymore. I mean handwritten. Although I don't go out, I know, and I know that I know, that I'm actually not that dumb. Baron. No, no, no, it was the groundsman. He gave me a new model of mobile phone.

Keith, that letter I mentioned, it's a suicide note. He wrote it before he died. I've read it for many years now. I keep on reading it over and over. Nobody knows about these two letters. A couple of people know about them. But not you.

You have to. Really. You have to read. This. These. This suicide note.

Nut Wang wrote it. You can't have forgotten him! Green thumb. Red shorts. Lived next door.

Beverly is calling again to tell me to hurry up and come home. Come home, come home, come home but I can't. I don't dare I don't want to I'm too dumb I can't. I don't want to.

Mom's gone missing.

And you're back. Why'd you come back?

Your fourth sister, Barbie

PART 2
LITTLE BROTHER'S BACK

16. The Eternal Prosperity Pool

Sam was no longer in the driver's seat when Keith woke up. The truck was parked by the side of the road. He got out and stretched. The sky was turning a dusky orange. There was a cabbage field by the road and the smell of something charred in the air. He was used to it. A farmer might be burning hay and garbage, the snake killer singeing snakes. There was always someone searing garlic or ginger, lighting incense or spirit money, or baking sweet potato or taro. Occasionally there were fires. Fields burned, houses burned, people burned. Flames had engulfed one of the townhouses in the middle of the night.

That smell pulled him back to reality. He was wide awake. He wasn't in Berlin anymore, he was back home in Yongjing. He put the back of his hand to his nose and inhaled hard. The source of the smell was him, not anywhere in his hometown.

Where was Sam? Didn't he say he was going to buy *mī-suànn* vermicelli? Just before he fell asleep, Sam mentioned the best pig trotter *mī-suànn* place in town.

He looked around and saw the Eternal Prosperity Pool sign on the other side of the road. It was still there.

T, it's right here, the place where I learned to swim.

On the last day of regular classes in grade seven, his homeroom teacher wrote "715 days until the entrance exam!" on the blackboard. "Slackers will end up as meat packers." The class would only get three days' vacation, she announced icily.

After that everyone had to come back to school, in uniform, for the summer vacation maintenance classes. He hadn't had a good night's sleep since his switch from Class Seventeen to Class Two. After a term of rote memorization of model compositions, he now wore glasses to correct his myopia. On the road home from school he saw a few classmates from Class Seventeen under the bishopwood tree smoking and chatting about how they would spend their summer holidays. "Got hair down there yet?" the spirit medium asked. When the other boys bashfully shook their heads, he proudly said, "I do, wanna see it?" They did. They formed a circle around him and he undid his zipper and showed them his organ. "Like a stick!" someone yelled. "It's so thick! Look at all that hair! It's just not fair!" like a rhymed incantation. That obviously appealed to the hairy boy's sense of his masculinity. His stick was soon standing up. Keith looked at it, amazed. He wanted to reach out and touch it. In his eyes, it was more proudly erect than the bishopwood tree.

He had actually touched one when he was very young. The one in the red shorts.

He fell sick that evening. The doctor hooked him up to an IV and fed him pills. A fever lit a bonfire in his forehead that burned for several days. He couldn't attend summer classes, he had to call in sick. Mother said he must be bewitched. She immediately covered a little porcelain cup of rice with a garment of his and recited the spell to collect his wits. Then she lifted the garment and observed the distribution of the grains. A thick and mighty tree had appeared in the rice. After a gust of cold wind, something dirty was dangling out, something long and thick. No wonder he was burning up.

Sam and a couple of their classmates came over to see him. Everyone was envious. The summer classes were no easier than the regular classes. The teacher forced them to memorize fifty English words a day. She'd bought a new rattan cane. Summer holidays were too hot for her to keep hitting them. From now on the boys would hit the girls and the girls would hit the boys. Whoever dared to go light would have to inflict double the punishment. His classmates soon rushed home to finish memorizing all the English words they would get quizzed on the next day, except for Sam, who stayed to go through all the assignments with him. "Once your fever comes down, do you want to go to Yuanlin with me?" Sam asked. "Don't worry, my mom will never find out."

In their eyes, Yuanlin, which was right next door to Yongjing, had all of the charms of a metropolis. There was a movie theater and a busy railway station. There were supermarkets, parks, bookstores, clothing stores, fast food restaurants, neon signs. The "town" of Yuanlin totally satisfied their idea of urban civilization. Taipei was a train or highway bus ride away. Taipei! How he wanted to go there and have a look around. So he immediately nodded. Maybe they could hop on a train and fit in a trip to an actual metropolis.

After Sam went home, he went to sleep and dreamed about the bishopwood tree. When he woke up, he discovered that he, too, had grown fine hair down there.

The summer classes were harsh, the homework heavy. The cicadas roared hypnotically outside the window. There were daily texts to memorize and tests to take, and anyone who didn't make the grade had to hold their hands out and wait for the rattan cane to fall. All the students who had failed went up to the blackboard to stand in punishment. There was a row of boys and a row of girls. The teacher handed the cane to the first boy. Then, one by one, the boys hit the girls and the girls hit the boys. Some boys went light, at first. Incredulous, the teacher said: "What, you like her? Are you in love with her? Didn't I say that you don't come to school to fall in love, you're here to study? You're here to find other ways to serve the nation besides procreation! If you want to fall in love, get hitched, get knocked up, have kids, then I'll be pleased to put you out to pasture!" That boy conveyed all his rage and shame into the rattan cane, raised it high in the air, and brought it down heavily on the girl's palm. A purplish red welt appeared, her face contorted, her eyes flooded with tears. After the last cane had fallen, the boys and girls had to bow and say in unison, "Thank you, Teacher!"

Finally it was Sunday. Sam arranged a time and place to set out on bicycles for Yuanlin. He said that they'd better not take the main road, or someone might see them and tell Sam's mother on them. So they rattled down bumpy little paths through the countryside. The fields were fertile, each an appealing emerald green. Busy farmers were spraying pesticides, hence the heady smell of chemicals in the air. Two boys from Yongjing pushed the pedals as hard as they could, imagining an enemy hot on their heels. Like wind and lightning they passed the slough, the carambola orchard, and the public cemetery, where they rode through a dancing cloud of bright yellow butterflies. Finally they had reached the border of the township. They stopped and drank the rest of the water in the bottle. Not minding how sweaty they were, the butterflies settled upon them. In front of them was Yuanlin, behind them Yongjing. Then they pedaled over the invisible township line into a realm of prosperity.

Once they got there, Sam seemed to know his way around. They ate Yuanlin-style *bah-uân*, bought cassette tapes of albums by teen idols, watched high school students shoot pool at the pool hall, and bought a Japanese starlet's nude album. Finally, they bought a big bag of Taiwanese popcorn chicken and sat in the waiting area at the train station to enjoy it. They watched a train leave for Taipei. "My mother wants my brother to be a doctor," Sam said. "I'll be a teacher. I'm supposed to take her place. She's nuts! I don't want to teach. You want me to hit my students every day? No way. But my brother is in a worse spot than me, the poor guy. She's been on his case so much since he got into high school he can hardly take it any-more. At least she's given up on getting me into medical school. She used to want me to be a doctor, too, but now she says I'm too dumb: I can be a teacher instead."

Sam opened the nude album. The two of them watched the trains come and go as they flipped through, taking in the tits and the pubic hair. "Miyazawa Rie's really popular these days," Sam said. "I'm surprised she was willing to do this in the nude. I guess her mother must have made her."

Looking at her photos, Keith was wondering what the big deal was. His classmate did stripteases at temple fairs, wed-dings, and funerals for the family business, and she always took off all her clothes. Over the years he'd observed her breasts get bigger, her bum rounder. But unlike Miyazawa Rie, she didn't have any hair down there. Later on he asked her about it and it turned out that she had to keep it shaved. If someone saw hair, they might report it as an offense against public morals, and then the police would come for her. But if her skin stayed smooth it was no problem at all.

As night forced day into retreat, they set out for home, by a different route. Back in Yongjing, they went by the unmanned train station and around the chrysanthemum field, all the way to the swimming pool. The lights were glaring, the cement sur-faces bright blue. Only a few people were splashing around. It had opened its doors not long before, the only pool in town. An advertising truck was still shuttling around announcing the grand opening. "To show our appreciation, all tickets are 20% off. Grandmas and Grandpas, come get fit and have fun with your grandsons. Bring the entire family for a swim!"

"Keith," Sam asked, "do you know how to swim?"

He shook his head and thought of his mother's warning. "My mom said I'm not allowed to, because of the water ghost."

"Nonsense! Swimming is fun. I'll teach you, all right?" Whatever Sam said, Keith nodded.

One summer, years later, he was horsing around with T on the beach. Suddenly T pushed him into the Baltic Sea. Although it was August, the water was still chilly. Unable to feel the bottom, he panicked. It felt as if the cold water was invading every orifice, flooding his eyes, mouth, and nose. T grabbed him from behind and pulled him out of the water and onto the shore.

"How can you not know how to swim, having grown up on an island?"

Lying on the beach, he spluttered violently. He thought of his mother's warning when he was a boy. "Stay out of the water, a water ghost will get you!" Those water ghosts apparently specialized in dragging people down until they drowned. When he was struggling in the water just now, he felt like some malevolent force was pulling him down. It turned out that it wasn't just Yongjing that had water ghosts, the Baltic Sea had them, too.

"I know how to swim, I really do. But I have to be able to touch the bottom with my feet. And I have to wear goggles. The water has to be clear and blue."

T opened his eyes wide and smiled. "Water isn't blue."

"Yes it is. The water in the pool back home is blue. And I could always touch the bottom, so I'd never drown. You were trying to murder me just now."

Smoking a joint, T held him tight, attracting the gaze of other beachgoers. But he wasn't afraid. T was there. He felt really safe. He coughed another few times on purpose. T held him even tighter.

T, my first swimming teacher, the one who helped me get my feet wet, so to speak, was named Sam.

"Just bring yourself," Sam said. "Make up some excuse and meet me at the entrance to the pool." After dinner he told his parents he was going to a classmate's house to do his homework. He rode his bicycle like a madman to make it to the pool in time for his lesson. Sam had brought trunks, goggles, and towels. He told him to go into the change room and try on the trunks to see if they were too loose. Standing in the navy briefs in the narrow cubicle, he had an anxiety attack. His tummy wasn't flat enough. His skin was too pale. His limbs looked like sections of bamboo. The undeveloped organ beneath his abdomen didn't bulge, it disappeared. He finally summoned the courage to step out, to the sight of Sam in his briefs, on which his eyes rested. He thought of that exclamation he had heard at the bishopwood tree. "Like a stick! It's so thick! Look at all that hair! It's just not fair!" A fire smoldered in his forehead.

There were two pools. One was a standard-length pool, the other a shallow pool for kids. "You're gonna learn in the standard pool," said Sam. "Just between you and me, a lot of children pee in the shallow pool. One time I saw a lump of shit floating around in there. Don't go in, whatever you do." There were statues of boys peeing into the shallow pool, knockoffs of the pissing mannekin in Brussels.

It was really quiet in the pool at night, so quiet they could hear the frogs and the crickets in the nearby fields. A few people doing lazy flutter kicks made barely any sound. Sam already knew how to swim breaststroke, backstroke, and freestyle. He could even swim underwater, holding his breath and gliding over the bottom. The first thing Sam taught him was how to kick. "Don't be afraid of any water ghost," he kept saying. "Relax your knees." Sam eased him forward in the water, holding him under the tummy and by the thighs. When he accidentally kicked Sam in the groin, he immediately stood up. Sam smiled and winked. "I'll get you back for this if it turns out I'm sterile," he said. "Come on, let's continue."

They kept fibbing to their parents and sneaking out to meet at the pool that entire summer. By the end of the holidays, right before the start of regular classes, Keith could swim freestyle.

He still wasn't breathing too well, but at least he could stay afloat and make progress through the water.

Until . . .

That day, the clouds dropped a load. Lightning tore across the sky. The lifeguard blew his whistle. "Please come out of the pool immediately." Keith and Sam were too busy wrestling in the water to hear the announcement. They kept fooling around, letting the warm rain fall on their faces. When they finally climbed out of the pool they saw their English teacher. Lightning flashed from her eyes, striking them both down. She didn't say a thing, just dragged Sam out.

The next day she announced a change to the seating plan. Sam's new seat was right in front of the lectern.

When fall term began, the whole class changed places. Sam stayed in front of the lectern, while Keith relocated to a back corner, right beside the garbage can and behind a tall, bulky classmate who blocked the view. It was the worst seat in the class. The kid who sat there usually got the worst grades on the monthly exam. Before, the teacher had often praised his English, but now she totally ignored him. When she assigned class chores, he was responsible for disposing of the garbage and cleaning the can. Sam's bicycle had been confiscated. He came and left with his mother. He spent lunch hour in the teacher's office, reciting English vocabulary. During summer vacation Sam had carried him around on his shoulders in the pool. Now Sam was sitting far away from him, staring straight at the blackboard.

Thirty years later, amazingly, the pool was still here.

Crossing the street, Keith couldn't hear any splashing. Business was so good later on that laughing kids competed with the nearby insects to see who was louder. Now it was quiet again. Maybe because of Ghost Festival? Was it closed for the holiday?

A dead palm tree had fallen over in front of the entrance.

The gate was flaking paint, the ticket window crammed with refuse. The fence wall had disappeared. So had the water.

There wasn't a drop in either pool, just dry white tile. Cracked, filthy, and unable to piss, the mannekins looked as though they'd been pushed into the shallow pool. Weeds had grown in the cracks between the tiles until they were taller than a grown man like him. Hung with a busted lamp and a kite that would never fly again, the palm trees that lined the pool were sallow. The standard pool was empty, except for a rusty bike, a headless teddy bear, a moldy sofa, and a dried-up potted plant.

He sat at the edge of the standard pool and stared at the teddy bear, lost in thought. Where was the water?

"It closed down a couple of years ago. It couldn't be helped, business was bad." Sam sat down beside him holding a carry bag.

"I was often the only person who came in. I would spend the entire evening here by myself. It's a pity. If I had the money I'd buy it and swim here by myself."

Where was the water? He looked at Sam and felt dizzy again. It was like a hole had been drilled in the back of his head and all the fluid was draining out. His childhood had dried up. His adolescence had dried up. And so had the pool. Maybe the entire Baltic Sea had dried up.

Sam opened the bag to show him the big pot inside. When he removed the lid, sesame oil steam escaped. Shiny brown pig trotters were floating in a broth. He smelled the rich meaty aroma and looked at Sam. Time stopped. The setting sun was stuck in the sky like that kite in the tree. The vapor from the pot froze in the air between them.

Sam took a handful of *mī-suànn* vermicelli out of the bag. "Handmade. Who says that the White House is the only thing worth visiting Yongjing for? It makes me angry when they say that on the news. Okay, okay, there's nothing to see here, but at least we have handmade noodles." The noodles were dyed golden by the setting sun, like T's blond locks.

"Did I mention this is where I met your sister? Let's go, she's waiting."

17. *You're coming home*

You're finally coming home.

Imagine, the youngest son of the Chen family is coming home. Sampan Yang is ferrying you home.

The last time you came home was for my funeral. You rushed back to hold a wake for me. The next morning, the cicadas were crying, driving you away. Before you left you lit incense in my mourning hall and said a prayer for me. You were mumbling, so I couldn't hear the words, but I knew that you were bidding me farewell. I wanted to tell you to leave, as soon as possible. All right, you've said goodbye, now you can go. Hurry up, go! Reticent in life, I was silent in death. I tried as hard as I could to give you a sign, by lifting the tablecloth or extinguishing the candle in the mourning hall, to tell you I had heard your prayer. But the tablecloth didn't move, nor did the candle flicker. I couldn't move in my picture, I was freeze-framed. I couldn't move in the cooler, either, I was stiff. There was no wind or rain to do the deed, and all the cats and dogs and the cocks and geese in the neighborhood were trapped in dream. Trees and herbs were hushed, and ghosts were mute.

Suddenly the cicadas were deafening. When she called you prodigal, that's when you finally left.

I wanted you to hurry up and leave because I was afraid that if you stayed even a second longer you might learn the truth about what happened in the water cistern. You would see my true colors, and your mother's. All the things that we did to you, and everything that we didn't do. We didn't protect you, not even once. The cruelest people weren't your homeroom teacher or the police. It was us.

You never liked coming home as a boy. I often went out to look for you. I would sling you in my arms and carry you home. Folks say that at six months babies sprawl, at seven they crawl, and at eight they drool. But you did everything faster than anyone. You started crawling at six months. At seven months you stood up and learned to walk. You were in such a hurry. You crawled, walked, and ran. Then you turned towards the door, wanting to go outside. If we carried you back inside you cried. If you saw a locked door or a shut window, you wanted to open it. If we said you weren't allowed to go somewhere, you'd find a way. Your mother and I enjoyed scaring you. We said that there were ghosts out there—in the water, the bamboo, the field, or the road. If you go there a ghost is going to get you and then you'll be an SOG, a son of a ghost. That got your attention. Your elder brother would frown and burst out crying, but you opened your eyes even wider. You were fearless and curious.

You kept running outside like someone was chasing you. When Cicada made dinner, nobody could find you. I'd go door to door and the neighbors would say that they had just seen you running around but had no idea where you'd run off to. Sometimes I'd find you sleeping in a coffin in the coffin maker's shop, sometimes at the neighbor's dinner table, with a hot meal in your belly. Sometimes you'd be watching the snake killer kill a snake, sometimes waiting for the bats under a streetlamp. I'd take you home, but as soon as you'd finished dinner, you hurled your gaze out the window and would want to go out again. You could never stay put. Your gaze kept throwing out the anchor, but the claws could never find purchase in the mud, your body couldn't find a moorage. You didn't want what Yongjing had to offer.

You looked east at the distant mountain range, and you said you wanted to go there all by yourself. You pointed west and asked if that was the way to the sea. I nodded. Do you remember one time I came home with a pile of fish and oysters in the back of the truck? I had brought a load back from the coast. I told you all about it. The wind was so strong in the harbor, and the harbor so dark, that I dared not approach. The water must be full of ghosts. When you heard that you let my hand go and started walking west.

That was when I knew that your hometown was too small for you, that Yongjing would never keep you.

Later on, when the Wangs moved in next door, you started running over there. If you were not at the Wang place, I knew I could find you in the carambola orchard, where Jack's youngest son Nut used to hang out.

Jack Wang was quite the character. He was the guy who would sell whatever the world was short of, whatever people needed. When he saw me making deliveries in my truck, he wondered if we could go into business together. He uncapped a bottle of maotai. The quality, he said, was off the scale, but it wasn't for sale, at least not to just anybody. Jack had connections, he could sell it to connoisseurs. It was so rare he could name the price. We could make a killing. Never having heard of maotai before, I did a shot. But as soon as I saw the simplified characters on the label, I slammed the bottle down and spewed the liquor on the floor. Don't worry! said genial Jack. Friend of his in Hong Kong had a special supply channel. He brought it in from mainland China, hence the simplified characters. The logistics were complicated, but if you don't take a risk then how can you rake it in? Am I right? Quite a few high-ranking officials have ordered crates. They just need to be delivered. There won't be any problem. Nobody's going to go to jail just for enjoying a drink. Cheers! Jack said that the martial law, which outlawed goods from the mainland, was all talk. Or rather, it was just for the regular Taiwanese people, not for high-ranking officials, most of whom were born on the mainland. Those officials would sit at home, drink a cup of maotai, a taste of home, and head down memory lane. Unable to go home, they would drink a bottle. If they became maotai fiends, so much the better: then they could flit home, over the Strait to the other shore. Jack said the worst times are the best times for any businessman to get into the market and make big money. He heard the owners of the Yongchang Bookstore had moved to Argentina. Afraid that America had abandoned Taiwan, they'd made a run for it. That was stupid, if you asked him. You had to stay in the game to make your name. "Big Rig Chen," Jack said, "or should I call you CEO? Let's join forces. I'll supply it, you'll drive it. Together we'll strike it rich."

I asked him how he knew what the world was short of. He said you have to make folks feel like they lack a certain thing. If they buy "it," then they'll be healthy, wealthy, and wise, and every baby will be a boy. As for what "it" is, that depends on how good the businessman is at creating demand. A couple of years before, he'd made big money selling air guns. That's where the money for the townhouse came from. "CEO Chen," he said, "tell me, didn't you buy your family a gun, back in the day? You didn't have to eat, your kids got to go to school, but you just had to have a gun. It made you feel safe, right? Everyone felt the same way. And I made a killing."

Jack had two sons. His younger son was tall and wiry, like a betel nut palm tree, hence his nickname. Nut was the first student in the township to test into NTU. He graduated and did his mandatory military service, but he wouldn't stay and work in Taipei. He came home and said he wanted to farm the land. Jack gave him an abandoned carambola orchard to tend. "People say he's some kind of an academic prodigy," Jack said, "but I guess none of those books he reads ever told him about the palms on the old hundred-dollar bills. Talk about money growing on trees; in Taiwan trees grew on money. And Nut just doesn't know the value of money! He won't go out and make any, he just hangs around in the orchard. They say he's got a green thumb, but if you ask me he's a greenhorn. Bet he won't last more than a few months as a farmer. Young people don't understand how tough manual labor can be. I spent all that money sending him north to college so he could get ahead and make it big, and then he says that he can't stand the big city. At least my elder son Baron's got his head screwed on straight, just like his old man. He loves money, and he's a ladies' man. He's got what it takes to make it in business."

For the last carambola harvest, both families went to lend a hand. Wang's two sons, my two sons, and my five daughters. Beverly was heating water for baby formula. Her husband was off gambling somewhere. Betty and Belinda were helping out. Barbie and Plenty were swinging under one of the boughs. They always got along the best. Baron kept staring at my Plenty. Keith, who was in grade one that year, tagged along wherever Nut went, learning to pick the fruit. Cicada was cooking up a storm, pouring on the Fragrant soy sauce and clattering the spatula around the wok. She made enough pork fried noodles to feed an army.

We all sat under a tree slurping noodles. It smelled so tasty that wasps and bees, butterflies and flies, and canines and felines all came, too, for a bite beside baskets of starfruits. It was a bountiful harvest.

A gust of wind stole into the orchard. Leaves soughed and fell, skirts flew. Beverly's can of dried milk got knocked over and powder swirled, forming a white fog. The sky went dark, rain clouds devoured the sun. Well-aimed chunks of hail the size of ping-pong balls fell suddenly from the sky, pelting all the produce in the town.

People yelled and ran. Someone kicked over Cicada's wokful of fried noodles, which spilled onto the freshly picked starfruits. The air smelled of milk powder and soy sauce. Thunder crashed, lightning flashed, even more hail came hurling down.

As the heavens opened, everyone ran for the townhouses.

"Run," someone shouted. "Hurry up, run! Before it's too late!"

A ping-pong ball hit my forehead, fresh blood dyed my vision. I rubbed my eyes and caught sight of Nut curled up under a carambola tree. He was sheltering my baby boy from the hail that was shredding the flesh of the freshly picked starfruit.

Racing past by the chrysanthemum field on the way home, I saw white hail bursting out of the sky and a million bulbs shattering crisply in the air. The hailstones were obviously expert chrysanthemum pickers, separating a million 'mums from the stalk and scattered petals everywhere. Petal-laden torrents flooded the neighboring fields, dyeing swathes of collapsed rice corpses yellow, purple, and bright, bright red.

After the hail it rained, for three whole days. The rain formed posts, and the posts fences, confining folks at home. Farmers who tried to save their crops were carried away by the flood. That year's harvest was a total washout, as all the produce in the township was pounded into pulp by the hail and left to rot in the rain. The water level rose in the slough, spilling dead hogs, dogs, cocks, and trash onto the road.

Three days later there dawned a day without wind or cloud or rain. That was the bluest sky I'd ever seen. I looked up and reached my fingers into the sky-blue paint. On the road in front of the townhouse lay a few dead hogs, whose stinking corpses glowed in the sun. Holding my nose, I went to take a closer look. They were covered in the shards from the light-bulbs in the chrysanthemum field.

Everything was made manifest in the sunlight that morning. The rain washed up all the garbage that the countryfolk had buried in the field or dumped in the irrigation ditch, turning it into a gutter. The fish leaped out of the pond and died in the betel leaf field. The bishopwood tree lost half its leaves. The ceilings in the three-wing compound wept. Water seeped through walls in the townhouses that had been built only a few years before. Paint peeled. Standing in the sun, I stuck my fingers in my ears, but the rain had adhered to my hearing, like tinnitus. I wanted to dig it out.

If only it hadn't hailed. If only it hadn't rained!

It was because of that hail and that rain that Cicada saw.

She saw the youngest Chen with the youngest Wang.

18. Finding fire

Beverly ran up to the third floor and rushed from room to room, opening drawers and wardrobes, looking under desks and beds, lifting blankets and mattresses, and disturbing the dust that had been sleeping there for eons, until the air was thick. Unhappy at the rude awakening, motes of dust banded together and mounted an assault on Beverly's nostrils, triggering an allergy storm. Her nose tingling, she opened her mouth like a hippo: ahhhhhh! By the time the wind wave surged out of her oral cavity, her lips were as pointy as a bird's beak: choo! So much spittle flew it was raining in the room, waking up even more dust. Another counterattack set off even more sneezes: hippo, ah, bird, choo, hippo, ah, bird, choo.

Beverly laughed. A sneeze is just a sneeze. Why had she thought of those two animals?

Ah, right. There used to be a zoo behind the White House, with tropical birds and a hippo, just because Plenty wanted to see one.

Without her little brother to help her count, she had no idea how many times she had just sneezed.

She sat on the floor of Plenty's room, having pulled out all the drawers in the dresser. Redolent of camphor, mothballs assailed her mouth and nose, which were still grappling with the dust. When hostilities ceased, in the gaps between the sneezes, she heard a faint gnawing. She covered her mouth and nose with her hand to stifle an incipient sneeze and listened carefully. It sounded like someone was cutting wood with a tiny saw. What the hell? She was alone in her dead sister's room on the one day of the year when the Hellgate gaped. Who could be sawing? The sound was coming from Plenty's desk, which looked like it might collapse at any time. When she tapped on the top, the sawing immediately stopped. She knelt down, looked underneath, and saw a termite's nest. That desk really was on its last legs.

At that time, all the furniture stores were selling desks like that. Father bought seven of them, one for every child. It was Beverly's first desk. The body and the legs were painted brownish orange. There were two drawers with nail-on silver arch handles. The desktop was a world map, with the seas in blue and the countries in different hues. At the bottom of the map were rows of national flags, and under each flag an official name. Baby Keith memorized all of them. Beverly would test him by covering up the names. He often zoned out staring at that map, like he'd fallen into one of those seas of blue, until he pointed out one of the colored shapes at random and asked, "Beverly, where is this? I want to go." She helped him connect names to places.

Beverly sat down at the desk. The seas were faded, the flags mottled. It was completely out of date. She hadn't completed secondary school or traveled abroad, but she did know that China wasn't a begonia leaf anymore: Mongolia had been independent for ages. "Sister," Keith asked one time, "Do you want to come for a visit? The ticket is on me. Bring Betty and Belinda. I'll take you all swimming in the Baltic Sea."

"No way, don't waste your money," she said. "I'm fine here. I don't know how to swim, I'd drown. What if I became a water ghost in that whatchamacallit sea? There's no way I'd find the way home."

She looked around. Nothing had changed since Plenty's death. Her pastel dresses were still hanging in the wardrobe.

After her funeral Father had gone in and would not come out. When the sisters tried to collect her stuff, he gave them a nasty look, shook his head, and growled through gritted teeth. He did not have to say anything, they understood. Maintain the status quo and pretend the room would keep sneezing of a morning. She hadn't been in here in years. Why today? "What am I looking for?" she asked herself. Oh yeah!

Fire.

Sam told her to get a stove ready. For a firewalk. The word was a match striking her forehead, setting her brain alight. She ran up to the third floor and went rummaging through all six rooms. Soon the flames died down, leaving her at a loss.

She kept right on rummaging. "Silly Keith," she murmured, "didn't I tell you not to come back?" Achoo.

Plenty used to wake up sneezing. She had an allergic constitution, with pale, paper-thin skin that would bleed at a scratch and break out in a rash if she ate a sliver of shrimp, not to mention the morning achoos, which Keith counted several rooms away: one, two, three, four, five, six. Once Plenty finished sneezing, he finished counting, having woken the whole family up. There was no need for an alarm clock. After Plenty passed away the sneezing disappeared. The television and the radio were turned off. Keith did not say anything for months. Maybe that's when the townhouse went into sleep mode. It hadn't woken up since.

Keith was the one who found her body.

"Jeez, Keith, why'd you come home again? I don't have a stove in the house, only a brazier to burn spirit money in."

Beverly got up. Aware that their wood-gnawing scheme had been uncovered by a human, the termites nibbled with fervid desperation. This was where Beverly lived, a place with a cracked floor and a termite-eaten desk. But the home had not collapsed any more than the desk had. Though her own body was all cracks from head to toe, she was still alive.

She went into her little brother's room. There were cardboard boxes on the bed, on the floor, by the wall, and on the map of the world, leaving barely any space to walk around in. Every box was labeled in his handwriting. The American Novel (Freshman). Irish Drama (Junior). Jazz CDs. Drama props. Literary prizes. VHSs. When she saw that she shuddered. Are those old tapes still around? She could still hear her mother scream. She looked away. A stove, a stove, I came up here to find a stove!

All of Keith's Taiwanese possessions were in that room, along with a box his lawyer sent from Germany. Back from Taipei, Betty helped Beverly go through it. Books. A few pairs of jeans, shirts, and suit jackets. A model submarine. Pictures with T. T holding and kissing her younger brother. They were laughing so happily. Beverly and her husband had never taken this kind of intimate photo together. Keith and T looked good together, why had it ended up like this? There were also German gummy bears, honey-flavored. Another fragrance greeted her nose. Finally, there was a handwritten letter with a forwarding address and an explanation of the candies. They were his favorite kind. He'd asked his lawyer to buy them to send to his sisters. At the end he wrote, "Beverly, don't worry, I'm all right. I don't have anywhere to store these things for now. Put them in my old room for a few years. I'll figure out what to do with them when I get out."

She framed a photo her little brother had taken with T and put it on her bedside table. They were holding hands, eating ice cream, and grinning in swim trunks at the beach, in front of a really big submarine. Last time Sam came to her room to repair the window he saw the picture and asked her if he could take a closer look. He looked at it a long time. Finally, he looked up. "He hasn't changed, you know. The way he looks when he smiles."

She finally recalled a clay stove with a grill she must have left in the back yard. She'd cooked wings and drumsticks on it last Mid-Autumn Festival. She was trying to smoke the orchids to death.

She'd had enough of orchids, and of her husband's orchid orchard. It was to drive away the orchids that she'd raised chickens in the back yard in the first place.

When Little Gao showed up to see his firstborn, the baby girl she'd given birth to in the swamp spinach field, he said that he was going to go to the temple to swear on all he held dear that if the next baby was a boy he would give up gambling and take her to see his parents. His parents? She thought he was an orphan, but he turned out to be the eldest son of a farming family from the neighboring township. So she kept trying. She kept getting pregnant and miscarrying. She overheard him tell the snake killer that the Lady at the Foot of the Wall had answered his prayers. Obviously, the fetuses his wife was losing were girls. The year her daughter turned three, she finally gave birth to a strapping baby boy. She didn't have to go to see her parents-in-law, they came to see her in the hospital. They brought a red envelope and held their grandson. They accepted her as their daughter-in-law and asked about her family. But they paid no attention to their granddaughter, who was crying and fussing to the side.

Her husband really did give up gambling after she gave him a son, but he hadn't cured his addiction, just found a new outlet for it: orchids. It was the snake killer who gave him the idea.

Small and crafty-looking in his thick sunglasses, which he wore day and night, and single in middle age, the snake killer moved into this row of townhouses at about the same time as Beverly's family and opened up a VHS rental store. His nickname was on account of his hobby: capturing, raising, killing, and eating snakes. He had come to the right place. Although the township was pretty dull in those days, it had ample wasteland and farmland, tumbledown houses and smelly sloughs,

making it a paradise for the kind of crawling critter that makes
most people's skin crawl. You could count on them to relieve
the tedium from time to time, by scaring some poor farmer
half to death. Screams in the fields told you that someone had
seen a snake. If you saw one yourself, you ran to the VHS
store. The boss could subdue various kinds of snake with just
a net and a bamboo pole. He could name them, too, and
explain if yours was venomous or not and whether it was right
for making soup with or medicinal wine. If it was colored then
catch it and cage it. If it was fat then flay it and throw a feast
for the neighbors.

When the kids started screaming, Beverly would take them
to the "zoo" on the second floor of the VHS store. When they
saw the snakes they would quiet right down and look at them
in awe. They weren't just local snakes. The snake killer had
gone to Indochina to spend a small fortune purchasing speci-
mens and finding ways of repatriating them. Beverly stared at
a Thai snake, amazed. It'd been to more places than her! With
their intricate patterns, those exotic boas were a lot more inter-
esting than the potted orchids the snake killer kept on the
counter downstairs. As far as she was concerned, they were
boring, just a couple of yellow or purple flowers. She could
hardly believe they could win him a million dollars in prize
money. The snake killer made it into the paper for winning the
gold medal in an international orchid competition.

Her husband aspired to a hobby, too. He didn't dare kill
snakes, but growing flowers was so simple, anyone could do it,
even him. So he made himself a flower rack and threw himself
into orchid rearing. He bought a hundred blooming orchids
and put his million-dollar masterplan into effect. He had no
idea how to tend them. He watered them every day, until the
roots rotted and the flowers withered. The investment from
the first year was a wash out. The next year he bought even
more orchids, along with a book called *Orchid Primer*. He'd

start reading it and end up staring at his orchids. Like her, Little Gao was a junior high school dropout. He went to work at fifteen driving forklifts, backhoes, and trucks. He was skilled and strong, able to hoist heavy loads on his shoulders. Yet he was hard-pressed to turn effectively weightless pages with his fingers and lift the words with his eyes. Aerial roots, pruning, repotting, and all the other terminology went over his head. The flower outlook in his orchid orchard remained grim, while the snake killer won another prize in an international competition.

The year both kids were finally in school, Little Gao's orchids bloomed gloriously at long last. He'd managed to teach himself to moderate watering, to let the aerial roots grow outwards, and to prune the rotten roots and stems. He could change a pot like a pro. He put up a sunshade net and a rain shield. In terms of robustness and floriferousness, his orchids weren't up to a competitive standard, not quite yet. So he moved a karaoke machine in and sang upbeat Taiwanese ballads to his flowers, so hoarsely that when a pack of feral dogs started to bark in response, it was hard to tell the difference.

By day he was still making deliveries, but as soon as he got off work he went into the back yard to tend to his flowers. One time he took his orchids for expert appraisal, laying them down with fastidious care in the bed of the truck. For some reason, it reminded her of his proposal in the garment factory all those years ago. Hey Bev! Wanna go for a spin?

Little Gao took up another hobby to try to remedy the deficiency in his education, calligraphy. He made himself a wooden sign that read Little Gao's Orchid Or Chard and hung it over the back door. The kids told her "orchard" was one word, Daddy got it wrong. Would he listen? She flipped through a few of his calligraphy practice books, which had formed quite a sizable pile. Little Gao's Orchid Or Chard, over and over again. He'd written it a zillion times.

A few years later, a moth orchid from Little Gao's Orchid Or Chard finally won a prize. It was a small amount of money. But it attracted the attention of a professional judge, who came over to look at the rest of his collection. He offered him a high price for one of the potted orchids. But her husband refused. She was so angry she felt like hacking him with a cleaver. But he was unruffled when confronted. "I'm bullish," he said serenely. Several days later a typhoon hit central Taiwan hard. It blew everything in the back yard away, leaving not a single petal, pot, or grain of soil behind. Little Gao stood at the back door and watched the ruthless wind tear his or chard apart. She thought that he would go out and rescue the orchids. But all he did was say, "Go next door and borrow money from your father. I'll go buy new ones tomorrow."

He spent even more of his spare time and money on his new orchids. He built a solid brick wall and a transparent plastic roof to block the wind and rain. Soon he restored his orchid orchard to its former glory. Various moth orchids bloomed beautifully. By that point he and Beverly were sleeping in separate rooms. He put a cot out in the yard and snored for his beloved orchids. One day at dawn she tiptoed to the back yard to find him getting ready to shower one of his orchids with affection. He was masturbating in front of it. That same morning, she rushed to the market to buy a bunch of chicks. Raising chickens was one of her chores at the three-wing compound. She knew how quickly they would grow, and how much noise and shit they would make. It would be mobile fowl against fragile flowers. That was her masterplan for getting rid of the orchids, for once and for all.

Raising, slaughtering, and roasting chickens—she did it all in the back yard. But the orchids did not wilt. And her husband did not leave.

She was in the back yard shoveling chicken shit when she heard her brother had killed T. She sat down on the ground and cried. A couple of cocks that would usually crow like crazy were shocked by her sobs. They hid behind the potted orchids and watched her cry without so much as a squawk. Keith was so smart. He had gotten such a good degree and written so many books. He'd even gone abroad. How could it turn out like this? Sure, none of the Chen children had married well, but how could her little brother turn into a murderer? If any of them really wanted to kill their spouse, it was her.

She finally found the stove by a discarded flower pot and a sack of charcoal. Under the stove was a plaque with Keith's name on it. And the Great Wall of China.

Firewalk? How do you do that? Does Betty know? Oh, I forgot to let her know about Keith. And Belinda. I'd better tell them to come home. What about Barbie? Will she be willing to leave the White House when she hears the news?

She picked up her phone and sent messages to Betty, Belinda, and Barbie. "Hurry home, Little Brother's back!" Then she searched for "firewalk" videos. The top result was "Firewalk with the Yellow Emperor." It had over a million views.

She clicked it. A man was wearing a yellow gown and thick glasses with a wad of spirit money in his fingers and a smoking brazier at his feet.

It was their snake-killing next-door neighbor.

19. The day the night died

In the bed of the pickup truck lay a work ladder, a toolbox, an electric saw, and an extension cord. Sam answered Keith's question before it was asked. "I came back to do electrical and plumbing work. Everyone else left, I'm the only one who returned. It's actually gone pretty well. I get more jobs than I can shake a stick at. I repaired a water heater before I ran into you at the soy-sauce factory. You know her. You went to elementary school together, and to grade seven before you got stuck in Class Two. That stripper girl, remember? So her water heater breaks down. She asks me to go fix it. I tell her to take cold showers, for Christ's sake, it's hot out! She tells me she knows I'm not going to charge her for it, so she might as well get it fixed. She's a mother now. She said something about how times have changed, and there aren't as many invitations for her to strip as there used to be. The queen of striptease has taken off her crown. Now she's deep-frying chicken fillets on the street."

Keith remembered her all right, copying his homework, dancing buck naked. She saved his life one time by dancing.

Sam engaged the engine. "You didn't get much sun when you were in prison, did you?"

He didn't recall Sam being so talkative or having such dark and glossy skin. His arms were like the night, the moles like twinkling stars.

T, when I first met you, you, too, were black as the night. Black coat, black gloves, black hat, black boots, black cello.

Actually he first "heard" T's black before he saw it.

His first week in Berlin, he stayed in a little ground floor apartment in the east end that the writers' association arranged for him. It had a little window looking out onto a noisy street. One window, one door, one bed, one table, one chair, one room, one bathroom, one kitchen. With one of everything, it was a perfect bachelor pad. After nightfall booze fiends raised hell outside in a language he couldn't understand. It was all of five steps from the front door to a U-Bahn station. The floor would rattle with every train. It got cold out, but he always invited the world outside to come in and make itself at home by leaving the window *gekippt*, "ajar." The dictionary listed it as the past participle of *kippen*, "to tilt." It described the kind of window that opens from the top, a tilt-and-turn window. It kept people out but let breezes and voices shuttle freely in and out. No matter how cold it got he would leave it *gekippt*. He did not want to go out. He had not let himself get to know Berlin. Writing a novel at home, he first heard the city sounds stealing in through the window. All the sounds were new, of the language, the wind, the rain. He couldn't read anything, neither notices nor posters, neither signs nor books. Effectively illiterate, he finally understood his mother's angst. But for now he enjoyed being an outsider. He was only there for a short stay. He did not want to become a part of Berlin. He actively excluded himself from everything. He passed all the strangers by. He had arrived without ceremony and he would leave without fuss. He wouldn't bother anyone.

He could see it was raining out, but he couldn't hear the rain on the walkway. He could barely hear it with the window open all the way. That was Berlin rain. It was a far cry from Taipei or Yongjing rain, which turned into grenades when it hit the ironskin roofs, interrupting even the deepest sleep and frazzling nerves.

When the rain turned into snow, he heard Bach.

He sat by the window as the notes of a cello sonata came trotting in on snowflakes. The tone color was full. There were occasional mistakes that were corrected before the music could continue. The mistakes were honest. There was no attempt to cover up, and no regret. Keith imagined that the cellist was a child. But the Schubert that followed was so world weary, it sounded like it must have been played by aged fingers.

The snow fell for days on end. He stayed inside, watching it fall and writing. He didn't go out at all. Every evening after eight o'clock the traffic abated and the cello appeared. He'd get ready for it by making a simple supper. Lettuce and tomatoes with olive oil, a fried egg and stir-fried garlic shredded chicken, simmered rice. He'd sit by the window and wait for the cello. When the sound came in he dug in. He ate very slowly, reading a few pages from a book. By the time the cello faded away he would have finished the last bite. One night when the cello did not come, he finally realized how awful the meal tasted. Without a cello to hypnotize him, his sense of taste was wide awake. The cello was gone, so were the groceries. Oh no, he really had to make a trip to the supermarket.

He carried two big bags of vegetables, fruit, and frozen meat home through ankle-deep snow. His jacket was covered in snowflakes. Standing under a streetlamp watching the snow fly, he remembered waiting for the bats under a streetlamp in his hometown. There were no bugs or mosquitoes under the streetlamps in Berlin, let alone bats. But the snow here had a palpable vitality. Glittering in flight, the flakes were like little white bugs.

The road started trembling. A gust of wind blew out of the station, pouring a cello into his scarf, his hat, his ears. The cello was late, but better late than never. He walked downstairs as the commuters who had just gotten off the train rushed out, forming a wave that pushed him back up the stairs and drowned out the music. The human flood quickly dispersed, and the low notes of the Bach floated slowly back up to the street. The wind heard it, the rain heard it, he heard it. It wasn't a neighbor after all. It was subterranean. He walked down the stairs and saw T.

Of course he didn't know the cellist's name. And all he saw was a blob of black that had occupied a corner of the station, along with the bow rubbing across the strings of a black cello, producing that characteristically deep tone. He could not see the man in black's face or any of his skin. The man was look-ing down, concentrating on bowing. Commuters hurried in and out of the station. Nobody stopped to listen to the black blob play the cello. He was wearing an oversized black woolen jacket, as big as a blanket. Keith noticed a little sticker on the left-hand side of the instrument. Approaching slowly, he saw it was a sticker of a submarine. He took out the change from the groceries and put it in the case. *Danke*, he said softly. Then he went home, opened the window, and wrote. He ate a lousy home-made meal.

From then on he often went down to listen. By the time he was a regular, he'd made the acquaintance of the big black short-haired dog with shining eyes that cuddled under the jacket. It often stuck out its head and snored. When it woke up, it listened lethargically, not making a sound. One time he was sitting cross-legged against the wall, when the dog crawled out, padded over, and rested its head on his thigh. Maybe it was the cello, maybe it was the dog. For whatever reason, that dog lay its head on the lap of a complete stranger. Its expression still indolent, it went to sleep. Its unconditional trust pricked his eyes. His tears came flooding out.

Keith cried through the entire movement. When the cellist finished, he snapped his fingers and the dog opened its eyes and yawned. It padded obediently back. The cellist finally looked up and pulled his hat back, revealing a pale, smiling face.

He never imagined a face like that, with bright blue eyes, defined features, sandy blond hair, thin lips, a toothy grin. It was a candid face. Another wave of rush-hour commuters hit the station. He threw some spare change in the case and let himself get flushed out.

Now that the man had seen him cry, he decided to stay away. He would stay at home and listen with the window *gekippt*. The snow kept falling, but the novel he was writing came to a standstill. The story was stranded. He could not write a single sentence. He went out to buy a pack of postcards and stamps, noting that he hadn't gone to any of the pictured sights in Berlin. Why am I here? he asked himself. He had applied for a subsidy to come here for a six-month residence, but what for? He never went out. He kept everyone at a distance. Wasn't this about the same as his life in Taipei?

One time he went to a performance by a theater troupe from Berlin. Up on the stage, the performers shouted in German, jerked their limbs violently, hit the walls, threw themselves on the floor. He paid no attention to the surtitles, just followed the actors' bodies with his eyes. Those bodies seemed boundless. After two hours of shouting, their voices were just as loud and clear. They were just as comfortable naked as they were clothed. For the curtain call, the cast went back to being their regular selves, smiling goofily as the audience applauded. Keith looked just as goofy. He was stupefied, as if he had just seen a ghost. How could anyone, even an actor, throw himself first halfway around the world and then into a part, so completely? And after breaking all boundaries, yelling, crying for help, fighting, basically tearing himself apart, how could he immediately regain his composure after the curtain fell? I should go see what it's like, he thought.

Now that he'd come he couldn't write a single word. Facing notepad or laptop, he felt physically restless. There was snow outside but fire in his mind. He wrapped a pillow round his head to smother it. He chugged ice water and took a freezing shower to drown it. But it was just the same. Nothing seemed to quench the flame.

The flame was spreading down his body and taking shape. It was like a little finger that was tickling his bones and guts. He had to get out of the apartment.

In Taipei he seldom thought of going out. He lived in an illegal rooftop addition. The landlord had piled old furniture outside the door. Any prospective tenant who climbed up the stairs would hurry away at the sight of that pile. He was the only one who stayed. When can I move in? he asked. The landlord was taken aback. "I'll clear out the furniture," he said.

"I've always wanted to plant trees and greens up here. You can help me water them." The landlord did make an effort, but the pile never seemed to diminish. If anything, it grew, with every visit. The rent was cheap, the room cramped, and everything was beat up and gloomy. Surrounded by glittering new apartment complexes, the grungy old walkup apartment building seemed out of place. Keith felt cut off from the world, as if he entered a parallel space-time when he reached the roof. It was exactly the environment he needed. Outside the rain bombed the roof, inside a busted sofa and a crippled table quietly mated, giving birth to even more crippled tables and lame chairs. He wrote by the window, looking out at a silver water cistern. That was his view of Taipei. Watching that cistern, he wrote three books about the city.

He hadn't told his family he'd come to Berlin.

And after sticking the stamps on the postcards, he didn't know what to write. What was he to tell Beverly? Should he send his regards to Betty? If he sent one to Belinda would her news anchor husband intercept it?

The cello issued an invitation. He carried the postcards and a pen out the door and down the steps. He sat down by the wall. The black dog came right over to lie down beside him. The cellist was messing around, improvising a tune. He put down the bow and plucked the strings. The notes ricocheted off the walls and into his body, reducing the fire and relieving his itch. He started to write. "Dear Beverly, I'm in Berlin. In Germany. I got a subsidy. I'm here for a few months. How's Dad doing in the temple? I was going to go home before I left, but decided not to. I got kicked out, after all, and wouldn't want to disturb him. I'm fine. It's been snowing the past few days. It's really quiet here."

The black blob looked up again. That pale face was smiling at him.

Several days later the snow stopped. With the first warmth

of spring, the earth was in a hurry to cast off winter. The temperature rose precipitously during the day, as sunlight forced jackets deep into dressers. The bald trees on the street budded tender new leaves overnight. He went for a stroll with his dictionary, stopping at every road sign, store sign, and notice in the neighborhood. There was a plaque to Lenin on the wall of the next apartment building. He looked up all the words, but couldn't get the meaning to cohere. In 1895, in August, Lenin . . . A black dog sat down beside his feet. When he squatted down to pet it, a black shadow blocked the spring sun. A black jacket was trailing on the ground.

Still wearing a black hat, Black Jacket pointed at the relief of Lenin and said a bunch of things in German. Keith started flipping through his dictionary. Black Jacket chuckled and took off his black hat, revealing feathery blond hair, soft and loose. He kept talking, but this time he included a lot of English words.

The flame in Keith's body rekindled. There he was, standing on an unfamiliar street in Berlin, when he suddenly thought of Red Shorts in the carambola orchard and Sam Yang in the swimming pool. And all that physical friction after he moved to Taipei. He got an erection.

The black jacket, black cello, and black dog all followed him into his little apartment. He was about to open the window when Black Jacket embraced him from behind and kissed his neck.

My name is T.

Black T got lighter and lighter. He took off his boots, his jacket, his sweater, his pants, and his underwear. The night died on the floor of the apartment. There it lay on the floor, while White T's body stood tall in front of him. His skin was so pale and smooth. He was so thin. His hair smelled like floral shampoo. When his parents told him ghost stories, this was the sort of white apparition that he would imagine, except for the shampoo. He took that body in. The hair was so fair, the eyes so blue. Those eyes were looking intently at him.

"Are you a ghost?" he wanted to ask. "Are you real?"

Together, they caused the little bed to quake, as birds called on the tree outside and the dog dozed under the bed. He suddenly thought of a new storyline for the novel. The German dictionary on the table got kicked onto the floor. T carried him onto the table, which creaked under their weight. That reminded him of the termites in Yongjing.

Where are you from? T asked.

He had questions for T, too. Are there termites in Berlin? Have you heard the sound termites make when they gnaw wood? It's like someone is sneakily sawing the legs of a table with a tiny saw. If you heard that sound in a dream, you'd think that the source of that faint sawing sound was somewhere inside your body. It was like a certain organ was being surreptitiously sawn off, like a certain blood vessel was being secretly eaten.

"We're there," Sam said.

The row of townhouses stretched into sight. His was fifth from the left.

T, this is where I'm from.

Beverly was waving at the truck, with a stove at her feet. She lit the fire and the flames darted out.

T, you never made it back to your U-boat, but I've come home.

20. McDonald's fries in 1984

Betty was writing a letter to Keith when she got the message from Beverly. "Little Brother's back!" When did you get out? Why'd you come home when we kept driving you away? Didn't I tell you not to? Didn't you promise me you wouldn't?

She checked the High Speed Rail timetable. She needed to take the HSR to Taichung and a local train to Yongjing. If the connection worked out, she could be in Yongjing in two hours. She would call her sister from the station.

Two hours was so fast! It used to take her six. When she set out for Taipei to apply for a job, her father drove her in the truck to Yuanlin. There she would catch a highway bus, either a Zhongxing or a Kuo-Kuang. If she had a bit more of a budget she could have taken the train, but it took at least six hours in any event. If there was a traffic jam or a train delay, then it could take a lot longer. One time the bus cast anchor on the highway, starting and stopping, for hours on end. It took her twice as long as normal to get to Taipei. Having missed the interview, she asked the driver to let her out early when they finally made it into the city. She got out and looked around for a public toilet. Walking down a lane, she worried that her bladder would burst. When she saw a green space with big banana trees inside, she ran right in, pulled her pants down, and irrigated the trees with half a day's urine. It fell like a waterfall, drowning out all the noise. Afraid someone might see her, she covered her face with a banana leaf. She had always liked them. They had such distinctive ribs and veins. They had such a luscious lime hue when the sun shone through. They were so soft and broad, giving shelter from sun or rain. Mother used to boil them and use them to wrap *tsùt-bí-kué*, sticky rice flour cakes, tying each one up with string. They came out of the steamer trailing a unique fragrance that exuded a charity and tolerance that rid you of your troubles and made all of your organs stretch and yawn. The taste enveloped your body in a deliciously thick drowsiness. You could lie down anywhere and your dreams would be as sweet as a ripe banana.

After discharging the flood, she stood up and found herself in a dense banana orchard. She forgot she was a vocational high school graduate who'd come up to Taipei to seek employment.

All she wanted to do was pick a wholesome banana leaf and take it home for her mother to wrap *tsùt-bí-kué* with.

Leaving the orchard, she noticed how rural the neighborhood was. There was a rice paddy and a creek, a habitat for egrets. Had time and space warped in the half day, reversing north and south? Could it be that after twelve hours on the bus she was still in Yongjing? If so, the soy-sauce factory was to the right, and farther along the carambola orchard. To the left was a betel leaf field. In the center of that field rose a metal frame that was taller than a betel nut tree, and on that frame sat a stainless steel water cistern, full of water for irrigation. She climbed up the ladder and knocked on the cistern. It sounded hollow. Shush! There was someone inside.

For a time during her childhood she would knock on a cistern at night and someone inside would respond. Now that she was all grown up, she'd knocked on a lot of office doors without getting any response at all. She didn't have any postsecondary education. She couldn't speak any foreign languages. She stuttered or fell silent in interviews. She dressed in muted colors. So she started to prepare for the national civil service exam. She wasn't good for anything except memorization. She threw herself into the practice tests for six months, never leaving the house. Her mother told her not to bother. Be realistic, get married! She asked a matchmaker to arrange for quite a few boys to come over to meet her. She had thought about it. If she didn't pass the exam, maybe she could just get married. But the boys the matchmaker brought had no interest in her, the plain second daughter. They all liked Belinda better, or could they wait for Barbie or even Plenty to grow up?

Those were arid days, in which she realized from the apathy in the eyes of all those suitable boys how plain she was. Their dry eyes would gush as soon as they caught sight of her sisters. Each of them had her own allure. Beverly's chest rose like a mountain range, Belinda's nose soared like a skyscraper. Barbie was as fine and pale as a piece of paper. And Plenty was the most beautiful girl in all of Yongjing.

Plain Betty ended up passing the test. When she was assigned to Taipei, she rented a room above a buffet eatery in the vicinity of the banana orchard. Finally she had left home, and just in time. The water cistern in her body had grown so large she was about to burst. Everything in her hometown was too intense. The chrysanthemums were too garish, the phoenix trees too bloodily red. The pigs squealed too pitifully when they got slaughtered. She longed for something more insipid. So she came to Taipei to live a "bland" new life.

After getting married she moved out of the neighborhood. She and her husband scrimped and saved to buy a tiny flat in a densely populated residential area. Several years later she took the bus past her old place and got off to see if the orchard was still there. It wasn't, and neither was the paddy or the creek. Cracker Jack Wang had taken a shine to the area and bought it all up. The orchard was now the grounds of a prize-winning green building. There were solar panels on the roof that protected the environment by powering the neon White House logo, lighting up the night. She really didn't get it. What was so "green" about it? To build a fortress that only the Wang family could enter, what was environmentally friendly about that? There didn't used to be any fences around here. Kids used to play hide and seek here, and old folks would grab a stool and gather round for a chat and a cup of tea. No need for a banana farmer to guard the orchard, the locals were all banana farmers. They weeded and watered together, and everyone got to share in the harvest. There was no buying or selling. Did the judges who gave this building the grand prize ever see what the orchard looked like before the Wangs broke ground? Those banana trees were so healthy. There were no yellow spots on the leaves. The bananas were plump and pretty, every bunch. At the time, you could stand in the orchard after dark, look up, and see clusters of stars studding the nighttime sky.

"I'm going home to see Keith," she typed before heading out the door, but she could not bring herself to press send. Every time she sat down to write her brother a letter, her husband would go on and on. "Why write longhand, in this day and age? Don't you know how to send an email? Hasn't the household registration office gone digital?" What would he say if he found out that Keith was doing time for the murder of his German lover in Berlin?

Many years before, Keith had published a story in a literary supplement about a boy from Changhua who came to Taipei, where he entered a luxurious, gilded world and got hot and heavy with a lot of male bodies, all complete strangers. One night a stock-market mogul lay beside him, the next night a pop idol. He took hot baths in different hotel jacuzzis, until he washed away all of the dirt that a childhood in the countryside had left on him, until his features were indistinct. His face changed. He even smelled different. When he went home, nobody recognized him anymore. Her husband read it sitting on the toilet, his face wrinkling up like a pickled plum. He came out and spit the sour juice in her face. "Well it turns out that your brother is a pervert. I can't believe the editor thought this ghastly stuff was fit to print. What's the world coming to? Tell him to use a pen name, it's so embarrassing." Then he ripped the paper up.

This was actually the kind of marriage that she wanted, with a conservative husband from an older era. He was a civil servant, a nine-to-fiver just like her. He didn't like to go on vacation, he didn't long to go abroad. He would stay home on holidays and sleep. He didn't spend much money, he had a stable salary. She'd had two children with him, a boy and a girl, no surprise. Boring and predictable. A colleague had introduced them. She knew that she would marry him on the first date. He had no opinion about what to eat or where. His features were like a bowl of unseasoned broth, his emotions lukewarm. He was neither tall nor short, neither fat nor thin. He talked in straight lines, never went on tangents. His clothing was cheap. He didn't have it in him to dress stylishly. After they said their goodbyes, she struggled to drag his contours into mind. When their bodies came together after the wedding, it was only for procreation, not for pleasure. She never had an orgasm. They turned off the lights and had a quick wordless encounter. Soon she was pregnant.

She'd read Keith's stories. The bodies of the men and women in those stories were always humid, like a tropical rainforest. The rivers were treacherous with rapids, the tree trunks erect. Serpents slithered, leopards howled, birds chirped. *Her* body was a dry mesh sieve. Read into her body, the rainforest became a desert. The past few years she'd been frequenting cheap hotels by herself to watch the erotic videos that played 24/7 on the adult channel. She saw bodies intertwine. Adult film actors of different races and skin colors went in and out of each other's bodies, moaning with pleasure, authentic or faked. All those moist moans entered her ears and disappeared into the desert, until one time, the video switched to two men. She suddenly stood straight up in bed and clenched her hands into fists. For about half an hour, there weren't any women at all, just men going in and out of each other's bodies. Those men were so beautiful. Lake water flowed around in their limpid eyes, until the video suddenly switched back to one with a man and a woman. Heart pounding, she called the front desk. "About that video just now . . ."

"Oh I'm so sorry about that, a part-timer put the wrong one on. You're not the only guest who's complained. It won't happen again, please accept our apologies. We'd like to offer you a discount upon check-out?"

What was there to be sorry about? The lake water in those men's eyes had flowed into her flesh. It reminded her of rainshowers she got caught in while walking the dog. It would jump in the mud and roll around, dragging her in, too. The summer rain was warm, the mud contained heat. The dog romped, the girl stomped, while worms wriggled in the mud. Her body was conquered by pleasure. She didn't feel the least bit dirty. The men in that video made her feel the same way, like she was covered in warm mud.

It turned out that her body liked to watch boy on boy. She fell into the moist, faintly mildewed sheets on the hotel bed. Her flesh relaxed. And out of her throat came a cry that she had never heard before.

The thick boss and the thin boss, Ming and Ri.

After Keith went to prison his lawyer sent a box of his personal effects. There were a lot of photographs. One of them made her yelp. In it T was kissing Keith's cheek as a black dog sat at their feet looking up at them. She kept on looking through the photos. A lot of them were of them with that dog. It looked exactly the same as the dog that Grandma had gobbled up. It had the same shining black eyes. It cocked its head the same way when it took a snooze. She scanned the first photograph at the office and managed to save it in her phone. She only looked at it when she was alone.

Keith, I've been meaning to ask, who's been taking care of that dog since you went to prison?

She got on the HSR underground. The train started speeding south. When it came above ground, night had just fallen. She was really hungry, but decided to wait until she got back to Yongjing.

The view changed rapidly. On the outskirts of the city, she saw dried riverbeds, dilapidated factory buildings, new luxury apartment complexes, and a Daoist temple in a vibrant hue of maroon. The train went in and out of tunnels. Ripples of light and shade made her drowsy. She suddenly remembered the dream she'd had the night before.

It was about a saw. Not an electric saw, now that she thought about it, but an old-fashioned saw with a wooden handle and sharp teeth, which were unevenly spaced for the cutting of trunks and stumps. Her mother was there in the dream.

Freshly permed and lightly made up, her youthful mother took her to the big open-air market. The basket was full of groceries, maybe for a spirit offering. Betty could hear the faint, somehow furtive murmur of a saw.

Then Mom called the cops on her. "Betty!" she yelled. "Where are they hiding! Tell us! I know you know where they are!"

The saw kept sawing. Not wanting to answer her mother or the cops, she jumped over a ditch to find out where the sound was coming from. Next thing she knew, Plenty's smiling face smashed ferociously into the dream. It crashed into the camera that must be shooting the scene, causing it to hit her head. Still dreaming, Betty felt real pain. Holding a saw in her right hand, Plenty was sawing at her left arm. "Betty," she said, "I'm a desert, too." She cut the arm off but there was no blood and no wound. She picked it up with her other hand. "Deserts don't bleed," she said.

When the HSR went into another tunnel, turning windows into mirrors, Betty saw her frightened reflection staring back at her.

She used to report all her dreams to her mother, who had her own approach to analyzing all the objects and living beings in a dream and ascertaining whether it was auspicious or not. Mother's mother hadn't just handed down her wit-collection spell to her daughter, but also that complicated dream hermeneutics. It wasn't recorded anywhere, it was an oral tradition. The hermeneut relied upon recollection, cogitation, and emotion to lead her to the right interpretation. If you dreamed about a snake it meant you were going to have a daughter. A flower portended a boy, flowing water that a long journey was ill-advised. A dream about death was a prophesy of prosperity. A ghost meant that you could get married, a tree that you'd suffer a certain symptom, rain that you could scatter the seeds and wait for a bountiful harvest. The system sometimes produced contradictory results. Last time, a dream about water meant a trip was a bad idea, this time head north. Yesterday a dream about fire was bad luck, today great luck.

The morning Plenty went missing, Mother announced that she had dreamed about a saw. Someone had been sawing a coffin in her dream.

Mom, Keith is back. Last night I dreamed about a saw. What did you tell us about a saw in a dream? But you're dead now. Can someone still collect wits and divine dreams from beyond the grave?

The HSR swiped swiftly south down the island's western plain. Betty suddenly smelled French fries in the cabin. Her stomach growling, she remembered how Keith would ask her to bring him a Happy Meal every time she made a trip back to Yongjing. McDonald's had just opened its first branch in Taipei. According to the newspaper, the takings from the first week set a world record. She waited in line for the longest time. Finally she bought a meal. She took it to the bus stop by the train station and waited for the highway bus to come. French fries, hamburger, and cola kept her company for many hours. When she got home, the dinner table was clean and bare. The whole family was waiting for the McDonald's meal that she had bought in Taipei and brought all the way home. She remembered how her brother's brow contorted when he was chewing French fries. The hamburger was sour, the cola flat. It was like drinking caramel syrup.

The HSR was almost in Taichung. Time to get ready to transfer to the local train. She looked out the window, no longer able to see her reflection. Every time she went home, she felt herself getting lighter and lighter. The closer to Yongjing, the more spectral she became. By the time she got there, she was translucent. She searched online to learn that the first McDonald's in Taiwan opened in Taipei in 1984. That was her youngest brother's first year of elementary school, and the year those police raided Yongjing. She was like a French fry in 1984, getting soft, cold, and sour on the hourslong journey home.

Before disembarking, she called her phone out of sleep and looked at the picture of her little brother, T, and that black dog.

She swiped to a photo from an old newspaper that she had found after years of searching in the archives. It was from a story about the thick boss of the Tomorrow Bookstore. He committed suicide in prison.

She actually bought two meals that year, not just one, when she went home to see the folks. Late at night, she slipped out and paid a visit to the Tomorrow Bookstore. She wanted to introduce Ming and Ri to the American fast food that had just arrived in Taiwan. "It's made in the USA!" She treated Nut Wang, too. He was the one who rolled up the shutter for her when she finally arrived. After he rolled it down, they all went upstairs to enjoy the food.

She remembered it like it was yesterday. "It's really good," the thick boss said when he tried the first soggy fry. "Betty, let's fly to America someday and eat at McDonald's together."

21. Snake soup

Beverly takes a lighter to a fistful of spirit money. Tracing three clockwise circles above your head and three counter-clockwise circles in front of your chest with the smoking paper, she chants, "Right left, left right. Burn fire, burn bright. Straight back, pure heart. Burn bad, new start." She tosses the rest of the paper in the stove as the flames start licking at her fingers. Soon it's ablaze. You take a deep breath, close your eyes, and step across the fire.

She watches the video again to make sure she did it right. A YouTuber named Yellow Robe says:

"Firewalk with me, folks, to cleanse your soul. Walk that fire, you'll be on a roll. Just leap the flame and get back in the game."

She repeats the last part twice with a rising pitch.

When the ritual is over she wants to give you a big hug, but her arms stay stuck at her sides, she can't reach them out. Your friend Sam's there, too. "I'm going in the kitchen to prepare the pig trotter *mī-suànn*," he says.

Did I ever hold you? I can't remember. All I know is that your brother got more than his fair share of cuddling.

Before he was born, your mother had a dream about flowers. What kind? I asked. Purple, yellow, and red, she said. They were flowers that oozed wealth and respectability, with long, pointy petals. There were hectares of them. They had a strong smell, so strong she could still smell them after she woke up. This time she was sure it was going to be a boy. Finally the Chen family had a future, someone to bear the surname. After giving birth, she did not let him out of her sight, even her arms. She was afraid he would disappear, or that he wasn't real. Only when my mother, aunt, grandaunt, and granduncle had come to make sure that Saucy Cicada had finally had a son after five baby girls in a row was she willing to let go. My mother finally put money in a red envelope for her. The previous five times she didn't even show up.

When Heath was three months old, your mother's hand slithered into my pants. One is not enough, she said. If we only have one, his sisters will gang up on him. So we have to have two, we need to have another. When we did, we wouldn't have to worry about the elder sisters clamoring for a share of the family fortune. Your mother never dreamed of flowers while she was pregnant with you. She bound your brother to her bosom with a strip of cloth for a daily walk in the chrysanthemum field. She picked globe amaranth flowers at the roadside to stick in her hair. She even rubbed the petals on her belly, but she still didn't dream about them. "No wonder I never dreamed about flowers when I was pregnant with you," she used to complain. "I should have known that I was going to give birth to a pervert and a misfit!" She smacked you, too. Do you remember?

Did you understand why you didn't "fit?" No, you just got yelled at and hit.

After the hailstorm, Jack came over to discuss business. He listed all the damage that the hail had done on a piece of paper. Bulbs for the chrysanthemum lamps. Roof tiles and windowpanes. A natural disaster is a business opportunity! Anything that was broken would have to be replaced. He'd handle supply, I'd be in charge of distribution. Good neighbors would get rich together. We rode scooters through the countryside visiting farming families. We got a lot of orders by undercutting the hardware stores. He made nonstop calls. In a single day he sourced sundry products all around the island. Then I had to drive the truck north and south, east and west, delivering those products to Yongjing.

Now that we'd made a pile, Jack said we had to celebrate. We asked the snake killer if he had any prime specimen we could serve with wine.

The snake killer had a plump serpent from Burma. We could slaughter it and make a soup of it. When girls drink the soup, their skin will glow. When boys drink it their things will grow. He carried an intricately patterned snake out of the cage. The snake arched its body and opened its jaw to try to defend itself. With a practiced hand, the snake killer grasped its head and yelled: "It's showtime!" All the neighborhood kids ran over and formed a circle around him. He bound the snake's head with a rope and cut a ring around its neck with a pair of scissors, giving us all a glimpse of the meat. Then he slit it along its length and flayed it, pulling the skin down and off over a porcelain bowl to catch the blood. He cut out the black gall bladder, pricked it, and dribbled the bile into a bottle of medicinal wine. After removing the hemipenes, he sliced the body in cross-sections and simmered it with medicinal wine, ginseng, and jujubes. The steaming soup actually smelled like a snake silently slithering around your ankle, up your leg, around your waist, higher and higher until finally it mounted a vicious attack on your nose and mouth, fangs bared. Once bitten, you would never forget. It was the most unforgettable olfactory experience ever.

We set the big round table up on the front porch for the feast. Cicada brought out cabbage, three-cup chicken, dried sardines with peanuts, and fried noodles with oysters. The Chen and Wang clans sat around the festive board. Bottoms up! We did shots of raw snake blood and medicinal wine. "What's yours is mine and what's mine is yours," said Jack. "Next time we'll make even more money."

Keith, do you remember? The bizarre hue of the evening sky above Yongjing. The moon was dirty yellow, and the clouds shiny brown, like worn but religiously polished cowhide. Then stars parted the cowhide clouds and winked at me tenderly. The grasshoppers called gently, tickling my ears like my mother used to do when she cleaned them with a pick. My head and neck tingled. Everyone at the table, children included, must have felt the same drinking the high-proof snake soup that painted people's cheeks pink. A breeze tiptoed past, afraid of spoiling the mood.

Everyone seemed to let it all hang out. Everything seemed out in the open, just like the stars in that clear night sky.

I felt blessed. We often went hungry before you were born. There was never any chicken or duck on our dinner table. Now we were feasting on oysters and the flesh of a venomous snake. Everyone could eat well and would sleep well. My eldest daughter Beverly was a wife and a mother. She was living right next door. My two sons were growing bigger every day. I felt I had reached a milestone of fatherhood. I did not have to worry anymore that you would go hungry. I no longer had to try so hard to reproduce.

What escaped my notice was that Cicada stayed sober. She hadn't touched the snake soup or the medicinal wine.

She could not find you.

She said you must have gone to see Nut. You followed him wherever he went. The hail hadn't just destroyed Nut's starfruits, it had left the poor fellow battered and bruised. Just when he needed to rest and recuperate, you kept going over and bothering him.

She carried a bowl of hot snake soup over to the Wang house. She went upstairs and through the open door of Nut's room.

I wasn't there.

I didn't see a thing.

The only way I can reconstruct what happened between Nut and you that evening is through the oral testimony that Cicada waited through the night to blurt out the next morning.

This is what she said. Nut was lying on the bed with his hands behind his head and his eyes closed. His expression was odd, while you were all red. You were resting your head on his waist and your hand on his root. Nut was very hard.

She froze for several seconds. Then she put the snake soup on the table, walked over to the bed, and took you in her arms. You were burning up, and fast asleep. But you kept gripping his root. You wouldn't let go.

She pinched your thigh and twisted, giving you a snake bite.

You shivered a bit and finally released your hold on Nut. Nut was only pretending to sleep. He was awake the entire time. "No wonder people call him a prodigy," she said, "he's a freak of nature! He's hung like a betel nut palm tree before picking!" That's what she said. "But a lot of good all that education did him, he's a pervert!"

"Thank Heaven," she said, "thank Heaven I was kind enough to take Nut a bowl of snake soup. Otherwise I wouldn't have seen. I would never have been the wiser."

She carried you home in her arms, past the unruly round table where we were playing fists, a drinking game. She didn't say a thing. She would keep it to herself until you woke up. The snake soup and the medicinal wine took a long time to wear off. You slept for a dozen hours. Your mother hadn't slept a wink. Then you wet the bed. That was it, she'd had enough. She pulled the pin of the grenade she was holding and threw it in your face.

You woke up in pain. You were wailing, but Cicada kept whaling on you. I ran up to the third floor to see what was the matter. She told me what had happened the night before and went back to thrashing you, harder and harder. Then she turned and said it was my turn. All I could think of was you holding Nut. I sat at your desk and stared at the world map, paralyzed.

Many years later, your homeroom teacher came to the house accusing you of seducing her son. She demanded that we arrange for you to transfer to another school.

Your mother apologized for not raising you right. "Sorry, Teacher. He won't have anything to do with your son ever again."

"But I don't want to transfer," you said after the teacher left.

Your mother grabbed a chair and threw it at you.

"Have you forgotten," she yelled, "how you got Nut killed?

You pervert! Misfit! Freak! It's the middle of Ghost Month, and the sacrificial duck doesn't know it's dead meat. So why don't you do us all a favor and go straight to hell? I'm sure you'll fit right in.

You held your head high when your teacher called you a pervert, but the walls came tumbling down when your mother mentioned Nut. The look in your eyes caved in and the tears flooded out.

I'm sure you remember everything she said.

But there are many things that you never knew.

For one, I lived for years on borrowed time, time that only the snake killer would lend me.

Another is that we never held you. We hit you instead.

22. *Sticky with the autumn in Berlin*

Belinda's big black German sedan hurtled south.

She hopped in the car as soon as she heard that her baby brother was back. When she got on the highway she stepped on the gas. Flashing speed cameras didn't slow her down a bit. She could imagine the look on her husband's face, which appeared on television every evening covered in a layer of foundation, when he got the fines. He wouldn't frown when he saw the amounts. Not a single ripple would wrinkle his brow. His reaction would only register in his cold, unblinking eyes. The irises would fade behind a thin layer of fog, and icebergs would erupt out of his pupils, causing his crow's feet to spread.

She floored it. Since she was going to run into those icebergs anyway, why not do it at full tilt? Keith, I can't believe you're back!

He wrote a letter to every sister, telling them no need to visit, please don't come. But Belinda went anyway.

Her husband was taking a team to Berlin to do a feature. She begged him to let her tag along. He was unwilling. "I don't want anyone to know my brother-in-law in Germany is a murderer. Use your head, think of what those sharks will do when they smell blood. Thank God he's no literary celebrity. None of those books he wrote were bestsellers. Remember that news story about him winning that competition? It was just a mention, really. The reporter didn't bother to dig. If he had, Keith would have led him to you. And who would have been sorry then?"

"If you don't let me go, then I'm going to go on my own," she retorted. "Think about it, which is more likely to cause trouble, if I go alone or if I go with you?"

She contacted Keith's lawyer before she left. The jail held visiting hours every two weeks. She just had to apply in advance. She selected the day. Her husband said he would go along, too, but at the thought of paparazzi outside the jail he got cold feet at the last minute and arranged an interview with some political figure instead. The lawyer told her to bring her passport and be prepared to leave her personal possessions in a locker at the entrance. Wallets, credit cards, cash, keys, and mobile communications devices weren't allowed in.

Belinda walked out of the hotel to hail a cab, but she had to hunt for the longest time before finding one. The jail turned out to be only fifteen minutes away. She assumed it would be in some unpopulated area in the suburbs or exurbs, as far from the downtown core as possible. But no, it was in a regular residential neighborhood not far from the city center. The yellow foliage on the trees glimmered in the early autumn sunlight. The wind swished the fallen leaves around on the ground. She'd arranged to meet the lawyer at the west gate. He was waiting for her there. He had a common German name, but his face was Southeast Asian, with dark skin and penetrating eyes. His English was fluent. After introducing himself, he reiterated the visitation procedure. Observing the question marks in her eyes, he explained that he was an orphan. Originally from Vietnam, he was adopted by a German couple.

He stuffed her purse in a locker, slotted a euro, and took the key. They really meant it about not bringing anything in. She'd put euro banknotes in a red envelope for her brother, but it looked like she wouldn't get the chance to give it to him.

The lawyer mentioned that her brother had attempted suicide several times but his situation had improved after counseling. Even so, he'd refused to see her at first. Then Shakespeare changed his mind.

"Shakespeare?"

"Ask him."

The lawyer pressed the buzzer and went in. Their IDs were examined and exchanged for visitors' passes. A female guard took her to a small room and did a full body search. She even lifted her insoles to make sure the only thing she was carrying was her passport. After passing a series of guarded gates, she was led into the visitor's room. There she waited for Keith. The lawyer would wait outside. If she needed him she could let him know. The room was clean and white. White paint, white table, white chair, white lamp. It was cool, colder even than it was outside. Not even the warm orange of autumn was allowed in the window.

He was thinner.

He had crewcut hair and sunken cheeks. His skin was pale and dry, his forehead flaking.

She reached for her purse, only to realize she'd left it in the locker. She was going to offer him a container of cold cream.

She patted the flakes off and touched his lips. "They're cracked! I'll send you a tub of lip balm as soon as I'm out. I know what brand you like, the one you recommended to me. I'm still using it. I have one in my purse. But they didn't let me bring anything in."

He didn't say anything, just pursed his lips and smiled.

They faced each other, speechless. Her words ricocheted in slow motion off the white walls, forming a sluggish echo that caused the air to buzz. He waited until the words from her mouth and the white flakes of skin from his face had fallen slowly to the floor before he finally spoke. "How long has it been? And the first thing you can think of to say is about lip balm. You're really something."

Belinda laughed. Last time she saw him was at Father's funeral, which he rushed home to attend, only to be driven away.

"You Germans are so uptight. Here I was, hoping to bring you spicy hotpot."

"Yum. I haven't eaten that in ages."

"You don't have much time left in your sentence. You'll be out in no time. We'll go for hotpot then. My treat."

"Can't wait. Is your husband outside?"

"He . . . He decided to do an interview. It's for the best. I only realized how few taxis there are in downtown Berlin when I tried to hail one. Or was it just my luck? Anyway, I just kept walking, aimlessly. I thought I knew myself, but I didn't get anxious. For some reason it was like what you wrote in one of your columns in the newspaper. I was wandering around, when suddenly I felt so relaxed."

She could just keep walking like that, never to return to the hotel, or to her apartment in Taipei.

"You don't feel anxious in here?"

"Anxious my ass! You're the inmate, not me."

Keith laughed and stretched. Spittle had moistened the barrier between them, a little. Her shoulders relaxed, a bit.

Keith said he was fine. He was taking his meds. Lately his appetite had been better. The prison cafeteria served gourmet meals as far as he was concerned. He still didn't feel like exercising. He just wanted to stay in his cell. Everyone had his own cell, no need to share. He had a lot of time to read, write, sleep, and think. There was a library in the jail that lent out books. Of course they were German books, but he was studying German. He read really slowly, constantly looking words up in the dictionary. But he had all the time in the world. He could express himself to his psychologist in German now. Strange, he'd been too lazy to learn before he went to jail. He was in Germany, why wouldn't he learn German?

"I'm going to be in a play. Shakespeare's *Hamlet*."

A Berlin theater had approached the authorities about a penal production. They'd cast the prisoners and give public performances. The audience would come into the prison.

"What part are you playing? The ghost?"

"As if, someone else is playing the father. The director arranged for five guys to play Hamlet. I'm one of them. I am memorizing the soliloquys, in German translation. It's so hard. It's killing me! But it's been educational. I only realized I'm small fry compared to some of the guys when we started rehearsals. The guy who is playing Ophelia in drag killed three people. Another of the Hamlets killed five. I only killed one."

"And you didn't do it on purpose."

He looked up at the ceiling. Belinda had never seen such sad eyes. In each, a sea. It took everything he had to stop them from pouring out.

"When is the opening night? I'll come with Beverly and Betty. The plane tickets are on me."

"Please don't, I'm going to deliver a lot of soliloquies in German. If I see you in the audience, I won't be able to stop myself from crying. How could I continue? I even have to do a song and dance. You're not allowed to come."

"We can sneak in and sit at the back in masks and hats, silly. You won't even know we're there."

"How is everyone? Good?"

It was her turn to look at the ceiling.

You want an honest answer? Your five elder sisters were unwanted children. How "good" do you think it can get for us, in this lifetime?

Keith told her about the globe in the library, the one Taiwan was not on. And about an atlas. Had she seen all the garbage outside the cell windows? The inmates tossed it out on the ground. The janitors swept it up three times a day, but there was no end to it. One day he looked out and saw an atlas. He hollered for the janitor not to throw it away. Could you please let me keep it? The janitor ignored him and disposed of it. He was just curious. If Taiwan was in that atlas, could he find Yongjing?

When they said farewell, Belinda said: "I'll get your lawyer to keep me updated. We'll be waiting for you outside the day you get out. And then we're going to have some fun. Beverly and Betty have never been to Europe before, we can show them around. But first we'll take you to a spicy hotpot place, the hotter the better." She wanted to hug him but she just touched his face. He was still her baby brother. She'd held him as a child. Why wasn't she able to now? Maybe she was afraid. If she hugged him, something she'd been holding on to for dear life might pop.

The lawyer reached out and took Keith in his arms. He even kissed his cheek.

On the way out, the lawyer offered her a ride. She shook her head and said she wanted to go for a stroll. He held out his arms and she shook her head again, even took a step back. No, no, no, thank you, goodbye.

A glance at her watch told her it was still early. Her husband would not be back until evening. She had half a day to herself.

She wandered along the road to a park and decided to go in. A father sat on a bench reading while his two children rolled around in a pile of leaves and swung on a swing. Their laughter jangled like a metallophone.

She'd had two abortions in the first few years of her marriage. Her husband went with her both times.

"What are you crying for?" he said. "Didn't we decide we were going to be happy just the two of us? Look at your family. That's what happens when you have a bunch of kids."

Nut Wang's college classmate, her husband became a close associate of the Wang family. After Nut passed away, he paid many visits to Yongjing to write his biography, always staying next door at the Wang place. By that point, the Wangs had built a bunch of big factories in China. Her father had invested a lot of money. Wang's eldest son Baron said he wanted to marry Plenty and build a mansion, the biggest Yongjing had ever seen, for her to live in. Belinda's future husband brought a couple of his architect friends down from Taipei to draw up a blueprint. The rest was history. The White House got built according to plan and ahead of schedule. The biography was a bestseller. Invitations came knocking.

"Actually the one I was sweet on was Plenty," he told her years later. "With that face and that body, my oh my. Who could resist? But Baron had taken a shine to her, and I thought to myself, you're actually not bad. We're pretty much in the same league, went to the same university, about the same age. Decent looks. You didn't need a complete makeover, just a touch up. And it turned out that I was right. That fifth sister of yours, what an intense personality. Scary! I made the right choice. You're the 'perfect' news anchor's wife."

She left the park and ordered an Uber. In the Destination field she typed in Keith's old address, the apartment he shared with T. She got out, stood in front of the door, and read the names. Which flat did her little brother used to live in? What floor? She sat on the steps and took out the lip balm. She was applying it when she smelled something sweet. Right, Keith mentioned a candy factory. She closed her eyes and breathed it in. Honey. Her favorite flavor. She imagined somebody pouring honey on her head until she was drenched. After finding a pile of leaves to roll around in she was sticky with the autumn in Berlin. She let her nose show her the way to that candy factory, but she just went in circles, until her husband called. "Where the hell have you been? I've been waiting at the hotel. Got a death wish? Or are you having the time of your life in jail?"

What a lovely day it had been! Every time her husband beat her from then on, she would force herself to recall the day in Berlin, stepping on the fallen leaves, smelling honey, looking for the candy factory, all by herself in a city of strangers. She wasn't afraid of getting lost and didn't feel like going home.

She cruised into Yongjing. It really had been ages since her last visit. There were more chain supermarkets and convenience stores now, and a few new houses. Suddenly the White House stole into sight. It was still shiny and bright. It was even bigger than she remembered. She rubbed her eyes and looked again. Was it really *that* big? Or had her memory shrunk it to get it to fit?

She parked the car and killed the ignition. She smelled noodles. With peppery sesame sauce. She was famished. She had been trying so hard to lose weight that she hadn't had a single bite to eat today. Was that the Mainlander Noodles stand she was smelling? Was that guy from Sichuan still in business? His noodle stew was still her favorite. With the homemade chili sauce that used to set her tongue on fire and burn the back of her head the entire day.

"Barbie Chen!" she yelled at the White House. "Get your ass out here this minute. If I can come back, you can come out!"

A white Porsche coupé stopped beside her. Baron climbed out of the driver's seat and walked to her window. "I thought you looked familiar from behind. I was wondering the whole way if I was trailing your husband's car. Turns out I was right.

How is the anchor? Hi, Belinda, I just got back from Taipei, too. Are you here for Ghost Festival? Care to come in?"

23. Ionic order columns

Barbie thought she heard someone call her name.

Impossible. The window was sealed, and the curtain was so heavy. No sound could get in. Was it Keith? Beverly said he was back.

She hadn't washed in days. She must smell. She should take a bath, seeing as how Keith was here. Then she could decide whether to go out.

Go out?

She hadn't gone out since Plenty's funeral.

She thought she was the winner, because she was the bride, not Plenty. She played the leading role at the wedding. But Plenty had still upstaged her. Her funeral made everyone in town forget all about the wedding.

The White House had only been completed that summer. The exterior was white with gold embellishment. There were Greek columns and pediments and baroque roof ornaments. The fence wall was solid white, the railing gold, with a coiling chrysanthemum motif. The front gate glared golden in the morning sun. The garden was a knockoff of the Palace of Versailles, complete with a Fountain of Apollo and crossed canals in which plump koi carp swam. But all Baron could talk about was the columns. Barbie remembered him go on and on about them at the wedding. Ionic order columns, Ionic order columns, Ionic order columns. I, I, I! He said it so many times Ionic turned into iconic, then ironic. Whatever. A column is a column. Did I mention that the building materials were all imported from Europe? It's the first time they've ever been used in Taiwan!

In the back yard was a little zoo. There were cages of tropical birds with brightly colored plumage and ringing calls. There was a pool for a hippo. That hippo opened its mouth really wide, like it was yawning. It was always crashing into the wall of its enclosure.

On the wedding day, the White House opened to the public for the first time. The people of Yongjing flooded into the grounds of the imposing European-style building, the likes of which they had never seen before. The then most famous banquet chef in central Taiwan took charge of the kitchen. Five hundred tables were set out in the garden, but soon they were all occupied. More tables were set out until there was no more space inside. There was nowhere to go but the field next door. A startling pile of red envelopes stuffed with wads of New Taiwan Dollars, tokens of the guests' well-wishes, ended up filling ten big rice sacks. Politicians, mafioso, and stars of various stripes all came to congratulate Cracker Jack Wang on the marriage of his eldest son. Never before had so many black German sedans been seen in that small town. There was even a traffic jam. Every street was clogged with imported cars. That, too, was unheard of.

Baron set out from the White House with a procession of ten brand new black Benzes to the Chen household to pick up his bride. He and Barbie knelt down and bid farewell to her mother and father. The kneeling bride thanked her parents and knocked her forehead on the floor. After the ritual was over, she thought she would cry, but her eyes were dry. She couldn't stop the corners of her mouth from curling up. Plenty had lost and she had won: the future mistress of the White House would be her.

The guide cock that it was up to the bride to bring was specially selected, and sizable, with a proud plumage and a jutting coxcomb. The firecrackers that it was up to the groom to light were custom-made, and arranged like dominos in a kilometer-

long line from the White House to the Lady at the Foot of the
Wall, the fried chicken stand, the temple to Mother Matsu, the
chrysanthemum field, and the pool. It was as if there was no
end to it—as if the firecrackers would explode all the way to
the Muddy Waters, thence to the Taiwan Strait. The fan the
bride tossed from the sedan window as she left her childhood
home was bespoke, hand-embroidered lace from Spain. When
it fell in the doorway and opened, everyone in the Chen household heard flamenco music. With a three-meter-long train and
a bustier festooned with a hundred pearls by a Japanese artisan, her bridal gown was from the hand of an American
designer. Although the small town grew hectares of flowers,
Baron insisted that the wedding flowers be flown in from
Europe. The bride's tulip bouquet was from Holland. The
page boy who greeted the bride held a glazed tea tray from
Italy on which big Fuji apples were arranged. The stove the
bride stepped over when she entered the White House was
fired in the oldest wood-fired kiln in the country in Shuili,
Nantou County, and the tiles she walked upon were from
Tuscany. Last but not least, the bridal suite. The tiles in the
massage tub were from Portugal, the sealed windows from
Germany, and the waterbed from France. "The water in that
bed," said Baron, "is not from the tap, it's melted snow from
the Swiss alps."

The front door was flung open, giving everyone a glimpse
of the extravagant interior decoration. The furniture was
Taiwan red cypress, the sofa Italian cowhide. The carpet was
Persian. The centerpiece was a glittering crystal chandelier air-
lifted from Paris to hang above a black Steinway grand. The
pianist was playing Schubert. His suit of boa constrictor
leather should have given him away, but only when he looked
up did everyone recognize him as the snake killer from the
video rental store.

The banquet began at an auspicious hour with a toast of

Bordeaux red, California white, and Guizhou maotai. The newlyweds changed into special costumes, a red satin suit for the groom and a red sequined gown with a plunging neckline for the bride. They were leaving for Paris for the honeymoon the following week.

The Wangs had really cleaned up selling crackers in China. In just a few years, they'd made enough money to come home and build the whitest house anyone had ever seen. "You ain't seen nothing yet!" the groom yelled into the microphone. "We're going to make even more renminbi and plough it back into the township where it all began. We're gonna build the biggest building in the entire world right here in Yongjing! What do you say?"

The small town was swamped with hip hip hooray. The carp leapt out of the crossed canals, the corks exploded out of the champagne bottles. Nobody noticed how quiet the Chen family table was.

By the time the banquet was half done, the canals were floating with disposable cups and wine bottles. Local guests got out plastic bags and handbags to stuff with leftovers and Cabernet Sauvignon.

Then Plenty appeared. In a white lace dress. She waltzed into the White House smiling, found the Chen table, and sat by her baby brother, who had barely eaten a thing. The dishes were basically untouched. "Keith," Plenty said, "you're such a big eater, why is your bowl empty? Why haven't you served yourself? Look at all that food."

Cicada pulled her away. Plenty broke away, returned to her seat, and started to chow down. On the stage the groom was speaking, a singer was singing, and a dance troupe was dancing. Plenty clapped and sang along.

"What are you worried about? I'm fine."

When Barbie saw Plenty sitting there with a big smile on her face, she clutched at her dress and made fists.

"The bride will make a toast!" Someone passed her a glass of red wine. When she relaxed her hands, blood-red glitter clung to her palms. It sparkled in the sun.

Well before dusk, the fengshui master announced that another lucky time had arrived. The chef was getting ready to send out the desserts in the still scorching sun when the fireworks started exploding colorlessly in the dazzling sky, as volley after volley from the launchers mounted in the nearby trees startled all the roosting bats out of sleep. The roof was soon covered in a thick layer of gray ash. The wind picked up, blowing the ash towards the banquet, onto the fried sticky rice balls and into the dessert soup, flavoring the food with saltpeter. The falling ash gradually thickened into a slow-motion waterfall. A swarm of bats broke through that ash waterfall and scattered. The fireworks lasted for ten minutes. By then the bats were gone. So was Plenty.

The massage tub and the waterbed in the bridal suite, the chandelier in the living room, and the fireworks in the sky were all Plenty's demands.

Decades later, the jets in the massage tub were busted. Barbie had taken scissors to the waterbed, flooding the bedroom floor, the hallway outside, and the Persian carpet downstairs with melted Swiss snow.

Barbie filled the tub with steaming hot water, stepped in fully clothed, and lay down. A hot bath. After all, Keith was back. She hadn't turned the lights on.

If she did she would stare helplessly at the blood on her hands, the gory glitter from her wedding dress.

24. More lone gloves

Sam walked into the kitchen and brought the pot to a simmer on one burner and the *mī-suànn* vermicelli to a boil on the other. The noodles were done in no time. He drained them, dipped them in ice water, and served them in bowls of pig trotter and broth. He carried a bowl out and proffered it to Keith.

Keith, Beverly, and Sam each had a bowl. The trotter was bright brown, the broth thick. Although it looked delicious, and it was supper time, Keith did not feel at all hungry. It was just too hot. The room temperature dug a well in his back and drew water. He forced himself to eat a couple of bites. The noodles were slippery, the trotter buttery. It was indeed delectable. But after two bites the noodles turned into red hot coals in his throat. The silence swelled amongst them. Everyone thought he or she had something to say, or had to say something when there was really nothing to say. The heat and the silence wrapped their hands around the diners' necks, choking them. There was nothing they could do about the heat. Beverly and Sam slurped their noodles strenuously, and Keith tapped on the porcelain with his chopsticks, to keep the silence from growing.

Beverly really did have a lot to say. You've lost so much weight! Is that all you're going to eat? I'll go and slaughter a chicken and make you chicken stew. No? Have some more soup then! Ex-cons are supposed to eat pig trotter *mī-suànn* soup as soon as they get out of jail. I'm not sure why. Betty will be here soon. Belinda is on the way. Do you remember how we used to feed you milk when you were a baby? How silly of me, how could you remember? But I do. Mother said she needed to care for Heath. So she handed you over to us sisters to take care of. Later on she blamed us for raising you wrong. Why else would you have turned into a sissy?

Keith looked down at the crack in the floor. It seemed to have vitality, waxing and waning before his eyes. The peeling white wall looked like an abstract relief painting. An altar table was piled with Ghost Festival offerings, including boxes of

White House crackers. He frowned. Why would Beverly have bought this brand?

Beside Beverly's sewing machine were heaps of mittens of different colors. He picked up a red left-handed one and a black right-handed one. Mismatched, of different sizes, seams undone. Beverly finally thought of the thing to say. "This batch is to be exported to Europe. Maybe they'll even be sold in Germany."

T, do you remember all the gloves we found, that didn't make a single pair?

He and T took the U-Bahn in search of lone gloves.

Between the thaw and the cold snap of a Berlin spring, T walked the dog with one hand and him with the other, saying they were going to look for *Handschuhe*. He looked it up in the dictionary. *Hand* was hand and *schuhe* shoes—handshoes, shoes for your hand. Gloves. They took the U-Bahn on impulse, changing trains on a whim. T scanned the floors of the carriages and the stations. Thrilled when he saw a glove, he went right over to pick it up. Many of these gloves had been trodden on, and looked all beat up. But T picked them up like they were diamonds or gold. Keith helped, too. It wasn't that hard to find them. By the end of the day, they'd stuffed their backpacks with lone gloves from all around Berlin, of various materials, colors, and styles.

What are we doing collecting all of these lost gloves? he wondered.

Language was useless. T's English vocabulary was limited, Keith's German inadequate. He had his little pocket diction-ary, but it was not enough. In a long string of words he might only catch a few. It was like only spotting beans in a minestrone and trying to guess what it tasted like. T chattered torrentially, gesticulating wildly. When he saw confusion written on Keith's face, he laughed and kissed him. Nobody had ever kissed him in public before—under a blossoming cherry or a budding chestnut, on a U-Bahn bench or a park lawn, by the river, on the roof. Oblivious to everyone else, T just kissed him and smiled at him.

They took a ferry across the Wannsee to the quaint town of Kladow. He sat on the shore and wrote a postcard to Belinda. "I'm by the Wannsee in Berlin. It's really wide, like a sea." Last time he was back he visited her in Neihu, Taipei. They sat chatting over coffee by the window. He watched the white waterfowl soaring over Dahu Park as the silvery MRT train carriages snaked around the lake. His sister's husband suddenly opened the door. Lightning flashed in his eyes when he saw him there. He didn't look at all like he did sitting at the anchor's desk. Keith hurriedly took his leave. Belinda looked so sad, so hopeless and alone. Keith had seen this expression before, several times: when Nut climbed out of the water cistern, when Sam said farewell, and when Plenty watched the fireworks at Barbie and Baron's wedding.

In early spring, when the myriad things revived, the air was crisp, and lovers were fresh, T took him to a wood to look for *Bärlauche*. What was that, bearleeks? Bear?

Bright green leaves poked up through the moist litter on the forest floor. Ah, so that's what a bearleek was. T picked one, rubbed it between his fingers, and put his fingers under Keith's nose. It smelled vaguely of Chinese chives. The leaves were broad and bright green. T got out a fabric bag and started to gather them. With sunlight sifting down through the branches, a thin layer of mist, and chirruping birds and buzzing bees, the scene took him back to the carambola orchard when he was young. Suddenly he felt sleepy. The forest floor was magnetic. It pulled his body down. The dog had found a soft patch of shade and fallen asleep. Now he, too, lay down, closed his eyes, and started dreaming. When T's body pressed down on him, he regained consciousness, but his body was still stuck in the dream, unwilling to return to reality. T was chewing bearleeks and kissing him, conveying the taste to his teeth and tongue. In his mouth a forest grew.

Back in the apartment, T melted a chunk of butter in a pan and tossed in minced garlic and chopped bearleeks. After quick-frying the mixture, he poured it in a glass jar, which he put outside on the windowsill. T put most of the rest of the leeks in a tea towel, tied a loose knot, and spun it above his head, for centrifugal force. He blended the dehydrated leeks with garlic, olive oil, roasted pine nuts, and salt and pepper. He spooned the pesto into another jar, describing it as a bread spread, a noodle condiment, and a salad dressing. He cut slices of black bread, spread them with chilled garlic bearleek butter, a sliver of cheese, the fresh pesto, a couple of the remaining leek leaves, and finally a slice of ham.

He took a bite. It made him cry. How could a sandwich taste this good? The bearleeks awakened all the organs in his body, as if by magic. Just one bite and there was spring in his mouth, flowers in full bloom in his esophagus, and a warm sun in his abdomen. Transported back to that deserted wood by the lake, he wondered: Who is this stranger sitting across from me? How old is he? Where is he from? Where does he live? Why is he staying at my place? Doesn't he have a home? Why did he make dinner for me? Why did he play the cello for me?

Several days later T wanted to take him to an art gallery opening. Afraid of crowds and strangers and socializing, Keith shook his head. He tried to explain himself, but the more he said the bigger and bigger the question mark on T's face got. T yelled and overturned a water glass, which shattered on the floor. He put on all of his black clothing and left with his black dog and black cello.

So Keith went back to quiet, lonely days spent writing and making unappetizing dinners. He'd been forced to learn how to say farewell since boyhood. T was just a stranger. In any case his time in Berlin was about to end. He would soon go back to

Taipei. It would be for the best if he didn't get too involved with anyone, or tied down.

Late at night, the doorbell rang. Fast asleep, he didn't want to answer the door. But the bell kept on ringing, forcing him out of the covers. A dog woofed over the intercom.

T pulled the dog into the apartment and him out the door. "Tonight, it's just you and me, nobody else. It's a moonlit night, the stars are shining." They didn't talk the whole way. They kept their distance—a meter apart. They walked down dark alleys. They walked a long time. Finally they strolled down a lane lined with blooming Japanese cherry trees. Pink petals blanketed the asphalt. In the air hung a faint fragrance, so faint that he had to take a deep breath to smell it on a deserted Berlin street in the middle of the night. There were petals on T's black clothes. T reached out to him.

They walked hand in hand to an art gallery. T opened the door with a key, turned on the light, pulled a chair over, turned off the light, and asked him to sit down. In the center of the room was a sandhill. From the ceiling above the hill hung all the lone gloves they had found on the U-Bahn. T set up his cello and started to play. The gloves moved to the music. They even flashed. He'd put LED lights inside. Little trains and trucks started to move around. The trucks climbed the slope. At the rests in the music, the gloves stopped moving and the vehicles braked.

He clapped hard and the gloves shuddered. He touched the hill and felt soft, fine sand. There was a wooden track on the sand for the toy trucks. The woodwork was exquisite. T had done it all himself. At the top of the dune was a model submarine, lying motionlessly. It alone was not sound-activated.

It's the sand of the Ostsee, said T. The "east sea." The Baltic.

That was where he was from. "One day I will take you to my hometown. There's a U-boat on the beach."

When summer came, they went to the bearleek wood again. By this time bunches of little white flowers of six petals each had appeared among the leaves. From a distance it looked like snow in June. The *Bärlauche* were bitter now that they'd bloomed, they weren't there to pick them. They jumped into the Wannsee, which was shimmering in the sun. T's hair was even fairer now, the same color as the light. "Don't go," he said. "Let's find more lone gloves together."

By that point he had figured out that T did not have a place of his own in Berlin. He slept on the sofa of a friend's shared flat. Keith would soon have to leave the little apartment that the writers' association had provided. If he were to stay in Germany, where would they live?

They went to see a lot of places before finding a cheap flat in east Berlin near the city limits. It was a long way to the nearest U-Bahn station, but close to a candy factory.

Beverly's phone rang.

"Hello, Betty? Are you at the station? I . . ." Beverly looked at Keith and then at Sam. "I'll send someone over to get you. Stay put, he'll be there in no time. Have you eaten? We have pig trotter *mī-suànn!*"

Beverly's voice rang out, her decibels undiminished by age. All the Chen girls sounded like bells. When they laughed, cried, argued, cursed, or sang, the whole town could hear it. Keith could hear it halfway around the world, in the quiet of the morning in his jail cell in Berlin.

Sam wiped his mouth with the back of his hand. "Should I buy you a deep-fried chicken fillet on the way? Your old classmate the stripper makes it. You've only had a few bites of your vermicelli. Aren't you hungry?"

His old classmate the stripper's fried chicken?

He hadn't eaten fried chicken in such a long time. He really wasn't hungry, but maybe when he saw it he'd eat it. He nodded.

Watching Sam leave in his truck, he thought of something he'd never told him.

Their homeroom teacher, Sam's mother, came over one evening and accused him in front of his parents of seducing Sam. He would never forget. "My pride and joy was on the way to medical school at NTU until this little pervert showed up and ruined everything! What rotten luck, a frigging fag transfers into my class and sets his sights on my son! If word gets out, how is my Sampan ever going to get married?"

His parents promised to arrange a transfer as soon as possible and forbid him from ever speaking to Sam again. The next day, he couldn't help it, he wrote Sam a note, snuck into the classroom, and stuffed it into Sam's bookbag while the class was out raising the flag.

He'd forgotten. The flag-raising assembly was her chance to check every student's bag for forbidden items. That day she found two comics, a VHS tape, a movie magazine, a novel, and a note.

When the class returned, she got out her haul and punished every rule-breaker, every violator one by one with a rattan cane to the palm, a slap to the face, and an English composition. She spat curses as caustic as sulfuric acid. But she didn't take the note out. She'd hidden it away.

After class he rode his bike to the bishopwood tree.

All he wanted to say was: Thank you for teaching me how to swim. I'm transferring to a new school. Goodbye. But the person who came wasn't Sam, it was their teacher.

She brought two students with her, two hulking boys, to straighten him out. They grabbed him and kicked him.

They were choking him when his brother rode by. Keith cried for help, but Heath looked away. He pedaled even harder.

Slaps, punches, insults. He thought that he was going to die. And it was that stripper girl who saved him.

25. For the Glory of Yongjing

You have a lot to say, and so does your eldest sister. But the sluice in your throat stays tightly shut, blocking the flow of everything you want to say. A sandhill forms in your mind. Yes, there is a sandhill in your mind. There is a mountain in your elder sister's mind. She wants to tell someone about it, so much. But she is also reluctant to, as if telling would make it true. So she doesn't say anything. Silence is avoidance. The secrets she hides in her heart will die when she does.

I almost never talked when I was alive, because I, too, had a mountain to hide. It was a mountain that he and I arranged to go to together, a mountain we could never reach.

When you excuse yourself to take a shower, I recall that you're the same age as the water pipes. Your sweat is a mighty river, while the water trickles weakly out of the shower head. There is black mold on the tiles. The wooden shower caddy has collapsed. Do you remember? It's your brother's handiwork.

You change into a loose-fitting T-shirt and a pair of shorts. You pull up a wooden stool and sit by your big sister's side. Heath made that, too, many years ago. The structure is still solid, the surface just as smooth. The deafening clatter of the sewing machine drives away the silence. It's so loud there's no need to talk. She is rushing to fulfill an order. You just sit on the stool and look out the open front door. Outside, Yongjing has been occupied by night. The streetlamps have turned on, but night camouflages all the little black midges that take aim at your legs. When the sewing machine takes a breather, you hear squeaking. Geckos. You haven't heard them in years. You walk to the window. There's a light brown gecko hunting midges on the screen. A warm gust carries dust, heat, and moisture in. It caresses your face and your damp hair, brushes your ears, and kisses your stubbly cheeks. You think you hear someone speaking.

Speech—where does it come from? The brain? The throat? The heart? Sometimes it comes on the wind.

Your mother Cicada couldn't read or write, but she sure knew how to start a rumor. She had only to say the word and people would soon get wind of whatever secret she wanted to share. It would enter their mouths and ears. Messages would disseminate, whispers circulate.

She went to the market to buy groceries. While beating the pork peddler down, she let on that Jack Wang's younger son, fresh from college . . . yeah, that one, well, he isn't normal. He likes boys, the younger the better.

Then she whispered to the swamp spinach seller. You know Nut Wang? The prodigy. Yeah, him. Well, he's a lech. But he doesn't like girls. I hear he fancies young boys.

At the Lady at the Foot of the Wall, she blabbed to all the members of her sutra recitation group: I hear that Nut, the youngest one, the wastrel of the Wang family, the one who wears the red shorts, even in winter, well, he's only pretending to tend carambola. The orchard is actually just a place for him to take schoolboys and feel them up. Don't tell anyone, whatever you do!

The butcher at the slaughterhouse by the Lady at the Foot of the Wall was hosing the blood off the cement floor. The splashing provided cover for your mother to pass the secret on to him. You know the Wangs? They've got a son called Nut. Right, the one with the green thumb. Well guess where he likes to stick it? I hear he got into some kind of trouble in Taipei, that's why he came back home to Yongjing. Mum's the word! When the butcher turned the hose on high, the rush of water carried the blood to the Lady at the Foot of the Wall, where it swept the beans that Cicada had just spilled into the fields beyond.

You use a pen or a keyboard to tell your stories, your mother used her mouth to make things up. She added local color, even invented characters, to make the rumor seem more realistic. The more baseless the rumor, the more people in this god-forsaken ghost town would believe it. The rumor Cicada started was like a virus that spread through spit and mucus. I told you, you told him, and he told some stranger. Soon the bishopwood heard it, the irrigation ditch heard it, the fish in the pond heard it, the betel leaf field heard it, the chrysanthemums heard it. (Mum's the word, indeed.) Eventually even the skulking ghosts heard it. The rumor was swept up on a breeze. Soon everyone had gotten wind of it.

Of course I didn't spread the rumor that Cicada started; I never spoke. But I, too, eventually got wind of it. As it spread it mutated, evolving variant strains. In the most virulent, Nut was a pedophile, a monster who preyed upon prepubescent boys.

Your mom wisely eliminated any trace of you in her made-up story. You never appeared in any of the versions that developed as the story spread. There was always a boy, but he stayed in the shadows. That his features remained blurry, his outline hazy, was a story-telling technique to leave room for the imagination to run wild. It was an appeal, for sympathy, fury, and, of course, fear. You might well have inherited your story-telling talent from your mother. Remember her ritual for calming a frightened child by collecting his wits? She could tell a story at novelistic length just looking at the patterns in the grains of a cup of rice—a story of violent gusts, pouring rain, and ferocious ghosts. You wrote stories on paper, she made waves on rice.

The last few years of my life I lived alone in the temple. Every time you published a book your sisters would bring me a copy. With only a junior high school education, I was never a great reader. Those stories you wrote, they . . . ah . . . I didn't think I'd understand them. But I always . . . I don't know how to put it. Ghosts, too, get tongue-tied. I read them word by word, book by book. People with terminal cancer are just counting down the days, but every day is like a thick novel you can't finish reading, or living. Finally I finished. I finished reading but I couldn't sleep. Your words would appear in my dreams, and all those stories.

Do you remember the literary prize you won? There was a report about it in one of the literary supplements. You didn't tell us. Usually, those supplements don't get read in a town like ours. But a clerk at the township office saw it flipping through the paper. He read your bio and realized that you were from Yongjing. So he entered your name in the household registration system and looked up your address. The mayor happened to be gearing up for reelection. He was about to launch his campaign and had to take advantage of every opportunity to rally support. His employee put the clipping from the newspaper on his desk and asked him for instructions. A follow-up identified you as the emeritus mayor Heath Chen's baby brother. Heath had gotten elected by a landslide on the other party's ticket. If he hadn't gotten convicted of graft, he might still be the mayor now. If the current mayor got a photo op with the previous mayor's brother, he could give the false impression of cross-aisle cooperation. They could spin it to steal votes from the opposition and keep him in power. So they immediately decided to issue a certificate of merit and a plaque to one of Yongjing's most outstanding native sons.

When they came knocking at the door, your big sister Beverly happened to be at home.

"Hello Miss Chen, is your little brother home?"

She was busy treadling at the sewing machine. "My little brother?" she answered. "He won't be out for another couple of years. My mother just went to visit him today."

"Ah, Miss Chen, I think there might be a misunderstanding. I mean your other little brother." I stood up from the wicker chair and said you were in Taipei and hadn't been home

in the longest time. The clerk showed me the clipping and con-
gratulated me. "He won a big prize, you know. It's a lot of
money. He made it into the newspaper, for goodness sake. We
would like to reward an outstanding local young man for his
amazing achievement." They wanted you to come home to
receive a commendation.

We couldn't find you. The phone number you gave us was
no longer in service. We really didn't know where you were living. "No problem," he said, "can you accept it on your son's
behalf? We just need to take a photo together." That clerk even
mentioned how grateful he was to Mayor Chen for taking him
under his wing. This was a chance for him to express how
thankful he was to the Chen family.

The new mayor appeared in the doorway and the clerk
passed him a big plaque with the words: "Keith Chen, Take
Wing, For the Glory of Yongjing." Underneath, a crude eagle
soared over the Great Wall of China, on which the township
mayor's name was carved, in a much larger font than was used
for yours. Beverly, the mayor, and I helped hold the plaque for
an awkward group photo in front of the townhouse. Then the
mayor shook my hand, bowed, and whispered: "Your vote
means a lot to me!"

I looked at the plaque, lost in thought. I went there many
times. The year the authorities allowed relatives to visit one
another across the Taiwan Strait, I went on a business trip with
Jack Wang. We flew to Hong Kong, en route to Beijing. Jack
said Beijing was the place for us to make a pile. But what
would we sell? He said whatever people lacked, that's what
we'd sell.

So we took a walk on the Great Wall of China. Our handler
brought several young ladies to accompany us. Wang quoted a
line from a poem by Chairman Mao: None who hasn't seen the
Wall can call himself a man. "Since we're here," said Jack,
"let's enjoy ourselves. Put your arms around those girls, that'll

make a man out of you. Look at how skinny they are. They look malnourished. They must not be eating well enough. Here's what we're going to do. We'll sell food, splash a few Japanese characters on the packaging. I know they like to holler slogans about resisting Japan and killing the Jap devils, but in their hearts they envy the Japanese. So we'll disguise it as a Japanese food product. They'll sell like hotcakes. After we find a factory, equipment, and financing, we're going to make that pile. We'll go back to Yongjing to renovate our ancestral abodes. Then we'll build mansions." Later on, after the city of Beijing turned into a giant silver water cistern, I told Jack he could have the girls and the Great Wall, I didn't want any part of it.

When your mother came home after visiting Heath that day and saw that plaque, she sat on the terrazzo floor and cried. After years of trying, she'd finally had two sons. Now one was in jail and the other was AWOL.

Unbeknownst to us you were in Germany. The next time we heard from you, you were "getting married." To a German. Who was over a decade younger. And who happened to be a man.

A typhoon blew through Yongjing the day we heard you'd tied the knot. Your mother threw a temper tantrum. She took the plaque up to the attic to hand it over to the wind.

It's always the wind, no matter what. A rumor-monger, the wind comes out of nowhere and ruins everything.

Do you remember going to the movies at the Lady at the Foot of the Wall? One time there was a sudden gust of wind that blew over the screen. And your mother found you in the fleeing crowd. You were still sitting on Nut Wang's lap.

26. Neither in the hills nor in the wind

Sitting on a stool, Keith leaned back against a soft hill of gloves. He was sweating profusely even though he was just lying there doing nothing after taking a shower. He must have looked uncomfortable, but he fell asleep immediately. Soon he was dreaming.

Splashing down a winding waterslide, he raced towards the exit and plunged into a sea. Down he went, heading into a bottomless abyss. He couldn't tell if he was plumbing the Eternal Prosperity Pool or the Baltic.

The Chen children can fall asleep anytime, anywhere, thought Beverly. We aren't choosy about the material or the location. Wood, grass, bricks, cement. On a sofa, in a waterbed. Under a tree, by a field, in a car—no matter where, that's a place to lay our heads. Sitting, lying, or standing, reclined or curled up on our sides, we can always get to sleep. Even when there isn't any place for us in Heaven and Earth, at least we can escape into sleep. Sleep your fill and all will be well, Mom always said. Heaven is great, Earth is great, but Sleep is Fate.

When Beverly and her husband moved in with her parents, Little Gao's back-yard orchid orchard had to move, too. That was where Cicada liked to sleep most of all before she passed away, in that orchard. After lunch, when Beverly's sewing machine grew particularly insufferable, she walked out back, sank into the reclining chair, and entered into a conversation with the orchids and the chickens, just by snoring. Her nostrils were like trumpets and her mouth like a tuba. Each exhalation was a blaring note. She was louder than the sewing machine. When she snored, even the cock with the lustiest cry would lie down in the corner of the yard, stick his feet up, and fall into a stupor. That was the best time to grab it. Beverly would take the opportunity to tie up its feet. By the time it woke it was well on its way to turning into a pot of stew.

After that mountain disappeared, Beverly and her husband were completely broke. No, they weren't just broke, they had a mountain of debt, and an empty nest. The kids were working in China and came back only once a year. Her parents were the only ones left next door. Just move in, Father said, there's only a single wall between us. Your mother needs someone to fight with. I don't give her that luxury, I'm not that much of a talker. She just isn't happy. If you move in, you can save rent. You just have to remember to schedule arguments with your mother.

Little Gao had put up all their savings down as collateral for a bank loan to buy a mountain in Nantou County to the east of Yongjing. Without asking her in advance. She remembered that mountain. It was a long, long drive to get there. They got to the end of a forest road, where the bamboo grew thick and the grass rank. There they had to leave the car behind and go on foot. They followed a twisting path, blazing a trail through the bush with axe and machete. They walked a long, long time. The underbrush scraped Beverly's arms, while the "biting cats"—stinging nettles—bit her calves. They only bit her. Her husband went smiling the whole way, without a scratch.

After emerging from a dank wood, she stood at the foot of the mountain that her husband had bought. He measured it with his hands, drawing the boundaries of their property, from this here plum tree at the front left to that there plum tree at the back right. "All this is ours!" he said. The slope was an untended tea plantation. The tea was growing wild, glowing green. The plum trees were blossoming: white petals around yellow-tipped stamens. Chubby bees were busy collecting nectar. She and her husband walked up to the plum tree at the top, where a tea table and stools had been set out. He made tea and did calligraphy, with leisure written on his face. She looked down but even higher mountains blocked her line of sight. She could not see the town in the distance. She couldn't see a soul. Water was flowing in the valley, wind was frolicking in the leaves. "The kids are all grown up," he said. "Let's build a cabin here. I'll keep cultivating orchids. You can do anything you want, and whatever you do, at least your mother won't be next door. We can grow our own vegetables, raise free-range chickens. We can steep tea and cook noodles with spring water." The wind plucked flowers as he spoke, depositing white petals in her cup. She looked over at Little Gao bent intently over his calligraphy, his face contorted into wrinkles, whether with age or concentration. A radio was playing by his feet. The sound of the announcer kept cutting in and out of static. "Next year is the year 2000. A new century is approaching. Are you ready? How are *you* going to greet it?"

She forgot about the biting cats and fell asleep under the plum tree. When she woke up, she wasn't on the stool. She wasn't in Yongjing, either. Little Gao was gone. She was lying on the grass. She turned on her side, then her front, and went to sleep again on a soft bed of dried leaves on moist ground. It was drizzling. Not too hot, not too cold. The humidity was just right. The soil smelled sweet. The myriad things hypnotized her.

So she kept dozing, unwilling to wake. That's all she wanted to do, sleep. That was how *she* would greet the new century.

Just over three months before the new century arrived, before ground was broken on the cabin, an epic earthquake struck just before two in the morning with an epicenter in Nantou. Little Gao had gone south to make a delivery that evening. Beverly was home alone in Yongjing, on the ground floor. She was doing a rush export job, drinking strong coffee to keep herself awake. When the house started to shudder, she rolled up the metal shutter and darted out. Her parents were soon standing outside next door. Her mother was screaming, and she didn't stop until the shaking stopped. By that point they'd been joined by all their neighbors. Glass kept breaking. Mother told her to call Heath, who was in China doing business with the Wangs, following in his old man's footsteps. She couldn't reach him. A call came in right after she hung up. It was Keith.

"Is everyone all right? Taipei is shaking like something else."

"We're all scared out of our wits. Mom and Dad are both outside. Everyone's fine. You know that the only one she worries about is Heath."

"That's a relief. Please, don't tell her I—"

The call got cut off. No reception. She wasn't able to make or take calls for the rest of the night.

When Little Gao made it home, he wanted to set out immediately for Nantou. She went with him. As soon as they crossed the county line they had to stop. The road was out. Along the way, houses had collapsed, mountains warped, rivers changed course. He insisted on going on alone to check if their mountain was all right. He told her to drive back by herself.

It was days before he returned. "It ain't slow going, it's no going!" was all he said.

Their mountain hadn't just warped on September 21, 1999. In just a few seconds the tea plantation disappeared, the plum trees disappeared, the entire mountain disappeared.

Little Gao picked up a pair of scissors and went into the back yard to prune and pot. Pots had been tossed on the ground, and spikes had split. He didn't say a thing. His hands were shaking so much he cut a few intact blooms by mistake.

The mountain was gone, and the new century would soon arrive. Now that they were bankrupt, she had to return the rental and move back in with her folks. He would move the orchids himself. He moved them one by one, as if he were carrying pots of gold, from this back yard to that.

Now Little Gao's orchid orchard was piled with posters, billboards, and banners from Heath's campaign. Keith's For the Glory of Yongjing plaque was there, too. Chickens shat on the posters, pots were stacked on the plaque.

Beverly found it looking for the stove. She hadn't seen it in years. In a typhoon that tore through Taiwan a few years before, Mother moved all their junk to the roof and consigned it to the wind. Around a crate of long-expired Fragrant brand soy sauce, she arranged Father's old newspapers, a box of Plenty's old shoes, her own old dresses, boxes of books, a moldy mattress, and Keith's plaque. As the wind picked up, Mother started reciting scripture with palms together in prayer to Heaven. When she finished she stared at the cistern. As her eldest daughter, Beverly understood the expression in her mother's eyes. Her mother wished the wind would take it away. Best if it took all the cisterns in Yongjing.

After the typhoon, she and her mother went up to the roof to find that the wind really had blown everything away, except the plaque, the cistern, and a box containing dozens of copies of Belinda's husband's biography of Nut Wang, *The Greenhorn in the Red Shorts: The Death of a Straight-A Misfit.*

Before he became a news anchor, Belinda's husband had come to Yongjing and moved in next door with the Wangs. He took a sound recorder everywhere he went, hoping to interview Nut's old classmates, relatives, and friends. He even interviewed Beverly.

"He was tall and thin," she said. "In those days, not many boys got that tall. So that was special. Must be why everyone called him Nut. He was really polite. He worked really hard taking care of that carambola orchard, and gave us a few big basketfuls of the fruits. He loved to read. He was always reading in that orchard. I recall he was planning to build himself a little cabin there, a place to put his books. Maybe because he read so many books, he could say things that went way over people's heads. He was good friends with the two bosses at the Tomorrow Bookstore and often hung out with them."

"Did you ever visit the second floor of the bookstore?"

She shook her head hard. What she neglected to mention was that this was a question for her second sister, who was always going over there as a student. After Betty found a job as a civil servant in Taipei, she'd bring the two bosses a present every time she came home.

Another thing Beverly didn't mention was the rumor that Nut was a pervert who preyed on little boys. At the time her own son was less than a year old. Nut commented on how cute he was and offered to babysit. She didn't take him up on it. She held her child closer, looking up at that towering young person with fear in her eyes.

There was no mention of the rumor in the biography. All of the small-town conspirators who had spread it back in the day kept their lips collectively zipped many years later. They talked and talked, until the claims they made were over the top. They talked until people got arrested. They talked until people died. Then everyone who'd talked sewed their mouth shut. If nobody talked, nobody was to blame.

"It was a crying shame," everyone told him. "We're playthings in the palms of Fate. Yongjing lost a good young man."

Keith was shaking wildly. He suddenly stood up, with a heavy fog in his eyes.

Kicked out of his dream back into the real world, Keith didn't know where he was. In Germany? In prison? Where am I? Who is this old woman?

Keith, I may be an old woman, but I'm also your big sister.

Beverly could relate, because she suffered from chronic insomnia after the earthquake. She wasn't afraid of quakes, but as soon as she fell asleep she would dream of that mountain, the one the big quake pushed over. She would wake in the middle of the night, a shower streaming from her eyes. Dream and reality would have gotten so tangled up she would have no idea where she was.

She wasn't going to take Little Gao's word for it. When enough roads had been repaired, she went to see for herself. She drove into the hills to try to find their mountain.

There was no sign of the road they had taken. "Didn't there

used to be a road here?" she asked a local. "With a dense thicket of bamboo at the end of it."

"It's all gone and there ain't nothing left. See how bare all those mountain slopes are now? The trees and grass and the waterfalls are all gone."

She still didn't believe it, so she went on foot, letting memory lead the way. She couldn't see any biting cats underfoot. She hadn't taken more than a few steps when she found herself at the edge of a precipice. Another step and she would have fallen into a raging river. This was nothing like the terrain she remembered. There was no bamboo, no biting cats, no plum trees, and no mountain.

The mountain was gone. Something in her body had caved in, leaving a gaping hole. What would she do? She did not feel like going home. But where to go? She drove around in the hills of Nantou, stopping in front of an old house. The posts and walls had collapsed, and the second floor had fallen to the ground. There was a relief carving of a pair of lions on what had been an upstairs wall. One of the heads had fallen off. The handiwork was exquisite, she could see that, even without the head. The headless lion reminded her of the collapsed head she had held in her hands in the garment factory. So she drove to Shalu. The building was still there, but from the looks of it, it had been left empty for years. A fellow seamstress had mentioned that the factory had moved to China. Apparently, it was exactly the same, in construction, specification, and installation. The only difference was the size. It was several times bigger. She walked behind the building, hoping to see the dormitory. But it was gone. There wasn't anything there except a mound of moldering fabric. The hole in her body gaped even wider.

Ever since, she had had two recurring dreams. One went down and the other up.

Going down. There is a serious tectonic slippage in the depth of night. In just a few seconds, the fault swallows the mountain. The slope plummets, along with the plantation, the plum tree, the table, and the stools. Sleeping beneath the tree, she plummets, too, with Little Gao's orchids, her sewing machine, her savings from Shalu, the garment factory, and a headless corpse. Everything falls into the black earth.

Going up. A severe typhoon land warning has been issued. She stands on the roof of the townhouse amongst the things that Mother has arranged for the whistling wind to take. The wind comes and blows everything away, all of Mother's offerings to Heaven. The soy sauce flies up, and so do Plenty's shoes and Father's old newspapers. Now it's her turn. Beverly gets ready. Her toes leave the ground. Then the wind stops, the typhoon is gone, the warning is lifted. She, a box of books, and Keith's plaque have stayed in place. She can't walk away or fly away. Not even the wind will have her.

When she wakes up from either dream she is neither in the hills nor in the wind. She's been here in Yongjing all along.

Keith looked so sad. His eyes were stuffed with question marks.

"Keith," she wanted to say, "here you are, just like me. You went all that way, but you ended up back home. It's like you never left."

But she didn't say anything. The Chens can really sleep.

Actually what they do best of all is clam up.

Another thing that Beverly had neglected to mention, to anyone, was what else the wind refused to take, in addition to the plaque, the box, and the cistern. There was another box, of VHS tapes.

27. The temple theater

"Excuse me, are you Betty Chen?"

Betty was leaning on the platform railing under a cloudless

evening sky. The full Ghost Festival moon was big and bright. Betty counted one, two, three, four, five stars in the sky, then took in the fields and farm buildings around the station. Points of light were floating in a banana field. Oh, fireflies! How long had it been? One, two, three, four, five, six, seven—she counted seven stars on earth.

When the local train arrived just now, she and a girl in a high school uniform with long hair and pimples were the only ones who disembarked. The girl kept her eyes glued to the screen. In the weak light, she looked pallid and exhausted, like a celluloid ghost. Then she noticed Betty was checking her out. "Isn't that the lady who was abusing seeing-eye dogs on the evening news, Household Registrar Chen? What's she doing in Yongjing?" She frowned, as if she was the one who had seen a ghost. She sprinted over the skywalk and out of the station.

"I'm Sampan Yang, but everyone calls me Sam. Your big sister Beverly asked me to pick you up. I'm sorry, my pickup's a bit beaten up. I hope you don't mind."

Betty followed Sam out. The outer wall of the station was covered in naïve art, probably by students from Yongjing Elementary. One painting was entitled Rainbow Station: blooms and bees, a train chugging down the track, and green hills under a red sun. She looked east and traced the silhouettes that were still visible so late at night. When Nut was on the run from the law, he hoped to find an escape route east, all the way to the Central Range. He would hide out in the mountains.

All the buildings in the vicinity were single-story, including quite a few ironskin homes, each with a metal frame on the roof for a cylindrical silver water cistern that shone with an uncanny luster in the moonlight. It reminded her of the rooftop addition Keith lived in before leaving for Germany. She was shocked to see all the junk the landlord had piled on the roof, not to mention how squalid the living space was.

"Please let me give you some money. Don't live in such a scary place! We can go apartment-hunting together." Keith shook his head and opened a bottle of red wine. They toasted each other and watched the bright lights of Taipei slowly wax and wane. Flushed, she got up and pressed herself against the water cistern, to cool herself off. Holding it, she understood why her little brother would want to live in a place like that. It was like a haunted house.

She hopped in, fastened the seat belt, and recalled who he was.

"Were you my little brother's classmate?"

"You remember me? I used to go to your house to do homework. Maybe I made an impression, though I was all of thirteen at the time."

"I remember your name."

She also remembered his parents in the living room trying to force Keith to switch schools. After they left, Mother threw a chair at Keith. Then she threw another at Father.

"Are you hungry? There's pig trotter *mī-suànn* at Beverly's house if you want. Or I can get you something else. It's a special occasion, after all. Would you care for a deep-fried chicken fillet? I'm going to go order one for Keith."

He swung onto Main Street, drove past the elementary school, and turned right. When he stopped at a stand across the street from a 24-hour 7-Eleven, the boss lady hollered: "Sam Yang, you busy beaver! You here to help me sell chicken?"

She looked familiar, but Betty couldn't recall who she was.

The aroma of the chicken drummed a rhythm on her slack tummy.

"Please get me one, too. Here's the money. I'm going to pop into the convenience store."

He refused to take it. "We'll sort it out when you get back."

All the convenience stores in Taiwan look exactly the same.

Standardized interior decoration, the same lighting; even the cashier bore a resemblance to the one at the store near Betty's flat in Taipei. All trace of the Tomorrow Bookstore had been wiped away. She walked to the back, stopped in front of the fridge, and pretended to choose a drink. There was a door by the fridge. If she opened it and stepped through, a flight of stairs would lead up to the library. Another flight led up to the bedroom.

As a vocational high school student, she used to come to the Tomorrow Bookstore on weekends to stand in front of the shelf and read. One time she fell into a long novel until closing time. The thick boss came over and asked, "You've been standing here reading the entire day, I'm feeling tired watching you. I was going to offer you a chair, but I didn't want to disturb you. Guess what? We're closing now."

She hurriedly put the book back on the shelf and realized that the metal shutter was already rolled halfway down. Why hadn't she heard? She bowed and apologized, "Sorry, sorry, sorry. I'm leaving now."

"No rush. Would you like to stay for dinner? We're having Japanese noodles."

She kept shaking her head, but the thick boss wouldn't take no for an answer. "Don't worry," he said. "We may be bachelors, but we wouldn't lay a finger on you." She followed him up the stair to the second floor. The thin boss brought out a bowl of hot soup noodles and said: "Make yourself at home! How nice to have some company for a change."

The noodles were fine, tender, slippery. The thin boss's parents ran an export and import business, and had access to a lot of Japanese food products. The noodles were from an old shop in Tokyo.

The walls were lined with bookshelves, the shelves with books. The thick boss said that nobody in Yongjing bought books, but they could at least move magazines. Forget about selling literary books, absolutely nobody was interested. So they only ordered books they were interested in. They brought them up here, added them to the collection, and read them themselves.

"You're welcome to come up here any time you want."

One shelf was for English and Japanese language-learning books. The thick boss said that they were trying to save money for further study in Japan or America. They didn't rake it in, but they made do. They could save a bit of money every month by keeping their expenses low. Maybe in a few years they would have enough stashed away to go abroad.

Betty became a regular on the second floor. She would take it upon herself to help make dinner, saying that she'd grown into an amazing cook growing up in a three-wing compound. No dish was too hard for her to make. Give her any ingredient, and she could do something with it. If she was there, they turned the kitchen over to her. She would turn whatever vegetable and meat they had on hand into a gourmet meal for three. They would talk about books over dinner. She liked novels, not romance novels but depressing literary novels. The thick boss liked foreign-language novels. He enjoyed guessing what the original was from the odd locutions in the Chinese translation. The thin boss liked Japanese writers. He was training himself to read them in the original.

At first the two of them held hands only under the table. But after she became a friend, they put their hands above board.

When Betty was hoping to find work in Taipei after graduation, they pulled strings to get her an interview. But she didn't get the job, or any job. "It's okay," she said, "I'm good at taking tests and memorization. I'll study for the national civil service exam." When she got the news that she had passed, she ran to the bookstore and threw her arms around Boss Ming. "My mother said I'd have to get married if I didn't pass," Betty said crying. "Thank goodness! Oh thank goodness!"

After she was assigned to Taipei, she would make a trip to a bookstore near NTU to pick up a box for the bosses every time she went home. The boxes were tightly sealed and really heavy. "No problem," she said. She'd been shouldering heavy loads with a yoke since she was a kid. It was no trouble.

One year at New Year's she went right to the bookstore from the station. The thick boss was closing up when she arrived with a hefty box, which she delivered to the second floor. There, she saw a stranger squatting in front of a shelf. He immediately rose when he saw her. He was surprisingly tall, so tall he had to bend down to talk to her. "Hello, you can call me Nut, everyone does. We're neighbors. You probably know my elder brother."

Three decades later, Betty came out of the convenience store without having bought a thing. Her arms felt sore, like she had just carried a box of books all the way back from Taipei and up to the second floor.

She got into Sam's truck and smelled fried chicken. He turned down a little lane and passed the Lady at the Foot of the Wall, which was now leaning on a towering tree with broad-spreading branches and luxuriant foliage. It used to be a cracked old bishopwood tree. Then a strangler fig seed germinated in the crack and wrapped a mesh of roots around the trunk. It grew and grew, until the younger tree had enclosed the old. It was a strange sight, a bishopwood inside a banyan. There was no trace of the hog abattoir, except for an obelisk, the Beast Spirit Memorial. Cicada had told Betty its story. So many pigs were killed there by day that when the wind rose at night, the neighbors would hear the howls. The wind only stopped carrying the pigs' cries of pain after this monument to their departed spirits was erected.

She had not been back in such a long time. Now the square was enclosed by a mural wall. She didn't remember seeing it before.

"When did they build it?" she asked Sam.

"That was the mayor, something about 'Painting Yongjing.' It was supposed to be a tourist attraction. They built the wall and hired an artist to come and paint it." Betty wondered why everyone was so keen on "development." An empty lot was in want of a house, and a boundary of a wall or a fence. It was apparently angst-inducing if a wall was blank, better cover it in bright colors. Sam drove so slowly she had the time to figure out the theme of the mural: the history of the temple. There was an open-air stage, a projector, and a screen. A film was showing.

When she was a girl, puppet plays and folk operas were often performed in the square. If the Lady granted your wish, then you showed your gratitude by hiring a troupe to put on a show. The local children would all crowd into the square to watch after school. Later on, after such folk productions fell out of fashion, the grateful faithful would hire a striptease troupe instead.

Oh, now she remembered, the lady who was selling fried chicken, was she the one who used to strip?

The first film she ever saw in her life was shown here at the Lady at the Foot of the Wall.

"Have you ever seen a film?" the bosses asked her. "Uh-uh," she said. Yongjing was too small for a movie theater. If you wanted to see one you had to take the train to Yuanlin. She didn't have the money, and her parents would never have allowed her. "But what if," the bosses asked, "we brought a movie theater to Yongjing?"

The bosses made a proposal at the township office. They would find a venue, set up a screen, and give their neighbors the opportunity to see a film. They ended up deciding on the temple square. The street in front was not an important thoroughfare. They could block it off for a few hours, it wouldn't impact anybody. The square could accommodate a hundred people. Which was about right.

When the towering screen and the hulking projector were in place, the Foot of the Wall Theater held its first screening. At the time the popular movies were works of political propaganda. The first film was a war movie about how the nationalist government had led the resistance against the Japanese. The square was packed. There weren't enough chairs. Many people brought their own from home, but it was too crowded to set them all out. Folks were jostling for a good seat. Sausage stands and ice cream sellers did a brisk business that summer night. Betty also remembered a grilled hard tofu stand in a dark corner. You could buy chunks of tofu on a bamboo stick, crouch down, and grill it yourself on a little stove, one of several such stoves puffing out a smokescreen for crouching lovers to kiss behind. Before the screening began, there was a general clamor in the square. Children cried, adults cursed, and mosquitos ganged up on everyone. Suddenly the projector shot a ray of light and an image appeared on the white screen. Hundreds of pairs of eyes opened wide. Even the mosquitos that were feasting on people's arms and legs pulled their proboscises out and looked up at the play of light and shade.

The thick boss described the scene: "It's like everyone in Yongjing just saw a ghost."

She and the two bosses sat by the projector and watched the film. She was crying. The movie was propaganda. Her tears were in line with the patriotic ethos of the day. But she wasn't crying because of the story. She was crying because she couldn't imagine how the massive machine she was sitting beside could have wrapped distant movie stars, voices, sounds, and songs into a roll of film and flung them with light onto that white canvas sheet. That was incomprehensible to Betty, like magic. Although she had heard so many ghost stories growing up in the countryside, she had never seen one. The first time she saw a film she trembled head to toe. She covered her mouth to stop herself from screaming. That must be what seeing a ghost was like.

That first time, the bosses sat together and she sat to the side. People were projecting strange looks their way, so the second time they showed a film, another resistance flick, she sat between them. A couple of kids ran over to ask: "Betty, which boss are you falling in love with, the thick one or the thin?" So the third time they showed *another* patriotic war film, they made sure to sit in three different corners. Near the climax, when the hero was getting ready to sacrifice himself for the nation, all eyes were glued to the screen but hers. She stole a glance at her two friends. She wasn't the only one who wasn't looking at the screen. The thick boss and the thin boss were looking at each other across the square. She cried a second time.

The moonlight that night was just the same as it was tonight. Tonight a full moon was hanging high above on the strangler fig, just as another full moon had hung on the bishopwood tree all those years before. Its leafy branches blended the silvery moonbeams with the rays from the projector and the savory smoke from the sausage-seller's coal-fired stove. A white mist filled the square, turning it into a fantastical lake of fluid light in which motes of dust glided effortlessly around on wings. When a breeze came to visit, ripples appeared on the screen. If you listened carefully, peeled away the film score, and extracted the coughs, you could hear hogs howl.

Betty was crying because she was angry. She was furious. Why, why, why? Why were the thick boss and the thin boss only stealing glances at each other but not at her?

28. Hippos are dangerous

By the time Belinda parked the car, the golden gate was creaking shut behind her.

How long had it been since her last visit? The mansion was shining in the moonlight, an uncannily pure white. It was flawless, without a trace of air pollution or acid rain. It appeared as if it would always be as pure as the driven snow. From a distance, it looked like a snow-white cliff had erupted out of the plain. From close up, the golden paint on the gate reached out to poke your eyes with sharpened nails. She gathered the Wangs had a painter on call. If paint peeled, if dust collected, or if smog dulled its luster, there was someone around to touch it up.

Baron Wang sat on a bench in front of the "Basin" d'Apollon, lit a cigarette, took a long drag, held his breath, exhaled a white ring, and sighed. "You don't smoke anymore, do you, Belinda?" he asked.

At eighteen years old, when she was studying for the university entrance exam, pressure would nibble at her body like termites. She used to take a notebook behind the house and around the fishpond, memorizing English vocabulary along the way. One day, Baron offered her a cigarette. "Miss Chen, nicotine will perk you up," he said. "You'll learn those words twice as fast."

She took it and let him light it. She noted a sticker of a naked woman on the plastic lighter. He taught her how to inhale, hold her breath, and exhale. She did as instructed. The smoke stole into her chest and fumigated several of the termites. Her feet left the ground, her head grew wings. She felt like jumping into the pond and swimming with the fish.

"Wow, you're really something. It's your first time, but you didn't cough at all. Sweet."

She looked at him out of the corner of her eye, but didn't reply, just took a drag and memorized three more words. When she was a girl she sometimes used to ride with her father in the truck. The hired movers used to tease her. They were the ones who'd taught her how to smoke. They watched her cough until her tears were like a waterfall, then rolled around on the ground laughing. It took her a few times to get the hang of it.

Father frowned and snickered when he smelled the smoke on her, but didn't say a thing.

"Don't worry, Miss Chen. Take it easy. With those grades of yours, you're a shoo-in for the top university in the country. You're going to follow in my little brother's footsteps."

"Will you please quit calling me Miss Chen, like you're younger than me? And, you idiot, the footsteps you follow in are supposed to be your father's."

He fiddled with the knob, letting the flame wax and wane. Then he stuck two cigarettes in his mouth and lit them. After exhaling, he said, "I call you Miss Chen out of respect, you know. Hicks like me may not be good at school, but at least we know how to respect people who are. Look at my little brother, he's about to graduate from university. He'll stay in Taipei and work. I'm so happy for him. He even wants to go to America for further study. I'm envious. Look at me, I suck at school, all I can do is follow my old man around. It ain't easy, you know, being dumb."

She grabbed the lighter away from him. The striker was hot to the touch. Taking in the naked lady, a tart with blond hair, pale skin, and big tits, she recalled a mover in her father's employ fiddling with himself with a lighter just like this one in his hand. Just a few seconds later, a white liquid spurted out. "Is that the kind of girl you guys go for?" she asked.

"Not me, I like intellectual girls. Women with beauty and brains. Just like you."

How long ago was that? Now she was in her late fifties. Baron must be in his sixties by now.

She sat down beside him and grabbed the cigarette out of his mouth. She was about to wrap her lips around it when she thought of her husband. Thinking better of it, she stuck it back. She noticed the globe he carried around in his midsection. "How'd your gut get so out of hand?" The last time she saw him was at the studio. Her husband did an exclusive interview with "renowned businessman Baron Wang." For the first time Baron was in front of the camera sharing the secrets of his success. He laid all his family's products on the table, crackers, instant noodles, candy, and health food. During a break in the recording he came over looking mischievous. It was the same expression as he'd had by the fish pond.

"Miss Chen, come on, I need a referral."

"What referral?"

"A doctor."

"Come on, do you get sick? Didn't you just tell my husband you're never going to die, eating all those crackers? What was it? Anyone who eats your crackers will live to a hundred years old?"

"At least. I'm asking where you get your nip and tuck. Your skin is so smooth, and you've sure kept your figure. Forever eighteen. I'm impressed."

That wasn't that long ago, was it? Look at how big his gut had gotten now. But time had not left many marks on his shiny face, whether at the corners of his eyes or on his forehead. He went to the same clinic as her husband for regular injections.

"I don't have to go on camera every night like your husband. He's the most senior handsome news anchor in Taiwan, and he just gets better with age. Of course he has to stay in shape. Unlike a businessman like me. The bigger my gut, the more contracts I get." He passed her the cigarette. "Relax, I won't tell your husband."

She took a drag. Looking at the fountain of Apollo, she remembered the moment when her future husband's architect friend showed a photograph of the Palace of Versailles to the Wang family. Plenty was there, too. When she saw the fountain, she said she wanted one. The architect, who had never been to France, asked a sculptor who specialized in Taoist figures to make it just like the photo. He made an Apollo in a four-horse war chariot emerging from a sea of monsters and Tritons based not just on the photo but also on his imagination. The stallions were indeed spirited, he got that part right. But Apollo looked a lot like the red-faced Lord Guan, the patron saint of businessmen and mafiosi. And when you pressed the button, jets of water spurted not only out of the stallions' mouths and the mouths of the sea monsters and Tritons, but also from Apollo's eyes. A truly phenomenal amount of water spurted out of the foundation the day of Barbie's wedding, melted snow from Europe that was rumored to cure every ill. Many wedding guests brought buckets to collect water to sip at home. A lot of them tossed in spare change and made a wish, hoping to get filthy rich.

The words *Basin d'Apollon* had been carved on the base. She had learned enough French to see that *bassin* was short an "s," but she didn't say anything. After all these years, the second "s" in *bassin* was still absent, and Apollo still looked like Lord Guan, except for the water marks on his cheeks and down his sides. He, too, looked old.

"Want to see the jets? I haven't turned it on in years."

"Didn't that museum in Tainan do one a couple of years ago?" Belinda asked. "I hear it was a full-scale model, and they hired a French artisan to make it. I was wondering why Baron Wang didn't hold a press conference to remind everyone the first fountain of Apollo in Taiwan wasn't in Tainan, it was in Changhua? 'At my house!'"

Baron leaned back and laughed. "Belinda, imagine what would have happened. A bunch of reporters would have come over to shoot the fountain. Then your younger sister would have appeared in the window upstairs and come charging out to make a scene. That would have been the end of me. Please, a businessman's most precious asset is his reputation. When that's ruined, you're ruined. You don't get a second chance."

When that's ruined, you're ruined? You don't get a second chance?

She looked up at Barbie's window. With the black curtain, it was the White House's only dark side.

"My sister, has she . . ." Belinda said, choking on the words. Barbie was as loud as ever today on the phone. *"Mom's gone missing!"* She couldn't be doing that bad?

"Belinda, don't tell me you made a special trip home to see Barbie." Without replying, she tossed the butt into the fountain and exhaled the last mouthful of smoke.

"Can I park my car here? Please don't tell my husband. You know how much trouble he can be." She looked at her watch. The evening news was almost over. Soon he would be driving home. He would call as soon as he saw the empty stall in the basement garage, if not before.

He was one of Baron's groomsmen. The moment the hippo ran out of its enclosure, he grabbed her hand and pulled her towards the White House. They ran upstairs. "Hippos are dangerous!" he said.

If only she'd known that the danger wasn't the hippo, it was the person who'd taken her hand.

She was seriously considering marriage. The man who'd taken her hand was not just a bestselling author, he would soon be anchoring the news.

Why not him?

What else could she do?

One thing she learned in university was that all she was good at was memorization for written tests. Ask her to go up to the front and give a presentation and she would stand there, tongue-tied in front of her peers, unable to snip the stitches that had sewn up her lips. Grammar and writing came easily to her, but she couldn't keep up in speaking. Her hand wrote fluently, but the well of her mouth ran dry. She didn't make any close friends in four years of university. Her roommates were all party girls, while she didn't know how to have fun. After graduation she switched jobs three times in six months. She forgot why. She just remembered feeling lost. She was an editor at a publisher, a clerk at a translation agency, and a secretary at a foreign company. All three jobs were hard going. She was expected to interact with people, but she just couldn't. She avoided dinners or other events at which she had to socialize or network. One time a foreign author visited the publisher. The boss asked her to interpret. She understood everything the author said, but as the syntactic patterns silted up her mind, she could hardly translate any of it. "Weren't you an English major?" the boss asked. "Your English is worse than mine!"

Her father told her to come home and take a break. He had her do the bookkeeping for the truck delivery business. However much she was making in Taipei, he would pay her more.

So she came back and worked for her dad. If Keith had any questions about his homework he would ask her. If she felt like studying English, she rented a VHS next door. She'd watch a Hollywood film two or three times, forcing herself to shadow the actors. Her little brother shadowed the actors, too. He was really good at it. He could quickly pick up on the idioms of the different characters. He hadn't studied much English, but he could repeat the lines really clearly. "When are you going to take me to Taipei?" he asked.

She wanted to, but she was afraid.

"Marry me," Mr. Bestseller said, "and I will take you back to Taipei. I will buy you a house. It won't be as over the top as the White House. But I'm certain you'll like it."

He must have seen through her. He must have known how bored she was with bookkeeping. Indeed, she often had to suppress the impulse to suffocate herself with a pillow. So he made an offer she couldn't refuse. "Will you be my assistant?" he asked when he was interviewing people for the biography of Nut. "It's a snake pit out there, and you grew up in it, you're one of them. You can help me stalk prey."

While chatting, they discovered that they were only a few years apart and had majored in arts at the same university.

He must have heard something about her. "You know Belinda? What good has going to NTU done her? She's ended up back here in Yongjing. She isn't hard on the eyes, but the matchmaker can't find any country boys who are willing to step up to the plate. She's out of their league. And look how old she is! In a few years it'll be too late. Her youngest sister Plenty's getting married already."

After the biography was published, he drove down from Taipei and presented her with a box of books.

"Let's get married. We'll leave this God-forsaken place together." That was his proposal.

She kept her mouth shut, but he knew, and she knew, that she didn't have to say it: she'd already accepted.

Yes, he saw through her. She would make a Good Wife for sure. A Good Wife who would keep her mouth shut. She would be a piece of furniture, an ornament. She sure looked good on him. She would be the great woman behind the great man. In pain, she would stay tight-lipped. She wouldn't tell a soul. She wouldn't have a soul to tell.

Baron pressed the button, and surging water columns shot out of Apollo's eyes. But the stallions, the Tritons, and the sea monsters stayed dry. Apollo looked like he was crying alone in the moonlight.

"Something must be stuck. I'll call the plumber tomorrow."

"No need to repair it, who are you going to turn it on for?" Strange how she spoke so quickly to Baron, and never got tongue-tied. She felt articulate. "I should go."

"Do you want me to drive you? I haven't been back in ages, either." She looked up at the black curtain.

"I wouldn't have driven down if my parents hadn't asked," he said. "It's a pleasant surprise to see you. Sure you won't come in and have dinner? Don't you want to say hello to your sister?"

She shook her head. She was hungry, and had a hankering for the foods she hated most of all. Would Beverly have any eggplant at the house? Maybe she could buy bitter melon on the way home. Or starfruit?

"I want to walk."

The golden gate creaked open. She walked out, telling herself: don't look back don't look back don't look back. She knew Baron's gaze was stuck to her. Just like it had always been.

Of course she looked back anyway.

She saw the black curtain on the full-length window tremble. Barbie's pale, puffy face poked out of the shadows. Barbie looked down and saw her husband smoking by the fountain and staring straight ahead. She followed his gaze and saw the golden gate, almost closed. Outside the gate stood a woman.

Belinda.

Belinda's phone vibrated. It was her husband. Didn't he just finish delivering the news? She turned it off.

She was really hungry. She wanted to eat bitter melon, raw.

Then she remembered the honey gummy bears from Berlin in her purse.

Keith.

She grabbed a handful and stuffed them in her mouth. She looked at Baron, then at Barbie. Barbie and Belinda hadn't seen each other in nearly thirty years.

She remembered the last time. "Did the hippo escape from its enclosure?" Barbie asked. "If it's out there, I'm not going anywhere."

29. *Those are all wild swans*

Where was he?

He tried to guess by listening. The tide. A sewing machine. A crowing cock. Mother's snores. A roaring hippo. Knuckles knocking on a water cistern. A barking dog. Clapping hands. A cello. Rain.

He rubbed his eyes. T. Beverly. Gloves. Crackers. A stove. Stools. A crack. Spirit money. Ash. Flaxen hair. Night. The moon. Swans. Leftover vermicelli. Golden lashes. Fresh blood. Thick fog.

By smell? Pig trotters. Pills. Humidity. Soapy skin. Smoked fish. Raw seawater. Seawater in hair. Honey. Sugar. A script by Shakespeare.

All these clues were like tiny tangled strings that had knotted up his mind. They were like snakes, hundreds of them, of different sizes, colorations, and species. They were writhing around on his body. Flicking their tongues and biting.

Why would he think of snakes?

He got bitten by one when he was a boy. He was rolling around on the grass when he felt an excruciating pain. A snake had sunk its teeth into his hand and wrapped itself around his arm, refusing to let go. He tried to pull the snake off with the other hand, but it was too strong. His brother was bawling. Other kids were screaming and running away. He thought of a trick his neighbor had taught him: he found the anus on the abdomen towards the tail and jabbed his finger in as hard as he could. The snake immediately relaxed, released his arm, and fell to the ground. He looked down at the bite marks on his palm.

He'd come home today feeling dizzy, with a shooting pain. Just like that snake bite.

He knew where he was. The house he grew up in. The place where he started out. Square one. The home he had exhausted himself leaving. Which didn't want or welcome him.

He saw his sister's gray hair and swans on the sea. The images superimposed, he couldn't concentrate. He had his meds in his backpack. Had he taken them since he stepped off the plane?

He stepped onto the porch. The stove was cool, the receptacle full of ash. It was windless, the air sluggish. A few cars went by, trailing hot gusts. There was a silver disc in the sky, a full moon. Looking left, at the end of the road, he saw the White House. In jail, the White House sought him out in a dream. Plenty was standing in front of the Golden Gate, yelling at a group of reporters. "I'm going to start cutting, are your cameras ready? I'm going to do it riiiiight *now*." The knife cut into her wrist, blood came spurting out, cameras clicked. Her features were indistinct, and after slitting her wrist she disappeared. The blood that dripped onto the ground had a vitality all of its own. It spread out, now growing like a vine, now spraying like a fountain. Soon the fence wall was coated, the basins brimming. The carp went belly up. The blood kept on spreading until it coated the columns and the exterior walls, turning them an obscene shade of red. The blood in the dream was luminous and viscous. The wall glowed, and felt like it had been smeared with gelatin.

"Doctor, why do people go home?"

That was his question for the psychologist in the German jail.

Safety, belonging, relaxation. To sleep, shower, and watch TV.

He asked his lawyer if he'd ever gone back to Vietnam.

The lawyer told him his story of homecoming. He could not speak a single word of Vietnamese, but he had contacts, and was able to find the orphanage he had lived in as a child. Adopted at three years old, he had absolutely no memory of the place, no *déjà-vu*. He thought that the visit and his donation would fill the hole in his heart. But when he got to Vietnam, the hole got even bigger. His German parents were all emotional. They were hugging the orphanage personnel and crying. But he felt detached, as if it had nothing to do with him. Even his homosexual partner got caught up in the moment and thought of adopting a child, while Keith's lawyer felt like running away. He wanted to leave Vietnam on the next flight and take that hole inside him back to Berlin.

Keith had read about selective or repressed memory in jail. In extreme cases people could go and delete painful chapters from their *Bildungsromans*, leaving only the beautiful and the good. When Keith thought about his hometown, he would naturally dwell on the positive. Like that summer night when his mother made citrusy *aiyü* jelly and served it with longan honey on the front porch. They all sat outside looking at the stars, listening to the crickets, and waiting for the fireflies. Ma sat in a rocking chair and counted the stars: one, two, three, four, five, six, seven. But he had not forgotten all the ugliness and the dirt, all the deaths and departures that he had caused, all the times when his mother threw punches or shade. When she beat him, her fists were like knives, her feet like swords. But the fiercest of all was her mouth, which burned his ears with Taiwanese profanity. He never resisted or talked back, because he was ashamed of himself, because he thought she was right. She was right to hit him and to say all those things about him. That he was perverted and abnormal. That he'd ruined the Chen family. That he'd never fit in. That giving birth to him was a sin. That she should have just had the one son.

So he did as she wished, he left. He went far, far away, with no plan to return. He even gave up his passport. He made a clean break.

But today he had come back home. He still didn't have any answers. Why do people go home? Where is home? He came back neither for salvation nor out of repentance, still less to find an answer. Coming home was not out of a duty. He found it stifling. But he had to come home.

He really had nowhere else to go.

"Let's get married," T said. "You'll get a residence permit.

Then you can stay. In a few years you can apply for a German passport."

"Get married?" Germany did not have gay marriage yet in those days, but there was special legislation allowing homosexual couples to register partnerships. T's expression was resolute. Playing with T's flaccid penis, Keith thought it over. Marriage would be a certain rupture, which would uproot him from his island home once and for all. It was a tempting offer. He would get a completely new identity. He could start from scratch in a place without friends, without family, without a personal history. He could start a new life with a stranger. He smiled, nodded, and said yes. When T heard it, he soon got hard in his palm.

Before they registered, T suggested a trip to Laboe to meet the folks. His mother was a teacher in a music school, his father a functionary in the harbor authority. In two days it would be Christmas. Why not spend the holidays with his family? They arranged a dog-sitter and took an express train to Hamburg, a slow train to Kiel, and a bus to Laboe. It was a roundabout route, with an abrupt change in window scenery, from the cityscape when he dozed off to the deserted snowy landscape when he woke up. When they got to Laboe the snow suddenly stopped. It was a dreary day. He saw a woman walking a dog on the beach of a quiet bay. When she saw T she rushed over and hugged him. Then she sized him up. The dog sniffed him warily, like he was an extraterrestrial lifeform that had just crashed on the shore. The sea was calm, though he could hear waves, faintly. T pointed out to sea. "Can you see them? Those white dots? Those are all wild swans."

T's home was a seafront cabin. It was two stories tall with a sloping roof. The exterior walls were off-white, the window frames Greek blue. There was a swing in the yard, hanging from the bare bough of an apple tree, and a bench with a view. T pointed at an upstairs window. That used to be his room.

He'd watch the big ships going out to sea with binoculars, guessing their destinations.

As soon as he went inside, he sensed it, that T's parents did not welcome him. Cold handshakes, evasive gazes. The only cordial presence in the room was the flashing Christmas tree. T and his father had a fight over dinner. He and T left that evening.

From then on T was *heimatlos*, homeless. At the time Keith didn't understand, not really, but now he did. He could even relate to refugees who risked their lives to find safe harbor when their homes were demolished, when their countries collapsed. They were homeless, helpless, rootless. Cut off, stripped away. Wandering in exile, forever.

That's how he felt when he drove to Laboe after killing T.

His eldest sister Beverly stood by his side and gazed up at the moon with him. His sweat was like rain, like a waterfall. The midges had left a lot of puffy red spots on his skin, tiny hills. The moon was rising slowly in a cloudless sky.

"It hasn't rained in ages," she said.

The day that he and T registered their partnership it was raining Berlin rain. The agency was in east Berlin by a little lake. They had the certificate in no time. They didn't bring witnesses, only an interpreter from the PRC to help him understand the procedure. "Congratulations!" the interpreter said. "Welcome to Germany!"

There was no ring, no suit and tie. They walked to the lakeshore, hand in hand. "This is the Weißensee," T said, a "white lake" in the rain. Someone was out on the lake in a rowboat. "We should come here this summer for a swim."

His sisters found out that he was "married" when they read his newspaper column about the sights and sounds, the knowns and unknowns, and the pleasures and pains of Berlin. One week he wrote about a pair of "newlywed" men kissing in the rain on the shore of a lake. "They didn't bother to bring an umbrella," he wrote. "They were waiting for the summer."

Betty called Beverly to give her a heads-up. "Thank goodness Mom is illiterate. But you'd better dispose of today's paper to make sure that Dad doesn't see it."

Belinda was drinking her morning coffee when she remembered today was the day of Keith's column. Nobody in Yongjing would read the literary supplement, would they?

Mother may have been illiterate, but a lot of her neighbors could read. The pork peddler could read, as could the swamp spinach seller, the potted plant purveyor, and the mechanic. They said it in a whisper, as a joke. They said it with furrowed brows, in disgusted tones. The wind came up, and blew the words in the column all around.

"It hasn't rained in months," said Beverly. "The ditches are dry. The township office announced water rationing, all those fields of flowers and fruits will have to go fallow. The old man is *not* snoring. Everyone is going to die of poverty, or drought."

He was so thirsty. He needed a big glass of water to wash down the pills.

Looking left, he saw a thin form set out from the White House and approach in heels that clattered on the road. When whoever it was saw him and Beverly standing there, the rhythm of her footfalls quickened.

Looking right, he saw the chrysanthemum lamps turn on, drawing a yellow halo over the field and tracing the townscape. As the light grew, it drove away the darkness and painted the paths through the fields yellow, the country roads gold. That light was like spindrift. A pickup truck was surfing through it towards them.

Keith was again reminded of the swans. The swans that came slowly near, that bobbed white as snow on the black swells of the Baltic Sea. He counted on his fingers, but he didn't have enough. He got a different number every time. But every one was pure and bright, like stars in the sky at night.

There was another thing he had never told his sisters, and

wouldn't tell anyone. If it hadn't been for those swans, the next one to die by his hand after T would have been himself.

30. Digging up the red flowers

One moon, two moons, three moons, four moons, five moons.

One swan, two swans, eight swans, fifteen swans, five swans, six swans, no swans. All the swans died.

Eight hippos, twelve hippos, one hippo. Good hippo, jumping hippo, roaring hippo. Sisters, brothers, can you hear the hippo roar?

There are five moons in my world.

This evening there are a million moons stuffed into the sky. A million, you heard that right, blinking quickly on one after another. I counted them one by one on my fingers, to a million. No mistake. There are too many of them, it's crowded up there. Moon on moon, jostling against one another, dissolving into one another until they fill the entire sky.

Forming a single massive moon.

I need a supermoon to see clearly. I want to see what you all look like now. Can you hear the hippo roar?

Mother took me to Yuanlin to get gold jewelry made for the wedding. Having accepted a huge engagement gift, she couldn't scrimp on my dowry. "What's so great about Yuanlin?" I asked. "Mother, I'm going to Paris for my honeymoon. Paris! I'll buy you all the gold you want while I'm there."

"The Jian Cheng Jewelry Shop has been famous since the Japanese were here," Mom said. "A lot of folks from out of town go there to get their dowry jewelry done. What's so great about Paris? Can you get there by train? By motorbike? What do you know about Paris, you silly girl, you've never even been!"

Mother bought bracelets, pendants, necklaces, and earrings, all of them old-fashioned, all of them pure gold. "Only this is 'classy,'" she said. "You have to wear things like this to get married in style."

I asked if the boss could make a gold necklace for a hippo to wear. It would have to be a chain.

Sisters, brothers, there is a hippo's roar in your auditory memory. It's low, like a brass instrument. It sounds lot like Mother's snores.

Keith, when you were rehearsing Shakespeare in prison, the director brought a couple of brass instruments for you to blow on. And though you weren't trying to, you found a chord that sounded like a hippo's roar.

I put on all of the gold ornaments in the shop and looked at myself in the mirror. I was radiant. The golden earrings were doing chin-ups on my earlobes. The skin of my chest was dyed gold. Junior would like it for sure. He loved my chest.

Yes, I called Baron Junior.

Junior said his family had made a killing on the stock market. "We're tycoons now," he said. "Business is booming on the mainland. The crackers are selling like hot cakes, in the millions, maybe in the billions. So tell me, what do you want?"

My skin is really sensitive. If I wear cheap trinkets I break out in a rash. One time I wore the gold necklace that Beverly's husband gave her and red flowers instantly bloomed on my chest. Beverly cried up a storm. "You liar!" she said. "You said it was twenty-four karat!"

But pure gold suited me just fine. My skin is happy to rub against any real gold ornament, the red flowers won't bloom. Glorious golden light.

Hippo skin looked really thick, a hippo couldn't possibly be allergic to a gold chain, could it? The boss of the jewelry store had no idea. He'd never seen a hippo. How big did they get? At the time I'd only seen a photograph. I said a grown hippo might be bigger than the entire store. The boss said he would have to use a lot of gold.

"No problem, it doesn't matter how much gold you need, my fiancé is a stock market tycoon." One cut, two cuts, one cut, two cuts.

The snake killer next door said he could get his hands on a hippo.

The snake killer could get his hands on anything. All the townhouse residents knew that no matter what you wanted you just had to ask him and he could figure out a way. Actually, you didn't have to tell him, a lot of the time he already knew. Sometimes he wanted money, but not always. You had to pay for a snake to make a soup, extra if he slaughtered it. You had to pay to rent a VHS. You had to pay for him to play the piano. But an antivenom was free. It didn't cost Mom anything to sleep with him, that was free, too. If you couldn't do your math problems, you could ask him, no charge. If you couldn't do your English questions you could ask him, same deal. When the doctor couldn't do anything for my rash, he gave me a snake-infused medicinal wine and a salve that forced the red flowers into retreat. He didn't take any money at all.

Right, none of you know. Only Beverly and I know that she was sleeping with the snake killer. Beverly found out pretty early on. She walked in on them. That's why Mother took a particular dislike to her. She would nitpick all day long. When Beverly quit school and left for Shalu, Mother breathed a sigh of relief.

I found out later on, but I didn't see it with my own eyes.

I discovered a couple of Mother's dresses hanging up in the basement. One cut, two cuts, one cut, two cuts.

Right, you don't know there was a basement. Only one of the townhouses even had a basement, the one that belonged to the snake killer.

It didn't hurt, it really didn't. One, two. A supermoon

shone, on the blade, with a glaring light. It was Keith who discovered my body.

You couldn't find me. Only he knew where I would go. Every time either of us got hit, we would both go to the ditch along the chrysanthemum field.

"Plenty," he said, "they all say I'm a pervert."

"It's good to be a pervert, silly!" I told him. "Let me tell you, when I marry Junior, I'm going to have a lot of money. When the White House is built, you can move in with us. There are so many rooms. I'll support you, you little pervert. I'll take you to Paris. We'll buy Chanel."

We never went to Paris together, you went to Berlin on your own.

It didn't hurt, it really didn't. I didn't understand your expressions of fear when you saw me take a razor to my skin. It wasn't like I was a ghost.

But now I am.

One cut, two cuts, here and there. I cut myself in different places to see how much blood would flow. It really didn't hurt, it was a thrill. The blood flowed like water, so beautifully moist. I've been a ghost for so many years now, but I still miss that feeling of razor ripping skin. How could you not understand? I don't understand why you all wouldn't want to grab a razor and slice.

The first time was because my arm had broken out again. It was so itchy I couldn't stand it. I scratched the red flowers until they were grayish blue. Which only made them itchier, and sore. The pain came from deep inside the skin. I wanted to know what was under there. Why did I grow red flowers so easily? There happened to be a utility knife on the desktop. I'd be fine if I cut myself open, that would stop the itch. I could dig up the red flowers hidden under my skin and pick them one by one. The blade slid across my arm, leaving a fine line from which bright red blood flowed. It didn't hurt. I saw the blood and forgot the itch. I never knew how beautiful blood could be. Hoping to pick red flowers, I ended up drilling a well. I had no idea how much red well water there was in my body. It used to trickle out every month, but it stopped when I was seventeen. That was no big deal, I had a big chest. And Junior just loved my chest.

One, two, three, four, five, six, achoo! Every morning when I woke up I would sneeze like crazy. Several rooms away Keith would be counting at the top of his lungs. When he finished everybody was awake.

Keith, you're standing by the road with Beverly by your side. Belinda is shuffling towards you. Betty just hopped out of Sam's truck.

Keith, the snake killer packed a box of VHS tapes for you, no fee, for free. You didn't even have to ask. We waited until the rest of the family went out to pray before putting a tape in the player.

By the side of the road, in the moonlight, nobody knows what to say. The supermoon starts to shrink, rapidly.

One cut, two cuts. Arms, thighs. Next time I would try my ankles. What part would release the most blood? Where was I the most humid? None of you have any idea what to say.

Betty says, "You're too thin."

Belinda says, "I've been eating this candy, from Berlin."

Actually Betty and Belinda haven't said a thing. But that's what they are thinking. Only I can hear it.

Barbie is pacing back and forth and talking to herself in her room in the White House. I can hear her even here. Now she's yelling: "Mother's gone missing, Mother's gone missing! Mom! Where did you go?"

The supermoon keeps shrinking, until there's only a single moon left.

A head with a plastic bag over it, pupils dilating.

Beverly looks up and sees a stormfront.

Keith, do you remember? The hail that shattered all of the

lamps in the chrysanthemum field when you were a kid? The next day, we sat by the field and saw the shards. The next night, the land was dark. Black clouds menaced. A chilly wind scurried. Whooshing, it was issuing a warning, that something big was about to happen. How could we know that Mother would inform the police? At the time we didn't know a thing.

A cool breeze blows up all the trash, dust, and fallen leaves in front of the townhouse into a little tornado. Beverly points up at the clouds, as if to say: I think it's drizzling. Looking at her little brother and two younger sisters, she really wants to say something. Her mouth opens, her voice box vibrates. She doesn't want to hide the words inside.

"It looks like rain," she wants to say.

But she doesn't say a thing. There's a chasm in her body, into which all the words fall.

Whoosh. Such a chilly wind is unseasonable in high summer! The same wind blew when Nut disappeared, when the Tomorrow Bookstore ceased operation, when the hippo escaped, when I vanished, when Keith was subpoenaed, when Father died, when Mother died, when the townhouse burned, and when we heard Keith had killed a man in Germany.

Shush.

The wind comes and shushes the geckos and the termites, the frogs and the crickets, shutting every mouth in the town of Yongjing.

PART 3
DON'T CRY

31. The maze of palm prints

It looked like rain.

Heavy cloud had piled up into a thunderhead that rumbled in the Central Range to the east as night bore down on day. Weeding in the field, Cicada saw an earthworm wriggling out of the ground. "That's a sign of rain," her mother used to say. She poked at the worm with her sickle. Actually she didn't need to watch for worms. Her hair could forecast rain. It had a natural curl. Other girls had to try to get the wavy tresses that to her came effortlessly. On humid days, the waves would grow into angry swells, which Mother would take a comb to. But like a little ship on stormy seas, the comb soon sank into a sea of curls, which clogged the teeth or snapped them off. Mother would sigh. "What'll we do? Look at your hair! You're a bride to be who looks like a ghost. Thank Heaven the eldest son of the Chen family is honest, he won't back out, and the matchmaker is on our side. She compared the Eight Characters of your births, the signs under which you were born, and your ancestries, but thank Heaven she didn't tell the Chens that the ghost of the lady who hanged herself in the bamboo is from our family. Ignorance is bliss. Nobody will find out. Shush. If anyone told, who would dare to marry you? As a widow, I'm just glad someone is willing to marry my daughter."

Cicada was eighteen years old, and about to get married to the scion of the Chen clan, formerly the richest in the township.

After the Japanese left, the nationalist government came to Taiwan and instituted land reform. Many hectares of land were forcibly appropriated by the government for well under market value. The Chens were no longer big landlords. Mother drew an invisible map in the air. "It used to be," she said, "that all the land as far as the eye could see and beyond belonged to the Chens. It's tough for a girl to marry into a rich clan, especially when the groom is the eldest son. But now they're not big landlords anymore. That's why they don't mind their son marrying the eldest daughter of the late owner of a soy-sauce factory. Otherwise they'd never consider you. The matchmaker says he's tall and slim, with a symmetrical face and a high-bridged nose. He's a junior high school graduate, honest and quiet. He looks studious. What's not to like?"

She'd seen him twice. The next time they'd be married. She knew next to nothing about him. His name was Clifton Chen, and people called him Cliff. He wore high-rise suit pants and a starched white shirt. With a book in his hand, he didn't really look like a hick or a hillbilly. The second time they met, they had their picture taken. The photographer asked her to get a little closer. When she did she noticed his spidery fingers and manicured nails. She looked farther down and for the life of her she couldn't see any dirt on his toes. His feet looked soft and pale, without visible corns. He didn't talk much. But once she got close, she could smell his breath, which was fresh, without a hint of decay, and his body, which was faintly fragrant, though exactly what he smelled like she couldn't rightly say.

She had never met a man like this before. The hired help wore shabby clothes. Their armpits smelled like a dead hog, their breath like rotten meat. There was gunk and grime around their nails. Their teeth were like gravel, and their hair was like greasy iron wool.

A few drops of rain fell onto her forehead. She heard her

mother call her. The wind was blowing too hard for her to hear what she was saying, but she could guess: "Go take in the laundry, it's drying in the courtyard!" The ground was wriggling with earthworms now, and the air was thick with low-flying dragonflies and swallows. Wait a minute, those weren't swallows gamboling in the air, they were bats.

She knew how to catch bats and make a tasty soup. It was during her second meeting with Cliff that she told him about deep-frying cicada nymphs, which were easy to collect in the early morning right after they crawled out of the ground. They were scrumptious. Goggles told her.

Goggles wore thick-rimmed spectacles, but everything else about him was small and thin: eyes, nose, mouth, build. Hired as an apprentice mover, he was now in charge of selecting, transporting, and washing the soybeans. He was really keen. He could speak Japanese, Taiwanese, and Mandarin. Apparently, he could even speak English with American soldiers he met when he went up to Taichung to visit the wholesaler. She had grown up with him. And actually, she'd learned everything she knew about the making of soy sauce, and a whole lot else besides, from him.

More raindrops now. The harder the rain fell, the louder Mother yelled. Cicada lay the sickle down and ran into the courtyard to take the laundry in.

But the clothes, sheets, and pillowcases that should have been hanging on the bamboo poles were nowhere to be seen. The pouring rain clattered on the roof of the soy-sauce factory, burying her mother's voice. She did not bother listening, she knew what Mother must be saying. Move your ass, you sluggard! How are you going to be the daughter-in-law in charge of a big three-wing compound if you keep slacking off!

She rushed soaking wet into the house, where echoes of her mother's shrieks in the factory finally struck her eardrums. Suddenly a pair of hands reached out to offer her a towel.

Goggles' hands were a world away from Cliff's. Cliff's were pale and soft, while Goggles' were dark and callused. Mother'd taught her to read palms and faces, to judge Heaven and measure Earth, to reconstruct the past and infer the future. A banana tree's health is in its leaves, a person's life is in his palms. Illiterate Cicada could make her way in a small town like Yongjing with skills like this, especially with her tack-sharp memory. She couldn't read the scripture in the temple, or understand it, but she could commit it to memory on one hearing.

She had not had the opportunity to read her future husband's palms, but she often studied Goggles'. They were really complicated, a chaos of starts and stops, a mess of intersections. It was hard to apply Mother's teaching to those palms. She couldn't read the length of his life or what was waiting for him further down the line.

She always read his palms looking down. She didn't dare to look up, because she knew that he would be looking intently at her. As the soybeans in the vats silently fermented, she grasped his hands and fell into a maze of palm prints. She read and read, murmuring the whole time. She was always talking. Goggles liked to listen.

After she got married, she would not be able to read his palms anymore.

She took the towel and dried her tangled hair. Her mother told her they would go to the beauty salon in Yuanlin to get it straightened before the wedding. On the table sat a stack of clothes that had been hung out on the bamboo pole, all sorted and neatly folded. Goggles was always one step ahead of her, and not just today. He was the first to finish the accounts, and the first to figure out when a vat had finished fermenting, when it was going to rain, and when the cicada nymphs would crawl out of the ground. She told him she was getting married. He didn't say a thing. She thought maybe she had said too much. She didn't need to say it. He already knew.

The pouring rain was a herd of wild horses running circles around them. "Congratulations, Saucy!" he said, smiling. "I'm quitting."

He gave her another towel for her to wipe her body with. Once she was dry, he left. That was the last she saw of Goggles.

She stood in front of the mirror and examined her rain-bombarded hair. When the Japanese were still in control of Taiwan, the air-raid sirens rang and an American bomb tumbled out of the sky, leaving a gaping hole in the ground. When he said that he was quitting, she heard another siren. How would she tell Mother? About the hole in her body. She knew what she would say. "Shush! Don't say anything. If you don't tell, nobody will know. Ignorance is bliss."

The next day she and her mother rode bicycles to Yuanlin to get their hair done. When they passed the bamboo grove, Mother looked left and right to make certain there was nobody there. Then she faced the grove, put her palms together, and prayed.

"Shush," Mother said, "you can't tell anyone, no matter what. The lady ghost in the bamboo grove is your grand-mother. My mother."

32. I'm just here to practice my routine

The townhouse was too damn hot. The unconditioned air was thick and turbid, like a flammable gas. A single spark would turn everything to ash. In the jail in Berlin, Keith often had a vision of gas making a shady deal with fire, then exploding and burning. Walls would fall, iron fences would melt, and paper would combust. Fierce flames would run wild. When the blaze burnt out, and nothing was left but ash, wind and rain should come and consign it to nothingness. But tonight the wind was late, and though thunder sounded distantly, the rain kept standing Yongjing up.

When Sam said that he should be going, Beverly asked him to stay. "You bought too much fried chicken for us to finish by ourselves. If you don't help eat, it'll only go to waste."

She dragged the big round table onto the porch so everyone could sit down and eat fried chicken outside, where there was at least a bit of a breeze. The chicken fillets had been dipped in flour, deep fried, and sprinkled with plum and cayenne powder. The skin was crispy, the meat tender and juicy. With the first hot and spicy bite, your scalp would flush and your nose would run. Keith hadn't had it in years. It tasted so good it awakened his appetite. He took big bites and looked around to see that everyone else was too busy doing the same to talk, until Beverly broke the silence with a few pleasantries for Sam. Betty and Belinda followed suit. Sam replied politely. Of course they had an objective in keeping him. If there was an outsider at the table, each could play the gracious hostess to the hilt. They kept taking wild free throws, missing on purpose. Nobody wanted to hit the basket. It was for the best that those balls did not go in. The social niceties were hollow but harmless. They could talk about the weather, the sunrise and the sunset, the falling leaves, the wind, the rain, the full moon, ghosts, and fried chicken. They could say thank you and don't mention it, as long as they didn't have to have a heart-to-heart. Indeed, politeness was a means of keeping one another at a distance, or pushing one another away. Nobody could pull in to shore, good manners left them all adrift. Afraid of isolation, they spit out speech, liquid language that solidified like the threads that spiders spin in air. Like wandering islands, they'd clearly lost touch, but they could still hear each other calling out, and at least they still had these threads of civility to keep them connected. But they would absolutely never ask, "How are you?" They were family, after all. They knew each other too well. They knew they were all ashes and dust, waiting for the wind to come and blow them away. They wouldn't ask anything so hurtful.

"That lady at the fried chicken stand looked so familiar," said Betty.

"You must have seen her before," said Sam. "She used to do striptease. Everyone in her family did, her grandmother, mother, and aunt. But now anyone can watch a striptease on a mobile phone any time they want. Business got so bad she switched to selling fried chicken. She used to be Keith's classmate."

Betty remembered seeing her doing a striptease at a temple fair.

Of course Keith remembered his classmate the stripper. He saw her at the Lady at the Foot of the Wall, at weddings, and at funerals, dancing that dance. On auspicious days of the traditional farming calendar, she'd do a lot of shows in a single day, rushing around to the different venues. With no time to write her homework, she always copied his. Assigned a composition, he wrote his own with his right hand and hers with his left, with a different tone and idiom. The teacher never noticed. He kept on doing her homework for her in the grazing water buffalo class in the first term of junior high. It was absurd in retrospect. Weren't they living in a conservative town? How could folks let a little girl take off all of her clothes at marriages, funerals, and other events? He'd watched her body changing on stage over the years, bathed in rippling rainbow light. Her chest gradually swelled, hair started growing in her groin and armpits. By the time he switched out of that class, her breasts had risen up into lofty mountains.

After school that day, the day Keith tried to slip Sam a note, the teacher cornered him under the bishopwood tree. The teacher's scorching palms left red welts on his cheeks. "You pervert! Homo! I went to your house to warn you to stay away from my son. But I guess you just don't listen, or you don't want to? Whichever it is, I bet I can make you."

The two enforcers she'd brought with her kneed him in the

gut. One of them prodded his butt with the mouth of a Fragrant soy-sauce bottle.

"Does it feel good? Want another poke in the ass?" When he tried to break free, the bottle fell to the ground and shattered. One of the boys picked up a shard and closed in on his face. He saw his elder brother Heath, but Heath took off.

"Hello Teacher!"

It was his classmate the stripper girl. She leaned her bicycle against the trunk and greeted the teacher with a dazzling smile.

"I hope you don't mind, I've come here to pray and practice. A few days from now my family has a gig here. I hear someone won big at the gambling table and has come back to show his gratitude."

Her face coloring, the teacher roared, "Who the hell are you? What year are you in? What class? Scram! I'm disciplining one of my own students. If you tell anyone you're dead meat!"

"Don't worry, Teacher, I didn't see a thing. I'm just here to practice my routine. Just pretend I'm not here."

She flung her bookbag on the ground and started to hum the tune to Lîm Kiông's hit Taiwanese song, "Marching Forward," "The train is underway, I'll see you all again someday. Mom and Dad, this ain't the end. So long, farewell, all my dear friends." She shook her booty as she stripped off her uniform under the bishopwood tree.

The dumbfounded boys relaxed their hold on Keith, who raced into the banana field behind the tree while he had the chance. He ran and ran and ran, past the ditch, the slough, the rice paddy, the pool, and the carambola orchard. He knew he couldn't stop, and must never look back, there was a ghost on his tail. Mother had told him if he ever saw a ghost he must run and run and run, until he left it in his dust. He ran to the station hoping to catch the next train, so he could escape this hellhole, never to return, but he knew the train would never come, and he had nowhere else to run. He collapsed sobbing by the side of the road, moments before a station wagon came racing by. The driver slammed on the brakes and rolled down the window. It was the snake killer. The stripper girl was in the passenger seat. She scrambled out of the car and took him in her arms.

At the sight of Keith all bruised up and unable to stand, the snake killer bundled him into the wagon and drove him to a big hospital in Changhua City. Keith remembered how fast his neighbor drove, going well over the speed limit and running every red light. He looked back and saw Yongjing receding in the distance. Clasping his hand, his classmate sang songs and told jokes. He looked back again and noticed a cage in the back, with several big snakes inside. Probably carsick, one of them spit out a plump frog. It was still alive. It shook itself and leaped around.

The emergency doctor said he had a broken rib and needed to be hospitalized. By the time he was discharged, everything had changed. The White House was built, with a fountain of Apollo in the garden. Before he left, Plenty was getting married to Baron Wang, now Barbie would be the bride. He went back to school, but the teacher was new. Sam had transferred to another school instead of him. He rode his bike to Sam's house, but it was empty, with a "For Sale" sign on the door. The stripper had gotten knocked up. She was out of school, but still dancing. "My mother says I can perform for about three more months before my tummy gets too big. I have to save some money. It's expensive to raise a child."

Sam swallowed the last bite of his spicy fried chicken and a gulp of ice water. "She's a grandmother now," he said. "She has a bunch of kids and another bunch of grandkids."

T, you remember my classmate the stripper, don't you?

Having moved into the little flat that smelled of candy, he and T soon struggled to make ends meet. He had transferred all of his Taiwan savings into his German account, but after paying a year's rent up front, the account was empty. He and T registered as a couple, and with the new sticker, a German residence permit, in his passport, he could get a job. But what could he do? His phobia of crowds made it hard to go out and work, and he couldn't even speak German. Maybe he should try learning German? He took a class but all the students were Scandinavian kids, carefree and cheerful. Their laughter was limpid, without impurities. They made plans to go clubbing on the weekend. He felt he would contaminate them with his company. When he forced himself to laugh along, rainclouds floated into the sunny classroom. But without German, what job could he do to support himself? He found the pressure hard to bear. It was as if a pair of spiny cacti had taken root in his shoulders. Any move and his muscles would explode in pain. When an invitation came in from Taiwan for any kind of writing, he accepted it immediately. But the manuscript fees would never pay the rent, and his books didn't sell that many copies. In tough times writing is not a skill that you can live on.

Don't worry, T said, he would stop going out in search of lone gloves or to play the cello. He would get a job. He would find ways to make money.

The first way was handmade, and homemade, clay animals: seals, trouts, Kiel herrings, eels, all animals that lived in the Baltic Sea. The figurines were palm-sized, a staid grayish brown, but delightful. The scales on the fish were finely done. T made a big batch in the living room, put them in his backpack, and went out to sell them. It wasn't worth renting a stall in the market, and he'd have to give his friend a cut if he put them on consignment. The easiest way to generate cash was by acting.

By acting? In a play?

T made a stack of little cards, on which he wrote the same

message. Keith tried to translate it with the dictionary, and though he couldn't parse all of the sentences, he figured out the gist: "I am deaf and dumb and out of work. I made these myself, ten euros apiece. Thank you for your support."

T headed out with a full backpack to catch the RE. The Regional-Express was a commuter train, with tables for passengers to work at. As soon as he got on, he put a figurine and a card on every table. When he was done, he would go table to table inquiring with his deep blue eyes to see if any passengers were willing to buy. The deaf and dumb sketch worked. He could sell a dozen a day. The most popular animal was a goofy seal.

Then T got a job posting stickers. An advertising company gave him a bag. All he had to do was ride around on his bike and post the stickers up along busy Berlin streets. He stuck them to transformers, fences, lamp posts, utility poles, leaving no space uncovered. By the stickers that he was hired to post he would put his own design, with a submarine and a hand flipping the bird.

T took the dog out and hunkered down by a bank machine with a sign around its neck that said: *Ich habe Hunger*. I'm hungry. By the end of the day, the hat was full of pocket change.

T also found a part-time job as a cashier in a fast-food restaurant. If a customer paid the exact amount in cash, T wouldn't enter the order in the register, he'd just pocket the money. There was so much traffic in the restaurant that nobody noticed his sleight of hand.

In the evening he worked as a waiter at a strip club. One evening a film company rented the venue out for a shoot. They needed extras. T signed himself up and signed Keith up as well. At the thought that he could see a film production at the place where T worked, and make a bit of money at the same time, Keith decided to go through with it.

It was an episode in a crime series. An undercover cop was trying to get close to a stripper under the glaring lights. He and T sat at the same table watching the striptease with rapt expressions. Under the table they were holding hands.

After the production wrapped and they'd signed the remuneration forms, Keith noticed a little submarine sticker on a few of the cameras, tripods, and lights.

They left the club at dawn. It was nippy in the early summer morning. T took his jacket off and handed it to him. All he had on underneath was a vest undershirt. T was thinner now, his cheekbones and jawline more sharply defined. Instead of taking the bus, they decided to walk all the way home, hand in hand. On the way he told T about the stripper he went to elementary school with.

T lost it when he heard about the teacher. "She doesn't have the right to be a teacher!" he yelled angrily in the empty street. He continued with a string of harsh, but reverberant, imprecations. Keith enjoyed trying to swear in German. The words scraped the throat and scrubbed tooth and tongue. He liked hearing them, too. Abrasive as coarse-grit sandpaper, they ground away some of the encrusted grime of the past.

Walking down those deserted streets, he felt for the first time that the language barrier had been dismantled. T understood everything he said in English. He understood everything T said in English, with a lot of German words mixed in.

The cello was fun to play, and they wouldn't have met without it, but T couldn't make much money with it. The rent hot on their heels, they packed the cello up. They didn't go looking for lone gloves. They had no time to pick bearleeks in the woods.

The two of them spent several years in bohemian poverty. When money was really short, T signed up for a hair show. He let a stylist show off his chops, and collected his blond hair to sell to a wig shop. "Don't worry!" T said. "We still have a cello to sell."

There were cacti weighing on T's shoulder, too.

Keith went through a naturalization process, gave up his Taiwanese passport, and got a German passport. T said it was so nice that he could stay.

He found a job, too, as a waiter in a Taiwanese eatery. Now that both of them had an income, their lives had a bit more stability. They bought an old car off a friend. Finally they had some savings. T suggested another trip home.

So they drove back to the Baltic Sea and stayed at T's friend's place. They drank wine, ate fish, went swimming, and licked ice-cream cones on the beach. T's old house was just up the way, but he never looked in that direction, not even when they passed by. He didn't mention his father or mother. His friend took their picture in front of the U-boat. Having just smoked a joint, T was laughing really loud. He kept on hugging and kissing him. T's friend was laughing and smoking, too. She took off her bikini and sunbathed in the nude. Back in the day, T said he wanted to take the train to Berlin and never come back. He asked her to go with him. "Thank goodness I didn't, or I only would have realized he was gay after we got there. Ha ha ha!"

Thinking back now, he wondered if there was a clear point in time when he and T started to fall apart.

On the way back to Berlin they took turns driving, but they weren't speaking. When they were almost in Berlin, T began to cry.

Back in the flat, they had a few days of hot and muggy weather. The wind smeared their skin with sticky strawberry pralines from the candy factory. Things seemed the same. But he had a hunch that something wasn't right, something was broken. He sneezed unwrapping a caramel. He crumbled a cork into a bottle of wine. A plate struggled free of his hands and fled to the floor. He saw blood trimming his fingernails. Boiling hot water suddenly sprayed out of the shower head. T held him close at night.

T would sob in his sleep, with his elbow hooked around his neck, stifling him. He found smooth pills in T's pocket.

Riding the RE train to sell a batch of open-mouthed, roly-poly hippos, T had a run in with a gang of dark-skinned drunks. They got into a fight, the figurines were thrown on the floor. T returned home with bruises all over his face, cuts on his arms, and a broken toe. "Fucking foreigners!" he kept muttering.

The fast-food restaurant caught T stealing and summarily fired him. The strip club went out of business.

The black dog got sick. Several days later it died.

The only job T had left was posting stickers. When he went to collect the stickers one time, he was asked if he wanted to join. The organization was trying to attract young Germans like him. All they had available was a gofer job, and the pay wasn't great, but if it worked out a full-time position might come up.

T joined.

His style changed dramatically. He no longer clothed himself in night. Fashionable threads appeared in his wardrobe. He got a slick hairdo.

Keith discovered numerical combinations in the stickers that T was posting. Soon a pair of small tattoos appeared on his upper arms, 18 on the right and 44 on the left.

33. Damn needles of rain

When she gave birth to her fourth daughter, Cicada was twenty-five years old.

Pain. The previous three daughters had been born on rainy days. It started to rain that day when the midwife arrived at the three-wing compound to deliver her fourth. In between screams, Cicada shook her fists at the sky and cursed the weather. Lying in bed, she watched the rain, imagining each drop as a needle cast down from Heaven, aimed right at her groin and ass. The raindrops were needles, not arrows. Arrows would pierce her skin and split her organs, killing her. But these damn raindrops were needles that would keep pricking her without doing her in. It was slow torture.

Another girl. The midwife handed the fourth daughter to her and went to tell her mother-in-law, who was waiting outside the door. Mother-in-Law just put on her *geta* clogs and went shopping. The *geta* clattered crisply across the courtyard. Cicada lay in bed feeling like she was the ground that her mother-in-law had just walked across, leaving her with broken bones and pitted skin.

"It hurts like hell, Mom!" Every time she gave birth, she would think of her mother. But her mother wasn't there, nor was her husband Cliff. There was just her and her fourth daughter.

Her mother had told her a lot of stories about pain. They were both illiterate, but great talkers. Their voice boxes never stopped vibrating, their mouths spitting out a high volume of language that echoed around the factory. The walls had absorbed their ceaseless chatter for years on end. When the workers took bristly brushes to the walls to scrub away the grime for spring cleaning, the residues of all their conversations fell off into their ears.

Mother said labor pain wasn't pain at all. "When I gave birth to you, of course it hurt," she said. "But compared with other kinds of pain, giving birth is nothing."

When Cicada's mother was a girl, *her* mother got gang-raped in the bamboo grove. A farmer found her naked, pressed beneath a man while another waited. The farmer chased those men away with a hoe, wrapped her in a rice sack, and took her home. But her husband's family would not let her in. They told her to go home. "I want to die," she told her young daughter. "I'm going to go hang myself in the bamboo. Don't tell today," she said. "Tell them where they can find me tomorrow." The daughter did as she was told, and went along the next day. She saw a thin body hanging from a thick stalk of bamboo. As the bamboo started to sway in a gust of wind, so did her mother's corpse. The bamboo made a very strange sound, like someone was scraping it with a knife. It had a rhythm, like a song. The wind beat at the bamboo leaves, like another song—like singing and weeping. She sat listening to the songs, while the keen wind split all the bamboo in the grove and sharpened the ends into points to gouge her with. That was pain.

Another story. For a firewalk ceremony at a temple fair, a thick layer of black sand was spread out in the square, with spirit money on the sand. Barefoot men lined up, each holding a statue of the deity and waiting for the right time. They were all men, both elders and teenage boys. Women were not allowed to firewalk. The fire was lit, and the men raced one by one over the piles of burning paper. One man hesitated, but when an elder cursed him, he hurried into the fire, only to trip and fall and drop his statue, which rolled into the flame. Everyone was aghast. "Save the god!" they yelled. Nobody was going to save that man. So Cicada's mother rushed in to pull him out. "Cicada, oh Cicada, let me tell you, they cursed me for that, for breaking the prohibition, for contempt of the court of Heaven. But Cicada, that man was your father. Who else would have saved him? You don't remember him, do you? All of his skin was burnt. He wailed for several days at home before giving up the ghost. His eyes were open when he died. I tried to close them but they wouldn't. A temple elder said I had angered the spirits by stepping into the fire, that I was to blame for your father's death. Actually I, too, wanted to wail: woe is me. The soles of my feet were badly burned, but death did not put me out of my misery. Do you know how painful it was? My feet still hurt to this day. I imagine they will keep hurting after I, too, give up the ghost."

Holding her bawling fourth daughter to her bosom, Cicada was seething. "I'm the one who's in pain, not you!" she said. "What are you crying for!" She could have tossed the infant outside in the rain.

Cicada was too tired to sleep. She was so hungry, for a bowl of white rice topped with lard and soy sauce and a piece of fatty pork belly, but she couldn't eat a thing. She wanted to speak but her mouth was dry. All the things she wanted to say filled her chest until curses spilled out. She cursed her newborn for crying. She cursed Cliff for not making enough as a farmhand to support a family. She hit her daughters. Soon they all looked afraid of her.

When Cliff heard it was another daughter, he sat on the edge of the bed and took the baby in his arms. "Don't cry," he said, avoiding Cicada's gaze. "That's a good girl. The next one'll be a baby brother."

But Cicada had a premonition that the fifth child would be born in another rain shower.

Only after marrying into the family did she realize that the Chens, once a rich land-owning clan, were not only broke, they were also deeply in debt, because although all their land had been appropriated, her mother-in-law maintained the same style of life as before. She bought Japanese pearl necklaces, pure gold earrings, jade bracelets, and silver hair clips for herself and the most expensive fruits and the fattest pigs to offer to the ancestors and the goodfellas.

As the wife of the eldest son, Cicada was responsible for sweeping up the spirit hall, honoring the ancestors, performing rituals at all sorts of festivals, and cooking three square meals a day for her mother-in-law. The daughters-in-law used to take turns, until the mother announced that the two daughters who'd given birth to sons didn't have to. So that task fell to her alone, to the daughter-in-law who could only give birth to girls.

It was only when they didn't have money for groceries that

Cliff went out into the fields to work. Cicada went home to borrow money from her mother. Her mother stuffed a wad in her hands, but she could only give her so much. She needed money to keep her own household running and get Cicada's younger brothers married. Studious Cliff spent all his spare time reading and teaching his daughters to read and write. But what good would that do? Cicada tossed out the few books on his shelf. She had no use for them. Could you support a family with a book? Could you plant rice in a book? Could you feed pigs with a book? If you threw them one, would they even eat?

She cried into a blanket that was too thin to stifle her sobs, which her mother-in-law heard through the wall. "There she goes again!" she yelled. "She's crazy! The damn matchmaker didn't mention that the lady who hanged herself in the bamboo was her grandmother. Must be inherited. Madness breeds madness."

When Cicada was honoring the ancestors, the incense suddenly flared up. "There it goes again!" Mother-in-Law screamed. A fire in the burner meant the ancestors were displeased.

Cicada stood there spellbound. Holding a child in one hand she reached toward the burner with the other. It was strangely thrilling when she pinched the flame.

If her mother-in-law hadn't run over and left red-hot slaps on her cheek, she would have let the flame swallow her fingers whole. Without fingers, she wouldn't have to hold incense, cook, feed the pigs and the chickens, sweep the floors, or weed the fields. She wouldn't have to hit the kids. Or hold them.

34. To a man

When Sam stood up to go, Beverly, Betty, Belinda, and Keith all panicked. What were they going to do? If Sam left, there wouldn't be an outsider to exchange banalities or beat around the bush with. They would have to face one another. But the pig trotter *mī-suànn* and the fried chicken had run out, as had their polite formulas. They had no reason to keep their guest.

Keith saw Sam out. The sky cleared, the wind died. It was humid and hot, yet another starry summer night.

"How'd you meet Beverly?"

"At the pool. She used to work there. She'd sweep up, deep-fry hot dogs, and scoop ice cream. After I moved home, I went swimming there almost every day. I'd buy an ice cream. There were two or three cool cats around the pool, if that. Nobody else patronized her stand. I guess I struck up a conversation out of boredom. And while we were chatting, I realized she was my junior high school classmate's elder sister."

Moonlight sprinkled gold dust on his dark skin. His facial muscles turned lines to furrows and back to lines. Crumbs of fried chicken clung to the corners of his mouth, and bits of pork and noodles lodged between his teeth. A sun hung in his forehead, a moon in his smile lines, and stars in his crow's feet. As they talked and laughed, there were stars and raindrops, there was day and night. There was an oily sheen on his lips, and ample moisture in his sweaty nose. His face was fertile, like an untilled field. The worm-turned soil was rich, the vegetation rank. The seasons cycled comfortably. Keith imagined that his own face must be worn out, a wasteland on which not an inch of grass grew. The lines on his face must contain the grime of years, so he didn't dare smile. Smiling would activate his facial muscles, put pressure on his wrinkles, and squeeze out too much agony.

"Do you want me to take you to the fried chicken stand to say hello to your old classmate?"

Keith thought it over and shook his head. His three elder sisters were waiting for him at home. He had to face them.

"Sorry Sam, for keeping you so long."

"Don't be silly, I was hungry. There was fried chicken to eat!"

"Thank you. What a funny coincidence that I met you at the soy-sauce factory today!"

"No need to thank me, old friend. I'm always here. I live at my old house."

At the thought of that house, Keith felt a pair of sweaty hands at his throat, and a soy-sauce bottle jabbing his rear end.

Noting the change in Keith's expression, Sam said, "Don't worry, my mother is long gone. My whole family emigrated to Canada. I'm the only one who came back. When I told her she was pretty pissed. The angrier she got the more of a sense of achievement I felt. Oh, here I go again. I caught the bug from Beverly, I just talk and talk. It's annoying, isn't it?"

Keith shook his head. "Don't stop, Sam. Listening to you I don't feel so sleepy. Otherwise I could lie down right here. Tell me more." Keith's gut turned over as it ground up the fried chicken into a thick stew of sleep. Hot and spicy, it sloshed around in his body.

So Sam said more.

He started with "Sorry." Back in junior high school, his mother suddenly announced they were moving. He had to switch schools immediately. He had no idea what had happened. A few years ago he finally heard from Beverly what his mother had done.

Growing up, he did whatever his mother said. He tested his way into the top high school in Taiwan, and then the top university major. After his elder brother got a Ph.D. at UBC, the whole family emigrated to Canada. Sam went to graduate school in Vancouver, too. He met a girl there, his doctoral classmate. They did research in the forest, observing owls from a bird blind. He told his mother that he was getting married. Mother took one look at the girl and said her skin was too dark, she wouldn't allow it. Sam didn't dare translate what his mother had just said into English. So, after a pointed glance at her son, she looked the girl in the eyes and said it herself. And then she switched back into Mandarin. "I let you take a graduate degree that wouldn't open up any job opportunities, and now you bring this kind home."

"This kind?"

Sam's elder brother could tell the time had come to announce that he was getting married, too. To a man.

"Imagine her expression! It was hilarious! I finally realized I felt the happiest when my mother looked like she was going to lose it. I wasn't that happy when I got my Ph.D."

"So . . . what about your wife?"

"We got a divorce." His face was still a fertile ground. His nose and eyes were healthy trees, unburdened with weeds. "It didn't work out. We never fought, we stuck it out for years, but it was exhausting. We talked it over for a long time. I guess I got to know myself at long last, through those conversations, through her. All those years, I was just a mama's boy. I was in such a rush to get married, just to spite her, not because I'd thought it through, let alone because I knew what I wanted to do. Was that really necessary? As for my mom, it was enough for her to have my brother there to piss her off, especially because he and his partner were so happy together."

Keith wondered whether he had gotten to know himself through T.

"I saw one of your short-story collections in a Chinese bookstore," Sam continued. "The author's name looked so familiar. I picked it up and it really was you. There was a story about my mother, right? That psychotic teacher who clobbers the students with a rattan cane, that was her, wasn't it? It all came back to me. Strange, I had forgotten Yongjing. When I read it, I decided to leave, to move back here. The day we signed the divorce papers, my ex-wife and I went for a walk in the zoo. I watched a hippo open its mouth to let the zookeeper brush its teeth. That brought something back, too. Soon after we moved away, my brother and I snuck out when my parents weren't home and took the train back to Yongjing. Walking around, we saw a hippo by the road. It had fallen over in a rice paddy. Its mouth was hanging wide open. Such an absurd sight, and I had forgotten it. When you think about it, it's ludicrous: a hippo in Yongjing! How was it possible? Or am I misremembering?"

Keith couldn't help smiling. Yes, it was absurd: a drunk hippo wandered down Main Street and ended up passed out in a field by the side of the road.

He'd told T the story. That's why he made that last batch of hippo figurines. To T, it was a tragedy. He'd never seen a drunk hippo; the only kind he knew how to make was a cute one. Trampled on the RE train, those hippos tallied with Keith's memory of the one in Yongjing.

"We spent the whole day in the zoo. When we said goodbye she cried. But those weren't tears of sadness. I understood that she was saying thank you."

Keith felt like he, too, understood. He'd seen the same expression of gratitude, on T's face. When he stabbed T, T did not yell out in pain, he smiled. His smile was appreciative. T did not even yell out in pain when he pulled the knife out. T rushed at him and punched him with his bloody fists. The knife entered T's body again in the next scuffle.

"Go, now!" T said.

Later on, during the police interrogation, his mind was a thick fog. Pills T'd fed him were having an orgy in his body. He'd been tied up for a long time, denied food and water. He was almost asphyxiated. T's fists left dark clouds on his skin. T sliced off a rectangular strip of skin from his arm with a razor. Maybe because of all the medication, he felt no pain. When he saw T holding that flap of his skin, he thought of Plenty.

Before she died, she announced she wanted to "perform" for him. She picked up the utility knife on her desk and cut her wrist. Blood flooded out. "Don't tell anyone," Plenty said. "It doesn't hurt at all." She had iodine and gauze ready to disinfect and wrap herself up with. "When the scar forms, I'll cut it open again." He remembered her smiling. She looked so happy.

Sam said he was raising bats in the back yard. When he moved home, a lot of the critters he had grown up chasing were gone. There were no yellow butterflies or bats that he could see, and far fewer snakes and frogs. The cicadas droned feebly in summer. A lot of trees that once provided habitat for bats had been cut down, all to clear the ground for the White House. Sam wanted to restore the bat population. He'd done his homework and was raising a few bats in his back yard as a pilot project.

"Remember to look me up sometime. Come see my bats."

Sam drove off into the night, leaving behind whirlpools of dust that invaded his eyes. He closed them and rubbed them.

Then he opened them again. The sampan had passed. And all that was left was the gleam of a full moon.

35. Japanese vitamins

Is it good to be a ghost? I say it's great.

I was so dry when I was alive. My skin was a desert. My nails were stones, my tresses dried vines. Now I can snuggle in the moss. I can relax on the leaky walls in the old house and roll around in the moist dirt. It's the comfiest after a summer rain, when soil and water mix together into the sweetest mud. I don't know whether there's a place anyone goes to after death called Heaven, but to me that mud is Heaven.

It's just that it seems like forever since it last rained in this ghost town.

I was a precocious girl. My breasts swelled rapidly. One day I left the house in the morning and my uniform shirt still fit but the moment I got off school the seams split, shooting the buttons like bullets at a couple of boys who were always staring at my tits. From that time on, the boys forgot that my name was Ciao, they started calling me Plenty. There was plenty to look at and hold on to. The nickname Plenty spread through the school. It went over the walls and sped down streets and lanes. In the end everyone in my family was calling me that. My breasts grew bigger and bigger, until I couldn't find my size in a bra. Mother took me to get one custom-made in Yuanlin.

Barbie was so envious. She didn't need to say it, I always knew. We ate the same things every day, we did all the same activities. We went to the same elementary and junior high, we drank the same water. We went to bed at the same time and got up at the same time. Why was I so full, and she so flat?

I liked my nickname. I liked the look on people's faces when they looked at me. The packers and movers who worked for my dad stared at my boobs and stood up down there. When I got bad marks at school and held out my hand for the teacher to hit, it didn't matter whether the teacher was a man or a woman, as long as I arched my back and occupied the teacher's gaze with my chest, their arms would suddenly go soft, and the cane would fall lightly on my palms. The neighbor asked Mother what tonics she was feeding me, why was I looking so good? Matchmakers came to the door to arrange engagements several years in advance, saying there were a lot of respectable families who were willing to wait. A lot of upstanding young men wanted to marry me.

The neighbor's eldest son Junior—as I mentioned, I called him Junior—came over to discuss a business proposition. He said my tits were the talk of the town. All the girls wanted to be me. He wanted me to tell people it was because I took a certain brand of Japanese multivitamin. He would be responsible for sourcing and selling it. Who cared what was in it, as long as it didn't kill you and had a Japanese label. He proposed a sixty-forty split. He would handle everything else, all I had to do was say I took those Japanese vitamins. I said sixty-forty suited me just fine, but it would be sixty for me, forty for him. He said it wasn't worth it, why didn't we just forget it then. I said he could feel my tits, ten seconds a side. Then we'd split it sixty-forty. Sixty for me, forty for him.

Ten seconds for the left side. I counted down slowly.

Ten seconds for the right side. I counted down quicker and batted his hand away.

"Oh, you're good," he said, satisfied. "Your dad sure isn't as good a negotiator as you. He's a total pushover, letting himself get ordered around and manipulated by my dad like a fool."

When I went with Mother to get groceries, I told the pork-peddler lady that I took those Japanese vitamins. When I went to the Lady at the Foot of the Wall to pray, I told the keeper I took the Japanese vitamins that my mother bought. That's how I filled out like this. When I went to school, I told my girl class-mates that I was pretty big after the first bottle, who knew I would get *this* big if I kept taking it. "It's such a pain," I said. "They're so big that I can't get a regular bra that fits me. I had to go to Yuanlin to get one made. It's expensive! The auntie who measured me said she had never seen boobs this big."

Sales were stupendous. Junior kept on ordering new stock. I saw "Japanese" vitamins on the desk in Barbie's room. I told her it was all a lie. "Those vitamins are useless, don't waste your money." That's what I said. She got angry and said it wasn't fair. Mother'd only bought them for me and hadn't let her take any at all. Now it was too late. She told me to go to hell. She said I'd been taking those vitamins all along without telling her. It was bad enough to be a daughter. It was even worse to get betrayed by one's own sister.

I was angry, too. "Take them then," I said. "Maybe ten bottles will do the trick."

So I made some money with Junior. Mother seldom gave us girls an allowance. No problem, I had Junior. He could make money like nobody's business. He knew what would sell. By going into business with him, I wouldn't have to ask my parents for money.

Junior and I got a bottle of French champagne to celebrate the success of the vitamin venture. As if we understood how to drink it. We snuck up to the roof not even knowing how to pop the cork. By the time we finally got it open it had warmed up in the hot sun. Did we care? When the fizzy yellow water slid down our throats it was sweet. It tasted pretty good. When we finished I was dizzy. "We're just getting started," Junior said. "When we make it really big, I'm going to take you to Paris, and all over France."

Junior was drunk. "Did your family ever buy an air gun?" he asked.

That talk of burglars running amuck in Yongjing, killing and raping, that was all bogus. It was a rumor that Junior and his father spread. It was easy to spread a rumor in a small town. You make up a couple of stories. Bribe a few families. Slip the police red envelopes. Create some disturbances in the night. When everyone in Yongjing was scared to death, Wang Senior started taking orders for air guns. "If a burglar comes in the door, just stand your ground, aim, and shoot. That's how to subdue the bad guy and keep your family safe." That was the pitch, and it worked. His dad made a pisspot full. That's where they got the money to buy a townhouse.

As we drank, Junior said he wanted to do it with me. I said no way. He had to marry me first. I wasn't that dumb.

He said he couldn't wait. Staring at my breasts, he got really big and hard down there. He had to shoot or he'd explode. He said when they were selling the air guns he'd often go off with his father and help make a commotion. He'd just hit puberty. Running around in the evening feeling horny, he thought of a trick. He'd walk up to a three-wing compound, shine a flashlight in the window, and wait for a girl to appear. If one did, he'd stay and wank in front of her until he shot his load on the glass. There were no streetlamps at all in Yongjing in those days. It was so dark at night that nobody could see his face.

"Please, Plenty, do it with me. There's nobody on the roof, nobody will see."

"You go make it rich and build a house for me. Take me to Paris. Then I'll do it with you. Every day. Any time." At the time Dad was going on business trips to China with Wang Senior. The two shores, the Nationalists and the Communists, started allowing people to cross the Strait to visit family in '87. Two years later, Wang Senior and Dad went over to prospect the market on that pretext. In June that year, there was a big disturbance in Beijing. Father said no way, no way he was staying, it was too scary. He fled home to Taiwan. The whole of Beijing was a silver water cistern, he didn't dare go back. From then on, Wang Senior only took Junior along to sign contracts and build factories. Not long after that the Wangs came back saying that everyone else had pulled out of the market, now was the perfect time for them to get in. They'd made the right arrangements and pulled the right strings. Any crisis was a commercial opportunity. They were going to get filthy rich.

The Wangs didn't actually get their start selling crackers, they brought out cookies first. The packaging was covered in Japanese. "Chinese people have it tough," Wang Senior said. "They look hungry. Like they don't get enough to eat. So we'll sell them sweet. They'll eat sweet and forget how bitter their lives have been. With food in their bellies, they'll forget their cares, and we'll clean up." Wasn't it a bad idea to sell Chinese crackers made to look like Japanese imports? "Of course they say they're anti-Japanese," Wang Senior said. "But every last one of them feels a secret admiration for all that Japan has achieved. Eating Japanese is being Japanese. Everyone's going to buy them."

So many cookies sold they had to expand the factory. Having scored with sweet, they tried their hand at salty. "Nutritious and sanitary, White House Crackers are perfect for any kind of spirit offering. When adults eat them, they can't go wrong. When children eat them, they'll grow up strong."

After making it big in China, they made a killing on the Taiwan Stock Exchange. In the late '80s the index took off. By the early '90s it hit ten thousand. Wang Senior imported German sedans for his two sons.

"Nut was a dumbass," Junior said. "Whatever his dream was, he was dumb. What good did going to university do him? He died so young. Look at me, I'm living high on the hog. I've made a shitload. Have you seen that book, the biography of my little brother? The author made a hell of lot of money off his death. Did Nut make even a single penny off his life? Moron. I'll break their legs before I'll let any of our kids go to university."

He asked if we could get married now. He wanted to try the titty fucking he had seen in Japanese adult videos on me. Titty fucking? I asked. He stuck his pointer finger between my tits and moved it up and down. The instant he touched me, my cleavage started itching like crazy, turning into a flowerbed. I covered that bed of roses up with my jacket right away.

"When I get married, my old man's going to build me a mansion. Whatever you want, tell me, I'll stick it in." The blueprint was drawn up and the ground was broken. I wanted a fountain. I wanted a zoo. I wanted a hippo to put in the zoo. Wang Senior gave my father and mother a big engagement gift. A Chen-Wang wedding would be the union of our two clans. The best materials would be used in the White House, and all the construction workers in the county would be hired to build it at top speed.

"Now can we do it?" he asked after the engagement ceremony.

He raced the German sedan to a big hotel in Yuanlin and
dropped his pants as soon as we got in the room. He said he'd
been hard the whole way. He was really big. And hairy. They
didn't call him Wang for nothing.

He wanted me to suck him off but as soon as I got close
enough to smell it, I barfed on him. Then on the carpet. And
on the bed.

I begged him to wait. "Please, I've not been feeling well
recently." Okay, he would wait.

We tried again. This time he wanted to try titty fucking. I
asked him to take a shower and wash himself with soap, until
he'd washed away the smell. He did as instructed. He still
reeked, of smoke, booze, and meat. I still felt nauseated, but
this time I managed to stop myself from throwing up. He got
me to lie down and squeeze my tits together. Then he stuffed
his huge meat into the crack and started to thrust it in and out.
He was moaning, but when he saw the weird red flowers, he
went suddenly flaccid and jumped off.

"You know I get these allergies," I said.

After the allergy attack had passed, he announced that we
didn't have to do oral, or titty fucking. He wouldn't indulge his
kinks, at least not this time. He wanted to do it down there.

In my room.

But I was dry. Really dry.

Too dry. He tried to thrust himself up into me, but I was like
a desert down there. Patience exhausted, he slobbered on his
palm and rubbed it all over himself. When I saw that I closed
up even tighter. He tried to force it in but was immediately
beaten back by my sobs and cries. "Stop! I'm dying! It hurts!"

He said of course it hurt the first time. It would be over in
no time. He lay on top of me and kept trying to get it in. I
started screaming. "You're hurting me!"

I totally forgot that Barbie's room was right next door. And how could I know that Barbie had stuck her ear to the partition wall?

I was dry every time. We tried many times and it was always the same. He said he'd never seen the like. It was unbelievable! He had fucked a lot of women, why couldn't he enter me? How could he marry me now?

I never told a soul that my period stopped when I was seventeen.

The last time we tried he brought a huge bottle of lubricant. When he finally got it in, I started to sneeze and I couldn't stop. Several doors down my little brother started counting my sneezes, one, two, three, four, five, six, seven. The sneezes made me seize up, pushing Junior out. He tried to get it in again, but I got tighter and tighter. I kept spitting him out and sneezing. Keith kept on counting. Suddenly I farted, so loud it drowned out my sneezes. I heard Keith laughing. I couldn't help it, I started laughing, too. That fart wrinkled up Junior's glabella. "Fuck!" he shouted. Then he left.

I smelled my fart. And burst out laughing another time.

At that time how was I to know? How could I know? That while I was closed up here, leaving him unable to enter, Barbie opened up next door.

I was dry. Barbie was wet.

I closed up tight. Barbie opened wide.

So Barbie took my place. She was wet and willing. Sure, she didn't have big tits, but she didn't have red flowers, either. And she didn't sneeze. I can see her now. She won, the White House is hers. She just opened the curtain and saw Belinda.

Looking back, Belinda saw Barbie, too. Then Barbie ran back into the bathroom and threw herself into the tub. There she sits, in the lukewarm water. Her room is piled with newspapers and magazines, all reports about me.

Reporters were out in force for the Wedding of the Century,

when Cracker Jack Wang's son Baron would take a wife. Baron and Barbie stood under the crystal chandelier for a photo op. One of those photos went on the cover of a magazine.

But the media attention to the wedding was miniscule in comparison with the obsession with my suicide later on.

After I died, Barbie drove Baron's German sedan everywhere, snapping up all the newspapers and magazines with reports or features about my suicide. She piled them all up in her White House room. That way nobody would read about it. And then nobody would know.

But Barbie read about it every day, she still reads about it constantly. How Baron humped me and dumped me. How after I was cast aside, I put a plastic bag over my head and slit my wrists. How when I was discovered, the plastic bag was stuck tightly to my skin. How rumor had it that I had a baby in my belly when I died. She read and read. Eventually she installed curtains, sealed the window, and locked the door. She's still afraid of hippos. She doesn't dare to go outside.

She wakes up terror-stricken every night to the sound of a sobbing baby. The fool.

I spread that rumor, about me being pregnant with Baron's child, before I died. I let the hippo out of its enclosure, too.

36. Sewing up the five sisters' mouths

It was still too stuffy to go inside after dinner, so Beverly brought some stools out. The siblings sat barefoot on the front porch waving fans, fanning up more waves of muggy air. The geckos on the wall were chirping, as if they, too, were hollering: It's too damn hot.

"I never thought any of you would show up for Ghost Festival," said Beverly. "I didn't sweep up your rooms, or wash the blankets. It's dusty up there."

"Who's going to need a blanket?" asked Betty. "Please, it's like an oven."

"Beverly, will you please install air conditioning?" asked Belinda. "It's on me. How can you sew in this heat?"

"You think I enjoy it?" Beverly snapped. "I'm not like you. Your husband is so good at making money you don't even have to work."

"What's that supposed to mean?" Belinda replied. "It's not like you don't know my situation."

"What situation?" Betty asked. "You don't tell us anything."

"You live in a luxury apartment in Taipei," said Beverly. "And you've never invited us for a visit."

"You guys want to live in a luxury apartment?" asked Belinda. "Then let's trade places."

"That's not what I meant," said Betty. "I'm not trying to start a fight."

"Knock it off, you two," Beverly said.

"You're the one who started it!" said Belinda. "All I did was propose installing an AC system. Is it too late? Call the electrical appliance store. See if they can come this evening. This heat is going to be the death of me."

"Will Beverly's monthly electricity bills be on you, too?" asked Betty.

"I don't need an air conditioner!" said Beverly. "An electric fan is enough! I've not been as lucky in life as you two. You get to live in Taipei."

"The lucky one is the third," said Betty. "The daughter that eats life."

"You want to talk 'lucky,'" said Belinda. "All right, I'll talk lucky. If any of us is lucky it's you."

"Since when am I the lucky one?" asked Betty.

Keith listened as his three sisters finally dispensed with the formalities. Their repartee was spirited and sharp. They interrupted one another, there was a real back and forth. Their tones rocketed and plummeted. Voices and memories were superimposed. Tacky recriminations left the three sisters' speeches stuck together. It was a mixed up and messy situation. He couldn't tell who was who.

It appeared that he could also hear Barbie and Plenty.

He looked down and smiled. Whenever his five sisters got into a fight, it was like trying to douse a grease fire with a bowl of water, producing enough steam to devour the Muddy Waters and the Central Range. They could start a fight at breakfast or bedtime, at home or at school, and anytime, or anywhere, in between. The only one that could stop the five sisters fighting was Mother. She had only to yell and glare at them, and needles and threads would come shooting out of her eyes, sewing up their mouths.

If Barbie could hear her three elder sisters fight, she would charge right out of the White House and join the fray. Normally the sisters' conversations were dull, but as soon as they stepped onto the verbal battlefield, swords came unsheathed and arrows snapped onto strings. Like theater actors, they didn't need microphones to project their voices. They turned the volume all the way up.

Last time he came back was after Father died. It was late by the time he arrived. He said he had jet lag, he would stay up for the wake. His sisters could go to sleep.

It was quiet on that autumn night. Too quiet. It was like a cunningly arranged moment of repose in a suspense film. The protagonist lets down his guard, right before the dagger thrust, the screams, and the blood.

He sat alone in the mourning hall folding paper lotus flowers, ferries to the "other shore." He wrote T an email to let him know he had made it home. T immediately replied. He was going out for a graveyard shift. He was working as a security guard in a factory from dusk to dawn. He would ride home at five in the morning. If he saw a blank wall along the way, he would get out a bottle of spray paint and spray out his frustrations.

T said he'd find a wall to paint Keith's father's face on. Keith looked up, saw his father's photo on the wall of the mourning hall, and imagined T spray painting it on a wall along a Berlin street.

Beverly woke up at one o'clock. She walked in, picked up incense sticks, and prayed. Then she sat down and folded paper lotus flowers with Keith. Her bones and joints creaked like rusty gears. "It hurts here, and it hurts there, it hurts everywhere. My shoulders are killing me. My back is sore, too. What with funeral arrangements and a job I still haven't finished, I can't sleep. Are you hungry? I'll go make you noodles."

"I'm stuffed. You've fed me quite enough already."

"Well, I'm just worried about you. Have you been getting enough to eat in Germany? You're so thin. And there's something else. I've been meaning to ask you, but I don't know how to say it. Oh, my aching neck!"

He gave her a massage. There were landmines everywhere, which exploded at the slightest touch. She kept yelping.

"Beverly, then why don't you try this?"

He got a joint out of his backpack, a present from T. He, too, had suffered strange pains the past while. It hurt to write. It hurt to hold the plates in the restaurant. It hurt to walk. T asked him to give it a try and it turned out to be really effective. The smoke immediately drove the pain away.

"What the hell! Is this what I think it is? How'd you get it through customs? You're asking for a whole lotta trouble!"

"My German friend told me I'd need it on this trip home. He insisted I take it when I was leaving for the airport. Come on, give it a try! Don't worry. We're in a roadside mourning hall, the police aren't going to hassle us."

She lit it, took a hit, held her breath, and exhaled slowly. As the smoke swirled lazily around, she smiled. "I know I'm a boring old woman now, but let me tell you, I was practically a juvenile delinquent. I dropped out of junior high school just cause I felt like it. Did I ever tell you about how the seam-stresses in Shalu taught me how to smoke?"

"Only about a million times. Should we be smoking in front of Dad?"

"Don't worry. He was pretty easy-going the last few years without Mother around to nag him about everything. Every time I visited him he was smoking and gambling. 'Can you gamble in front of Mother Matsu?' I asked. 'My diagnosis's a certificate of immunity,' he said. 'The goddess is very forgiving, you know. Terminal liver cancer, for Heaven's sake! With her blessing, I'll win money for sure.'"

He looked up at his father's photo. Easy-going? He couldn't imagine it. His father almost never talked. He didn't smile or laugh. He had a hard look in his eyes.

"Beverly, what was it you were meaning to ask?"

"This is really dope. Is that what the kids say nowadays? I feel so relaxed. I think I'm talking louder now. I was just won-dering what to do about all those things in your room. Do you want me to throw them away?"

"You mean my old books?"

"Yes, but I was thinking of the box of VHS tapes."

It was a present from the snake killer. Mother had found it in his room, taken a tape downstairs, and put it on. When she saw two men making out, she let out a terrified lioness's roar. Weird, didn't she throw them out? What are they still doing here?

"Why wouldn't she have tossed them?"

"Beats me. They keep on popping up. Not even the typhoon could blow them away."

Beverly had watched those VHS tapes, too, while the tape machine was still working. She watched one and couldn't help watching another, and another, until she'd watched them all. She really enjoyed them. They transported her to another space-time inhabited by happy men of different skin colors. She thought that maybe Keith had left them here on purpose, to answer questions that were too hard to ask.

With the two of them taking turns smoking it, the joint was soon a butt. The stars in the autumn sky were resplendent, the cool breeze refreshing.

"After the funeral, you just stay in Germany, don't come back." Beverly was folding the golden sheets into pretty weird-looking flowers. She looked at him pointedly. "Did you hear what I just said? Promise me."

Beverly flicked the butt onto the floor, stood up, stubbed it out, and stretched. There was fog in her eyes. "I'm going to hit the sack, I'm exhausted. Watch out for cats and dogs. I forgot to just now."

At two in the morning, Betty appeared.

"I just heard Beverly's voice. What a foghorn! Has she gone to bed?"

"What, did you all arrange to take turns staying up with me?"

"Don't be silly. We can't even arrange to get together for dinner." She sat down to fold the flowers. When she saw Beverly's she frowned. "They're hideous. If we burn them, Dad will laugh his head off when he receives them in the after-life, won't he?"

"Are we a family of insomniacs now?"

"I was just thinking about what Mom's going to do when she wakes up tomorrow morning and finds you here. When I thought of that I couldn't sleep."

"Don't worry, you know I'm used to getting slapped around. If she yells at me it won't be news, either."

"Is that all you remember, getting hit and yelled at? She really spoiled you, you know. Have you forgotten? She just can't bear to lose face. Today she was complaining about how Heath never comes home from the mainland, not even for his father's funeral. She said it loud. She was saying it so the neighbors would hear. Actually everyone knows where he's hiding out. So what if he doesn't come back? I don't particularly want to see him, either."

The road in front of the old house was noticeably wider, and smoother now that it had been paved. Suddenly a heavy motorcycle streaked past. It was going way over the speed limit, so fast it left a red and white afterimage.

"Beverly mentioned that street racing is a thing here now. She said that if any bikers swing by we'd better stay out of sight."

"We're sitting here in a mourning hall. They're the ones that should be scared, right?"

"Good point. Ah! What are we going to do? Mother is going to wake up in a few hours."

"I'm not scared. Why should you be?"

"Have you really forgotten how she doted on you?"

Of course he remembered. His sisters weren't allowed to eat dinner until he and Heath had tried it. The two brothers were always getting new clothes and shoes, while the sisters had to wear hand-me-downs. If they didn't fit they were altered, and if they were out of style they couldn't complain. If they were watching a soap opera and he said he wanted to switch channels, Mother would holler at them to let Baby Keith have his way. When his bicycle got stolen from school, he got a new one the same day. When a sister's bicycle was stolen from the station Mother caned her and berated her. "Last bicycle I'm ever buying you!" she yelled. When their parents went on a trip, they only took the two brothers along. The two brothers went to Yuanlin for piano and mental math lessons. No need for the daughters to take lessons, they were just girls. They were only going to get married off.

"All right then, I'll go see if I can get to sleep. It's all

Beverly's fault, she woke me up. Keith, can I . . . would you mind if I visited you in Germany?"

"Anytime!"

"You said it. Don't complain when I show up at your front door. After Father's funeral is over, go back to Germany and take good care. Don't come back again."

He looked behind the mourning hall at just before three. And as expected Belinda was coming downstairs.

"I kept hearing footsteps downstairs, like a pneumatic drill! How can anyone sleep!"

"Must be rough for someone used to living in the lap of luxury to have to bed down here."

"Piss off, Keith. When are you going to grow up? I assumed you would have living in Berlin. Hey, have you been watching out for strays? There's a lot of them in the countryside."

"Why exactly do we have to watch out for them?"

"Isn't it because a dog or a cat will turn the corpse into a zombie if it jumps over the casket?"

They both went to take a look at the cooler and imagined their father as a zombie. It tickled their funny bones. They both laughed.

They sat back down and folded paper lotuses. The bamboo basket on the floor was getting pretty full. How many was enough? If they burned them would Father get them?

"Is he good to you?"

Keith nodded. Belinda looked him in the eye to make sure he wasn't lying. He nodded again.

"That's a relief. Don't be like me, stuck for a lifetime."

"Have you ever wondered . . ." Suddenly he didn't know how to finish.

"I think about it every day. But what am I going to do? Come back here and live with Beverly? Could I stay with you in Germany? Or maybe I should head over to the White House? Hole up with Barbie in that room and never go out?

Forget it, he knows I have nowhere to go. In retrospect, Betty was smart to marry such a boring guy. I can never remember what her husband looks like, no matter how hard I try. Boring is good. Boring is the best."

Modified motorcycles and souped-up scooters rumbled down the road. Two teams were hooting and howling and revving their engines, ready to go head to head across a thin white line. The first pair of speed demons throttled up. Screeching tires left skid marks on the blacktop, and thunder in the ears. They went whizzing past. In no time they came roaring back. When they saw the mourning hall they swerved and averted their eyes. With death as their shield, Keith and Belinda obviously had nothing to worry about.

Next up, mixed doubles. A pair of bare-headed girls rode pillion, gripping the riders with their arms and thighs, their long hair flapping, and laughter ringing, in the wind. One of them was slashing the air with a watermelon knife, and screaming, all the way. When she passed the mourning hall she sneezed.

Just like Plenty. The way she looked before she passed away, youthful, voluptuous, long-haired, pale-skinned. Red lips, big eyes. A sneeze volcano.

The biker gangs were gone. Belinda said she was going back to bed.

"Keith, the last time I saw Father at the temple he wanted me to tell you to just stay put in Germany, don't come ever back again. He was really frail by that point, and so sick he couldn't keep anything down. We weren't allowed to tell you then, but now that he's dead there's something you have to know. Dad was always reading your books. And he told you not to come back."

In the morning, Mother woke up and drove him away. All he could do was burn incense to his father and leave. Beverly, Betty, and Belinda gave him a ride to the train station, with

Belinda behind the wheel. The previous night the three sisters had talked nonstop. Now they had nothing to say.

Soon the news of T's murder reached the small town.

"Remember Cliff Chen, that guy who got his start wholesaling betel leaf? Well I hear his youngest son killed a man in Germany." That's what people said. And now Keith hadn't kept his promise. He'd come back even when he said he wasn't going to.

His three sisters were still fighting.

Betty's phone rang. It was her husband. "I think I just saw you on TV."

Betty walked inside and turned on the television by the sewing machine. "Household Registrar Chen looks down on seeing-eye dogs," said Belinda's husband in a rebroadcast of the evening news. "Here's a citizen journalist's video of an incident that had netizens foaming at the mouth today."

The three sisters all went quiet. They sat down in front of the television, lips pursed.

Obviously, Mother wasn't the only one who could sew their mouths up.

37. With a snake, a dragon, a phoenix, and a tiger on the roof

Heath, too, saw Betty on TV.

He always watched Belinda's husband deliver the evening news. He never missed the rebroadcast, either. He kept thinking that if he made a comeback, the anchor could do an interview.

It couldn't be Betty, could it? It just looks like her, right?

On the wall of his room hung an "ink treasure," a gift from Beverly's husband. A while back Heath needed orchids for the garden, so he went home to buy some. Little Gao was in the back yard doing calligraphy. Heath couldn't help a sigh at the sight of the banners and posters from his campaign. "Don't worry," his brother-in-law said. "If you run again, you've got my vote."

Then he wrote four words on a piece of rice paper for him. Heath framed it himself. He did everything from scratch, from sawing to sandpapering. He hung the ink treasure on the wall.

"Hell make a comeback."

Neither of them noticed the missing apostrophe.

He found the four words heartening. It was as if he was just biding his time, waiting for his opportunity to reenter the political arena.

He was once the township mayor, for goodness' sake. He was elected by a landslide. But he didn't survive the construction scandals he got caught up in in less than two years into his term. He exhausted his appeals and went to prison.

Mother was unwilling to see him off. He knocked on her door, only to hear her sobbing inside. The door was locked, and she would not come out. The woman who said she wanted to be the mayor's wife would not see him off, either. They were engaged, but when the news broke she broke it off and wouldn't take his calls. He left messages until her number was no longer in service. He got up at dawn on a foggy morning. He packed his bag, put on his best suit, and waited for the police to come pick him up. When he walked out the door, he saw his father waiting to say goodbye to his eldest son. Father looked like a ghost in the fog, especially with his liver cancer. He looked gaunt. But he was smiling. Heath had never seen him so relaxed.

He opened the bag, took out his Mayor Heath, At Your Service vest, and put it on over his suit jacket. He had bought the suit on that trip to Paris. He'd bought a dozen. This one was the most expensive. It was pure cashmere wool. He thought he looked very smart in it, even though it made him sweat a waterfall in the steamy heat of Yongjing. The night before he smelled mildew when he took it out of the wardrobe and saw how dark the light gray fabric had gotten. He showed it to Beverly at the sewing machine. "It's growing mushrooms!" she said in Taiwanese, meaning it was all moldy. He was due to start serving his sentence the next morning. There was no time to get it cleaned.

So he stood in a moldy Parisian suit, smoking with his father by the side of the road. The yellow ribbons that Baron had promised him were nowhere to be seen.

Baron promised him many things.

When the judgment was handed down Baron got off scot-free. Because *Heath Chen* was the name on the bottom line. Because it had nothing to do with anyone at the Wang Foundation. "Don't worry," Baron said. "I'll get a crowd of people to tie yellow ribbons to their arms and come to give you a big send-off. Belinda's husband will send a reporter to do a live interview. Imagine, a crowd of ribbon wearers several hundred or thousand strong. You will go to prison in style. The day that you come out, that's the day you'll make your comeback."

Baron told him they could pay a bit extra for actors who could cry on cue for the camera. It'd be more effective from a PR standpoint.

But that morning, there were no yellow ribbons waiting for him in front of the townhouse. There was just him and his father.

Him running for township mayor was Baron's idea. "The Chens and Wangs are one big family. Your sister Barbie's a basket case, but have I abandoned her? No, I still take care of her, I'm her husband. We're brothers-in-law, we should help each other out. Don't worry about the money, I'll fund your campaign. I promise you, you'll get elected by a landslide. These country people will vote for you if they get their hands on some cash. All you have to do is promise to open doors for me. I've got a property to rezone. And I'll need a permit to develop it."

Soon the district prosecutor had him in his sights. "No sweat," Baron said. He would hire the best lawyers to prove that due diligence had been done on the environmental impact assessments, and that everything was above board. Heath had nothing to worry about! So Heath did not worry. After all, the Wangs were like Teflon, nothing ever stuck. They always got away with it, whatever it was. A graft scandal broke after the Wang headquarters in Taipei won a green building prize. It was all over the news for quite a while, but in the end Jack and Baron escaped unscathed. The panels on the roof kept sucking up the sun by day. The building never stopped shining at night.

Heath burst out crying when he got in the cruiser. He hadn't done anything wrong. Why was he going to prison? When Nut Wang was thrown in jail, Mother told him it was Nut's own fault. He was a pervert, he had it coming. But Heath hadn't done anything wrong, he wasn't a pervert, so why was he "guilty?" Everything he had done was for the good of Yongjing. And why didn't the Wang Foundation have to pay a price? Why did he have to be the fall guy?

He made a lot of improvements during his short tenure. Wherever there was a blank wall, he had artists paint his portrait on it. His mom liked those portraits. She put on a bespoke peach cheongsam and stood proud beside one for a photo op. When Heath was elected, firecrackers were set off three days and three nights. "Congratulations!" everyone said. She felt like it had all been worth it raising him. Finally he had made it. Occasionally people asked about her youngest and a typhoon would pass over her face. "He's dead," she would coldly say.

This was how Baron talked him into running. "You're the eldest son," he said. "Your mother had five daughters. She kept trying to have a boy until she had you. Are you going to spend your whole life working in a coffin shop?" Yes, he was a coffin carpenter. He was actually happiest sawing and sanding, until Baron said that as township mayor he wouldn't have to make dead people's money anymore, he would bust his ass for the greater good. They'd do it together. When they made it big, they'd build a house that was even bigger than the White House. "Trust me," Baron added, "no girl's going to marry a guy that makes coffins for a living."

Father was dead set against him running. He'd gone to China with Jack Wang and invested everything. Trusting Jack completely, he didn't check the fine print or the transfers. In a few years Jack was rolling in dough, while his slice of the pie had somehow gotten eaten. Father warned him against working with the Wangs and told him he was a spoiled brat. "You can't do anything, but at least you can do carpentry. Focus on that, not on what you think you want. You'd be a disaster as mayor."

So there he was, crying like a child in the back seat of the police cruiser. Every time he cried his mother used to swoop in to take care of everything. One time when he was staring blankly at the homework on his desk, his mind a wilderness, Betty came in to offer help, but he burst out crying, dripping tears onto the page. Mother came in and slapped Betty on the cheek. Another time, she shielded him, and no one else, when they were caught outside during a hailstorm. Yet another time, in junior high school, a classmate made fun of him. "Everyone says your little brother is a homo. That means you are, too." He came home in tears. The next day Mother switched him to another school. When he couldn't get into a high school, even a vocational one, he moped around the house feeling sorry for himself. Mother paid a visit to a private school and got him in with cash and gifts. When he did his military service, she handed over another red envelope to a township representative, who pulled strings to get him the cushiest assignment, pouring wine and lighting cigarettes for the officers. When he came home wanting to get married, he resented the country girls the matchmaker introduced him to. They were too earthy. He wanted to marry a girl who looked like Miyazawa Rie.

But Mother wasn't there for him the day he went to prison. It was Father who shut the door of the cruiser. He didn't say a thing. He didn't wave. He just stood in the doorway of the old house and watched the cruiser leave. As the car sped off, the fog swallowed him up.

The scene was just as bleak the day he was released. There weren't hundreds of supporters, let alone thousands. Not even his parents were there. No yellow ribbons fluttered. He left by himself, without ceremony. He took a bus.

He did not go home, he went straight to Baron to beg for help. "Please give me a job. I'll go to Beijing. Shenzhen would be okay, too. Or even Jinan. Just get me out of Taiwan, I need somewhere I can lie low." Until everyone in Yongjing had forgotten that he had gone to jail. Then he could make a comeback, run for township mayor again. He knew all Baron had to do was spend a bit of money, to get people to look away and find themselves unable to remember what they knew perfectly well. "Baron, please, help me. I helped you, didn't I? You must have made a lot of money!"

In the end he didn't go anywhere. Baron offered him a storeroom in the White House. He went to work as the groundsman. He swept up the fallen leaves. He pruned the trees. He tended the crossed canals and fed the carp. He cleaned the fountain. If any paint flecked off any corner of the mansion, he ran back to his room, opened a can of white or gold, and rushed off to touch it up. He was also responsible for cooking and serving Barbie's meals. He took them upstairs and knocked on the door. "Barbie," he said, "it's time to eat."

He could still hear Barbie moan. Baron was originally going to marry Plenty. But later on he suddenly stopped coming for Plenty, he came for Barbie instead. Barbie moaned really loud. And so did Baron, so loud that Heath felt itchy all over. The only way he could relieve the itch was by fiddling with himself. He had no idea that Barbie was moaning so loudly so that Plenty would hear next door. He worshipped Baron for making Plenty sneeze and Barbie moan like that. He wanted to be Baron when he grew up.

Now he was the one who visited Barbie's room, which she was completely unwilling to step out of in spite of all the refuse she'd piled up in there. Sometimes she would go berserk. Late at night, when he heard the snores like cracks of thunder in Barbie's room, he would tiptoe in with a flashlight to collect the tray and try to pick up the garbage. What a stench! Strange-looking mushrooms were growing on the walls. He shone the flashlight on Barbie, who was sleeping on the floor. Her hair was white, her legs distended. He did not know what ghosts look like but he guessed that if a ghost saw his sister it would get scared for sure. That ghost would assume it had seen a ghost.

Still watching TV, he heard a car. Baron had not been home in a long time. Why would he come back for Ghost Festival?

He kept watching. Belinda's husband looked so handsome. He sounded authoritative. Belinda was a lucky lady. And the rest of the family? Everyone was down and out. Keith was a pervert and a murderer. What a disgrace! At least Belinda had married well. When he made his comeback, her husband would seek him out. He had been practicing his new stump speech for years.

After the story about Household Registrar Chen, the anchor announced: "It's Ghost Festival today. Have you prayed yet? Next we have an exclusive interview with the Yellow Emperor, who will tell all our viewers about how to navigate the various taboos and make it through the spookiest month of the calendar in one piece."

A man in a full-length yellow robe appeared walking out of a temple to address a gathering of over a thousand devotees, all of them prostrate on the ground in the same color shirt. "Yellow Emperor, save humanity!" they all cried out in unison. "Deliver all sentient beings from suffering!" The camera zoomed rapidly out to show the entire temple in flamboyant maroon. The design was ridiculous, with a snake, a dragon, phoenix, and a tiger on the roof. The camera cut to the head shot of the yellow-robed man. "On Ghost Festival, when all the ghosts come out to roam, Yellow Emperor is at your service, helping you keep your family safe. You, too, can avoid calamity and make a heap of money during Ghost Month."

Heath's bowl and chopsticks fell to the floor. He knew who that was.

The Yellow Emperor was his old neighbor the snake killer.

How was it possible? Didn't he die in the fire that killed Mother?

38. Bliss and piss met

"Why is all that junk still piled up in the back yard? Just recycle it." "Who would bother recycling Heath's campaign posters? Quicker to burn them." "He's still your brother, for better or worse." "He's your brother, not mine. He still owes me a bunch of money. Burn the whole pile." "Burn it for the ghosts." "Only ghosts would want it." "Not even ghosts would." "Heath bummed money off you, too? He came asking me for money, he wasn't borrowing. I knew I'd never see it again. He even said we should take better care of him, cause he's the eldest son." "That doesn't make him any less of an idiot. Has he ever shown you that 'ink treasure' Little Gao gave him? 'Hell Make a Comeback?' He can go to hell!" "You know how outrageous he was as mayor? He plastered his face all over the town. All that talk about painting Yongjing, and all they painted was his face. Mom was standing there beaming, as if her eldest son had finally made something of himself." "He begged my husband to interview him. I almost threw up when I saw it." "He even had thousands of cases of mineral water made with his face on every label. He was handing bottles out. In this day and age!" "There were Mayor Heath canvas bags, ballpoint pens, and betel nut boxes, too." "Don't tell me these ghastly things still exist." "In another pile, in his room on the second floor." "Where's Little Gao?" "He's died and gone to Paris!" "Paris?" "Would anyone buy his orchids?" "Only a ghost." "Not even a ghost." "Tell Barbie to hurry up and come over." "Today she was yelling 'Mom's gone missing!' over the phone. It's annoying." "It's not like you don't know her situation." "What situation, exactly? Who doesn't have it tough? Who isn't unhappy? But what good does going into hiding do?" "I want to go into hiding, too. Where should I go?" "Into the hills. Didn't you buy a mountain in Nantou?" "It's all gone." "Gone?" "I just saw Barbie." "What? You went to the White House?" "Did Heath let you in?" "Or Barbie? She wouldn't answer the door when I knocked." "Where are we going to sleep this evening?" "You really want to spend the night? Aren't you going back to Taipei?" "It's so late. Better stay."

What a racket!

To Keith, his three sisters were like bacon in a skillet. Crimson, crispy, fat splattering. They hadn't fought in a long time, they couldn't with their own husbands: Beverly had nothing to say to Little Gao, Betty had trouble remembering what hers looked like, and Belinda resigned herself to the anchor's fists. The bacon had been lying flabby in the fridge, quietly waiting to hit the hot oil. The moment it did it sizzled boisterously, rapturously. I know where your scars are, you know where I hurt. I expose you, you trample me. Words confined for years slipped out. Body heat erupted, mouths spewed lava, spittle scalded. The sisters kept turning on the heat. The air smelled meaty.

Keith felt like an outsider, unable to enter the fray. He couldn't fight, he didn't know how. He lacked fat or oil. When his shriveled body encountered heat, it smothered the flame and fouled the pot. He and T had never fought.

Stuck in that hermetic little East Berlin flat, they worried about bills and rent. He couldn't concentrate on writing, T had no chance to practice cello. They were used to solitude but had no time for it. How could they possibly not fight? They were both locked up tight. They choked back words, they swallowed questions. Instead of getting things out in the open, they always said they were fine. They smiled through breakfast.

T got a new hairstyle. He didn't ask. New clothes appeared in T's wardrobe. He didn't ask. The stream of T's questions dried up. He didn't ask. When they entered each other's bodies, he discovered tiny tattoos on T's biceps. He didn't ask. After they untwined their bodies, T turned away, crying. He didn't ask. T got a windfall. "Don't worry about the rent," he said. "Why don't you quit your job and focus on writing?" He didn't ask. T took pills. He didn't ask. T bought American sneakers with a big N on each upper, each pair a month's rent. Where did T get the money? He didn't ask.

Until he saw an Internet news clip of a far-right demonstration. Neo-Nazis were carrying torches and flags down a Berlin street. T was marching in the crowd, waving the tricolor.

He was wearing dark sunglasses. Black jacket, black pants, black shoes. Night had fallen upon him once again. A capital A was embroidered on his jacket in a gothic font, along with some other symbols that went over Keith's head. When a reporter approached him he didn't shrink back. He wasn't at all evasive. He spoke calmly into the camera.

He had never seen T like this. That evening, insomnia crept up on both of them. He finally asked, about the demonstration. T's body split the night open. He changed clothes, went out, just disappeared. Several weeks later he returned just as suddenly, early in the morning. He made a big breakfast, including a fresh bearleek pesto. He served it with a smile and said everything was fine, he was home. How was the novel coming along? He hugged and kissed him. A few days later he disappeared again. This time he shut off his mobile phone. The next time he reappeared a glare had replaced his smile. "They know I'm with a man," he said. "And that it's a foreigner. They know."

"Who?"

"They'll come looking for me. We have to move."

"Who!"

Next thing he knew T was choking him. "You idiot, you don't understand anything."

That evening at three in the morning, the doorbell rang. He picked up the handset and heard cursing. The doorbell kept screaming. T lit a joint with trembling hands. The next morning, they came out to find their bicycles gone and the car splattered with red paint. *Schwuchtel* had been written on the windows, along with a swastika. T told him to go inside, he would clean the car. He'd be back in a second. "Don't answer the door. Don't let anyone in no matter what. Don't call the police." T repeated that he'd be right back and not to worry.

The car drove off. T didn't come home. For the longest time. He didn't answer calls or emails. The doorbell stayed quiet for a few days. Then one evening, a brick broke the window. He waited until morning to clean up the glass. There was an N on the brick.

He finally learned what those symbols meant rehearsing Shakespeare in jail. The N on the brick, and, according to some, also in New Balance, was for Nazi.

The embroidered A on T's jacket was for Adolf.

1 in 18 represented the first letter of the alphabet, and 8 the eighth. 18 was code for Adolf Hitler.

44 meant DD, Deutschland den Deutschen. Germany for the Germans.

But at the time he had no idea. T burst in with rope and tape, grabbed him, and choked him. It took him back to that time when his teacher trapped him by the bishopwood tree. The rope was to tie him to the chair, the tape to seal his mouth and nose. T started to pack his bags. He said he was moving to another city and wasn't coming back. This time was only to say goodbye. "Pay the rent yourself. Pretend you don't know me."

When T saw the broken window, he yelled: "What did you do that for?" How could he reply with a taped mouth? T pummeled him, took off his pants, forced himself in. Then he saw the brick and apologized. "Sorry, sorry," he said, crying. "I know who did it. It's them." Then he hit him again.

How long was he tied up for? In court, he was unable to give a clear answer. T kept force-feeding him pills. He was in a daze. He remembered shitting and pissing on the chair, he couldn't help it. T wiped it up with a towel, then rubbed it on his face. T cut him with a razor.

T kissed him. "Sorry," he said. "I love you." "Goodbye." T ripped off his clothes. T helped him change into clothes that he'd soiled. T hit him. And himself. T threw him into a wall. Then himself. T played the cello so hard the strings broke. A neighbor pounded on the door. "Knock it off, for Christ's sake!"

T asked him non-stop questions while adding layer upon layer of tape. He would cut a slit for pills only to seal it again. He wanted to answer T's questions, but how could he? He wanted to ask, "What the hell happened?"

Then T severed the rope with a razor, grabbed a carving knife, and stabbed it at him. The two grappled on the piss-and-shit covered floor. The knife entered T's body. His hands were all bloody, he was covered in blood, piss, and shit. He pushed the broken window out and honey rushed into his nostrils. Ah, honey-flavored candy. As the scent of the candy mingled with the stench of human filth, holy and lowly mixed, bliss and piss met. He was tired, so damn tired. T told him to leave, but he was just too tired. He lay down and fell asleep.

How long did he sleep? Perhaps a long time. Maybe only briefly. When he woke up there was blood all over the floor. T was lying in it, eyes open wide. He was smiling, but slackly. Was that really T?

Go!

He remembered T had told him to go.

Where?

He found T's mobile in his pocket and the keys to the car. He gazed in T's eyes. He knew where to go. There were murky waves in the blue irises. He took the murder weapon with him. He would drive to the Laboe and kill himself on the beach.

39. Swimming with the neighbor's cat

Ingrid got up for good at five in the morning after a sleepless night. She'd gotten up several times during the night to make sure her husband was still breathing. He'd stopped snoring. Everything had changed, not just the snoring. She quit smoking. The cat went missing. The potted plants all withered. It didn't snow or even rain the whole winter. The wall clock died, freezing the hands.

She didn't tell him about the train she was going to take, the trip she was going to make. She made up something about a concert that the music school had arranged far enough away to require a hotel stay. He didn't reply, just kept eating his bread and drinking his beer. He didn't finish either. His appetite was a shadow of what it had been. He used to drink two big cans of beer with dinner. Now half a can was enough. Sometimes he forgot.

The seagulls got up even earlier than her on that chilly March morning. They were circling over the beach and screaming when she left to catch the bus. The wind off the sea gusted so fiercely she had trouble keeping her footing. She took in the Kieler Förde in the light of dawn. Many years before, during a severe winter, the Förde froze, the churning seawater crystalized. She led T onto the ice. She told him if they kept going like this, they could make it to Kiel. T kept smiling and yelling: "Mami! We're walking on the sea!" When he let go of her hand and raced away she couldn't catch him. She slipped and fell. T saw her sitting on the ice and laughed. Then he disappeared into the snow.

She ran into a neighbor on the bus. They greeted each other civilly and talked about the weather. The neighbor's tone was cautious. She chose her words carefully, for fear of mentioning T. Since T's death everyone in town had been acting so polite. They avoided the topic, stuffing their eyes with a sympathy that disgusted her. She found it estranging. The report about T's death had mentioned homosexuality, Neo-Nazis, and Taiwan. She imagined her neighbors and relatives talking about it behind her back. One time she couldn't help asking a neighbor she was particularly close to: "Are you all talking about my son when I'm not there?" "Ingrid, no," her friend replied, "we really don't. The things in the newspaper, they're just too frightening. We don't know what to say. We don't even know where Taiwan is."

Today she was off to Berlin.

Will I be able to get off the train when I get there? she wondered. When she received the notice, she wanted to go, alone. She didn't know why, just that she really wanted to go.

That day, the day everything changed, the police knocked on the door, told her about T, and asked some questions. They'd let her know if anything came up. Soon after they left, her mobile vibrated and T's number appeared on the screen. The police must have made a mistake. My son's not dead, he's calling me! She took the call, but it wasn't T. It was him.

She rushed out and found him by the U-boat. He was crying and saying sorry, but beyond that they couldn't communicate. He was badly wounded. His face was all swollen. His clothes were really thin for the weather. There was sand in his hair and a knife by his feet.

She had the whole day to herself. The moment she disembarked at the Hauptbahnhof she felt like a smoke. She hadn't had a cigarette in a long time. Why would she have such a strong craving now? She also felt sleepy. The weather was fair, the spring sun surprisingly hot. She'd go find a quiet park somewhere, sit on a bench, and sleep.

She took the U-Bahn, with no particular destination in mind. She transferred and got off when she felt like it. She thought she should see Berlin, the city her son had roamed around in. But she had no idea what part of the city he called home. She didn't know what he was doing here, either, or that he'd married that Taiwanese man. She'd only seen him twice. The first time was several years ago at Christmas. The second time was by the U-boat. Today would be the third. How was she to face him? No, she didn't want to face him. She had brought a hat in her purse that she'd rehearsed wearing in front of the mirror at home. Pulled down, the brim covered half her face.

Cafes had set tables and chairs out on the sidewalk. She chose one at random, ordered a cappuccino, took a bite out of a cake. At the bottom of her backpack she found a flattened cigarette, but she didn't have a lighter. Holding it between her fingers, she wanted to smoke it, but not really. After eating the cake she reclined and snoozed. When she woke she went to a shopping center down the street. Spring was in the display cases and on the hangers. She grabbed a few floral print dresses to take into the change room. But she'd only tried one on when she felt sleepy again. The cubicle was wide enough. So she sat right down and had another snooze. She bought the dress, came out of the center, and noticed Asian restaurants along the street. She chose one, again at random, and ordered soup noodles. After eating she felt like sleeping *again*. She asked the waiter if there were any parks nearby. She yawned all the way there. Children were playing and dogs barking. She found an unoccupied bench, lay down, and went to sleep. When she woke up it was about time to set out.

Her shoulders no longer felt so tight. Berlin had relaxed her. In Laboe everyone knew her and she likewise. She even knew all the neighborhood dogs and cats by name. Here, nobody knew her. She could go to sleep in public and nobody would notice or bother her. Nobody would ask her why she hadn't lit the cigarette. Nobody asked her if she was all right. Nobody mentioned the weather. Nobody knew where she lived. Nobody knew her only son had died. Nobody knew her pain.

When she got to the jail, she had to leave everything in a locker outside. She told the guard she didn't need anything, just the hat. Could she please just wear it in?

She found him in the program. He was one of the five Hamlets. She was surprised at the size of the audience. Why would so many people come to a prison to see convicts put on a play? They had to pass multiple security checkpoints before entering the prison proper. Finally they followed a guard towards a red brick building. There were so many floors inside, with a lot of cells, a lot like the prisons she had seen in films. Before the performance began, the director came out to explain that this particular building had lain empty for years. He'd spent a long time applying to make use of the space and communicating with the authorities before getting permission. The actors had three months for memorization and rehearsal. Most of them had never read Shakespeare before. Some had picked up other Shakespearean plays in the meantime.

She took a place at the back and put on the hat. The lights came on. The actors lined up on the stage and started to recite their lines. She'd read Shakespeare in school, but had forgotten all of it, except that she found it boring, reading it on the page. But read out loud, with the modulations in tone, it was charming. He said his lines intently in a loud voice.

Each time they finished a scene, an actor invited the audience to follow him to another corner of the jail. She always brought up the rear, and sat at the back, as far away from the stage as possible.

He had a lot of scenes, a lot of soliloquies. She didn't understand why the director had gotten so many actors to play Hamlet. During one soliloquy he was sobbing by the end, his shoulders heaving. What was he was crying for? Was Hamlet supposed to cry in this scene? But then she brushed her cheek with her hand and found she, too, was crying. Could he see her?

The performance lasted over two hours. During the last scene, the wooden swords slashed and stabbed, penetrating every character's body, until everyone was dead. Her gaze never left him. He was lying on the ground sobbing quietly.

The curtain fell. There was applause, then a standing ovation. She didn't dare stand. She didn't want him, or anyone, to see her. A rain shower had fallen on her face.

The director gave a speech. It was opening night tonight, he said, so they'd prepared some simple snacks. The audience was welcome to stay after and enjoy them with the actors. She stood up to leave but ran into his gaze on the way out.

She walked up to him not knowing what to say. A welter of images formed in her mind, but not a single sentence. He was trembling, and still crying. She kept him at a distance of two or three paces and got a good look at him. The abrasions on his face had healed. There was no sand in his hair. He looked healthier now.

If you don't know what to say, then don't say anything. She walked out, not daring to look back.

Back outside, she wondered if she should have said something and if so what. What did she have to say? What if anything needed saying? Taking the U-Bahn to the hotel, she went in the wrong direction, then got on the wrong connection. She was going in circles in the unfamiliar city. But she was in no hurry. She was even enjoying herself. She imagined being lost forever never finding her way back to the hotel, never going home. Nobody would find her.

Suddenly T didn't seem quite so far away. He must have felt the same way during his time in Berlin as she did now.

Finally she got back on the right line. As soon as she sat down T appeared.

Right in front of her.

She lay on the floor and stuck her head under the opposite seat. Passengers stared, then looked away. What did she see? A sticker with a submarine and a hand flipping the bird.

When T had started acting up as a teenager, Ingrid found his behavior impossible to comprehend or handle. He put the neighbor's son in hospital. He went swimming with the neighbor's cat, held it underwater, and put the body on the owner's dinner table. He threw a girl classmate headfirst into a wall. He threatened the teacher and principal with a knife. He got into a fight with his father and stabbed him with a sharp pair of scissors. While baking his mom a cake, he set the kitchen on fire. The firefighters found him laughing. It was so beautiful, he said. She took T to Kiel to see the doctor, but the only thing that settled him down was art. He was always drawing, especially that U-boat. He said he was going to pilot it somewhere, far away from Laboe. He drew and drew and a hand flipping the bird appeared by the submarine.

She lay on the floor of the U-Bahn carriage and wept.

T had taken this train.

She knew what she should have said in the jail just now. Now she knew.

What she really, really wanted to tell him was: "Don't cry."

40. *So that even Paris could hear*

The wind has come, cramming air through the cracks in all the windows in the town. Deep in the night, the town is yawning, getting ready to go to sleep and say farewell to Ghost Festival in a dream. Yongjing hears the whistling wind, like a whispered threat. It reminds folks of ghost stories they heard growing up in the countryside: a will-o'-the-wisp lighting up the graveyard, spirit money ash sailing out of the brazier, a shadow hanging around in the bamboo grove. I've come whistling into the townhouse, too. There's a strong chance of precipitation in central Taiwan according to the weather report. After a long drought, the town might see rain.

My three eldest daughters and youngest son walk up to their old rooms and wake up the dust out of a long slumber. When Beverly goes to clean the bedding, it's like dipping the cloth in ink. Better not risk the duster. The partitions are too thin for sound-proofing. The sisters can carry on a conversation through the walls.

· "Beverly, the house down the way, the place that used to rent out videos, it's still all sooty. What gives?"

"Right, and the 'For Sale' sign has been hanging on the upstairs balcony railing ever since the fire. Who would buy it?"

"Even if they cleaned off the soot, who would buy it if they asked around? It's an 'inauspicious abode,' if not a haunted house."

"Who knows? I hear there was an investigation, but nothing came of it."

"Even if it wasn't an inauspicious abode, even if it hadn't burned, would it sell? The real-estate market is bad enough, in a place like this."

"What's that sound?"

"The wind."

"No, it's not."

"Yes, it is."

"Shut your mouths and listen up."

Shush.

Can they hear me pass through the wall?

"Termites," Keith says, touching the world map, his finger on Germany. He was always looking at the map. He would point at a country at random and tell himself he was going to go there for sure some day, and he was never coming back. He put his ear to the map and heard gnawing.

Keith's voice is hoarse, torn. It passes through the wall and into his sisters' ears. Beverly thinks of a ripped seam, Betty a split white hair, Belinda a cracked high heel.

"Why don't you go to sleep? You just got here, you must have jet lag." "Yeah, go to sleep, we can talk tomorrow." "All three of you can go to sleep. I'll go down and close the door."

"Were any of you here when it started?" Keith asks.

Nobody answers. They don't know how. They all think they know something, but actually they don't. Only I know. Only I saw.

Keith, you can't hear me, so you will never know that it was your mother who set the fire. When she heard that you were going to jail, she went down into the basement of the snake killer's place. Pacing back and forth, she decided her time had come. You don't know, and I didn't know when I was alive, that the snake killer had a basement, the only one in the row. Plenty knew. After Baron decided to marry Barbie instead of her, she had a full body breakout, a rash from head to toe. The snake killer opened a secret door, took her down into the basement, and uncorked a bottle of medicinal wine. While he was daubing it on her, Plenty saw your mother's dress on a hanger.

She lifted it when the snake killer wasn't looking, put it on, and went to see her mother. When Cicada saw her, her eyes flashed lightning, her voice thundered. Plenty threatened her. If she let Barbie marry Baron, she'd tell everyone what she'd seen in the basement. As if Cicada could tolerate a threat from

296 · KEVIN CHEN

her own child. "Go tell your father!" she howled. "Tell him! He'll be happy to hear it. Barbie will marry into the White House. As for you, everyone knows Baron had his fun with you. Haven't you heard all the nasty things he's been saying about you? Who's going to marry you now?"

After the wedding Plenty kept trying to do herself in. Cicada thought it was a passing phase. They would visit the matchmaker and find another suitable boy. But the silly girl went on cutting herself. She held a suicide press scrum in front of the White House. She cut her face and breasts in front of Baron. She even left a pool of blood in the basement for your mother to find.

When she heard you'd gone to prison, Cicada hid down there, unwilling to come out. She seemed to hear every mouth in the town saying: "She had a bunch of girls, then finally two boys, both jailbirds." She told the snake killer she wanted everything to burn. The basement, the snake killer and herself, the past. She was a failure as a mother and as a wife. Both her sons were convicts. Her husband was dead. She had no reason to keep living here. She was too ashamed to keep living here.

The fire broke out in the middle of a windy night. In an instant the snake killer's house, every floor, fell into a sea of fire. The fire spread quickly on the first floor, from VHS to DVD. The snakes and other critters on the second floor all got burnt to a crisp.

Woken up by the fire siren, Beverly opened the window, looked out, and was shocked to see the fierce tongues of flame. A water column spurted out of the hose into the house, black smoke billowed out of the house into the sky. Barbie heard the siren at the White House, but didn't dare open the curtain. Was the White House burning? Great, all those old newspapers were flammable, they would burn for sure. She imagined her own body catching on fire. That must be the scene that Plenty most wanted to see. Plenty had asked her, her tone cold, with question marks in her big eyes: "Barbie, why? Tell me why? Didn't we always get along the best?" Jealousy. She never admitted it. People only ever looked at Plenty, not at her. Plenty was the prettiest and the most delicate. She had the biggest boobs and the richest suitor. She even had a better singing voice. Barbie wasn't pretty, buxom, or sensitive. She didn't have any suitors. She envied Plenty her allergic constitution, her pale, dainty skin. Everyone doted on her. The hippo was Plenty's, Paris was hers, too. And the White House and everything in it, including the fountain of Apollo, all hers.

"Your sister is so dry," Baron complained. So, she opened her own body up and moistly invited him in. He complained about the size of her tits. She said she had everything else, and was up for anything. He could do whatever he wanted to her. "Then I'll screw you in the ass!" he said. She immediately nodded. When he did the deed, she moaned so loud that Plenty heard, so loud that the whole of Yongjing heard, so loud that even Paris could hear. "Shit!" he said. "I'm going to marry you. I haven't met a girl yet who let me fuck her butthole. Not even the ones you pay for are willing." She had won! The hippo was hers.

"There's a fire next door!" Beverly called Barbie to say. "At the snake killer's place. I think Mom's inside!" She'd already called Betty and Belinda to tell them the same thing.

As the fire department slowly got the blaze under control, animals kept crawling out, an iguana, a pangolin, a civet cat, and a boa constrictor. The boa hung on to the outside wall, until the heat forced it off. When it fell the firemen fled. Finally, a giant eagle burst out of the billowing smoke, wings aflame. Onlookers gasped as it flew into the wind coming out of the east, trailing fire across the sky above the town. It looked to be heading for the hills.

Two charred bodies were found downstairs and identified as the snake killer and Saucy Cicada. That was the first the townsfolk had heard about a basement.

41. U-995

Listening to the termites, the wind, the geckos, Keith plummeted into an abyss of sleep. Pity there was still no island rain. He'd come home to hear it.

There was rain in his dream, along with sand and tide. The seawater was cold, the sand gritty.

After killing T, he drove the car alone all the way to Laboe. The night was deep, and everyone in town had gone to sleep. There wasn't a single solitary soul on the beach.

A huge Second World War submarine lay on the beach, a U-995 that, from a distance, looked like a giant gray whale, solitary and sublime. At night it was illuminated by ripe mangos, tinted lights that turned the boat's steel skin a bizarre golden hue.

By the U-995 lay a little grassy dune. As the sea wind scoured his exposed skin, his body shook. He fell on his ass and sand got in his wounds. They still hurt. That meant he was still alive. He lay his head down on the grass. It looked dry and yellow, but it was actually nice and moist. There were a lot of fine white feathers in the grass, and tiny bits of white shell. Looking at the U-boat, he imagined T lying on the floor of their little flat. He hadn't closed the door. T hated the police, so he could not call them. He left the door open so the neighbors would.

The previous summer they ate ice cream and smoked weed by that submarine. Laughing, T told him a story about it. When he was fifteen years old, he had a decisive battle with a classmate he'd fallen foul of right beside it. They weren't allowed to bring any weapons, just their fists. The boy was much shorter than T, but he was stout. He hit T into the ocean, then charged in after him and held his head underwater. T held his breath and stopped moving, feigning death. When the boy let go, he jumped up and counterattacked. Having grown up in the ocean, he knew where it was deep and where shallow. He knew where the rocks were. He picked one up and knocked a hole in the short boy's head. Then he pulled him out to sea.

And then? Was the short boy all right?

T kept laughing. An expression of victory appeared on his face. That boy stayed in the hospital a long, long time. "Too bad he didn't die. Moron!"

He got out the knife from his backpack, the one that had entered T's body. How do you use a knife? he wondered. To kill yourself? Do you slit your wrists and then lie down? Should he put a plastic bag over his head like Plenty did? Roiling the dark brown sea, the tide called out an invitation. Maybe he should just walk into the water and drift into the deep.

Nobody could find Plenty, except for him. He went to the ditch and saw her half-submerged beside several hogs in the foul water. It was really hot, and she had sweated a lot, so much that the plastic bag was stuck to her face. He tried to shake her awake, but she did not respond. He hugged her and cried. His crying attracted passers-by, who spread the word. By the time their parents found them, he had cried himself to sleep. It looked like there were two bodies lying by the ditch.

He looked out into the Baltic and saw little white dots in the distance. Wild swans.

One, two, three . . . . He kept on counting all the way up to thirty. He counted again, up to twenty. Then he counted a third time, to thirty-five. The white dots were bobbing up and down, floating further and further away. He fell asleep counting. Maybe he didn't need to kill himself with the knife. His body heat escaping, he sank slowly into the sand. He would go to sleep and never wake up again.

Even later in the night, he felt a furry, no, a downy, sensation, and a water bird's call. He opened his eyes to the sight of

a blob of white. It was pure white, like a fluffy cloud on a
sunny day. Like cotton.

He got slowly up and found himself in the clouds. That
lamentation of swans had come ashore and gathered around
him. Several of them were right beside him. They were nuzzling
their heads into their bodies, snoozing. One of them stepped on
the knife, glanced at him, and quietly preened itself with its
beak.

He had to suppress a laugh. He had just killed his partner,
what was funny about that? It was something about the
plumage, so extremely white, and glimmering in the night. They
were not afraid of him in the least. They trusted him so completely they had gone to sleep by his side. Suddenly he didn't feel
lonely anymore. It really was amusing. The youngest son of a
central Taiwanese country clan, he was lying on a beach in the
north of Germany in ripped clothes with excruciating wounds
that would soon begin to fester. He had not taken a bath in a
long time. There was even dried shit on his skin. But here he
was, surrounded by swans in the dead of night. It was just too
absurd. Laughter bubbled up to his mouth from deep within
his body.

He thought of the hippo the day of Barbie's wedding.

It was by far the biggest animal in the zoo. Baron had asked
the snake killer to get one for him. The snake killer said he had
a way, just leave it to him. The workers dug a really deep pool
for the beast. The day it came to town, Baron had a new bride,
Barbie. At the wedding reception, Plenty pulled Keith away
from the Chen table, saying to come see the hippo. They
walked to the back yard. The tropical birds were screeching,
wedding guests were shrieking, all of them drunk. The guests
were standing by the hippo enclosure. The hippo opened its
mouth wide, exposing sharp teeth. When it did, they poured
sorghum liquor down its throat, along with French red wine
and German white. They tossed in Japanese apples and prawns.

"The hippo's mine," Plenty said.

Still in his boaskin suit, the snake killer was feeding the birds. "I know how to open the enclosure, if you want," he said.

When the fireworks went off, the guests left to go see. The snake killer winked at him and showed Plenty how to unlatch the gate. The hippo waddled slowly out. It'd had a lot to drink. It swayed back and forth and took a look at Plenty.

"Go," she said.

The hippo started to trot towards the banquet tables. They heard screams and crashes. The hippo must have bashed over quite a few tables and stepped on a few toes. Guests fled the scene.

The wedding fireworks had ended, but the fireworks in Plenty's eyes had just begun.

Watching the hippo trampling the round tables, they couldn't help laughing, Plenty and Keith.

After smashing around the White House grounds, the hippo lumbered along Main Street all the way through town until it fell over in a rice paddy.

Keith sat up. He had to pee. So he peed sitting down. He was used to it. The sky started to lighten in the east, until the sun showed its face, its light tinting the swans' plumage pure gold. The swans turned toward the sea and eased elegantly into the water. White stars appeared again on the shimmering surface.

He felt in his pocket for T's mobile. He entered the passcode. He knew the code for T's bank card, too, and the balance. What side of the bed he slept on and how many light brown moles he had in his crotch. But the T who tied him up, hit him, and raped him, Keith didn't know him at all.

It was raining, a sunshower. He took in the swans on the sea and the U-995 on the beach. The submarine was getting rained on. It would never dive again.

He found Mama in the contact list.

He started to cry as soon as he pressed Call.

42. If only I had kept my mouth shut

Keith was sleeping fitfully. Sweat flowed down in rivulets, which converged into a torrent that poured into the sheets. He was soaking wet, having sweated a sea. His dreams were a muddle. Something sharp was thrust at him. He woke up with a start.

What a racket! Trucks kept racing by, roaring through the wall. He headed for Plenty's room. With the windows onto the balcony, it might be a bit less stuffy.

He wasn't the only one who thought so. Betty was sitting on Plenty's bed looking up at the moon. In the light her wrinkles appeared even deeper, but relaxed, uncovered, honest. Belinda's skin looked too smooth, as if the wrinkles had been ironed out. It was twilight in her eyes, high noon on her skin. The effect was like jet lag.

"It's so hot, isn't it?" she said. "I can't sleep, either. I just went downstairs and took a second shower, but look at me! I'm all sweaty again." When he sat down by her side, the bed frame groaned. Apparently, the termites were awake. Maybe they'd had a sleepless night, too.

"Betty, what time is it?"

"I don't know either, I can't find my watch. It doesn't matter. Every time I come back it takes me a while to adjust. The time here is different, it's slower."

"What's with all these trucks?"

"Beverly mentioned the Wangs built a warehouse, a 'satisfaction center' for the biggest e-commerce platform in central Taiwan. It's news to me, too. Since it was finished trucks have been driving past all night long." Right then another big truck raced by, shaking the surface of the road, and the floors and walls of the townhouse, too. He imagined the products those trucks were hauling converging in Yongjing from all around the world. Globalization had arrived, it's just that the locals had no idea. They still had no sense of "prosperity." They were in a time zone all of their own.

Finally, a cool breeze. Like those trucks, it was rushing along, plundering and looting as it went, never looking back. The breeze that blew into the old house brought thick clouds that hid the moon.

"Before I came home yesterday I visited a lot of places. Did you know that the swimming pool is closed?"

"I heard. Beverly used to work there."

"I also went to the carambola orchard. I couldn't believe it was still standing." At the mention of the orchard, they both fell silent.

Keith was thinking, it's all my fault. So was Betty.

They had never talked about it. About what happened in 1984. The year the first branch of McDonald's opened in Taiwan, the year Keith turned eight, the year Nut Wang gave up a high-paying job in Taipei and returned to the countryside to tend carambola.

Keith liked Nut a lot. After school he always ran over to the orchard to see him. Tall and thin, Nut smelled of sweat, and his skin was wet. His teeth were shiny, and he had such fine hair on his tummy. He always wore a pair of red shorts. He was always reading. He read Keith translated novels. He played the guitar and sang American folk songs to him. Keith enjoyed grabbing Nut down there. Nut would pat away his hand. "No, you don't, you're just a kid." So Keith waited until Nut took a snooze before attempting another audacious grab. Nut got really hard. He had no idea why.

Another memory, from when Nut was recuperating in bed after the hailstorm. After who knows how many bowls of snake soup, Keith stumbled muddle-headed over to the Wang place and up to Nut's room. He started to play around in Nut's lap, until his mother suddenly walked in with a bowl of soup. She didn't say a thing, just gave him a stern look, took him in her arms, and carried him home.

Saucy Cicada saw a couple of posters on the walls of Nut's room. She couldn't read them, but she knew they would raise a tsunami.

When films played at the Lady at the Foot of the Wall, he sat on Nut's lap, reached his hand back, and grabbed Nut's groin. Nut gently detached his hand, pointed at the screen, and said: "Watch the film." He tried another couple of times, until Nut gave up and let him stroke it. The thing in the red shorts swelled up again.

"It's all your fault," Mother said. "*You* got Nut Wang killed! I only called the cops when I saw you and Nut messing around."

She told the police she saw Communist Party posters on Jack Wang's youngest son's bedroom walls. She heard he was reading banned books, too.

Before the cops came for him, several friendly-looking outsiders showed up. They discovered that Jack Wang's youngest son, the one who was nicknamed Nut, often went to gatherings at the Tomorrow Bookstore.

Agents tracked down Betty in Taipei.

"Miss Chen, we'd like to ask you a few questions. Do you deliver books to the Tomorrow Bookstore in Yongjing?"

Betty had no idea that the boxes she was moving from Taipei to Yongjing contained banned books by leftist writers and magazines published by the Tangwai movement, the informal, and illegal, opposition to the Kuomintang.

"We know you're not a part of this. As long as you cooperate, you'll be fine." It was a veiled threat. "It's 1984, after all. We're not going to make a big deal out of it, we'd rather keep it hush hush. All you need to do is give us some names. Tell us the names of the other members of the reading group. The group that meets on the second floor. Who are they? What books do they read? What's on the walls?"

She couldn't recall the names of any of the books, but she had seen Marx and Lenin on the walls, in addition to Chairman Mao, Generalissimo Chiang, and Chiang's son Chiang Ching-kuo. They used to aim darts at Mao's or Chiang's eyes. When she mentioned Chiang Kai-shek she realized she had wet her pants. She was shaking too much to hold it in.

"Who are 'they'? Tell us. Who are the members?" Nut and the two bosses, Ming and Ri. She didn't understand the books they talked about. She just went there to eat and chat. She hadn't joined any reading group. Tangwai, democracy, socialism, freedom, she didn't understand any of it. All she did besides delivering boxes was bring them McDonald's French fries to eat.

"Thank you for your cooperation. Don't worry, nothing's going to happen to you. We've looked into your background, and obviously, you don't have any direct involvement in this case. And as I said, we're more relaxed these days. There's a lot of international pressure on Taiwan now, we're supposed to clean up our human rights act. It's a delicate situation. Actually, we're just hoping to avoid trouble. But I must say, Miss Chen, that if this had happened a decade ago, heads would have rolled."

She sat at home in a daze all afternoon before she thought of warning the bosses. She took the night train back to Yongjing, but the agents from the National Security Bureau had beaten her there.

That morning Cicada got up early and went to the Lady at the Foot of the Wall. They would be reciting sutras for the snake killer. He'd won another championship. He was going to take the winning orchid to the temple to thank the Lady for her assistance. As a sign of his sincerity, he hired Cicada's recitation group and the Three Sisters Burlesque to come perform. Cicada told the snake killer something big was going down that morning, she wanted to stay out of it. Could they do it first thing in the morning?

None of the singers had gotten enough sleep. Sleepy-eyed, they were still wondering why they had to wake up at such an ungodly hour. Surely the Lady would prefer to sleep in. But they'd gotten up anyway, as that snake killer sure was generous when he handed out the red envelopes. The ladies put on their costumes, set up the microphones, turned the amplifier all the way up, and started reciting. Cicada sang the loudest, really belting it out. She was practically roaring into the microphone.

Right next to the temple was an abattoir. The butcher was standing there holding his knife when he heard, or felt, the blast from next door. "Fuck!" he cried. "Why are they reciting scripture so early?" He stuck the tip in and the pig squealed. The way it cried before it died, it was as if it was competing for volume with Cicada and the other ladies across the way. The louder the pigs squealed, the louder the ladies sang, pumping up their decibels. By now the pigs were squealing on the same beat. After a brief tug of war, they complemented each other rhythmically and harmonically. Divine exaltation and bloody butchery were the two parts of the most bizarre song in history. The secret police heard it. It was an even bloodier morning than usual. Listening to the chanting from next door, the butcher felt sleepy. He was too tired to clean the killing floor.

The blood formed a river, which flowed towards the temple. Still facing the microphone, Cicada felt something wet underfoot. Looking down, she found herself standing in a river of blood.

The Tomorrow Bookstore was cordoned off when Betty finally made it. She saw the thick boss and the thin boss being pressed into police cruisers.

Betty slapped her face, again and again. "It's all my fault. All my fault. All my fault. If only I had kept my mouth shut. If only . . ."

But by the time the police charged into the Wang household, Nut was long gone.

The snake killer had shaken Nut awake in the middle of the night. "Hurry! Rip up all your posters. Best if you burned them. Take all the books you can carry and hide."

Nut ripped up the posters and took the books. But where could he hide? Where could he hide the books?

"Don't worry," the snake killer said. "I've got a safe place. I guarantee that they won't be able to find you, for the time being." Indeed, when the police arrived, he was nowhere to be found.

They did not find any of his books, either. His room was empty.

Betty had not mentioned that Nut and the bosses weren't the only members of the reading group. There was a fourth.

"Betty," Keith said, "it's almost dawn. I want to go pay my respects to Dad."

It was raining, finally. The raindrops rode the wind onto the balcony and into the room. Betty and Keith felt the threads of rain on their faces, but neither wanted to get up and close the window.

Betty didn't mention that the fourth member of the reading group was their father.

43. Two suicide notes

Father, Mother:

Let me first apologize.

I didn't make it. If you are reading this, I'm dead. After I finish writing, I'll give it to the snake killer. He promised he'd take care of it and that if anything happens to me, he'll turn it over to you. Of course I hope everything will work out. But I have a feeling it won't.

Father, sorry. I know that you greased all the palms and pulled all the strings you could to get me out. Now I'm out. But the two bosses of the bookstore are still in custody. I'll see if some friends can help get the word out. If it makes the news, then they might make it out, too.

Mother, sorry. Really sorry. Baron was never as good at school as me, but he's sure got a brain for business. He's going to make you really proud someday.

They went to work on me when I was in there. They're very good at their jobs. They don't let you sleep, and they know how to hit you without leaving a mark to get a confession. But I knew they didn't have anything on me, my room was empty. Without any direct evidence, they had to let me out. So I'm out. If only it were that simple.

The snake killer has hidden those books of mine away somewhere, I don't know where. He'll return them if he can. If something happens to me, please tell him to dispose of them, to avoid implicating anyone else. Thank him for me.

I'm not afraid of death. My only fear is not being free.

I'm not going to cry, even though I know I might die at any time.

I'm afraid for the two bosses. Father, Mother, help them if you can. It pains me that all I can offer you is:

My condolences.

Your son,

Nut

Dear Cliff:

Of course I hope you never have to read this.

You must have heard I got out. You know as well as me that they won't give up so easily. I can't go see you now, I don't want to get you in trouble. You're just a few doors down, but a world away. Thank goodness you're all right. Thank goodness they didn't find you.

One of the conditions for my release was that I have to keep a record of everyone I talk to, everywhere I go, everything I eat and read. I have to report back to them. So I really can't go and see you. Sorry.

I'll get this letter to the snake killer somehow. If anything happens to me, he will pass it on.

The person I find it hardest to let go of is you.

The days we spent together in the cistern are the happiest of my life.

Whenever your youngest slipped and fell, had a nightmare, got hungry, he would cry. Don't cry, I would say. That-a-boy.

Cliff, I'll say the same thing to you: Don't cry, don't cry, don't cry. I haven't cried. Really. And I won't. So please, Cliff, don't.

Yours,

Nut

44. Homo Crime Duo Busted

The bosses got arrested. Everyone was looking for Nut. Where could such a tall guy hide?

He was not in the carambola orchard, the fishpond, or the bamboo. After searching every barn, the police concluded that he had caught wind of the manhunt and fled Yongjing.

There was a notice in the newspaper with the headline "Homo Crime Duo Busted." "The owners of the Tomorrow Bookstore in Yongjing, Changhua were operating a front for a gay porn operation. After hours, they shot and sold depraved adult movies, harming public morality."

The police seemed to have pulled out. Without all those outsiders around, the small town was quieter, though not quite back to normal. The chrysanthemums were blooming, the betel leaves evergreen.

Cliff Chen was gone.

Cicada couldn't find him anywhere. There was a pile of betel, both nuts and leaves, waiting for delivery. But without him to arrange the schedule, everything was a mess. Nobody knew how to do the books.

Cicada saw a shelf of books downstairs at the snake killer's. She was illiterate, but her memory was tack-sharp. She'd seen those books before, up in Nut's room. She told the snake killer Nut could go to hell for all she cared. She just wanted to know where the hell Cliff had gone.

The snake killer didn't let on where the hell Cliff was. But he knew what the hell had become of Nut.

"Ask your daughters. I told them to take turns delivering meals." Girls would stand out on the road at night, so they had to go by day, wearing low-key clothes and looking relaxed. The deliveries couldn't be too regular or they'd attract attention. They had to select dishes without a strong smell that would give them away. Sometimes they went alone, sometimes in pairs, with one keeping watch and the other making the delivery. Sometimes they rode bicycles, sometimes scooters. Sometimes they walked. However they went, they couldn't rush. They knew the small town like the palms of their hands, including all the secret paths. They knew how to get to the carambola orchard by a roundabout route.

On the roof of every residence in the countryside sat a silver water cistern. Farmers mounted them on frames to irrigate their fields. Nut was hiding out in the one in the orchard.

One day, Betty and Belinda went to the market to buy groceries, to the Lady at the Foot of the Wall to pray, and to the Fragrant soy-sauce factory to eat with their grandmother. They snuck out the back door and took a path to the orchard. Betty climbed up the cistern and tossed in toilet paper, a lunch box, clean clothes, and newspaper clippings.

She almost fell off when she saw her father.

Inside the cistern.

The next few days, the sisters delivered two lunch boxes.

Nut and her father were talking quietly inside the cistern. It was often suffocating. Their limbs would go numb. But their hands stayed tightly clasped.

Only on moonless nights did they dare climb out to piss, shit, and stretch.

Nut pointed east. "Cliff, we have to get out of here. There are lots of hiding places in the Central Range. They'd never find us there."

Cliff nodded.

They read the clippings and hurled silent curses at the sky. The bosses had been saving money to study abroad. Now everything was ruined.

They would leave the next day.

The summer cicadas cried in the trees, like a warning.

That day the sisters brought Keith to the orchard to beg Father to come home.

Betty climbed up and tapped. "Father, Mother wants you to come home. There's a mound of betel nut and leaf in the living room. The books are a mess. Only you can sort it out."

Nut and Cliff knew what she was telling them. She meant that "they" knew, that "they" were coming.

"Cliff, please," Nut said, "go home. If we get caught together, it'll be the downfall of both our families. If I get caught alone, it might be easier to explain. Don't worry, I'll make it out. Alive."

The sisters would never forget the expression on Father's face when he climbed out.

Father's gaze stayed inside the cistern. Before he climbed

down, he looked down and said a few words. The cicadas were too loud for the kids to hear what.

Cliff took Keith in his arms. Resting his head on Father's shoulder, Keith saw a head emerge at the edge of the cistern. He felt his father's eyes sweat.

After Cliff came home and took a shower, he sat down, did the books, and arranged the schedule for the next few days. He made a lot of calls. He made sure every driver got his paycheck.

It was so hot that afternoon. Everyone sat down on the porch around the round table to enjoy a feast. It was an ordinary day, but Cicada really went overboard, as if she was making the mother of all spirit offerings. Ghost Festival was still a few weeks away. Then again, the Hellgate would start to creak open in a couple of days.

Everyone ate, nobody spoke. Keith started crying, saying he wanted to go see Uncle Nut. "They caught him," a neighbor riding by hollered. "I hear they got him!"

Why was the rice so hard, like pebbles in Cicada's mouth? The bowl was suddenly so heavy she had to put it down. She looked down and saw blood on her feet.

Nut was released, but several days later a chrysanthemum farmer discovered his body in the irrigation ditch.

Another notice appeared in the newspaper: "Not Straight Enough? Straight-A Misfit Chooses Suicide Over Prison."

Many years later, Keith would find Plenty's body in the same ditch.

The snake killer had two letters.

He turned them over, as promised. To Jack Wang.

45. Where did that wind come from?

The rain stopped. The sun rose.

Beverly cooked up a big pot of congee, fried eggs, cabbage,

tofu crisps, and grilled sausage. Belinda put on one of Beverly's loose-fitting dresses. She left her hair loose, too, and didn't apply makeup. Squatting down to eat, she could not recall the last time she felt so relaxed. She took a cracker from the table, took a bite, and frowned. "Have you guys ever wondered why the Chens ended up with a tumbledown house in Yongjing and the Wangs with the White House, that headquarters in Taipei, and a private jet to fly around in when Dad and Jack Wang started out together, selling these god-awful crackers in China?"

"Because Jack knew everything," her father answered before blowing on her congee to cool it off for her. It was too damn hot.

Of course Belinda didn't see or hear him.

Their timely ascent of the Great Wall gave them a commercial advantage on the competition. That summer Beijing was in chaos. Cliff said he was pulling out, he wasn't going to invest. He'd gone to the square and seen hundreds of thousands of Nut Wangs. Jack was apoplectic. He had stuffed a lot of red envelopes, greased a lot of palms, or they wouldn't be where they were today. "Don't worry about those young people," he said. "We're businessmen, we should keep our minds on the bottom line."

"Forget it, Jack, I quit. I'm out. If something happens, it's going to end in tragedy. It'll be even worse than it was for us a few years ago."

"You're talking to me about tragedy? Was it your son who died or mine? We come here to do business, and here you get all sanctimonious on me. All these pretty girls and you won't touch any of them. Don't think I don't know. You don't fuck women, not even your own wife. But you were fucking my son."

Cliff never went back to Beijing.

Now Betty squatted down beside Belinda to dry her white hair, which had no place to hide in the morning light. Beverly squatted beside Betty, forming a circle of crones around the crack. She peered in as her congee steamed, then looked up. The three disheveled sisters gaped at one another. With the Hellgate wide open and all, someone might mistake them for ghosts if they went out for a walk.

"Let's go visit Father after breakfast," Beverly suggested.

Famished, Keith wolfed down five bowls of congee and chomped on tofu crisps. The night before he had finally heard the island rain. He got so hungry listening to it. After he finished, he walked outside.

The world was glistening after the rainstorm the night before had washed all creation clean. Without the films of dust they had carried through the long drought, the leaves glowed green in the rising sun, which dyed the clouds gold. The birds cried good morning. The fresh smell of mud hung in the air. He saw the White House in the distance and blinked. It was still an absurd sight.

On their way to pay their respects to Father, they met a lot of relatives Keith did not recognize at all. His sisters had to tell him who they all were. "Say hello to your aunt!" "Hurry up, greet your uncle!" "This is your grandaunt!" "Have you forgotten your granduncle?" His brain did not have a folder for all these faces. They all smiled kindly, patted his shoulders, and asked, "How long have you been back?" All he could do is shake his head, smile, and nod. Why was everyone so old?

At the clump of bamboo, the siblings all stopped and paid their respects. They actually had no idea why. They were only doing it because Mother had told them to, starting when they were young. It had become a reflex. They had to put their palms together and pump their hands up and down every time they passed.

By the soy-sauce factory they looked up at the mottled canvas mural of the emeritus mayor. When had the factory shut down? None of them could remember. When was the last time they had eaten a meal made with Fragrant soy sauce? They had all forgotten.

"Beverly, you're taking us the long way!" "No wonder it feels like we've been walking forever." "Nonsense! Anyone from Taipei or Germany can shut up now. I am the only one here who's still from Yongjing. Follow me." "No way, we should have taken a right turn back there. At this rate it'll be evening before we get there." "I'm going to find my own way!" "Didn't the path used to go that way?" "Okay! We'll see who gets there first!" "All right, race you!"

Not knowing which elder sister to follow, Keith decided to go off on his own. Actually, he turned out to be the only one who remembered the shortcut, and he was the first to arrive. His bickering sisters were all out of breath when they finally made it, one after another. To the carambola orchard. That's where Cliff's cremains were scattered.

They lit incense, set fruit on a plate, faced the orchard, and prayed. A rusted frame was all that remained of the water cistern.

They cleared away the fallen leaves, piled spirit money on the ground, and lit it. With the flames licking at the sky, Beverly and Betty put their palms together and said: "Father, Keith has come back to see you. Please bless him and watch over him."

Keith also put his hands together. "Father, I'm back. Please give Beverly, Betty, Belinda, and Barbie your blessing." He was trying not to cry.

T, I'm home.

They hear a vehicle approaching.

A maroon SUV is rolling slowly towards the orchard. Belinda can tell that it's a Porsche. She even knows which model it is, because it's the one her husband drives. She is shocked. She hasn't thought of him since yesterday afternoon. Looking at Beverly and Betty, she tries to remember what their husbands look like, and what hers looks like for that matter. But she can't.

That SUV is out of this world. Lines of flashing LED lights in a rainbow of colors hang off the sides, golden figurines dance on the roof: a dragon, a phoenix, a snake, a tiger, a hippo, a giraffe, a pangolin, and an eagle, all moving left and right and up and down. To top it off, a scrolling marquee at the front brings the following good news to Yongjing: "THE YEL-LOW EMPEROR IS HERE TO SAVE HUMANITY!!! HIS YELLOW HIGHNESS WILL DELIVER ALL SENTIENT BEINGS FROM SUFFERING!!!" The exclamation marks stop flickering, and the animals freeze when the SUV stops in front of them, but that doesn't make it any less eye-catching. The maroon paint job is so saturated that it sucks up all the color in the vicinity. Wherever it goes, the surroundings must look pale by comparison, as if their only reason for existence is to set off this SUV.

The window rolls down and, lo and behold, there sits the Yellow Emperor they saw on TV. He's wearing sunglasses and smiling, showing a glaring set of pearly whites. But to them, he isn't the Yellow Emperor, he's their neighbor the snake killer, who operated a VHS rental store on the first floor of his town-house.

Betty recalls the huge, vibrantly colored temple she saw through the HSR window on the outskirts of Taipei. Beverly is reminded, too, of a lot of friends who believe that the Yellow Emperor has the power to cure cancer, relieve pain, and make sure the next child will be a son. Some say he has thousands of spectacled cobras at his beck and call.

In the passenger's seat sits their mother.

Cicada can't recall how long it's been since she visited Yongjing. Once upon a time she promised that she was never coming back.

But yesterday someone called the temple saying that her baby son was home.

Cicada puts on her shades and gets out of the car in a gorgeous hot-pink dress with pure gold accessories. Her hair is white, her cheeks ruddy. Her three eldest daughters and her youngest son are aghast. "What's wrong?" Cicada wonders. "Seen a ghost in Ghost Month? Frightened, are we? Need me to help you collect your wits?" When they were growing up, every time they couldn't get to sleep, didn't want to eat, or got a bad mark on a test, she would collect their wits for them. All she needed was an article of the child's clothing, a porcelain bowl, and white rice and she could conduct the ritual anytime, anywhere. She learned it from her mother. She filled the bowl with rice, tied it tightly with the garment, raised and lowered it thrice before the chest and behind the back of the afflicted soul, then held it to the forehead and cast the spell: "Earth Mother, Father Sky, collect the wits of this frightened child. Sleep well, sleep tight, everything's going to be all right. Earth's vast, Sky's great, your luck will turn, just you wait." With a pinch of the child's earlobe, the ritual was complete. She had only to uncover the bowl and observe the patterns in the grains and she could discern the child's previous existences and his or her destiny in this life. He or she had to wear the garment. A good night's sleep was guaranteed.

Now she is honored in the temple as Madame Immortal. Every time she collects someone's wits, she receives a thick red envelope. The earliest available time slot on the online appointment booking system is early next year, almost six months away. Politicians, business tycoons, and celebrities spend a fortune to jump the queue.

The daughters can't think of anything to say. A second ago they were arguing incessantly, now threads have sewn each pair of flapping lips into a seam. Why do they look so old? Cicada can't get over it. They are dressed so shabbily. They are hoary-faced, weary-eyed. They look even older than her. Cicada imagines she could breathe hard on them and they would turn to ash. Soon the wind would come and blow them away.

Her youngest son's expression is the most complex. He is looking at her with tears welling in his eyes.

Suddenly a sweet and sour taste gushes in their mouths, as if they are drinking bowls of starfruit soup.

A stiff gust scares the swallows from the trees. Keith looks up. Hey! That's not how swallows fly. Those are bats!

Where did that wind come from? From the Taiwan Strait or the Central Range? The wind that just blew through Yongjing set out from the Baltic Sea, from the dry box in the White House, and from the treetops in the carambola orchard. The wind was layered, containing speech. The wind blew a message into Cicada's ears, for her to preach.

I called the cops, she wants to say, not because of you, my baby boy, but because I found out about Cliff and Nut. The Yellow Emperor, she wants to say, I mean the snake killer, our neighbor of many years, is actually Goggles, an apprentice at the Fragrant soy-sauce factory I met a decade before I married your father.

Have you eaten yet? Have you gotten enough to eat? I used to worry that you'd go hungry. That's what she wants to say. But that's not the message that the wind wants her to relay.

Her youngest son's tears are streaming down. The wind comes again, pouring words into her ears. She hears them. So clearly.

The wind tells her to tell her youngest son: "Don't cry." That's what the wind from the Baltic Sea, from the suicide notes in the White House, and from the carambola orchard keeps saying: Don't cry. Don't cry. Don't cry.

Cicada drums up her abdomen.

She causes her throat to quake.

She opens her mouth to speak.

THE END

AFTERWORD

I always wanted to write a "ghost" story.
When I was growing up in Yongjing, ghosts were rumored to be everywhere in the countryside—in the slough, in the bamboo by the field. My elders mentioned ghosts to scare us kids: if we weren't good, a powerful ghost would show up to discipline us. Kids loved to talk about ghosts, too. We traded stories about spirits of the swimming hole. Don't spend too long on the toilet, we said, or ghostly hands will reach up and grab you. Never leave a doll by the bedside, or an evil spirit will show up in the middle of the night, possess the doll, and start dancing.

But what exactly is a "ghost"?

When I was a child, my sisters teased me by calling me "a ghost who loves to cry," in other words a crybaby. That would make me cry even louder. "I'm not a ghost. I don't want to be a ghost!" Wiping away the tears, I cocked my head and, in my naivete, I thought: Wait a minute! Being a ghost might not actually be that bad. Able to walk through walls, ghosts are powerful. They can scare people and choke them. They can even possess their bodies. I started laughing. I was a crybaby who wanted to be a ghost.

Although I heard a lot of stories, I never saw a ghost, or felt one, until I did my mandatory military service. When the lights went out in the high mountain base at which I was stationed, two other soldiers and I sensed a paranormal power. Instead of freaking out, I thought of a scene in Haruki Murakami's *Dance,*

Dance, Dance. As the narrator and the matinee idol Gotanda drown their sorrows in drink, a "third presence" appears in the room.

> Someone else was here besides Gotanda and myself. I sensed body heat, breathing, odor. Yet it wasn't human. I froze. I glanced quickly around the room, but I saw nothing. There was only the feeling of something. Something solid, but invisible. I breathed deeply. I strained to hear. It waited, crouching, holding its breath. Then it was gone. (Translated by Alfred Birnbaum. Vintage, 1994, p. 301)

The next morning, I set about trying to explain the previous night's apparition with science and logic. Reasoning failed, and no theory could explain what we had experienced.

I didn't see anything, I just "felt" "something." Was that a "real" "ghost," or was it a ghost like dead King Hamlet or Du Liniang, the heroine in *The Peony Pavilion*?

Do you become a ghost only after you die? Or can you qualify as a ghost while you are still alive?

Having written *Ghost Town*, I still have only a vague idea of what a ghost is. I'm still full of the question marks that prompted me to write the novel in the first place. There was no other way to answer the questions except by writing. While I was writing, I got some guidance from William Faulkner: "The past is never dead. It's not even past."

So the past is like a shadow that follows us wherever we go, and everywhere there are memories and sorrows we want to bury, to cover up, there must be ghosts. Maybe you and I are ghosts.

* * *

I always wanted to write a novel about "crying."

I was a crybaby, a ghost that loved to cry. The ninth baby in my family, I cried when I was hungry, when I was full, when I went to bed, and when I woke up. My seven sisters took turns coaxing me—there, there, sweetie pie, don't cry—but no one could get me to shut up. After I learned to read, I cried when I read books or newspapers. I cried when I watched TV and when I listened to the radio. I even cried in my sleep.

After I grew up, I cried at films, and at lively or lonely scenes. I cried when I read novels, lyric essays, and poems.

To write the chapters in the novel that are set on the shore of the Baltic Sea, I visited the small coastal town of Laboe on a winter day in February. There I saw a man sobbing forlornly on a beach next to a submarine, a stranded metal whale. He buried his head in the sand, and kept hitting the ground with his fists, as wild snow-white swans gathered on the sea.

I sat on the icy cold beach and listened, to the sea, the wind, and his cries.

* * *

I always wanted to write a novel about hippos.

When I was a child, I used to meet a crazy woman on my way to school. Her hair was long and tangled, her clothes ripped, her eyes wild. The words that poured from her mouth were a mystery. In the middle of summer, she wore a heavy winter coat.

One day when I met her on my way home, she'd fixed her gaze in the distance. "There, by the field," she said. "There's a dead hippo." She pointed at the faraway rice field. I noticed many scars on the insides of her arms. She must have slit her wrists with razor blades.

Later she disappeared.

I rode my bike around Yongjing, looking for hippos, looking for her.

* * *

I have been writing stories about Yongjing for a long time.

Last time I went home was for a referendum on same-sex marriage proposed by a conservative Christian group for the local elections that were held on November 24, 2018. After flying all the way back from Berlin to vote, I spent only one night in my hometown. I am from Yongjing, but I no longer have a "home" there. I was born on Bade Lane. I grew up in a townhouse on Hulian Road. In junior high school we moved to Zhongshan Road. The old houses were all still there, but no room belonged to me. I couldn't have found a desk to write on.

Yongjing still looked the same; the past echoed in my mind. I took a slow regional bus to the deserted train station and walked slowly into town. I thought I was going home. I realized how rash I had been to walk; people in the countryside tend to drive or ride motorcycles. I walked past the pool where I had learned to swim, and stepped inside with a hum of horror in my throat. The pool was run down, and the water had dried up. I sat by the dry pool, a moldy ruin into which memories of swimming in the cerulean water of my youth crashed. Is memory reliable? I wondered. Are these memories real? Does my childhood still exist, somehow? Does eternity? What about Yongjing? Why was I writing about it?

I stayed at my older sister's house that night; it was clearly the house I had lived in as a child, but everything looked strange to me. After dinner, I wandered the streets. I saw the Temple to the Mother at the Foot of the Wall, the elementary school, and the Everyman Bookstore. There, a man with long hair in a ponytail stopped me: "This is a flyer," he said, "for tomorrow's anti-gay referendum. We need your support."

I just stood and stared. I wanted to remind him that not so long ago men were forbidden to wear their hair long. "Under martial law, the state would have cut your hair," I wanted to say, "and labeled you subversive. Here you are on an island of freedom, spreading hate in the street and rejecting people who are different from you." This is what I actually said: "Can you please stop discriminating against people like me? Because of people like you, we can't go home."

To him, it was all ghostspeak. What did he care if I couldn't go home?

I started writing *Ghost Town* in Berlin in July 2018, and by the end of April 2019, the novel was complete. I excavated memories of Yongjing the whole time. I always wanted to escape from Yongjing, but I kept writing about it. Sometimes everything around me seemed to come unmoored, including me. When I looked down, my skin and flesh grew blurry, even transparent.

Afraid I had become a ghost, I sent the manuscript to my editor and hit the sack.

I slept peacefully.

I knew that a ghost would appear. I knew that Yongjing would glide into my room in Berlin and lie down by my side.

K.C.

TRANSLATOR'S NOTE ON NAMING

Anovel begins with the title for the translator, too. The title of this novel begins with the word 鬼, ghost, pronounced *gǔi* [kʷei] in Mandarin, the national language, and *kuí* [kʷi] in Taiwanese, also known as Hokkien, the language that Kevin Chen's folks grew up speaking. 鬼 appears in many words and idioms in Chinese languages. As the author mentions in his afterword, a crybaby is "a ghost who loves to cry." Alcoholics and drug addicts are "booze fiends" and "drug fiends." I made up the word "ghostspeak," a calque of 鬼話, meaning bullshit or nonsense. The idiom 什麼鬼—literally "What ghost?"—translated idiomatically as: "What the hell?" Hell is, after all, where ghosts dwell, most of the time.

The Chinese title 鬼地方 is another ghastly idiom. It could mean something like the popsicle stand that one blows, but it's usually more unpleasant, more like wasteland or hellhole. The title, however, could also be read literally, as "ghost place." In Chinese, nouns aren't marked as singular or plural, so the title could also be translated *Ghost Places*. All the places in the novel, or in our world, are ghastly, each in its own way. So why did I settle on *Ghost Town*? For two reasons. First, because, like the Chinese title, it's ambiguous, though in a slightly different way. A ghost town is haunted or deserted. Second, because the narrator of the first chapter says he's from a small place that is a ghost place, or a small town that is a ghost town in my translation. Small towns like Yongjing and Laboe are deserted, because of population outmigration—because people like Keith and T leave, never to return. Small towns are also haunted by "actual" ghosts or by "symbolic" ghosts, whatever it is that ghosts represent. Big cities like Taipei and Berlin are haunted, too, particularly in the middle of the hottest month of the year, the seventh of the traditional calendar, when the lone souls and wild (or hungry) ghosts who have nobody to mourn them pour through the Hellgate to wander through the world.

The holiday had to be named, too, but ghosts of translators past had done the work for me. It's typically known as Ghost Festival, an occasion for both Daoists and Buddhists to conduct ceremonies of "universal deliverance." The "deliverance" in question is, in Mandarin, the "crossing" of a body of water, usually a river or a sea. Philosophically minded Buddhists associate water-crossing with transcendence, with leaving this vale of tears behind and reaching the other shore of Nirvana, only to realize that "you" were "there" the whole time. Ordinary believers wish for deliverance from whatever personal hell they are in so they can get to wherever they want to be. In *Ghost Town*, Keith just wants to go home, and his childhood chum Sampan Yang is the one who ferries him there.

Beyond the title of the book and a name for the festival, I also had to come up with the characters' names. Given that most Taiwanese people have English names, like Kevin Chen himself, this seemed natural enough. But there was another reason for giving the characters of *Ghost Town* English names. While I respect translators who romanize names, I personally find it impoverishing because names in literature are often significant. They certainly are in this novel. The *shān* in Ashan, the patriarch of the Chen clan, means "mountain," so I thought of a synecdoche that could serve as a name: Cliff. The *chán* in Achan, the matriarch, means "cicada," and Cliff and Cicada happen to contain a "k" sound, which is compensation for the loss of the Mandarin rhyme (Ashan, Achan). The first three sisters' names share a character, as is traditional in Chinese families: Shumei, Shuli, and Shuqing. So I invented a familial naming tradition, Beverly, Betty, and Belinda, names that suit their respective personalities. To break the girl curse, Cliff and Cicada depart slightly from tradition with the fourth daughter, Sujie, hence Barbie. In naming their fifth daughter Qiaomei, they depart totally from tradition, hence Ciao, who is known as Plenty from high school on. Big brother Tianyi and little brother Tianhong turned into Heath, who never leaves his rural home, and Keith, who leaves home the first chance he gets. Keith Chen the character may remind you of Kevin Chen the author, and he should: Keith is Tianhong, Kevin Sihong, in Mandarin. Beyond the Chen clan, I gave Mr. Wang the cracker manufacturer the nickname Cracker Jack, and his sons the names Baron and Nut. Baron seemed an apt name for a childless stock market tycoon, and Nut for a misunderstood idealist who never cries, never cracks, who keeps his head in the clouds, or in the stars, until the bitter end.

Nut never lives to see social liberalization and political democratization, but Taiwan's history since his death in the mid-1980s has been sweet, and salty. So it's fitting that *Ghost Town* serves up a feast of Taiwanese treats. I tried to translate the names of these treats literally and descriptively, like the *bah-uân*—"meat circles," those saucer-shaped dumplings with a minced pork filling—that Keith and others enjoy. Reading about these delicious dishes, you may come to feel that Taiwan isn't so ghastly after all. To tens of millions of people, including myself, it even feels like home.

D.S.

ABOUT THE AUTHOR

Kevin Chen began his artistic career as a cinema actor, starring in the Taiwanese and German films *Ghosted*, *Kung Bao Huhn*, and *Global Player*. Now based in Germany, he has published several novels and collections of essays and short stories including *Attitude*, *Flowers from Fingernails*, and *Three Ways to Get Rid of Allergies*.